Good

Men

Hard Times

By C.W. Broesamle

"The man in the Arena"

"It is not the critic who counts; not the man who points out how the strong man stumbles, or where the doer of deeds could have done them better. The credit belongs to the man who is actually in the arena, whose face is marred by dust and sweat and blood; who strives valiantly; who errs, who comes short again and again, because there is no effort without error and shortcoming; but who does actually strive to do the deeds; who knows great enthusiasms, the great devotions; who spends himself in a worthy cause; who at the best knows in the end the triumph of high achievement, and who at the worst, if he fails, at least fails while daring greatly, so that his place shall never be with those cold and timid souls who neither know victory nor defeat."

Teddy Roosevelt

"The most terrifying force of death comes from the hands of Men who wanted to be left Alone. They try, so very hard, to mind their own business and provide for themselves and those they love. They resist every impulse to fight back, knowing the forced and permanent change of life that will come from it. They know that the moment they fight back, their lives as they have lived them, are over. The moment the men who wanted to be left alone are forced to fight back, it is a form of suicide. They are literally killing off who they used to be. Which is why, when forced to take up violence, these Men who wanted to be left alone, fight with unholy vengeance against those who murdered their former lives. They fight with raw hate, and a drive that cannot be fathomed by those who are merely play-acting at politics and terror. True terror will arrive at these people's door, and they will cry, scream, and beg for mercy... but it will fall upon the deaf ears of the men who just wanted to be left alone."

– Author Unknown

Chapter 1

The iPhone blasted out the terrible wail of the alarm and dragged me from my slumber. It was the radar alarm sound from my phone that woke me no matter what as it reminded me of the incoming alarm I had often heard when deployed. It was a sure-fire way to wake me and my wife, Rae, no matter how tired we were because of our pasts. We both are combat veterans of the Iraq and Afghanistan wars and honestly lucky to not have too much mental baggage from those days. That cannot be said for tens of thousands of others who served their country, giving so much. I slid my covers off me and realized it was another brisk morning on this fall day in October.

"Damn, it is a little nippily this morning" I said to my wife.

"Ugh I don't want to go to work today, why do Mondays suck so bad" she replied.

"Me either, shower?" I said shuffling to the bathroom.

"Yeah, let me get the coffee going and I will be in with you." She said.

The shower was nice and a fantastic way to get my old muscles going after sleep. I am no spring chicken anymore, that is for sure, 55. Where had all the years gone? Sure, it seemed like only yesterday and I was getting out of bed with my mom yelling at me to get going. She had passed a few years back and I sure would love to have her around to yell at me again. I doubt she would have liked the Covid scare or the way the area I grew up in had changed and gotten. So many homeless people in and around my California hometown. I grew up in a rural area of southern California where my father still lived despite me trying to get him to leave that crumbling state. As a kid and young adult there was maybe a handful of homeless people in and around the area, now there was a handful in just a block. Times had surely changed for the worst and it didn't look like it was going to get any better anytime soon.

The economy was not recovering despite the election of the long shot Independant candidate winning in a landslide. Two years after he was elected, the recession was turning increasingly into a potential depression with inflation at a record high. With the wars still raging in the middle east and Ukraine and our congress continuing to pour money out to them, it is no wonder we have not seen it get worse. Russia had yet to take more than half of Ukraine and the threat of nuclear war had been present for years now with threats often coming from a devastated Russia. Top this off with Israel fighting for their very existence with most of the Arab states in the region. They had threatened to use their nuclear arsenal against a few of the Arab states and it was a surprise to me that it had not happened yet.

I looked at my iPhone after I got out of the shower and ready for the day. I had put on my jeans and vans with my normal everyday carry items, or EDC as those in the carry world called it. My EDC was an old Zippo lighter, two different knives, a pair of throw away handcuffs, a Swat-T, two extra magazines for my SIG320 X Compact, and my gun. I had been carrying a gun in one form or another since I joined the army in early 1992. It was no wonder that I had even made it through basic training at Fort Sill, Oklahoma with my young and dumb attitude. I had become a 13Fox, a fire support specialist at the time. You might be thinking that it was a fire fighter job, but it was not, it was calling in artillery, close air support and Naval gunfire. I got to blow stuff up from the units I supported, and it was pretty cool until my buddy got me to look into Special Forces.

It was while I was in Korea in 1997 that I was talked to by my best friend Mark, and the bug was put into my ear. I found out that Special Detachment Delta, also known as Combined Arms Group or even the unit, was looking for people and had a recruiting team in country, so I went and applied. They had a mini selection process set up where there was a run, swim, and physical fitness test sort of process. Then if you did well on that they sat down and interviewed you. At my interview they told me they liked what they saw but that I needed to have some Special Operations time under my belt before they would let me attempt to proceed more. I thanked them for the opportunity to get this far and licked my wounds from not getting any further. It had taken me two more years to get into the Special Forces as an 18E Communications Sergeant, after selection at Camp Mccall, North Carolina, Airborne, the Qualification phases and language at John F. Kennedy Special warfare center and School, then forward to 1st Special Forces Group at Fort Lewis, Washington. Man was I fit then, getting put on a ruck team. From there I grew as an operator, communicator, and shooter.

"Honey what is on your mind this morning?" my sexy wife asked me. "You seem a thousand miles away."

"Sorry love was looking back at my career in the Army" I responded.

"Oh my what brought that on" she continued.

"I am honestly not sure, just popped into my head. What do you have going on this morning? Any IEP's?" I asked. She was a Gifted teacher at the local high school and an IEP is an Individual Education Plan.

"Not today, just pulling kids in to talk to them about the college application deadlines' she said.

"UGH Yuck, I hope they aren't going to get a basket weaving degree" I said laughing.

She punched my arm and said, "You know I try hard to not let them go do things that are not purpose driven."

"I know, I know. You are a great teacher and mentor my love and you rock at helping these kids figure out their own direction. I hope you know I like giving you shit right?" I said with a little snark in my voice as I wrapped her in a hug and gave her a kiss. She kissed back and smiled as she looked up at me and said, "Daydreaming and giving me shit in the blink wink of the eye hmm? Are you looking for trouble today my love?"

"No just me being me, sexy" I said with a little laugh and a smile as I let go and smacked her on the ass. As I did this our youngest came around the corner with bedhead hair and a look of not being awake or impressed with us. "Morning kiddo" I said to him. He grumbled as he replied "morning" and continued on his way to our bed. Owen was ten years old and usually got up and dressed then went in and crashed on my side of the bed until I woke him to put his shoes on and take him to school. I heard our other son, Anthony, who was a senior in the same school my wife taught at. "Hey boy you sleep well?" I asked as I looked around the corner from the kitchen.

Anthony replied "Yeah Dad after I finally could fall asleep."

"Took you a bit to crash out son? Things on your mind?" I asked.

"Yeah, I am tired of stupid dumb people at my school that are siding with Russia and the Arab states in the wars and against everything that the US stands for, or at least use to stand for. That and calling be a dumb ass for joining up with the Army. I can't wait to be done and away from almost all of them." he said.

Anthony was Rae's son from her first marriage, and I saw him as my own son after helping raise him for the last 13 years. We, Rae and I, had met while in the Army, she helped my unit move around Iraq during a deployment and caught my eye as she was talking to me in her flight operations center. We courted and got married while on a rotation to Afghanistan where she again helped move units around theater. I had two older sons, David the oldest and Donnovan the second oldest, from my previous marriage who currently are both serving in the armed forces. David had stayed with my ex-wife who is Canadian and joined their Army. Donnovan, yes two N's, is in the American Army and had lived with Rae and me until he left to serve. Anthony saw how well his older brothers were doing in the military along with how well my wife and I were doing and decided to join too despite my best efforts to talk him into going to a tech school.

Owen seemed to be leaning in a different direction than his brothers, which I could understand because he had not seen much of the military lifestyle that the others had seen. Time would tell where his direction would take him, I just hoped that we did well to raise him in spite of the public schooling.

My phone brought me back to the current time as it alerted me it was time to get the little one going out the door to school. Rae yelled she loved me as she headed into the garage and jumped in her 4Runner as I was getting the little man up and going. He was not a happy camper this morning and I could understand why as it was colder today and a Monday. We got into the Sequia SUV, backed out of the garage, and headed to his school. He enjoyed getting a ride to school in the morning and most times my work schedule allowed this to happen. He took the bus home after school and to be honest he could walk to school since we are no more than a few miles from the school; however, the school does not like to have walkers. Just another factor of this new day and age compared to when I was in school, and kids would walk or ride their bikes from miles away to school.

"Have a great day at school buddy, I love you" I said as I dropped him off in the line.

"Love you too Dad" he responded as he bolted from the SUV and headed into the school doors.

After pulling out of the school lot I headed over to the training facility that I owned and operated on the outer lying part of town connected to the old Air Force base. After retiring from the Army, I went into the consulting business and helped train private military contractors, law enforcement, and government agencies in various aspects of combat applications. Being on the trigger was just one little part of the skill set in operating in a stressful hostile environment. I was thankful to have gotten to go to SFARTAETC, pronounced safartac, which was advanced reconnaissance target analysis exploitation techniques course and a slew of others at Bragg, which is now Fort Liberty after the whole 'woke' movement needed to get rid of the names of bases that had what they called rebel traitor names. Society had gone crazy trying to erase history, like something truly out of the book *1984*. With all my training and knowledge gained from years of operational experience I had decided to get a degree in security management and try to score in the industry. I was lucky and knew a few of the right people to get my foot in the door. After a few years working with these guys, they pushed me to start my business. It was a remarkably successful company with a high flow of income, not to mention I was happy to continue what I loved to do also.

I pulled up to the gated compound and punched in the security code at the outer gate. I could hear the electric motors hum as they pulled the gate open, and I saw the second gate in front of me as hydraulic bastions lowered into the ground for the first gate. It had taken me years to get the compound to this level of security, slowly using the capital gained from the business to develop and create with. The compound was on 40 private acres that attached to the airfield, had a headquarters building, a training building with dedicated training rooms, two shoot houses, three covered firing ranges, out buildings, Large storage buildings, and a bunk house. In recent years I had consulted with an old friend to develop the necessary hangars to field a small air wing since the compound was attached to the airfield. The Headquarters, training building and bunk house were all connected by a tunnel system. The compound also had a sizeable bunker under it that very few people knew existed. By far it was something I cherished to have as mine. I had 12 fulltime employees, 4 of them maintenance guys just to keep the compound in tip top operational capacity.

I drove through the gate and stopped once inside the bastions and waited for it all to close behind me and then for the inner gate to open. The process only took a few minutes, and I was on my way up the drive to the headquarters building and my office. I waved to Adam as I drove past him. He was the maintenance manager and oversaw the other three maintenance employees, Miguel, Steve, and Todd. I pulled up to the building and parked and got out of the SUV and walked to the door. The door abruptly swung open and startled me.

"I am glad you are here" said the Operations manager Craig.

"What the fuck! You trying to give me a heart attack or get yourself fucken killed?" I exclaimed as I relaxed my draw hand that had instinctually moved towards my gun after being startled.

Craig threw up his hands and said, "woe boss sorry damn. I saw you pull in from the window and needed to catch you right away with this crazy shit going on."

"What crazy kind of crazy shit would make you risk startling me like this? I didn't have my radio on the news this morning as the boy likes to listen to music when I take him to school, and I had not moved it. What the fuck is going on now?" I asked.

"The stock market just crashed and the talking head on the news is saying they hit a level 1 circuit breaker.' Craig said.

"Ok and what the fuck is that? I remember something about an automatic stop if it drops too much or too fast. Is that what happened?" I asked.

"I don't know I ran out when I saw you pulling in here as they started explaining it on the TV" he said.

"Well let's go see how the fuck this day is going to go then. Do we have a big training day scheduled today? I remember the local PD guys are coming out, anything else going today?" I asked as we went inside, and I could hear the TV blasting away with breaking news.

"No, we just have the local PD guys scheduled today and this week is a slow week as we are gearing up from the Canadians to show up next week" Craig replied.

"The Protective Services guys again?" I asked.

"Yeah, their team with I think 20 of their trainees are scheduled for a two week go" he said.

As we entered the lobby, I heard the talking head on the news say that they had released Level 1 and immediately the market crashed more than 12% causing a Level 2 circuit breaker. He explained that a Level 2 was like the Level 1 and they would halt all trading in all markets for another 15-minute cool off period. I took out my phone and messaged my wife telling her to look at the market. We had been seriously preparing for a bad turn or situation for years, and things like this always made us start thinking. I got a response from her saying that it was a long time coming and that the toothpicks holding it all up seemed to have broken today. I had to giggle reading this which made Craig look at me sideways.

"Rae wrote that the toothpicks finally broke and it made me giggle sorry" I said.

"Yeah, I am surprised it took this long for something like this to happen with all the crazy shit in the world the last three plus years honestly" Craig responded while listening to the TV.

He was referring to the crazy election of a third-party candidate to become the 47th President of the United States that happened almost three years ago. The year leading up to the election saw widespread demonstrations much like the BLM movement, this time supporting the Palestinian's and Hamas of all things. Chanting 'From the River to the Sea' in the name of peace to support Palestine against the Israeli war fighting Hamas that started after a brutal attack four years ago. Since that attack Israel has been fighting Hamas and then many of the Arab states surrounding them. This on top of a stalemate war in Ukraine where Russia had invaded and continued to fight ever since. With these wars and the US congressional end fighting back and forth with no real allegiance since the White house was controlled by an independent, caused our economy to roll and twist like a flag in the wind.

"I bet it crashes more and they shut it down for the day when this cool off period is over. What do you want to bet Craig?" I asked.

"I am not taking that bet at all because that is what it going to happen. Shit, I think it is the start of something much worse." Craig replied.

"Yeah, I think it might be time to think about circling the wagons. I guess we will see what the next 72 hours brings and go from their hmm buddy?" I said.

"Damn do think it is going to get that bad?" he asked.

"I truly hope not, but it is bound to happen since there has never been a real fix and the can has been kicked down the road over and over again" I replied.

As I spoke those words the announcers on the news said the cool off period was ending and trading was about to resume. This entire time we had been standing in the lobby outside our offices kind of just frozen in time waiting to see if the train wreck got worse. Stephanie walked in and stopped and looked at us with a puzzled look, she is the companies Logistical Manager.

"Umm what do we have here? What is going on that has you too looking at the TV so seriously and oblivious to things around you?" Stephanie asked.

"The markets are crashing!' Criag announced.

"What?" she said with shock and a little anxiety in the voice.

"Yeah, they just did like two cool off periods and are opening the market again right now." Craig said.

The news announcer was looking at the screen as he spoke and looked a little white in the face. He turned to the camera and said that the market had reached a Level 3 circuit breaker, and it was closed for the day. He looked back at the screen and then the camera and said before the S&P 500 had stopped trading it had lost a total of 26%, The NYSE had lost

28%, and the Dow Jones had lost 27%. He announced that he was going to go to their financial expert as the camera cut to another female reporter who honestly looked very shaken.

We all stood like statues as we watched her stumble for words and then say that a downturn like this had not really happened since 1987 in what was called Black Monday. Since that time, they had built the circuit breakers to help prevent such a huge downturn in the market and during Covid it had helped stop a serious downward slide, but this was nothing like it. She stopped talking and looked like her mind was scrambling for words, then said that it was unprecedented to see all the markets plunge so hard so fast all at the same time with little to no prediction of it happening. The main announcer thanked her, and they cut away from her at this point.

I looked at Craig and said, "Get everyone together, the entire staff including the maintenance team for a meeting in the conference room ASAP." I then turned and walked into my office and closed the door. My mind was racing as I put my day bag down and took my glasses off and rubbed my face. Was it finally going to crumb at our feet? Was this the day? My mind was awash with thoughts of doom, and I had to shake it off and call the wife. I pulled out my phone and at the same time turned on the TV in my office to watch the talking heads of the news spin this market crash.

My wife answered on the third ring. "Holy shit my love! This is a huge crash and they stopped trading. Looks like the toothpicks didn't break they exploded in a big way hmm?' she said.

"Yeah, this looks pretty bad my love. I am glad we have been slowly preparing but damn I didn't want to see it actually happen" is all I could muster.

"You think it is the start don't you? What do you want me to do? Have you called the older boys yet? I know it just happened but, well I guess you called me first." she said.

"Yeah, I called you sexy, but I am still kind of stunned because no one has been saying anything about a downturn, and bam! And the way it crashed doesn't look good. I mean we have seen it go wonky but this, it is just, crazy" I said.

"Yeah it is wild, and we have seen it go crazy and thought it might be starting. What are you thinking then?" she asked.

"I already called a meeting with all here at the compound. I am going to talk it out with everyone and see what they all think then go from there. I think either way we will know more as the day goes on, I mean it is only a little after eight thirty love...shit." I said.

"Yep, good morning us" she said as she laughed.

"I love you sexy and will let you go. I will call if anything needs to be discussed and you do the Same, eyes on a swivel today love ok?" I said.

"Ok my love, sounds good. Be safe" she said as she ended the call.

Putting the phone back in my pocket and looking towards the TV, I could hear the talking heads on there discussing the downturn as they were calling it. One was talking about March of 2020 and the Level 1 circuit breakers being triggered four separate times, but it had helped make the market stop the rapid decline or crashing like it had today. Another mentioned SEC rule 201 and other breakers that stopped trading of certain stocks that fluctuated too much in up or down trading and made to pause. They all seemed shocked it was going how it was and trading stopped today already.

I turned from the TV to head across to the conference room and see if everyone had made it in already. As I walked in and looked around, I saw Craig, Stephanie, and Luke sitting in their places around the large conference table. Luke is the company's intelligence specialist, and he was very connected to many of the known alphabet soup agencies.

"Hey boss man" Luke said.

"You see this shit Luke?" I responded.

"Yeah, and my people had no clue. So that is not a good thing. I will save it for when the rest get here, but not good boss." He said.

"Okay." I said as I looked on to the rest of the group assembling in the room.

Paul was sitting in his spot, he is a dynamic entry specialist, well really our demolitions guy at the company. As I built the company, I knew I was going to have to teach and have explosives go with it, and as such I had gotten all the required permits and licenses from the ATF. Bill was also in his chair watching the TV with a serious look on his face, he was in charge of our weapons and the armor here at the company. Along with the permits for explosives from the

ATF we also have a Class 3 license and manufacturing stamp for building weapons and needed parts legally. With this comes spot visits from the ATF and that is all in Bill's area of the company. Next to him was Troy, our IT wizard which helps our team out in today's global market for sure. Next to him was Jeff, our lead instructor at the shoot houses and honestly all classrooms taught material. It was a sizeable job and Jeff had it well in hand with Frank his assistant instructor. Frank was next to Jeff, and they seemed to be in a side conversation of their own. Frank could easily be the lead, but Jeff had taken the job before Frank and thus got the higher title, much to Jeff's chagrin. Adam had his maintenance crew down with him, he liked to sit to the side and not be at the big table. I often had to ask him to join us with his guys but had come to let them sit together as a group to build their team bond. Miguel, Steve, and Tod all worked maintenance as part of Adam's team. After seeing they had all made it to the room, I cleared my throat to get their attention.

"UMM, thank you all for dropping what you were doing and coming to this sort of emergency meeting." I started as I looked around the room. "None of you are strangers to dynamic situations yourselves as you are all combat veterans and friends of mine. That being said, it looks like we might have a start to an event we all know has been building and could happen. Those that might not know or have not listened to the TV as you came in here, the stock markets are in total chaos after they crashed today, and trade was stopped. The talking heads are goin on and on about how the circuit breaker worked from letting a total collapse happen. We are in the heart of what could be the opening phase of a meltdown of the markets worldwide. Luke, what are your people saying?" I finished looking at him.

"Boss, everyone else" he said as he stood up. "Honestly, my people are a little shocked and stunned at the moment. They did not see this coming and are looking to see exactly what they believe triggered this much of a slide. I get an underlying tone that they are all scared boss and that isn't how most of them operate if you get what I am saying." he told me and looked at the others. "I looked and it seems to have started with a rapid sell off of bank stock, which is really nothing new, but then it cascaded, and everyone was selling bank stock then it avalanched and BAM" he said.

"Ok so it just happened to be bank stock that started it, but it went viral and here we are?" I asked.

"Yeah, to me but I am not remotely an expert, it looks like that. After speaking to others in my circle I think this might be the start of something very bad. One guy said that we could see runs on banks as early as an hour or two from now. I have reached out to see if I could get a line on what the White House response might be but we both know they are just a figure head now since it is a third party in there. I love the guy's message and drive but damn if he has little to no congressional support these days. So, his fed chair could push one way or another, but congress will surely have a say too. So we might look to see if anything else happens and go from that point. Either way, this is not going to turn out good in my view boss" he ended and sat down.

"Ok thanks for looking into it and keep doing what you do Luke, if you see any key things, please let me know so we can go from there. Stephanie, how are we sitting logistically if things went completely south?" I said as I looked her way.

"Well, that depends on what you define as going south honestly. Though I will say we are well stocked in all things and have the stocks we have all talked about should this world as we know it collapse but is that ever going to be enough?" she said looking around and stopping at me.

"No, most likely we could never have enough. So, we are stocked how we have planned but you think we should get more should this be a true collapse if we have the chance?" I asked.

"Yes, I think we should go to extremes if we think that this is the beginning of the end" she replied.

"Ok, so we could always use more. What does that look like for everyone else at the table? Start thinking about not ever getting another thing after we get our last buys, what are you wanting now before that happens? Let's start with Craig" looking at him.

"Oh, sure fuck me and make me go first, right?" Craig said laughing at me.

"Yep" I smiled big at him.

"You are thinking like no shitting this is it, the crash and follow on shit hits the fan kinda thing then? Like we are going to the continuation of family plan? Is that what you are getting at?" he asked, looking me in the eyes very seriously.

"Ok everyone Craig hit the nail on the fucking head here. I think this could be a Shit Hits The Fan (SHTF) fucking deal. I am scared to say it but yes. I want to know what we as a group think we need to do in these decisive moments while we have a chance. We have a great plan and have known each other for years if not much longer. We all have talked at length about something like this happening, more so in the last couple years as the writing has seemed to be on the wall, now we are fucking here. So now is the time to say fuck it and give me a list of things we should get to cover all the bases. I know we have a lot already but let's get moving and get a list going. Steph can make it happen I am sure as long as things don't stop dead, which might happen but I doubt it. I think we have time, but it is going to get ugly. This is the Warno to get those moving that need to be moving this way, because I think it is here ok?" said while I looked around the room.

"Ok so beans, bullets, and gear then" Craig said questioningly.

"Yes, and anything else we think we need more of or want" was my response.

"Then can you give us say two hours to get our minds going and wrapped around this being real and let say we come back here with our lists and what we think we need to do' Craig said.

"Does that work for everyone else" I asked.

The head nodding and yeses around the room made it clear they all wanted time. "Two hours from now back in here. No fucking around people. Get it together and let's focus on the ball rolling and us making the best of what time we might have left. I will be in my office making calls and a list too. Questions before we adjourn?" looking around the room seeing none. "OK two hours let go!"

Everyone filed out of the commence room but Luke. He sat looking at me and at his laptop in front of him. "Boss, there are already reports of runs happening on banks. It is my prediction that within a few hours we are going to see widespread panic. I am going to call a few people and will be in your office in a bit to let you know what they think is going to be the federal response. It is not going to be good, it might be a total collapse" he said as he rubbed his face in pure concern.

As I walked by Luke, I patted him on the shoulder and said "Ok buddy. I knew it was fucking bad and most likely going to turn into a SHTF situation. We have prepared and will put the final touches on it. You got this, we got this the best we can." I walked out and didn't look back, heading for my office. I had to make some hard calls that I was not sure how they would go.

Chapter 2

Rae set the phone on her desk and opened Microsoft edge on her work computer and searched current news after she had gotten off the phone with her husband. Every headline started with 'Huge stock market downturn' and she could not help but roll her eyes reading it. 'More like the toothpicks exploded' she thought in her head. Wayne had been talking about this for years, hell ever since they got married really. On the first trip across the country to visit her parents she had given him hell for all the gear he had packed besides the suitcases. From weapons and ammunition to individual backpacks he loaded it all despite me giving him hell. I remember him telling me that what we took was all we would have if something bad happened, I might have even rolled my eyes at him saying this. All these years later I understand it and live by being ready.

It took him getting me to read a few SHTF books like *Light Out* by David Crawford and the *Going Home* series by A. American to slowly get me on board and with the program. During those times we had a small amount of gear and since that time we have done nothing but brainstorm and think through the processes of what if and purchasing more. With the purchase of gear also came the training for me. I served in the Air Force and then took the Blue to Green program offered and switched to the Army. I worked in flight operations and was not even close to a shooter or operator like my husband. I have been trained well, both by Wayne, and other people. I have been through most of the programs offered at his, our, company. His guys have gotten me up to speed, not completely up to their standards but they have accepted me in their circle and respect my abilities. I would have never thought all those years ago to be in this place and time, and thankful we had worked so ridiculously hard to get where we are.

My mind turned to our children, David, Donnovan, Anthony, and Owen, and what this will mean for them. The oldest David is in the Canadian Army, and part of JTF 2, an operator like his father. Donnovan is in 2nd Battalion, 75th Ranger regiment and an operator in his own likes. Thery both have had multiple deployments and combat operations under their belts much to the dismay of me and even Wayne, though he will never admit that. Anthony, my first born from my ex-husband, Wayne' stepson which you could never tell from the outside, joined the army a few months ago in the delayed entry program. He too is following in his father's footsteps as a 13Fox. The youngest is looking more into other fields as he was never exposed directly to the military like his brothers since he was born just before I had gotten out. Wayne and I had talked about the older boys and that if it was a no shit complete SHTF situation he was going to offer the boys a place to come, if they so choose.

As the years passed and we had both been out of the military, money had started to flow in from our hard work. Eventually Wayne opened his own company. The first couple of years had us tightening our belt and using the income to build the company. It was a goldmine I had no idea was there due to Wayne' knowledge, and honestly his leadership skills. He built the company from friends and acquaintances out of the military. Luke was about as close to a best friend Wayne would admit to having. They knew each other from the teams, and through the years had worked together off and on. Craig was in the same boat as Luke, a devoted friend that had been on the teams too. I had to laugh when I really looked at them all, most had been on a team or with a team of some sort and worked directly for Wayne, minus Troy, Adam, Miguel, Steve, and Tod that is. Those five had worked for me and were brought on board by me after the vetting process set in place by the company.

I refreshed my computer and looked at the headlines that started to populate the screen. It looked like some banks were starting to have panicked people pulling money from them. I was very thankful that we had started to invest a huge amount of our money in silver, gold, and platinum. It was hard to admit I was glad because I had fought Wayne on this aspect of the preparations as it seemed that we would want to have money in the bank to always use. He had assured me that we would be able to use credit if it came to that and pay it back by liquidating some of the metal resources. At this point I was glad because we would not have to worry about trying to pull money from our accounts as it looked like many people are currently doing.

My phone started to vibrate, and I looked at it and it was Wayne. "Hey my love. You see that people are already starting to panic and pull money from the banks?" I asked as I answered the phone.

"Yeah, Luke showed me a minute ago. Love, I am afraid this is going to spin wildly out of control way quicker than we had ever thought" he laughed and continued. "Way faster than any of the books we read had made it seem like. I am calling to ask if you think I should pull my dad in no matter what he says. I could send Craig out in a charter and have him snatched with his little bit of supplies and his dog. What do you think?" he asked me.

"It looks bad my love. Call your dad and talk to him, and if you need to go get him then do it. I hope you don't have to snatch him" I said giggling. His father would be pissed if Wayne did that.

"Ok sexy. We had a meeting here and are coming back together with lists of last-minute things we think we might need. Anything you can think of we will need more of" he asked me.

"Fuck! Yes, female products. I know we got those reusable pads for periods that are supposed to wash good but why not purchase everything they have locally or even online and get them sent here. I know the roads might get crazy, but does it hurt to try that way" I said.

"Nope we will get a local purchase crew together maybe even do the curbside thing and get all of them. Send me a text with the type you want, maybe get with the wives of the group and see too?" he said.

"Ok, I can do that and ask. Do you think the others are talking to their wives?" I asked him.

"I fucking hope so babydoll because we need to make sure we have all the bases covered. I have to go and call my dad and try to get him to see it is time to be here. Wish me luck." he said.

"Good luck my love" I said as I blew him a kiss.

"Thanks. Bye" I heard him say as the phone went dead.

His dad, Carl, was going to be a hard sell since he still lived in the house he had when my mother-in-law passed away. We had talked to him about moving here with us when she had passed, and he finally had told Wayne to leave it the fuck alone. His words exactly. He went on to explain to us that his friends and memories are all there, and I and Wayne could understand. I think it weighed heavy on Wayne that he did not have him closer, but we went to see him as often as time would allow. It would be a huge surprise to him if Wayne snatched him and gave him no options. I guess we will see what happens with that.

I opened my phone and looked at the Spouse text group we had created and used to keep up to date with each other. Susan was Craig's wife and we had been friends for years as were most of us on this list. Jessica was Paul's wife, Danielle was Jeff's wife, Amanda was Bill's wife, Rebecca was Frank's wife and my best friend, Bella was Adam's wife, and Maria was Miguel's wife. We had one male in the group, James, as he was Stephanie's husband and the reason it was the spouse group and not the wives group.

I typed out the following message: All, if you are not aware of the current situations on going with the stock markets and the banks, it is bad. We are currently looking at it as a SHTF event and initiating the plan. Please respond with things you may need/want or that you think the group may need.

Rebecca responded immediately: I am aware and making a list.

Bella followed: Yeah aware and thinking about things.

Maria sent: Yes. We need more food items. Making a list now.

James sent: Um no. What is going on?

Rebecca responded: Market collapsed and then people freaked and pulled their money out of banks.

James: Shit. Ok let me think about it.

Amanda chimed in: Ok so things are going to go like we talked about when planning all this?

Rebecca: Yes

Me: Yes

Amanda: Ok, I will think about anything more.

Susan joined with: Fuck. Fuck. Fuck. This is bad isn't it??

Me: Yeah Susan it is pretty bad.

Susan: Ok, working on possible things.

Rebecca: Should we meet?

Me: Let me get with Wayne and see. He mentioned something about a meeting in a few hours so not sure if he is looking for it to be all of us yet.

I Called Wayne to ask about the meeting and let him know that I was brainstorming with the spouses about what we might want/need. It rang three times, and he picked up, "Hey sexy, what is up?" he asked.

"I have the spouse group in a text group, and we are brainstorming about the needs/wants for the group. Do you want us at the meeting you are having or get a list and send it to you?" I blurted out.

"Fuck, I am sorry I had not even thought about getting you all involved yet' he said.

"That is why we are a great team my love, we pick up the slack from the other one" I said with a slight giggle in my tone.

"Ok, how about you get them all to send you what they want or think we need then get with me in an hour and we can go over it. I think no matter what we spend and buy anything and everything we are even slightly thinking about, what do you think?" he asked me with what sounded like a little bit of concern in his voice.

"I think you need to take a deep breath my love and know that we have this and no matter what we are going to make the best of whatever is to come. Don't start sounding stressed already love, you got this." I expressed with love in my voice.

"I love you sexy and I know we will get through this but it is crazy to me that it is truly here. I mean we have talked about this so many times, joked, rolled our eyes at things and the likes but damn, here we are. So get the list and call me in an hour. I think maybe we have the spouses call in to the meeting so we don't have a flood of people here anyways. Sound good?" he asked.

"It sounds good to me and I know we got this and so do you, it is just wild. OK, let me get with the group and let them know and we can go from there. I love you so so very much" I said longingly.

"I love you too baby doll. Head on a swivel just in case sexy. Talk to you in a bit." and he hung up.

I went back to the group text: OK everyone I need your list in 45 minutes so I can get it all together and send it to Wayne. He is thinking about having you all call in to the meeting. I will let you all know the number when I get it confirmed that it is the usual number.

Susan: I am sure it is the usual number for the meeting. I will get you the list I am thinking about soon.

James: Does it matter what we think we might need and or should I just go with what I think?

Me: If you think we need it put it on the list, Wayne always says better to have and not need that need and not have.

James: Right, ok.

Rebecca: Working on the list

Amanda: I will get it to you in a bit

Danielle: I just caught up in this text messages because I was on the phone with Jeff. He sounded a little scared. I had not heard that in him in a very long time. Will get list to you Rae.

Me: He sounded scared??

Danielle: Yeah kinda has me a little on edge to be honest. Have not heard that tone from him in a very very long time

Me: Ok, I got the same feel from Wayne too

James: Um they are never scared WTF is going on??

Me: They know that this is the real deal and the feelings are coming out because it is the real deal and they never wanted this. So everyone please think hard and put even the most wild thing you might think we need on the lists, it seems we are in for it.

Susan: FUCK FUCK FUCK....talk is one thing but FUCK it is here.

Rebecca: I agree Susan totally....UGH

Bella: Holy shit

Bella: WTF is going on.

Bella: This group never...Fuck it is happening??

Me: lol welcome to the party Bella

Susan: Better late than never right Bella??? LMFAO

Bella: Is this real? Like the shit is hitting the fan? The day seems normal here in my neighborhood

Maria: go turn on the TV girl, it is very real and getting a little wild because people are starting to freak out.

Bella: Freak out??

Jessica: Yeah they are pulling their money out of the banks and banks and ATMs are out in places causing more problems.

Me: Yeah I see it on the News right now. I just can't believe it is going this fast.

James: I can, ok I am going to focus on the list and get it to you in about 35 minutes

Me: Ok I will be waiting for all your lists and let you know if it is the regular call in number. I am going to get to work on my list but here if you need something.

As I was finishing that text message our son Anthony walked into my room at the school. "Hey mom, is there something going on everyone seems a little upset about something. Mr. Green was all in his phone and told Clarra to shut up when she was getting loud talking to her friend Debbie. I have never heard him like that mom" he said.

"The stock markets are closed due to a crash. People are freaking out and pulling their money from banks and they banks don't have enough money, so" I explained.

"So shit is hitting the fan for real and not like books or movies. What does dad think?' He asked me with a serious look on his face.

"He thinks it is for real and has started the first stages of the plan" I said.

"Real and started the plan. Like the plan? As in circle the wagons?" he said looking a little pale and concerned.

"Yes son, the plan, don't freak out and relax, do the things we need you to do, it is going to be ok." I said patting him on the shoulder.

"Hey, look at me" I said as I looked him in the face "We will get through this no matter what ok?"

"Ok mom. Do I need to get Owen?" he asked.

"No, you can head home since you have just the one class today and if I need you, I will write. Try to enjoy yourself and do your normal things and homework too. Nothing is stopping yet, so we continue to do the things we normally do day to day ok" I told him.

"Ok then. Hope you have a good day, I am going to head home." he said as he left my classroom.

I hoped he would be ok heading home and that things had not gotten too crazy yet. I felt bad for him with his entire future ahead of him potentially gone, but also knew he was a strong kid and would be able to navigate whatever lies ahead. I went out to the hall to monitor the kids as they changed classes. I caught a few faces in the crowd that seemed to understand what might be going on, but for the most part they had their heads in their phones or the million-mile stare heading to the next class. My teacher friend that I went to high school with taught German across the hall from me and was heading towards me. "Hey Chelsea, how are you doing" I asked as she approached.

"Did you hear about Mr. Green going off on Clarra? She just came to my room and was crying because he yelled so loud at her." She told me.

"Yeah, Anthony stopped in before heading home and told me. He said her and Debbie were talking like normal, and Mr. Green yelled at her to shut up. Anthony was a little concerned about the outburst." I responded.

"It is not like Mr. Green at all, I was a little shocked when she told me it was him honestly." Chelsea said.

"Yeah well I think it has to do with the stock market situation going on right now most likely. Mr. Green has always talked about investing in it, so maybe he is a little upset." I said.

"Stock market situation?" She asked.

"Yeah, it crashed earlier and they shut down the market, this got people freaking out and pulling money from the banks and since then it has started a real panic." I said.

As I said this to Chelsea my phone and watch buzzed, and I looked to see what was on my watch. It was Anthony calling me. "Hold on Anthony is calling me" I told Chelsea as I walked to my classroom.

"Hey kiddo you ok? You just left a bit ago." I asked with a little concern in my voice.

"Mom there is a line of people at the bank and people standing outside of it at the ATM and doors. They do not look happy." he said sounding more relaxed than I thought he would be.

"Ok, head home and relax son. We are working on the plan and if we need you to do anything we will let you know, ok?" I said to him.

"Ok mom just thought I should let you know. Should I call dad and let him know too?" he asked.

"No dad is busy talking to poppa out in California right now." I replied.

"Oh, I didn't think about Poppa." he said.

As I was talking to him my phone buzzed and I looked at my watch, Maria sent a list to me in the group. "I have to go kiddo, I love you" I told Anthony.

"Love you too mom" he replied as I cut the call.

Chelsea stuck her head in the room and asked, "Ok Rae what is going on?"

"I think shit has hit the fan like we, well Wayne brought up at wine night awhile back' I said.

"So, the market crash is that bad?" She said looking at her phone. "FUCK!"

I couldn't help but smile hearing her curse when she saw the headlines. "I hope it is not that bad, but it seems to be that bad and it is scary for sure." I said to her.

She looked at me super serious and said, "Does the invite still stand from Wayne?"

"As far As I know yes it does. We will know more as this unfolds for sure. Just make sure you have the stuff we talked to you about keeping on hand ok" I said.

"Ok, thank you." she said looking scared.

"It will be ok, we all will get through this" I told her.

The bell buzzed for the next class and Chelsea turned and headed out of my room as students started to file in. I knew the rest of the day was going to be crazy as my phone continued to buzz with the other spouses sending me their lists.

Chapter 3

Wayne sat down at his desk with the TV going strong in the background alive with talking heads all going on and on about the market and how this was most likely just a readjustment. Saying how for years it had been going upwardly. I smirked and turned to my phone and dialed my dad's number. It rang three times, and I thought it was going to go to voice mail when I heard the "hello" of his familiar voice. "Hey dad how you doing?" I asked him.

"I am a little sore today, the bike ride around the lake yesterday took a lot out of me" he responded.

"Oh, who did you ride around the lake with" I asked.

"Ed and Robin went this time. It was a nice slow pace I am just hurting from the normal places. Nothing new son." He said.

"I hope they are doing well. I called because we have a huge issue and I need to have you here" I said.

"Are the kids ok? Rae? What issue?" he said with serious concern in his voice.

I didn't think about how that might come off and felt bad with my wording and how it had upset him and responded, "damn sorry to freak you out dad, they are all ok. The issue is from the stock market collapsing this morning. It is very bad and I think it is going to cause the world to go crazy and make our lives as we know them now completely different."

"You scared the shit out of me. I thought someone had gotten hurt badly son. The market crashed?" he said.

"Yeah, they stopped trading it got so bad. Then people started pulling money out of the banks freaking out and well it has just continued on." I said.

"Ok so you want me to come to you because of this?" my dad said.

"Yeah dad. I know you talked about staying up with Ed and Mike and closing it down up the hill but I think it is best if you come hang out with us for a bit and see how bad it is going to get." I told him.

"I don't think I need to come out to you guys. That is a long ways and take a lot out of me." He said.

"A plane is going to land at Ryan airport and pick you and Chase up" I said. Chase is his little dog. Since my mom had passed away, he had kept a dog, which I think helped keep him going.

"A plane? You are serious, aren't you? Is it that bad?" he said a little more serious now.

"I will be honest with you dad, I talked to Rae and am asking you to come but in reality, will come snatch you if I must do that. I hope I can just come get you and bring you here, but if not and you are not willing to come normal, I will bring a team and get you. Sorry but this is that serious right now." I said sadly.

He raised his voice a little, "You are threatening to take me even if I don't want to come?"

"Yes dad" I said hanging my head a little bit. This might turn to shit I thought.

"Wow, if you are willing to do that it must be serious. When is the plane coming? I can get my things together and be ready if it is that important to you" he said.

"I can have a plane here and going wheels up in an hour or two at most. Then the flight time into Ryan is about two hours. I will come with Bill to pick you up and help pack things we should take. If this is as bad as I think it might be dad, could be a long time before you get to go back, if ever" I said.

"It is that bad then, ok. I guess I will see you later today then. And the grandkids too. Let me go start looking around" he said.

"Ok dad. Sorry to be like this but it will be better for all if you and Chase are here. Love you." I said.

"Love you to son' he hung up.

I sat back in my chair and took my glasses off to rub my face. That didn't go as bad as it could have but not as great as it could have either I thought. At least I didn't have to go snatch him. Now I had to plan on going myself instead of just sending Bill, which might have made it a little harder to sell to my dad and have him come willingly. I picked up the handset off the company phone on my desk and dialed the air charter company. It was run by a friend of mine, Mitch, who did both tactical flights and regular charters of fixed wing and rotary wing aircraft. He flew Blackhawks in the Army for years and had been friends with me long before he became a warrant officer, and I went to the dark side in Special operations. The phone rang twice and was answered by the attendant, "Aeronautics America, how may I help you?"

"Hey this Is Wayne from Bear Tactical, is Mitch around?" I responded.

"Oh, hello sir. He said you might be calling let me ring you through." the attendant said.

"Thank you" I said as I heard the click and a ring.

"Hey buddy" Mitch answered.

"Hey back at you. I take it you are aware of the news and situation then since your attendant said you had expected me to call?" I asked.

"Yeah, I am tracking the crash of the market and the run on the banks. Looks like the White House is going to go live in a bit with the President." he said.

"Shit I wasn't tracking that part, I wonder what He is going to say? Hey, I need a bird to take me and Bill to go get my dad in California. I know short notice, but it is important to me, can you swing it?" I said.

"Stop with the 'can I swing it' crap, you know I would do this for you come hell or high-water friend. The Cessna Citation Longitude will be at the departure area of your local field in 30 minutes. It was already on the way because we had talked about this before, and I knew you would want him there. Do you think I need to pull the fleet and re-establish it at your local airfield? Are you doing the SHTF plan?" he said.

"We started the plan implementation as of an hour or so ago. Are you wanting to pull it all in and do this? I asked him.

"I had hoped you would want to be a part of the plan as we had set it, but I was not going to assume you would go for it until you saw it was a sure thing. You know what assuming makes you" I laughed.

"Yeah, it makes you an ass, but you are already and asshole so..." he trailed off.

"Funny, Ok you know you and the family and the others you wanted to have are all welcome and things are already here at the compound stored, so come whenever you are ready buddy." I said.

"Ok then. I need to get off this and start to put it in motion. I am sure Melinda and the kids will be happy to see Rae and the boys. I will be in touch as we get closer Wayne. Be safe getting your dad" he said.

"Will do buddy. See you soon" I said hanging up. Damn he already knew I would be calling and had sent his bird to get us. I was truly blessed to have such good friends. I heard a knock at the door and Bill walked in. Bill and I had been friends doing things for years, he was a top-notch operator and a good friend. "Hey glad you stopped in" I said looking at him.

"Yeah, I figured you would be sending me to get your dad. I wanted to see was it going like the plan called for or if we are changing it up, or he said fuck off." he said sitting down.

"It is going to go as planned and we do not have to snatch him. I will be coming to make sure it doesn't change though." I said.

"Makes sense, when are we going and what do you want to pack out? I was thinking standard extraction gear just in case." He said.

"Yeah, I think we need to pack like we might have to go ground all the way back here, but It is not like the Longitude Can't handle the load and then some" I said laughing. We traveled all over the world in diverse types of transportation and the Cessna Citation Longitude is one of the nicer rides for sure.

"Yeah, I was thinking better to have than need and not have." Bill said.

"I agree, let's go to our team room and get the stuff we think we will need before the meeting. I think we have time to get it done since we have about thirty minutes or so." I said.

I slid my chair back and we both got up and headed to our team room. The company team room was built like most team rooms I had been a part of with individual bays for each person and their equipment. We had fifteen areas in the company team room with another team room set up for people coming to the compound for training. This area was secluded from the other team room which was in the Instruction building. This room was strictly for all of us that worked daily at the compound to train and teach others with a few extra bays for our personal guests or friends. In reality these other bays also served to help organize our team should the SHTF plan go into effect, and we had to go operational ourselves.

I had been preparing for years in the event that the world collapsed for one reason or another. The company compound was specifically built for the event that the SHTF. From the tunnel system interconnecting the buildings to the big, no big is not the right word, huge bunker too. I had spared no expense and sunk my entire TSP from my years in the Army into it along with other investor money from many of the guys in the company. From faraday proofing the buildings and underground system, two separate wells, solar, and so much more the compound truly was made to survive, as long as we could keep it in our possession and not get smoked by the lucky bullet.

As I walked in it seemed Bill and I were not the only ones that thought about making sure we had our kit set up and ready to go. The gear we wear when doing operations and honestly daily is referred to as 'kit' by many in the industry. Honestly, I was not even sure when or where I had first heard this term and how it had stuck with me, but it had and now was used from military to law enforcement, if you asked them what they had for kit they would describe all their gear. Over the years I had acquired a lot of different kits, and they had gotten increasingly refined as the mission sets changed and the operations that drove them did too. From direct actions to daily carry, after years of operational tempo my taste in gear changed and refined. I had turned into a Hailey Strategic fan years ago and honestly use a bunch of their products. In fact, the kit I was pulling out to get my dad was an older Micro Chest rig in grey with Thorax plate carrier. I honestly was taking two setups, one with plates and another without. Both had a Flat pack set up in the back. Both setups carried three rifle mags and two pistol mags with a big admin pouch up front and a hanging Med kit. I had the radio pouch set up on my weak side, which is the side without your weapon. So, If I were right-handed my radio would go on my left. For me this was the given and many would say this was optimal, but I never really harped on a person's kit as much as did they know how to use it when they needed it.

I also was taking an old tried and true HardHeaded Veterans bump helmet and one of their ATE ballistic helmets. I had learned through the years that it is better to stay out of a gun fight at all costs than to actually have to be in a two-way range. That being said it is also important to have the right kit for the right actions. So, I was going to error on the side of caution and take two different setups and hope to not need either of them. The helmets had a side rail system that I had my amplified Peltor ears attached to them along with a night vision mount on the front. I also had a Battery pouch set on the back of the helmets that helped run the night vision longer should we need that option. I ran an RNVG system from Steele Industries. They had started up about six years ago now and had treated me right. I have a lot of different night vision sets depending on the mission set and what I want to be able to see and do at night but the features of the RNVG really worked for me. I also had a few sets of NVGs to loan out.

When it came to weapons, I really leaned hard on the AR platform since I had a lot of years on M4's and HK416's along with many civilian variants. A few years back I went on a crazy buying spree and bought a rather large, well the company did really, number of different Sons of Liberty rifles. A ton of MK10 style and M4 style. I could spend days talking about their weapons and the service that Michael Mihalski gives to his customers. They are not cheap, but they will work in a fight and have a lifetime warranty, though if the world is indeed going to shit, will that matter much? Still a solid choice in a rifle and yet many others would do just fine in a pinch too. I had never been a 'brand snob' as much as I had been a 'know your tool and how to use it to maximum efficiency' type of guy and facilitator. Even a HiPoint can kill you, and the person that used it on you can upgrade to your kit. Needless to say, I was going to take the M4-89 SBR, short barrel rifle, in 10.5 with a SureFire SOCOM556 Mini2 can. It had a MAWL DA for night targeting should that be needed along with an Aimpoint Micro, 3 power magnifier, and Magpul back up sights. It was a real work horse for me.

I was choosing to go with my Sig Arms Scorpion 320 from their custom shop with a SRO sight on top and it had a custom threaded barrel if I needed to put a silencer on the end of it for semi quiet work. Contrary to what most movies and TV shows might have a silencer, or can as I call them, sound like, they are still pretty loud when shooting. They make the noise manageable to the unprotected ears but still loud and noticeable as a bang. I usually run this gun with the extended magazine and have twenty-one rounds ready at my disposal should I need them. The pistol was not my primary weapon, as the rifle was, and I have seen my pistol as a way to get to my rifle even in the everyday carry option. In operational missions it was a backup weapon to be used when and if my primary weapon fails to work.

All the gear I, or anyone else use, is just tools to effectively help the most important weapon we all have, our minds. Without the right mindset no amount of training or gear will get you to the end of a battle. Through the years I have seen to many men, strong men, crumble under the pressures the mind places on them in battle and operational tempos. The mind can eat away at you from the inside and take your edge away from you should it slip. It is the most trying thing to train anyone in the rhythm of battle, that mindset kills. I am different than most when it comes to mindset, as I think you must train your mind more than anything else to fight despite all that is happening around you. That you must look deeply into yourself and find that which drives you, keeps you grounded and guided. If your mind is not ready for the fight that might come to you, then you are doomed to lose before it ever even happens. Thus, men much stranger than me have fallen because their minds where never truly in the fight. In the end it is the man that makes the gear, not the gear that makes the man.

I had most of my gear packed into my travel bag when my iPhone went off. I pulled it out and looked and it was a message from my wife saying she was getting the lists together and everyone was hoping to call into the meeting to the regular group conference number if that was ok. I wrote back to her yes it was good, and I had lost track of time packing gear. That I would grab Bill and head to the meeting and talk to her in a bit.

"Bill meeting time you go to go over there?" I asked as I walked up into his bay.

"Yeah, just zipping the bag closed now" he replied.

"Ok, let's head to the conference room and see what we are going to have to do to get ourselves more prepared than we are and see where the market crash has taken us all so far today." I said as I looked at my Sunto watch for the first time this morning. Damn it was already time for the meeting which was 11:45 our time. This should be interesting as I had not been watching the news and been busy planning to get my dad out of California and back here to us.

I walked into the meeting room and the news was going in the background and everyone was looking at Luke as he was on the phone with someone. His back was to the group, and I caught him saying 'really, that bad' in a tone I had only heard him use during operations in places we should not have been doing things that needed done and but was not going well. He got off the phone and turned to the entire group quietly leering at him as the new anchor said the President was about to address the nation at any moment.

"Ok everyone, is the conference line open for everyone to call in." I asked. The speaker on the conference table erupted with 'we are' from the spouses it sounded like to me.

"I think we are going to be a little shocked at what the President is about to say to the Nation" Luke said.

I turned to him and said, "Ok what do you know?"

"As you all heard me talking to my contacts, the government has no way to handle what has already become a crisis in the banks. Small scale riots have already broken out in New York and Boston when the banks closed their doors and ATM's went dry. These are just the ones being reported on, my contact said that many banks throughout the entire nation have been ransacked and have no hard currency to give. He did not say exactly what the President was going to tell the Nation because he wasn't sure, but they are going to have to move quickly to try to slow the most likely economic collapse that will make the great depression look like a cake walk." Luke replied.

"Ok, so we are going to move forward as fast as we can with the SHTF plan because it has already started to go faster than we might have thought possible. Do we have a list of things from everyone to you Stephanie?" I said as I looked to her.

"Yes, the spouses thought of a lot of things that we could use more of but had, but some of the things had kind of not been thought of so I am glad they sent me to the list. I need everyone to meet me at Costco parking lot, Spouses I am talking to you. We will all be heading to various places to pick up what I already ordered for curbside pick-up. I have already placed a bunch of overnight orders online and they are already getting packed and shipped as we speak. This is going to sound harsh but work no matter how important you think it might be, is not anymore." Stephanie said as the News anchor stopped and announced the President of the United States.

"Let us all listen to this and see what we make of it after he is done." I said as the President took the podium.

"My fellow Americans, I have come to address you all as the stock markets have had a very sudden downturn which has caused many of you to panic and run out to the banks and pull your earnings from those institutions. I can assure you that there is no need to worry about your finances because they are insured by the government and safe where they are. The stock market has had up swings and down swings for many years and this sudden steep downturn was stopped thanks to the SEC safeguards put into place many years ago. Ladies and Gentlemen, we are still strong and do not need to let fears take hold and drive us to panic. The market will open tomorrow morning as usual, and things will move forward. I have fielded calls from other national leaders this morning and they assure me that their markets will open as usual and that this is just another bump in the road for the global economy. With this fear and panic sweeping the nation, I have ordered all banks closed for the remainder of the day today and all day tomorrow. This is to safeguard these employees and the institutions they work for from the people who have let fear and panic grip them into doing outrageous things. Together we will all get through this, as One Nation

Under God. May he bless us all in this trying time. Thank you." He turned and walked away from the podium to reporters shouting in pandemonium at his back question after question.

My mind was awash in thought when the speaker on the tables erupted, "FUCK! People are going to go even more crazy now." It was Susan's voice. She was one of my wife's close friends and had no problem speaking her mind.

"With out a doubt" was said by James on the speaker too.

I looked around the room as I started, "OK quiet down everyone. We have prepared and talked about this for many years. We have a plan, but we also know a good plan" everyone chimed in "goes to shit at first contact" I smiled and continued. "Yes, it does and we all have talked so much but never honestly thought it would come to this, maybe we did. But it was not what we had ever wanted, despite this, we are here now, and it is happening. It is happening faster than I thought it would happen really." I said this looking around and seeing heads nodding. "Bill and I will be going wheels up today to go help bring my father back here with us. I know the plan called for just Bill to go but I want to help assure my dad because he has never really been a part of the planning process. So, change one to the plan, Criag will be in charge as I head out with Bill. Stephanie is in charge or all logistical needs, Bill, I hope you have gotten with her on all the needs you have since you are going to be with me out in California."

"Bill got with me and said Craig could answer anything that comes up as could Jeff" Stephanie chimed in.

"Great, glad you are way ahead of me on this." I said as my cell buzzed and I looked to see it was the plane crew alerting me they were twenty minutes out from landing at the local airfield. "That is our ride to Cali to pick up my dad with a twenty-minute ETA to wheels down Bill. Craig we are going to get moving. Does anyone have anything major for me before I get a move on?" I asked.

Luke started, "I do boss. All my assets are saying that the bank run is just the start and that the word is out that the Fed is going to freeze the market and put a limit on how much anyone can move in and out of banks starting after the banks are to reopen. Different contacts with my assets tell me it is going to be a soup sandwich within hours of this announcement, if it doesn't leak before then. I recommend that anything we want to do with our finances be done as rapidly as possible. We need to start moving as fast as we can while still maintaining our attention to detail."

"So, this is going to get as bad as we hoped it never would in your optics?" I asked.

"Yes boss, rapid movements on our parts is in order in my professional opinion" was Luke's reply.

"Fuck me." I heard Bella say on the speaker.

"With that I will excuse myself and Bill from this meeting but hope you will all continue to talk. Set the plans in motion everyone. We built this business knowing that it might come to this, and sadly here we are." I said as I stood and looked at Bill. "Ready buddy?" I asked moving towards the team room to get my gear bag.

"Yeah, I will Call Amada on the move. I think she will be glad you are going to cover my six' he said with a snark.

"Sure buddy, that six needs a lot more than me to cover it" I said laughing at him.

"Fuck you, you know you want this prime sexy thing" he said shaking his but at me as we entered the team room.

"That boney no meat ass is far from sexy buddy" I jeered at him.

We went to our bays, grabbed our gear, headed for the Sequia, and threw it in the back. As we jumped in, and I had it started and rolling the phone rang in the vehicle system. It was the crew calling, "We are wheels down and pulling up to the passenger terminal right now." the female voice said. "We are five minutes out" I said and hung up.

"They must have had a tail wind and got here faster than expected" Bill said.

"Yeah, or the tower brought them in priority because they know it is for us" I said.

"True enough" was his reply.

We pulled into the private passenger terminal of the airfield and unloaded our gear bags and wheeled them into the lobby. The attendant knew us and gave us a greeting and a smile. "Hey guys, taking off on a trip with all this weird stuff happening I see."

"Yeah, sadly work never stops. We clear to head out to the Cessna Citation Longitude?" I said abruptly.

"Oh yeah you are cleared, good luck to you guys." He said as we walked out the terminal doors to the tarmac and towards the beauty of a plane. The Cessna Citation Longitude had a range of 3500 nautical miles with room for 8 passengers. I was lucky to have such great friends in my life, though it was not a free ride, it was always discounted to just operational cost when flying with Mitch's company. Benefits of a long friendship that I was not willing to take advantage of and often paid full price despite his bitches and moans at me.

"You guys wanting your bags in the passenger compartment like normal?" the crew member asked as we pulled them towards the plane.

"Yeah, we do thanks." Bill told the crew member.

"Okay then, welcome aboard." the crew said stepping to the side of the passenger doorsteps. Our bags barely fit through this tight little door and we both had to duck getting into the aircraft. This Longitude was configured with a latrine in the rear with a couch that pulled out to a bed, then a four-passenger seating area and a little open space near the front passenger door up front. It was a perfect configuration for our needs this trip since we packed big gear bags heading out. We had no longer gotten our gear bags situated when the door was pulled closed, and the planes started to move.

"Hey guys get seated, and we will clear for transition to take off and get this bird in the air" the crew member said.

"Ok we are ready when you are. I take it you know where we are going and need nothing from us?" I said with a little surprise in my voice.

"Yes, our boss gave us very specific details about who it was we are going to get sir." was the reply.

"Cut the 'Sir' shit with me, I worked for a living" was my reply. It was an inside joke from Non-Commissioned Officers, NCOs, about Commissioned Officers not really working in the Army.

"Ok, not a problem. Thanks for having us take you." he said.

"I take it you are part of the guys coming to the compound here rather soon?" I asked.

"Yeah, all of us are part of that package. Thank you for including us, I know I can speak for the entire crew and others, we are grateful to have a place to go since it looks like it is going to be bad." he said.

"God help us all if it gets too bad really. I am just glad we are going to have a chance to stay safe and help one and other." I replied as I felt us go wheels up and my phone buzzed. I looked down and saw it was my wife.

"Hey sexy wife" I said.

"Hello my love. Glad I caught you before you took off." she said.

"Well, you didn't really catch me before as we are wheels up already. What is up?" I asked.

"Oh shit, then get off the phone with me and enjoy your flight. I love you and be safe my love." she snapped.

"No love we can talk if the cell stays connected, which is most likely continuously, though I have not tried to do that much. What is on your mind?" I pushed.

"I know we can talk love, just was hoping to catch you before you went wheels up, you know I hate to talk to you while you are on a flight despite you reassuring me it is fine." she said.

"Love, it is fine. What is going on in that head of yours?" I asked again.

"That this is real love. Like it is happening. Right now, right here, life as we know it is changing, and most likely for the worst and never going to be the same. I just, well, never thought it would come to this. I am a little shocked that we are here." she finally let out.

"Yeah, it is like so many of the books we have read and yet so different too. Thank God, you have blessed me with understanding all these years and came to understand what I was hoping never to have to deal with, is fucking here." I said shocked in my own way. "I love you so much. I should get off here though and talk to Bill about our plan and options should it get crazy."

"Ok my love. Give your dad my love and I will talk to you when you are there. Be safe hubby of mine." she said.

"You be safe picking up those curbside orders sexy wife and watch your six please, I love that ass" I joked.

"Oh, I know you do, love you too" she said as she broke the connection.

Bill shook his head at me and said with a smirk, "what about my ass?"

I just looked over at him and closed my eyes to catch a quick wink before we got to California. I knew I might need the rest for this operation.

Chapter 4

I woke to my arm being shaken by Bill and the look on his face said it might not be a good thing he was waking me. "What is going on?" I asked as I shook the cobwebs out from my nap. "The crew needs to talk to you, something about California airspace being restricted" Bill replied. I got up and headed for the cockpit of the Cessna to see what was going on. As I got close the flight crew member looked at me and said that the Los Angeles Air Route Traffic Control Center announced they had to land at prescribed landing areas in California or face arrest. I looked at him and said, "ok so what exactly does this mean and what are you wanting to talk to me about."

"Here go talk to the pilot" he said moving out of the way.

I slid past him and stuck my head in to hear the pilot exchanging words on the headset. He was upset and told the other end that he was a private charter aircraft that had filed a flight plan and was going to a smaller airfield in the Hemet, California area. It sounded like the other end was not allowing this and the pilot was getting upset with this. He saw me out of the corner of his eye and smirked while pointing at a spare headset. I took the hint and put them on.

"Flight 1012 I understand you have an approved flight plan, but we have been informed that all airspace in California is now restricted to landing and departing at passenger terminal approved sights only. If you do not comply with this there is the threat of arrest. I am just a relay and complying with the wishes of the state government." I caught the controller telling the pilot. The pilot looked at me and switched to internal flight communications, "what do you want to do? You know we are a very capable crew and can go wherever you want to go."

"I know you are very capable and have flown us on other missions before, so the real question is what do you think this is about?" I asked him.

"I think they are trying to stop people from coming and going in and out of the state. Maybe they are trying to stop the outflow of money? I am not sure exactly what is going on because I have never heard or seen anything like this." The pilot said.

"Ok so if we go in and land and you dump us and go airborne again how long before you need to refuel? Can we do a turn and burn without refueling" I asked.

"I could do the turn and burn and even dump you and let you go out and get your dad while we hold on the ground. I am just not sure what the response is going to be if we land." He told me.

"Let me go fill Bill in and see what he thinks about this new development." I said, turning and heading into the passenger area. Bill was already breaking open his kit and looking at it all. "So, you heard it is not going to be as easy as we had hoped I see" I told him.

"Yeah, so how hot do you think a response could be in your hometown? I remember it being pretty small and not like landing in Los Angeles or anything." He said.

"I honestly don't know. I mean I think we could get to my dad's house and get him and his stuff back in an hour. Would they be responding in an hour? And if so, what are they going to do?" I said aloud.

"Ok fuck it, if this is going south like it seems, we go like it is a hot extraction and get loaded out as such. I just hope we don't have to get in a fight with local LEO on this." I said tuning to tell the pilot what we wanted to do.

"We go like it is a hot extraction. I will call my dad and tell him to be packed and ready for us to load him out. To pick us up at the airport cafe. You taxi in and wait in that area;

do you need any of our gear to hold the plane if it gets hot?" I asked.

He smirked and replied, "no we got this and knew it could be dicey and packed accordingly."

"Ok then, let me go call my dad and get him over waiting for us at the cafe and get kitted up. How far out are we and are you going to go low level then and just VFR into land and go hard like that?" I said turning.

"Twenty minutes out and we are going to go low level VFR and dark. I just turned the transponder off, and the controller is going crazy on the channel." I heard him say as I was walking into the passenger cabin and felt the plane start descending.

Bill looked at me and smiled, "Let the party start."

"I don't want to have it be a party Bill, hoping this is just a quick in and out and nothing special except whining on the radio." I said as I started getting my gear ready. I pulled out the hard plate gear knowing this could get hot if they are going to attempt to arrest us. As I looked around, I saw the crew getting gear out too and had to smile at how prepared Mitch's guys are. I pulled out my phone and called my dad and he answered on the second ring.

"Hey kiddo, you here already?" My dad asked.

"No we are twenty minutes away and the California government just closed the airspace and made planes land at certain terminals. We are coming in low and trying to avoid issues, but I need you to come meet us at the cafe at Ryan airfield dad. We are going to be in serious kit so don't freak out. Take us straight to your house so we can pack the truck with your shit and get out of here. I am hoping to avoid trouble" I told him quickly.

"I saw something on the news about restricting travel in and out of the state to stop the flow of money or something." my dad said.

"Well, we are going to be getting you and your stuff and out as fast as we can. I hope you have things packed. I also want you to get all the family pictures you want to keep dad, I will be honest and not sure when if ever you might be back if it is this bad." I said calmly.

"I have a pile of stuff already waiting son. I am ready too. Just need you to help load it all up." dad said.

"Ok fifteen minutes out or so if you can head over and be waiting for us. It could get dicey dad, just know we will do whatever we need to do to get you out." I told him.

"Ok, I am on the way with Chase, see you soon" he said as he hung up. Chase was his dog and was not getting left behind either. I put my helmet on and turned the ears on, they amplified the sound around me and cut out loud noises. They also had my radio plugged into them so I could hear communications and not allow others around me to hear. I then keyed up the radio and gave a radio check to Bill. He had me loud and clear and I then asked the pilot if he had me which he did. The last thing I checked was my pistol and rifle to insure they were locked and loaded. The first magazine in the rifle was loaded with Hornady TAP hollow points to stop over penetration. I hoped I didn't have to worry about using any rounds.

"Five minutes out" the pilot said in my ear as I felt the plane make a step bank and lose altitude.

I clicked my push to talk button twice to acknowledge his transmission and looked at Bill. He smiled at me and said, "here we go."

I felt the plane level out and then touch down. The pilot said he knew where the cafe was and had been here before in my ear. Again, I double clicked and started looking out the windows getting my bearing. I did not see anything that looked troubling to me. As we came around the corner of a hangar, I could see my dad sitting in his old silver Toyota tundra waiting for us in the cafe parking lot. So far so good I thought.

"Deploying door," I heard the crew say in my ear as we rolled to stop, and the door came open and the stairs deployed. I came out gun up and scanning. Bill directly behind me with a crew member behind him. I saw no threat and moved quickly to my dad and Bill and I jumped in the back. "Lets go Dad!" I yelled as he started driving away.

He lived about two miles away from the cafe and the airfield. The drive was easy, and we saw nothing out of the ordinary. I was hoping this went exactly the Same on the trip back. As we backed into his driveway, I got out and looked around. The neighborhood had not changed much over the years.

"Where is all your stuff at dad?" I asked as I hugged him.

He looked at me and shook his head saying, "Right inside the door. You weren't kidding about wearing serious gear. I bet half of that isn't even legal here in California anymore."

"No dad I would say I have more than twenty years of felonies on me right now according to this shithole state and their laws. Which you know I don't give a fuck about" smirking as I said it. "Bill get his stuff and I will hold the street unless you want to hold the street."

"I'll get his shit in the truck while you talk and watch" Bill told me moving to the door. He started making trips with plastic totes. He was on his sixth trip when my ears were filled with radio traffic.

"Bear elements this is Wings, we have a patrol pulling into the cafe area looking around. No lights but he is getting out of his unit and looking around. Will advise." came the radio traffic. I double clicked the transmit and looked over to Bill.

"Two more totes!" he yelled. I ran in and grabbed one and he grabbed one. And we moved back to the truck. "Bill, you drive, dad you ride up front with him." I said as I jumped in back and bill started driving off. "I locked the front door dad, and we are on the move. I hope this isn't the last time here, but it might be. I am sorry it is like this old man." I said as we moved down the road. I had the gate code for the side gate to the airport and was thankful it was not near the cafe. I told Bill how to get to the gate and he drove to it. I jumped out and punched the code in. The gate started opening and I jumped back into the back of the truck with the totes.

"Bear be advised the officer is coming near us calling out to us with his hand on his weapon." the radio chirped in my ear.

"One mike out Wings and I will put him on the ground as we load the plane and depart. Bill go directly to the loading bay door and I will get out and engage with verbal commands. I hope he sees he is out gunned and just lets it go smoothly. Here we go" I radioed as we pulled up.

"DON'T FUCKING MOVE!" I commanded as I exited the vehicle to the frightened look of the officer seeing me in full battle kit and rifle trained on him. "I AM NOT HERE TO HARM YOU OR ANYONE ELSE. DO AS I COMMAND AND WE WILL BE LEAVING SHORTLY! NOD YOUR HEAD IF YOU UNDERSTAND ME" He nodded his head and then moved his hands high above his head. I moved in close to him and kept him covered as Bill and the crew members loaded the plane.

"Please don't hurt me I have a family" the officer pleaded.

"I am not going to hurt you and don't even want to hold you at gun point, but this crazy world just doesn't want to stop today so here we are. I do not want to restrain you either. So, tell me why you are here?" I said as I lowered my weapon to the low ready knowing I had him complying.

"I got a call to service to check and see if a plane had landed here at the airport. I radioed the dispatchers that it looked like a private jet was here. They have not radioed back. That is all I know." the officer said.

"Take your left hand and unplug your ear bud from the mike so I can hear the radio traffic please" I asked him. He reached slowly and pulled the plug from the mike. His radio was alive with chatter. I heard the jet engines whining to life and knew we were soon to be moving out. "Two Minutes" my ears said. I clicked twice in acknowledgement.

"Who are you guys?" the officer asked as I saw him stiffen from a radio call.

"They're asking if you are 10-4?" I said.

"You law enforcement too? I mean you know the calls and are a pro so what is going on?" he said.

"I just came here to get my dad." I pointed at him loading the plane with his dog. "On the way here the air traffic controller told us we had to land at certain airports and couldn't come here. As you can see, I don't give a fuck what the government of California has to say about where I go or what I do"

The officer nodded at me, "so you just want to leave and be on your way no harm no foul then?" he asked.

"Yes" I said as my ear said they are ready to roll. I could hear sirens in the background now.

"Can I trust you to let you just walk towards your unit and not look back. I honestly didn't even want to go to gun, but I am leaving with my dad today, no matter what it takes." I said, backing towards the plane as it started to roll.

"Good luck to you folks. I am not sure what is going on, but you could have easily killed me, and you didn't. You have my word I will turn and call in and go to my unit. As long as I have your word I get to see my family tonight." he said sternly.

The officer turned and started walking as I went up the stairs and pulled them up and the crew pulled the door closed. The Jet engines whined louder as the plane started moving more rapidly. My ears came alive that the pilot was going to get us airborne, and we had best all get seated from this take off and flight path. I turned to see Bill already helping my dad into a chair with Chase looking at me all crazy. All I could think was thank God it was a levelheaded police officer that knew he was dealing with professionals and had not tried anything. As I sat back in my chair it more or less sucked me in from the force of the take-off and immediate bank.

"The Los Angeles Air Route Traffic Control Center is all over the radio now and they are looking for our signature in the air. I have not heard anything like this since 9/11. Why are they restricting air traffic?" the pilot asked over our radio channel.

"I can only guess that California is trying to cut their losses and stop their big money people from taking off to other places. How are we looking on fuel and how will this affect our return to the compound?" I asked

"We can get back no problem, but we can't be taking a huge detour or anything. I am not sure how Albuquerque Air Route Traffic Control Center is going to act when we come up to talk to them. If we have to we will just go dark all the way home. Either way we can make it work" came the reply.

"Ok, thank you for this. It means a lot." I told him.

"Stop, we know what we are getting into and that you have taken us into the compound with our families. So, this is part of the job now. We are all a part of this now." Came the reply.

"Got it. ETA to our local airfield?" I asked.

"One hour thirty-seven minutes give or take. I am going to stay at a low level then pop up and get radio coms with Albuquerque Air Route Traffic Control Center when we get in their zone. If they get silly, we will go low level and get home." He said.

"Ok. Keep me informed if it gets crazy, I am going off coms to talk to my dad." I told him as I took my helmet off and looked at my father. He was drinking a beer and smiling at me.

"Well, that was a little more serious than I thought it would be" my dad said sipping at his beer.

"Yeah, you and me both. Got ya a beer already from them hmm?" I said smiling at him. It was even a Bohemia, which he liked a lot.

"How could I turn one of these down with all the excitement? What was that about anyways? Is it really this bad that you are going to threaten a police officer?" He went on.

"Getting you at all cost old man, and yeah it is this bad. It is going to just continue from here on out. I just hope they don't try to intercept us at this point, though I think they most likely have more important things to deal with." I said looking out the window.

"Intercept as in fighters?" my dad asked.

"Yeah, and not much we can do about those besides do as they ask." I said.

"Well, here is to hoping nothing like that happens" he said as he raised the beer and drained it.

"I second that" Bill said as he was putting his kit away.

"Thanks for getting me son, and thank you for risking it too, Bill. Have you talked to your brother son?" my dad asked.

"Fuck! No, I have not, have you?" I said.

"I talked to him earlier today when all this started, and he said not to worry that it was just another downturn. He said it was going to be fine and that the government would take care of it like always. I asked if he had supplies if it goes bad, and he just laughed at me and said I was being like you." my dad told me.

"I am an ass and didn't even think about grabbing him while we were out this way. I mean he most likely wouldn't come with me at this point because it is just starting, but they are already restricting travel in California, so it is only going to get worse from here. Add to this that it is mostly only electric vehicles now and all the trouble they have been having trying to keep the grid going. Who knows, I should call him." I said.

"He will have to take care of himself, but I hope you are willing to get him too if he asks" my dad said looking at me with serious eyes.

"You know I would try dad, but he is his own person and never wants to think about it being as bad as it most likely will get." I said.

As I finished my phone buzzed, I looked at the screen and I saw it was Luke. "Hey what is up? You don't call while I am on an Op unless it is pressing." I said.

"Boss shit is about to get extremely crazy. The air travel restriction that California put in place for air travel is going national in twenty minutes with another news conference. Not sure how they are going to spin it but the reality is they do not want people to head for the hills. All my sources are saying things are about to go very sideways. Major cities are seeing riots and looting already in the streets with opportunists taking full advantage. My sources inside the Fed are saying that the crash is the start of a complete economic meltdown. That they are scrambling to try to stabilize it all, but the bank run started a precious metals run, and it has not stopped. This is the real deal boss. I thought you should know right away." He said with a tone of shock I had not heard in his voice.

"Thanks for the heads up, get with Criag and Stephenie if you have not briefed them. Let's get the liquidation plan rolling if Stephanie has not done that yet." I told Luke as Bill sat forward in his seat trying to listen.

"Liquidation in motion" Bill said quizzically.

"Will do Boss. See you soon" he disconnected.

"Yeah Bill, all of Luke's sources and informants are saying it is going to completely melt. They are putting a national flight restriction up in a bit with a news conference he said." I replied to Bill.

"Wow" my dad said.

"Well then we are going to be busy for sure." Bill said as I got up to go talk to the pilot.

"Hey" I said as I looked in on the pilot.

"What is up" he asked.

"Have you come up on the Albuquerque air control net yet?" I asked.

"I just did and was listening to the chatter. They are letting all the flights head to their destinations, but new flights must go to certain airports only. It really does remind me of the air traffic after the 9/11 attacks. We are cleared into our local airport. Should be in about thirty minutes or less. You good?" He asked me.

"Yeah, we are all going to be good. I have staged vehicles there for us to take back to the compound. Should be enough room for us all if you guys are heading there too." I said.

"We are going to get this thing put to bed when we get back then head over. Protocols the same as always to get in at the compound?" He asked.

"Yeah, they are. You all know the drill and it will only get more serious from here on out it seems." I told him as I turned to head back to my seat.

I was honestly having a tough time understanding just how fast this train was moving. I had thought about this happening for years, talked to Rae about it often but it just was going so much faster than I had thought it possible. It was almost dinner time at home and already cities had started looting and rioting, air travel was getting restricted, precious metals had spun up in price, the banks had been closed, and that was just the start of what I knew since going to get my dad. It was going to be a lot more crazy than I had ever imagined it seems, I knew time would tell.

Chapter 5

After landing we loaded all the stuff out of the plane into the vehicles we had staged. Bill drove one of the company trucks to the compound with all my dad's stuff and I took him to the Sequia. I was sad for my father to see his entire life packed into storage bins but glad to have him here with us. Now I had to shift my thinking and look to the future for us all. I had the Patriot Channel on in the vehicle as we pulled out and they were going live to the White House press room for a news conference.

"Let's listen as the Press secretary is about to start," said the new anchor.

"Hello all, today, as we are all aware of, the stock markets have seen a downturn that has caused many to panic. This panic has created a fear that is now sweeping the nation for no reason. With concern the Federal government and this administration have started to implement measures we hope to help calm you the American people. The President earlier closed the banks nationally in hopes that it would slow the panic as people rushed out to try and get their money. This panic rush caused fear and thus caused people to take to the streets which in turn caused travel issues. With this in mind California was the first to try to restrict the panic in spreading with travel restrictions. Their efforts are in accordance with plans to prevent people from causing more issues and flooding out of one area and into another. Effective immediately, all air travel will be restricted to commercial carriers only." The press room got loud as reporters started to mumble among themselves to this announcement. "Settle down and let me continue before we turn to questions. "This measure means that air travel is restricted, nothing more but to keep the travel normal and not see a massive shift to private planes flooding to the airways moving from one place to another. This measure is being implemented to calm the public. Private travel by vehicle is not being affected or restricted as is the normal everyday flights from one place to another. This measure only affects private travel on private charters which is to help control the nation's monetary flow. I will now take a few questions." The press secretary finished, and I looked at my dad out of the corner of my eye.

"Well this is going to be a wild one" I said.

"Going to be? You mean it is getting weird right?" my dad replied.

"It sure isn't going like I had thought that is for sure" I said as the radio blared the pandemonium that was the news conference.

We could hear news anchors yelling over one and the other asking questions as the Press secretary yelled back to calm down and took a reporter's question.

"So as of right now private aircraft travel is suspended?" asked the reporter.

"Right now, the FAA is implementing the flight restrictions. All questions regarding what that looks like need to be fielded by the Department of Transportaion and the FAA. I can say that as we speak all private flights are being directed to land at designated passenger terminals or their intended destinations." the Secretary stated.

"We already experienced that didn't we son" my dad asked.

"Yeah, dad we did, and glad we are back on the ground and not having to deal with this drama in the air. Also, glad we have the capabilities we have because of the crews Mitch has to fly his birds, both fixed and rotary." I said.

"They seem very professional, and we sure got out of California in a hurry" was his response.

"Yeah, they can do much more than most that is for sure when it comes to flying" was all I could say.

My phone rang and the vehicle display showed it was Rae. "Hey sexy lady we are driving to the house right now" I said.

"Hey Rae" My dad said.

"Hey, I hope your flight was not too bad with all the crazy going on" she said.

"Not bad at all" My dad replied to her.

"Hey Wayne, you hearing all that is going on? Is it going to affect Mitch and his teams?" She asked.

"I am not sure how it is going to go honestly, let me get off here with you and call him" I said and hung up.

"You just cut her off?" my dad looked shocked.

"Yeah, she knows what it is about dad, not really cutting her off as much as doing what she wants me to do and needs to be done" I said as I called Mitch direct.

"Hey, things are going to be a little dicier now" Mitch said as he answered.

"I was calling to see what I need to do on my end to help it not be too crazy here" I told him.

"How are the controllers in the tower there? Can we grease the wheels to get all the birds in?" He asked me.

"I don't think locally will be the problem" I said.

"Ok, I am bringing in the planned group and assets. Most are already on the move. So the restrictions are not an issue there, but that last few will have issues and most likely have to go dark and fly in. Will this bring heat?" He said with concern.

"If it does it will not be local as they are all friends and now that I operate on a covert level at times. But these are new times so we will see" I said.

"Ok, I know the crew is bring the bird over you took the ride to Cali on now and the other assets are going to be arriving. I hope that what I asked for is enough" he said with reservation in his voice.

"Brother, we got this one way or another. When will I see you and the family?" I asked.

"I am getting everyone going after school today. I was going to wait longer but I don't think we can wait longer and still get out. I have a bird fueled and ready to go. It is only a few hours flight from here in Texas to you." He said.

"Your bird?" I asked him.

"Yeah the Hawk" he answered.

"Ok, just let me know when you are wheels up. We are going to be at the house for the night and then move to the compound as it gets worse, you guys want to get picked up and stay with us?" I asked.

"Let me talk with Melinda about that, might make it easier on the girls." was his response.

"Ok brother, talk to you later then. Safe travels" I said as I disconnected.

"Wow, he sounded calm considering son" my dad said.

"Yeah, dad this is not his first or even second rodeo" I said.

"I can tell this is going to be crazy from my perspective since you guys all seem like a well-oiled machine. I guess this is what you have been talking about for years coming to a sad reality isn't it?" He said looking at me with concern in his eyes.

"I honestly hope it isn't and we are just overreacting dad, but I think we are in for that wild ride" I said looking over at him.

"I grabbed your suitcase with all your overnight stuff dad, but is there anything else you might need? I already have a 90 day supply of your medications at the house and a 6 month supply at the compound so that is good to go. Anything else you need like special food for Chase? I have fresh chicken for him already" I said rolling my eyes at his spoiled dog.

"I see you rolling your eyes at me, and I know I spoil him." he said petting Chase.

"So, I think we have you covered for a while then?' I questioned.

"Yeah, it sounds like you really have me covered honestly. Now I can focus on the grandkids.

"Awesome, now I am calling Rae to see if she needs anything." I said punching the call button on the display.

Sher answered on the second ring, "Hello sexy man, are you on the way here? Owen is supper excited poppa is coming."

"We are getting close to the house, but I wanted to see if you needed me to pick anything up." I said.

"Nope we have it covered here. I started beef so green chili burritos tonight for diner" she said.

"Oh, that sounds good to me" my dad said.

"Glad it does dad, so I will see you guys when you get here" she said.

"Ok about ten minutes tops beautiful. Love you." I said as I got ready to hang up.

"Love you too sexy man" she said, and I ended the call.

"I hope you are ready to get mugged by Owen dad" I said smiling at him.

"Hard not to enjoy that son, hope Anthony is around too. Have you talked to Donnovan or Josh?" he asked.

"Not yet, but I am sure they are doing a bunch of stuff themselves with all that is going on." I responded.

"Surprised they have not called" he stated.

"Yeah, I thought Donnovan might have already called but not yet, I am sure they will touch base with me when they get the chance or are popping smoke to come here. Are you going to call Trevor?" I asked.

"I will call him when I get settled at your place. Will you take him in here if he wants that? Will you go get him?" he asked with concern on his face.

"It will depend on the climate, as in what the world looks like if he needs or wants that. Not going to be a simple flight to grab him now. And I honestly didn't think about him because he has always blown me off with the conversation of being prepared dad. I can't save him if he is not willing to help himself first." I said with a sad glance his way.

I turned down the road and pulled up to the house. It was a four-bedroom three bath place, so dad would have his own bathroom and room. It was in a nice neighborhood, and I liked our neighbors for the most part. We had a few issues with one of the neighborhood Karen wives, but we honestly didn't care about her or most of the neighbors beyond being neighborly.

"I know he has not been very open to being ready son, but he is family and your brother, and I hope you would try to get him if you can." he said to me.

"I love him and will do what I can for him, Christie, and Macy and you know that dad, it is just not something I had on my list as a priority." I told him.

The Garage door closed behind the Sequia while Owen came into the garage waving at us with a big smile on his face. It was a blessing to have children and come home to them so excited to see you and it was for his future and my other children's also that I tried to get us ready for what the world might throw at us.

My dad slid from the seat and let Chase go running over to Owen while I got out and grabbed his suitcase out of the back.

"Poppa!!! Yeah, Chase nice to see you too." Owen said excitedly as Chase excitedly licked his hands.

"Hey Owen, how are you doing?" My dad asked him.

As we entered the hallway from the garage Rae met us and got Chase in the house and showed my dad to the guest room, though he knew where it was at. "It is all set up for you dad, if you need anything let us know or you know where it is most likely. Glad you are here with us" Rae said.

The evening into the night went quick as we ate and relaxed from our quick trip and tried not to think about what was happening around the world but instead enjoyed the gathering of family and togetherness. I had gotten a few update texts from Luke throughout and they did not look good. Many reports of the big cities crumbling and riots in the streets. We stayed away from the news and anything that had breaking news on until the boys were off to bed as we planned to move forward normally until our town yielded to the inevitable.

As the boys got tucked in and I retreated to the living room I turned the channel to CNN with the volume low. My dad said he was tired and heading to bed too and Chase followed after him. Rae sat next to me on the couch and watched as report after report talked about the panic in the streets of America.

"Do you really think this is it, that it is going to not get better?" she asked me.

"It sure looks like this thing is not going to stop, but I am praying that it is not going to happen, but deep-down love, we are in it for real." I said rubbing my face. I could not believe it myself, after years of thinking it was going to happen, I was still having a tough time accepting that it was here, that this was it. Sure, I had thought it was going to happen and had a few scares in the last couple of years, but nothing like this. They restricted air travel already, which I was still trying to assess what that was about and had asked Luke to figure out exactly what the play was with the government doing this. As of yet he had nothing for me on this aspect.

"So, I go to work tomorrow, and the kids go to school?" she asked as we watched rioters in Albuquerque breaking into stores and banks on the local news. This was the closest major city in New Mexico to us and the compound. And it showed that we are not too far from the chaos and realities that this current market collapse panic created. It revealed the fear gripping the people as they came to the stark conclusion that they had no money in their wallets and only plastic.

"Yes, we move forward business as usual as a family until it is no longer sustainable to stay at here at home." I said.

"What is the point that we decide to not continue as usual then in your eyes?" Rae asked.

"I honestly am not sure love, I mean I did not think I would go grab my dad this quick, but it looks like it was the right move. I still am in shock and hoping I started the plan for no real reason." I said looking at her and seeing the worry I felt in my heart too in her eyes.

"I think we reacted perfectly, even if this blows over, which I think we both know is not going to be the case love. This is the start to something very shitty, and no matter how I look at it, we are going into it." she said as she pulled close to me.

"I am scared too" I said as I pulled her closer to me "but we have each other and the kids and the team love. We are going to be ok, sure it will get bad, but we have tried to cover all the bases in the last few years to create a plan to survive it all."

"I know, lets go to bed I want you sexy man of mine" she purred as she got up and walked away towards our room shacking her sexy ass.

"As you wish" I said jumping up and chasing her to the room.

Chapter 6

The morning started again as the alarms woke us. We did not hit the snooze today but instead got right up and turned the TV on to the news. As I grumbled and got up, I looked at my phone that read 0615 and had three messages from Luke. All three told the story of the night and the early morning panic in our government as the people of America started to tear from fear which in turn caused the administration to look to stop the spread of the panic with no real since of what was to come. As I was reading his last text my phone started to vibrate and showed an incoming call from Luke instead of a message, which troubled me. Luke only called if the information was urgent.

"Talk to me buddy" I said into my phone as I answered.

"Boss you need to get Mitch here as soon as possible if he is not already in the air. They are calling for all travel to stop starting at 10 AM Eastern Standard Time this morning. All the major cities have had most of the banks broken into, stores looted, people in the streets. You did the right thing yesterday and today it is going to get bad. I would recommend we circle the wagons and bring everyone in. This is no shit the real deal." He blurted out in a fast no nonsense tone that I know and trust.

"Wilco" I said hanging up.

Rae looked at me all serious now, "who was that and what is going on?"

"Luke it is not stopping and moving faster now, travel ban starting at 8 our time" I said as I punched in the speed dial for Mitch.

It rang three times and Mitch answered. "Hey dude, you are calling early." He said.

"Nationwide travel ban going into effect starting in about an hour is the word I just got from Luke." I told him rapidly.

"Ok I will get Melinda to get the girls up and going and we will go wheels up as soon as we can. I will be flying dark and coming straight to the compound area. I will see you there and thanks for the heads up friend." Mitch said.

"Stay safe and see you and the girls in a while." I said as the connection broke.

"Plans changing for all of us then?" Rae asked.

"I don't know love, I guess we need to accept the reality that things have changed, and we need to figure it out where we know we are going to be safe." I said.

"And that means the compound then. Do we tell everyone to come or is it at their own coming?" she asked.

As she finished, we heard the TV blare 'Breaking News' that the President was going to address the nation at 10 Eastern this morning and talk about the current market downturn the panic in the streets. I looked at Rae and she rolled her eyes at the announcer's tone, she really disliked, maybe hated, this announcer.

"I guess that settles it then, let's get everyone going and head out to the compound and start thinking about what this all means long term. We can figure out if we need to ask everyone to come when we get ourselves settled in." I told Rae.

"Ok I will get the kids up and tell them to pack the things they need, their stuff at the compound is already set and good to go right" she asked.

"Yeah, they have all the systems and games we have here there, they might need to update it there though, but our internet there is more state of the art than here anyways" I replied giggling a little. The boys loved to game, and honestly, I loved to game with them as did Rae, so our home system was surprisingly good, but I had an amazingly fast state of the art closed system that used Star Link and fiber optic in the compound.

"Do you want me to get your dad going too" she asked.

"No, I will go wake him" I said as I heard him coming up the hall.

"Wake me?" he said with a smile on his face looking at me as he walked into the door frame of our room. His guest room was just down the hall from our master bedroom.

"I should have known you would be up, yeah change of plans as it is getting worse faster then I had planned" I said.

"I saw on the phone that it was crazy this morning and it is shocking. I am glad you came and got me out of California, and I want to talk to you about getting your brother" he said.

"Dad, that might be a very larger order since they are going to put a travel ban in place here in a few minutes. We can talk about how to get him when we get to the compound if that is ok. You could call him and see what they are planning to do and that might help me think about a plan." I said to him.

"Ok, I will call him and see what they are doing. I know that his politics are not yours, but he is family son" dad said as he turned and headed to the bathroom in the hall.

My brother and I have been different for an exceptionally long time, as kids we played cops, robbers, cowboys, and Indians, with Star Wars and G.I. Joe, and even went shooting with my dad. He never liked to hunt while I did, I went off to the Army and he stayed in California and went to college and continued to play golf on a professional level. I am not sure at what point he developed his political stance, it might have come from his high school love and wife, Christie, but I am not sure. Either way, he fell in the middle but leaned left and stayed to the left with his wife who was leaning far left. Regardless of all this, I still loved him and his family dearly. His daughter Macy was very left leaning also but would sit with me at gatherings and ask me a lot of questions and show how smart she was and that she was a deep critical thinker. I would make every effort to help them, it was not a priority to me however, sadly, because he had not wanted to be a part of the compound when it was brought up to him.

"You know your dad is going to push that a lot right" Rae asked.

"Oh Yeah, I know sexy. I just hope he knows I will do what I can but that Trevor had a chance to be a part of all this from the ground up, and he wrote it off as not needed" I said.

"I know this, but your dad will want us all together regardless. Just don't get upset when he starts to push sexy man of mine." she said.

"No promises my love" I said as my mind turned to what was at hand, getting us going to the compound.

Most of our supplies and gear were already stored at the compound. That being said, we still had clothes and other things that we kept at home in case we had to get to the compound which was about 15 miles from home. Anthony had his car which he could load out whatever he wanted to bring with him, which most likely would be his Warhammer 40K sets. He loved that tabletop game that his older brothers David and Donnovan had gotten all of us into long ago. I would make sure he was armed today just to be sure and to add another gun to the convoy as we went out to the compound. I went out to eh living room and used my loud voice that I learned to project while in the Army training others to be better at what they do.

"Family Meeting" I boomed out.

I heard "Ok" replies through the house and even from my dad.

As everyone came into the living room, I had switched the TV to CNN and the announcers where babbling about the President addressing the Nation at any minute.

"Ok the President is going to announce that travel is restricted. I am not sure of the details as my sources did not know exactly how restricted it was going to be but state to state travel is banned starting at 10AM Eastern 8AM here. So, we are going to pack up our things and go live out at the compound for the foreseeable future everyone. I need you to go pack the things you want there as we might not be coming back here anytime soon, so pack accordingly. Anthony, pack your go kit in your front seat and make sure you have your weapons out of your safe locked and loaded just in case please. I am not going to sugar coat it to you guys as you know I try to tell you how it is always, our country and most likely the world is going to crumble into a panicked chaos in the next few days and what that looks like moving forward I honestly have no idea. I know we have each other, and an effective team built that is going to be at the compound. So, we will be able to deal with most problems." As I said this last part the announcers said here is the President of the United States. The family turned to the TV and listened.

"Good morning my fellow Americans. I have come to you early this morning as panic has swept into the streets of

America overnight. I asked all of you yesterday not to let fear drive you and your emotions and despite my pleas fear has swept our great Nation. This fear has caused panic and thus many banking institutions have seen capital pulled from accounts large and small and even the destruction of banking sites. The stock markets of the world have also seen a steep downturn which has caused greater fear not only in America but throughout the world. We have seen this fear causing people to leave their jobs and head home, many starting a journey to their countries of origin. Yesterday my administration started to restrict travel in order to help stem the fears from spreading and growing. Today I come before you with more measures to help stop the fear and break this continuing cycle. In just a few minutes the stock exchanges will open, and the American people will see that their fears were for not. Regardless of this opening, I have instructed that a temporary travel ban be in effect starting at 10AM Eastern Standard Time. This travel ban is to stop people from traveling to places to spread fear and unrest. It was a trying and tough decision to make since our great nation is founded on freedoms. These freedoms are God given and should not be treaded upon lightly. With respect to these freedoms, state to state travel is temporarily banned. This measure will not affect many in their daily lives and will stop the flow of people who are flocking to the cities causing unrest. There are many exceptions to this travel ban and the many agencies that will be enforcing this ban are being given the rules to be able to address you directly and not make me take more of your time than needed. These are temporary and will be in place a day or two as the market returns to normal and the fear that is gripping many subsides. This small inconvenience will help to stem the unrest and will not be noticed by most. Together we are stronger. Let us stand together and not let panic and fear drive us for it is not the American way. God Bless you all and God Bless America." the President ended, and the screen cut to the reporters.

"That was the President of the United States addressing the nation as more strict travel bans go into effect in just a little over 35 minutes from now. The stock market is set to open in 5 minutes under very trying times. I have been given the travel restriction rules and my producers are going to place them on the screen as I read them." the news anchor continued.

"Ok, well here we go then. I think we need to all get going and start packing the things we want. Remember boys you already have a second gaming system set up on the compound so no need to take any of that with you. I am going to watch and see what happens as the market opens while I am getting all my gear ready to go also. Questions?" I asked as I looked around.

"No school then dad?" Owen said excitedly as he jumped around a little.

"No school today buddy, go pack up like we are staying at the compound for a while ok?" was my response to him.

"AWESOME!" he yelled as he ran off.

"I wish I felt the same way buddy" I said under my breath watching him run off excited.

"Oh My God!" Rae said. Her words broke me from my trance as I looked at her to see what she was upset about. The TV showed the current stock market numbers down in the bottom left corner of the screen, and it was already more than eight hundred points down with less than a minute into trading. The news anchor face took over the screen as they broke away from the travel restrictions. He was staring at the camera with a blank almost stunned look. Rae, my dad, and I all watched as if it seemed like forever before he started to talk, and when he did his words and voice sounded broken and unsure.

"The markets just opened and are already, wait, um, they are already down, wait, um, the market was just frozen, and trading suspended as it opened and, well, it um, seemed to crash." the reporter said looking pale and stunned.

"Welcome to reality" my wife said to the TV as she turned and went to get packed.

"Damn son, it was barely open, what happened?" my dad asked.

"I don't know exactly what happened dad besides it has crashed and this is going to make things worse, far worse. We need to get our stuff together and I know you already are mostly packed. Do I need to get your anything?" I said to him as I watched the reporter try to explain what was happening while looking shell shocked.

"No, I am good and will go see how Owen is doing and Chase and I will help him" he said as he went off towards the boy's rooms.

"Ok" I said as I returned my focus on the news reporter. As I did my phone vibrated with an incoming call. I looked to see who was calling, figuring it to be one of the team members. I was shocked to see it was the Sheriff calling me.

"Hey Mike, how are you?" I asked.

"Cut the shit Wayne" he said and continued "The nation is going to shit, and I know you have a plan, so are you going to help me if I need help?"

"I have talked to you about this at length Mike and you know I will try to help with what I can, but I am not in the game of helping those who are not going to help themselves. So, what exactly are you asking here?" I spoke. I had helped Mike and Charles, his undersheriff, get elected when he was tired of the incumbent sheriff and his inability to stem crime in the county. I had spent many hours training his agency and talked to him at length with the county board on emergency preparedness. So, he knew I was ready and wanted my community ready as well.

"I am asking for your help if shit goes sideways Wayne. If I need help, your team will come to help us, me. I think you know me well enough that I would call only on you if the situation was dire, and I needed a solid team to pull us out of the fire. I know how to police the community; I do not know how to stop war or those who might bring war to our streets. I know I might not be sounding straight but I am hoping you get the meaning of what I am asking of you and your team Wayne." He said.

"I get what you are asking now Mike, and you have my word that I will try to help you if it is at all possible." I told him.

"That is all I can ask of you Wayne and hope that it never comes to this, but the city is not ready like you have told them and the county board over and over. People here in our county are going to go crazy with the travel ban restrictions the President just released, and I am not too keen on them myself, seems rather unconstitutional and glad we are not a county the borders another state because I don't think I would enforce this. That being said, I was just reaching out because I know you are ready for whatever is coming. You have our frequencies but are you monitoring them?" He said.

"We are going to start our radio room operations today and will be monitoring if you can't reach us on the phone." I replied.

"Thank you, Wayne, hope it doesn't get worse, but the market just crashed again so we will see." Mike said.

"I hope not too Mike, but we both know that hope is not enough." I said.

"Ain't that the truth. Talk more soon Wayne." he said as the line went dead.

I had been watching CNN's anchor struggle with the news that the market collapsed again upon opening as trading was stopped due to the circuit breaker taking over. It had not stopped the sudden and violent sell-off of all the major banks' stocks. And the anchor was talking with a financial analyst asking how this could happen and whether it not be stopped before such a steep downturn. Everyone was refusing to use the word collapse to try to stop the fear, and I found it ironic because the public knew what a crash looked like, yet we are still trying to play the word games that have plagued America in the past decade.

The anchor cut off the analyst and spoke directly to the camera, "All trading has been suspended for the day. It was just announced by the SEC that all trading is suspended

Tuesday. The announcement follows: Due to the opening rapid decline in the market and the current circuit breakers' inability to stop such a rapid and deep downturn, it is in the best interest to suspend trading for the day. The market will reopen Wednesday morning at the opening bell barring any issues that arise from the failed circuit breaker."

"That is wild" said the analyst before his mic was abruptly turned off mid-sentence.

"Again, the SEC has stopped trading today due to a faulty circuit breaker that was unable to stop the steep downturn. Their statement says trading will resume tomorrow barring any issues. Stay tuned as we bring you the latest information on the stock market and news across the world." the announcer said as it went to commercial.

"Fuck" is all I said as I turned and left the living room to go pack.

"They suspended trade today love" I said as I walked into the bedroom.

"Yeah, they are still trying to control it thinking it will stop. This is the real thing isn't it sexy" my wife asked.

"Mike just called me as the market was stopped and asked if I was going to support him" I told her.

"Damn, seriously? Like he knows it has started after all the times you talked to him about it?" She said.

"Yeah, just as if he knew I was the one to talk to about it all coming down." I said.

"What did he really ask for my love?" she asked me as he stood looking at me seriously.

"That if it went bad, I knew more about war than he did, and it was not community policing at that point is pretty much what he was saying. As in would I help him if it got seriously bad. Before you ask, I told him I cannot help those that do not want to help themselves first. That I would help if I could." I said, looking at her as she crossed her arms looking at me.

"You are not going to just let them fall are you?" she said.

"If they fail and fall, our community is doomed my love. As much as I dislike a large segment of our community, it is our future to make sure this doesn't get too wild here." I told her as I pulled her close to me reaching around and grabbed her by the ass and kissed her. As I finished the kiss looking in her eyes, "The future of our children and our children's children will rely upon the shoulders of good men. I hope I can be one of the good men love, that I can bring men together and create a community of good men."

"You are a good man sexy man of mine. I know you will do your best to create a future for us all." she said looking deep into my eyes.

"I can only try sexy. That is all I can do." I said letting her go and moving to pack out the little bit of gear I kept at home.

It took us another hour to get it all put how we wanted it and ready to close the house like we would not be returning for a while. I even went out and shut off the water and closed the return from the sewage. I had put in a valve to close out the sewage line because if it got really bad people did not understand that it could all back up into their homes. I was hoping to be able to come back home one day, and I honestly hoped I was wrong, and things would stabilize. As we left the house and headed for the compound, I looked around the neighborhood and prayed it wasn't going to be the last time.

Chapter 7

As we drove to the compound, I had gotten out a set of radios for each person in the vehicles, at times I tend to over prepare just in case. The old 'better to have and not need than it is to need and not have' thing. My dad knew I was always trying to be prepared but the level of my preparedness was exceedingly high in his eyes because he had never really seen me in operational mode much less the mindset of doing things like this. My mother and him had attended my graduation years ago for basic training, then they had come to see me get my green beret and long tab after graduating from Special Forces. Sure, they had visited a few times and he saw a team room or two, but he never saw me in operational mode, just tour guide mode and he was shocked at how thorough I was at going over plans and contingency plans.

I was the lead vehicle and had no passengers in case I had to get in contact and let the others continue to the compound. Anthony and my dad were the number two spot and my wife pulling up the rear with Owen riding shotgun. We had practiced this a few times in the last couple of years after the boy got his license and talked in detail about it as we prepared to leave earlier. Now as we drove, we started to see that the collapse and the issues it was causing were here in our hometown. We stayed away from the main roads in town and took the long route around, but it still went by a corner with two gas stations, a bank and a car dealership that was out on the edge of town. The bank had a bunch of people and they looked very agitated.

"Heads up the bank has people that look pissed, stay aware and if people approach us be prepared to go even if the light is red." I called out on the radio.

I got a bunch of 'roger' called out on the radios, even Owen called out which made me proud of him. As we got to the intersection the light was green and we rolled past the crowd. I could see the bank doors had been pushed in and lay all broke. The ATM machine looked like it was all broken open also. Then I saw the flashing lights coming our way and I was torn if I should pull to the side and that is when my years of following the law took over and I slowed and pulled over, but I did not stop just rolled slowly on the side of the road. I looked back and everyone was following suit.

"We are not stopping, just giving them room, and keeping going. Watch around you as we go." I called out again on the radio.

"The crowd is looking up now hearing the sirens and they are looking at us and the police cars" Rae called out on the radio.

Sure enough, the crowd was looking at us and our way because the lights and sirens were coming from this direction. It was not the police it was the Sheriff department responding with two of their trucks. I could not remember if this area was county or city here, but the Sheriff had taken the call or they were the first on the scene, either way the crowd did not run or seem to care as much that they are arriving. It was weird watching the crowd not really caring that law enforcement was coming. Maybe I had expected more from people in my own town, but I should have known better.

"Gun!! Gas station left side long gun" I heard from Rae on the radio.

"Everyone drive hard past me I am stopping and providing security. You know the route and what to do, we talked about this. Go! Go! Go! Dropping to S O frequency" I called out as I pulled more to the side and stopped with my nose of the vehicle angled away from the possible threat.

"Roger" Echoed in my ear as Anthony gunned it along with Rae and they vaulted past me and continued on.

I was wearing a covert chest rig that had three rifle magazines with my radio, combat belt with my standard setup, and I had my rifle tucked in at my right leg like I had most days in this vehicle. I slammed the vehicle in park then reached down and grabbed the pistol grip on the rifle as I was already opening and starting to exit the vehicle. I could see the first Sheriff deputy as he passed me looking at the bank just to the rear of my vehicle and not seeing the threat to his right.

The guy with the long gun was bringing it up towards the deputies' vehicle as I was out of the Sequia, to the rear, and had already deployed my rifle on target. I was torn at that moment; do I shoot and stop the possible threat or let it play out and see what happens. In that millisecond I decided not to depress the trigger and end the possible threat, instead watched as I changed frequencies on my radio to the Sheriff dispatch radio frequency. The threat just watched the deputies pulling up to the scene with his eyes looking to be on the lead unit.

I keyed the radio, "deputies responding to the bank call there is a threat to your right in the gas station. I say again deputies responding to the bank call there is a threat to your right in the gas station."

I could see the threat and he was just watching the deputies as they came to a stop. As they stopped, they ducked down and exited their vehicles and looked towards the threat. I guess my call had changed things as both deputies had long guns out and coming up. The threat looked surprised that they came out like they did and hesitated.

"Drop your fucking gun!!!" I heard echoes from the deputies as they zeroed in on the threat. I had the threat dead to rights in my aimpoint micro with the dot on his face. He distinctly showed fear on his face now seeing the two deputies aiming at him. He looked to be a MAM, military aged male, in his early to mid-twenties and Caucasian. He had an AR variant rifle that did not look too special with some sort of dot sight I could not tell from this distance what it was. The crowd at the bank was also stunned and started to scatter in all directions.

In my earpiece I heard a deputy transmit "410 to S O, 97, Code 3 one at gun point 10-3 the air. Break, who called with the warning." I immediately pushed the transmit key "Bear 017 to 410 it was me." All the deputies on the local sheriff department knew who I was, all my teams call signs, and most had trained at the compound or had one of my guys train them at their department range.

"S O to all units the air is 10-3 I say again the air is 10-3" came the dispatch response.

"410 to Bear, you on this guy too? I can see his weapon aimed in my general direction but not much of him" he transmitted to me.

"435 to 410 I have him if Bear doesn't." came a report from the other deputy.

"I have him and could drop him now, but he looks unsure and scared. You want me to start giving commands to mess with his OODA loop?" I asked. The ODDA loop is a person's natural response to observe, orient, decide, and act. Our OODA loop can be broken, and this can cause a hesitation or pause in any of the four cycles when something out of the ordinary happens.

"Yes. 435 I am going to move down my truck. If either of you think he is going to pop off a shot drop him." came 410's reply.

"Roger" our relies on the radio echoed and I immediately started to give commands.

"PUT THE FUCKING RIFLE DOWN!! RIGHT FUCKING NOW!! IF YOU DO NOT PUT IT DOWN, I AM GOING TO FUCKING KILL YOU!!" I commanded in my booming military voice. It made the guy with the gun actually jump and almost drop his rifle. As his head shifted my way so too did his rifle slightly. Most people that are not well trained will move their weapons the way their heads move, even well-trained personnel can fall prey to this. What he saw was a guy at the end of an SUV aiming a weapon with a weird looking can on the end of it smiling at him. I was smiling to throw off his OODA loop even more. It worked and he let go of the rifle and it dangled on his chest at a weird angle because he had some sort of sling. His hands flying high in the air like rockets as he looked at me now with complete fright knowing I had him in my sights the entire time and death was but a small squeeze of a trigger away.

"435 to 410, I have cover you can go secure him. Bear do you see any other threats?" came the call from deputy 435.

"Negative on threats. I am scanning and see none. 410 and 435 I have other urgent business if you are good here I am moving on." I radioed as I moved back to the driver seat and saw the deputy securing the guy that had the gun.

He looked my way and gave me the thumbs up. As I heard him transmit, "410 to S O, 10-2 the air we are 89 here with one 15. Break, thanks Bear for the assist." I gave him the thumbs up and switched my radio back to our family channel and listened. I did not hear any traffic on the radio so that was a good thing.

"Bear 006 this is bear 017, over." I called.

"Go for Bear 006" was the immediate reply from my wife.

"Everything is good to go here and heading your way. Are you secure at the compound yet?" I asked.

"We are secure and good to go here. Glad it is good there, we can debrief and AAR upon your arrival" she said.

"Roger that" was all I could think of as she had turned into her military self on the radio with the operational mindset that I knew she had from a few deployments down range.

As I drove on towards the compound, I reflected on how the situation at the bank had turned out to be far more serious than I had thought and that I was blinded into focusing on just the bank, which was not my nature, but it happened. I was also glad I did not have to pull the trigger on that guy because I did not need the headache that would come from it. The collapse of the markets had not stopped society and the rule of law, and if I had shot that guy, I would have had my rifle taken and the process started to see if it was justifiable. I knew the Sheriff would have my back and knew it would have been justified, but that was what stopped me from pulling the trigger if I was at all honest. I did not want to deal with the bureaucratic shit storm of killing a person right now as the world around us slowly collapsed. Well not as slowly as I might have thought it would.

I got to the compound and pulled to the gate. Then I punched in the code and watched the outer gate open along with the first set of bastions allowing me to pull up into the secondary area and the other gate with bastions behind it. It didn't take long for the outer gate and bastions to redeploy, and the second gate opened as its bastions retracted. The compound had a five-foot-high dirt berm around the perimeter with an eight-foot-high razor wire topped fence apart from the area attached to the airfield. That area has a ten-foot chain link fence with razor wire on it and a M50 P1 post and Beam fence from Ross 18 feet inside the outer fence. Three areas attaching the property to the airfield had the ability to move to allow aircraft of all sizes to come park in my area should that be needed. I had leased space to American Airlines to park a slew of their aircraft during Covid in my area. It made a bunch of money when things slowed on the contracting side. One area was capable of being opened for big shipments but rarely used since we could open both sections of the compound entrance at the same time to allow bigger freight onto the compound.

I had put a lot of thought into the compound with the hopes that should I need it, I could stay here for as long as needed and still be able to defend it from a more superior force. I had solar, wind, and was using the aquafer and was lucky to be able to tap into a geothermal area and generate energy from it. This gave the compound a multi-faceted electrical system. The use of geothermal energy gave the compound the ability to have continued energy almost indefinitely, and this source was not known to many people and utilized for the bunker system and tied to the battery banks from the solar and wind systems in case they had an issue providing the power to keep them charged.

I had five different drinking water wells on the property, and each was a different depth and possibly a different source of water. This was the hope when I contacted the well company to do the drilling and they assured me we had tapped at least three different water sources in the five wells. This redundancy was part of my military training where one is none. The company owner assured me that two wells was more than enough, but my money was still good for him to take and give me the other three wells reluctantly.

Needless to say, I had tried to cover all my bases and when I took on more of my friends and added to the team their experiences and knowledge went into building a better compound. Troy, our network specialist, was instrumental in getting the compound wired tight for all the technologies we wanted to run. Rae had worked with him in the school district and talked to him about his military service and eventually we recruited him. He was a communications and IT specialist in the Army for six years then got out and started working in network and IT. He helped integrate our systems and was part of our radio system and Android Team Awareness Kit (ATAK) setup too.

Craig, Paul, Jeff, Bill, and Frank had all served on a team with me at one time or another. Bill and Craig are probably the closest thing I have to best friends and had put up with my shit talking and grumpy self for more than a decade and stuck around. Not to say Paul, Frank, or Jeff are not good friends, just how it is in my head, I guess. These five guys and I are the heart of Bear Tactical and are the core team. All the employees of the company are well trained in shooting and have passed our courses, just these five guys had been operational in many parts of the world doing work on the sharp end of the stick.

The maintenance team was our second team, they all had operational time in the military and a few combat tours too. They did not operate at the level that the other five had, but they are a strong and formidable team, on top of that they understood the systems of the compound to the bare bones. Adam led this team and he could ramble off almost anything you needed to know about a system on the compound and this is what I had required of him. I found this team to be more valuable than my team because without them the compound could fail, and that was not an option for any of us.

The entire Bear Tactical team was tight and friends along with their families. We did many things together to try to build this kind of relationship that was not just work based but life based. Working together was second to being friends. And that is how I built this company, and it was a great cover to build this self-sustaining group of like-minded people. In essence I had brought us all together because we had the thoughts and knew one day, God forbid, we might need to pull together and weather the storm. It looked like the storm was here.

Chapter 8

The afternoon zoomed by as people and equipment started flowing into the compound. Mitch had arrived and landed the Blackhawk at the hangars I had built for him on the compound to support our air wing. Rae was happy to get Melinda and the girls to show her the housing for their family and employees. She had been to the compound on numerous trips as they developed the plan to bring the company here if things got wild in the world. Mitch has built Aeronautics

America much like I had built Bear Tactical, using friends and people he trusted and respected. The hard part for him was the maintenance teams for the air frames he used and making sure he had the right people both in like mindedness and in ability to have on the team. He had used Luke to vet a lot of the guys he did not know from personal experience, which for that part of the team was a lot.

Our plan was to bring him here and give us, my family, his family, and our teams, an advantage most would not have in a dire situation, air power. He had worked closely with me in every aspect of the air wing part of the compound. From the underground fuel storage and fueling stations to the air frames he desired to have besides his transport. We currently have two A-29 Super Tucano air frames, and a U-28A Draco with all the bells and whistles to go with them. It paid to be a government contractor and training facility with the right connections and money. He had spared no money on the platforms or the systems to run them and equip them. He had all his fixed wing pilots trained on both platforms and all their systems. We had his transport planes as well as his Blackhawk, which we spent a lot on parts and equipment to keep it air worthy well into the future. The hope was to have and never need all of these assets, but we had a very capable ability to do way more harm than most could fathom should we need this. And that was just with the air wing.

I have been purchasing government equipment and vehicles for years as the drawdown of our military added vast amounts of goods on the market. This was also helpful in the pricing of purchases because they were well used and did not cost top rate money to acquire them. GSA auctions, government surplus auctions and the likes helped me develop a nice fleet of vehicles to use for training purposes and also add to the SHTF plan. I also had two M-ATV assault vehicles, one M-ATV Utility vehicle, and three JLTV Close Combat Weapons Carriers. All of them had Common Remotely Operated Weapons Stations (CROWS) except for the Utility M-ATV. It was a huge jump to get this system and no small feat Stephanie had pulled off from using the company contracting leverage with the government.

Most of the equipment was stored away in the storage building, which was huge and resembled many of the big maintenance buildings on military bases. I had made sure to get this built and grounded to try to protect against a possible solar flare or even an Electro Magnetic Pulse (EMP). I had tried to insure that all of the things we had here at the compound would make it through such an event, but it was almost all hypothetical since the research on EMPs was not in depth. Then we had a nice above ground ammo storage bunker area left over from the Air Force base days which we had refurbished and maintained to keep all our explosives and such in, and a lot of the ammo too.

The security of this area and the entire compound was routed to the headquarters building and the operations room. It resembled a tactical operation room you see on a lot of movies with big screen TVs covering the walls and workstations. A section of the TVs had all the camera views that were placed around the compound. The system we currently used had augmented artificial intelligence (AI) used to help monitor and secure the compound. This allowed for less people to have to monitor the cameras and look for anomalies thus helping me keep the need for another full-time employee down. As more of the family members arrived this operation center would be manned at all times and become the hub of all things on the compound in the days and possible weeks to come.

The bunk house was more like a luxury hotel instead of a bunk house once you entered it. It was three stories high with rooms on all floors. Rooms ranged from single rooms to full-blown suites. I had worked with an engineering firm that specialized in hotels and developed this from the ground up hoping to never have to use it as what I was building it for, a SHTF lodge. The kitchen was state-of-the-art and developed to be more of a cafeteria than a restaurant. It was not used very often since we did not feed those that attended our courses but had housed them on the first floor in the single room area. From the outside this building looked like a plain barracks or older hotel which was by design. This building was big enough to house all of us coming to the compound and feed us. My hope was that we would not need to be here long term, but I made sure we could if need be.

The top floor was single and double rooms with the middle floor being all the larger suite style rooms and the bottom floor had double rooms and the likes for those with small families or just a wife or girlfriend. The first floor also had the kitchen and dining area and a game room with pool tables, foosball, dart boards, and Ping-Pong. Since it was built those that worked for me had been given the keys to their own room in the building and told to make it their own, however they wanted. The idea was to have it feel like a home away from home if we had to come live here at length. We had brought the boys here and they had all their gaming systems and things they wanted here already set up to try to make it easier if they had to live here.

As the evening approached, I was walking around the bunk house making sure everyone was getting settled into their areas. The only ones a little out of place had been the maintenance crews and flight crews from Mitch's group. They had assigned rooms, but the maintenance crews had not been on the compound as much as the locally based people had. A few of the families from that group seemed upset they were at the compound and that was to be expected because it had not gotten too bad out in society. I heard a few conversations talking about coming here was not needed and knew it was time to have a group meeting and set a few ground rules for the compound and try to build us into a family and not just people in their own worlds doing as they wanted, because I had a sinking feeling it was going to get very real and very bad before it got better in the world.

My phone buzzed at that moment, and I looked to see it was Luke calling.

"Hey Luke, what is up?" I asked.

"Boss I need to talk to you face to face ASAP." He stated.

"What is your location I can come to you." I said.

"In the operation center" he said.

"I will be there in less than five." I told him and hung up.

I called Rae as I started heading towards the exit of the bunk house and she answered on the third ring. "Hey love, what is up?" she asked.

"Luke needs to see me ASAP in the operation center. I think you should meet us there too. I am heading over now" I told her.

"Ok, I will let the kids know but they are already on their games." she said.

"Make sure they know about not saying they are at the compound with their buddies please before you come." I told her.

"Already had that talk with them and they understood." she told me.

"Awesome, see you in a bit sexy." I said.

"That you will" I heard as the connection broke.

I made my way over to the Headquarters building and into the operation center and saw Luke in his area. He waived me over and I saw he was on the phone. I could overhear him telling the person on the other end that they would be ok and continue with the plan they had worked out.

He looked up at me as he laid his phone down on the table, "Boss it is getting bad in the bigger cities. Riots are happening around the country with banks burning and stores being looted. Seventeen states have called up the national guard to institute the travel restrictions that the federal government has instated. One of my sources tells me that the federal government is going to address the nation and announce restrictions on accounts. She did not have details on what this means but I think you are smart enough to infer that they are going to put limits on people's accounts to try to stop the run-on banks. I have not had time to go help Paula and she is dragging her feet. I need to go grab her and her stuff and bring her here." he blurted out to me.

"Stop talking and get going, do you need anyone to help with that mission? Is it an extraction or just you needing to go help and put a fire under her kinda thing brother?" I asked him as Rae walked up close to me.

He rubbed his beard and looked at Rae, "Can she come with me? Paula respects Rae and it might make it easier with Rae along." Luke said.

I looked at Rae and she seemed as shocked as I was that Luke had asked, "you good with helping him my love?" I asked Rae.

"Um sure yeah, I am good to go with helping you Luke. Is Paula not wanting to come?" she asked Luke.

"She doesn't think the market going down like this is a bad thing and she doesn't follow the news at all, so she is clueless that the country is falling apart. She knows the plan, well this part of the plan, I have not told her all of what we have here as we have only been dating about a year." Luke said to Rae.

"I know your track record with ladies Luke, and that you try to compartmentalize this place and our SHTF plan, but it is time to shit or get off the pot about this girl. Is she the one you want here?" Rae said matter of fact to Luke.

Luke looked at her and held his hand on his heart, "Ouch, straight into my heart Rae. I want her here, maybe even need her here."

"Ok, that is good enough for me, is that good enough for you?" I asked Rae to try not to make this a big thing.

"Yeah, it is good enough for me" she said giving me a look I knew to mean I was in trouble.

I am not sure what I had done but it seemed like she was a little upset with me. I had this feeling ever since the radio call as I headed to the compound this morning after the bank incident. I guess we will have to talk about it after she gets back from helping collect Paula and her things.

"Did you catch what he said to me earlier babe" I asked her.

"I caught the tail end of it about the inferring that they are trying to stop runs on accounts. I take that they are going to put limits on account access." Rae responded.

"My best analysis is yes, they are going to put limits on spending or access to the account. What that looks like I am not sure, maybe like Greece did and limit spending and withdraws with daily or weekly caps." Luke said as he raised his hands in the who knows pose.

"Ok, why don't you two get out of here, I will go with at least a good sidearm and a long gun but go how you think you need to go." I said as I looked at my wife.

"I am going to go with the covert kit and my little sub gun" she said.

"Nice" Luke said.

"Don't forget radios and let Graig know your routes and plan." I told them.

"Wilco" they both said turning to talk to each other.

I heard Rae telling him she was going to go get her kit and meet him at his vehicle and he said ok and went to talk to Craig. I had not really noticed the hum of the operation center as I walked in but now, I noticed it. All the areas had people in them looking over things and even a person watching the camera bank. I looked closely and saw it was Troy. I should have known he would be watching his network of toys working. With my input on the security minded side of the camera placements he had developed the network and assigned the AI rules. The system really was state of the art and gave us text alerts if defined areas had intruders enter them. You could put a virtual fence anyplace you desired and if a person crossed that fence it alerted you to their presence. If we could keep the system running it would be nearly impossible for a person to sneak around the compound and not to know it. The best part was it worked day or night.

"How is it going Troy" I asked.

"Just like we had hoped." he replied.

"Anything I need to know or help with" I asked him.

"No everything seems to be good at this moment, I had been helping all of Mitch's people get settled in and connected to the system." he said.

"Great, thank you for doing all you are doing Troy." I said.

"No problem." he said looking at me.

I looked over and saw Luke leave after talking to Craig. Walking over to Craig he looked up at me and smiled.

That was possibly a good thing or a bad thing with him smiling I thought.

"Luke caught you and Rae off guard he told me" Craig started.

"Yeah, he did. I was not expecting that at all. Fucker got us both." I answered.

"That is funny. I think Rae will help though, lady to lady might be better than Luke's Viking approach" Craig stated.

I started to laugh, "Luke and his Viking mannerisms right. Viking smash and all that." He would play with all the kids of the compound family and chase them with his trusted nerf axe yelling this as he hit them with it.

"VIKING SMASH!" Craig yelled.

"Ok fucker enough of that, we will hear it a lot in the coming days I am sure." I said smiling.

It was nice to break the tension because we all felt it and knew that things had just started to get bad, and the worst was yet to come. Everyone in the room was smiling except for the few newer faces from Mitch's crew. That made me laugh a little more because it must be weird to hear a guy yell that in the operation center.

"Did he brief you on his plan to go get Paula then?" I asked Craig about Luke.

"He did and they are going to come up on coms in a minute." he said.

"Does his vehicle have an ATAK tracker on it?" I asked looking over to the ATAK system display on one of the mounted TVs.

"He has the TAK tracker installed on his personal phone as does Rae so we can track them personally." He told me.

"I knew this, but it slipped my mind. I guess the age is getting to me" I joked.

"Age is and attitude. Isn't that what you always say?" He jibbed at me.

"Yeah fucker, it is, and I am twelve at heart" I said smiling at him.

He started laughing at that and said, "well they are displayed with standard callsign on the screen. See Bear 6 and Bear 2 up there."

"I see them. Glad we will be able to keep tabs on them. I will go put my kit out in one of the Tahoe's and tell Bill to put his in there too for a Quick Reaction Force (QRF) in case." I told Craig as I walked out of the operation center and headed towards the team room.

I pulled out my phone and called Bill.

"What up brother?" Bill answered on the second ring.

"Luke and Rae are heading out to go pick up Paula and I want to have a QRF ready just in case." I answered.

"So, am I part of the QRF?' He asked me.

"Yeppers brother, me and you." I said.

"I will go grab my kit from the team room then, what are we using?" he asked.

"I am going to put it in the Tahoe with the covert light bars" I responded.

"So full kit then ready to hit it hard if need be?" he said more than asked.

"Yeah, and turn on your ATAK too. I am in the team room right now getting the kit together and making sure my ATAK is up, and I can see Rae and Luke on it." I told Bill.

"See ya in a minute" Bill said disconnecting.

I was making sure my MPU-5 was turned on and linked to the mobile ad hoc network (MANET) when I heard more than I saw Bill walk into the team room. Having this system was another great benefit of being a government contractor and one I was glad we had. I looked at my screen and saw I was connected and could see both Bear 6 and Bear 2. For the most part we did not use the zeros in the call signs when tracking or even calling on the radio. The zeros were more of a place holder than for use it had turned out. The thought long ago was that we could have a lot of people on the team and wanted to be able to go into the 100's if need be. It turned out I overthought it and really it wasn't needed but old habits die hard for me. As I was looking at the screen, I saw Bear 24 on my screen along with the others and knew that it was Bill.

"I got you up on mine, so I know you see me" Bill called out from his personal cubby in the team room.

"Sure do buddy" I said. "Let's get this shit in the Tahoe and ready just in case."

"Moving" came Bill's reply.

As we exited the team room and walked towards the row of vehicles a few heads turned our way and looked at us. It was a couple I vaguely knew from Mitch's crew. They looked a little shocked at the sight of us. I guess they might not be used to seeing guys with rifles and full kit, oh well they will get used to it soon enough I thought and continued to the all-black Tahoe. It had blacked out windows and a push bar. It looked like a police vehicle and was kitted out exactly like one with covert lights and sirens too. It was used as a training tool here very rarely as this Tahoe was a designated QRF vehicle in the SHTF plan. And my training of the local police and sheriff deputies helped allow for me to be on their frequencies. Dispatch knew my call sign and designation as a reserve law enforcement asset along with most of the team.

I started the Tahoe and turned on the radios while I stored my kit in the driver seat. I grabbed the handmike and keyed up, "Bear 17 to S O. 10-8 at my 42 for a possible 10-14 of Bear 6 and Bear 2 from his 42."

"S O 10-4" came the reply from dispatch.

A few minutes later my phone started to vibrate, and I pulled it out and saw it was the Undersheriff, Charles.

"Hey, how are you Undersheriff?" I asked.

"Cut the shit bro, what the fuck is going on? You never go 10-8." he cut me off.

"Nice to talk to you too." I replied.

"Seriously, what is up. This morning you helped my guys out and made sure they didn't get their bacon smoked and then ghost out and now you are going 10-8. I got it the world is going sideways and you have been preparing for this but what gives?" he blurted out sounding a little stressed and agitated.

"I am sorry I have not called you today honestly, that is a mistake, and you are a friend of mine and I should have called. I can't make that up now so I will tell you we are pulling people in and one of my guys is going to grab his lady and just so happens he wanted Rae to go help him." I blurted back.

"That incident this morning was just one of many today. Right now, we are debating if we need to secure Walmart and Stew's Club. Mike has been talking to the County Board and the City Counsel all day off and on as the shit has been getting a little wild here. People are upset they can't get money and that is causing issues, but they are still able to buy things with their cards, so it has not been too terrible. What do you know about all this?" He asked me.

"I know the market has crashed and people made a rush to get their money out of the banks. That caused more issues. I also know the government restricted travel and had talked to Mike about that when he called me. The part I know, and you might not is that they are going to restrict account usage tonight. Or that is the word on the street from our sources. We have pulled everyone in to see what happens. I told Mike I will help those that help themselves, but I was not going to go out of my way to help those who are not willing to help themselves. Does that make sense?" I said.

"Bro are you serious? They are going to cut people off from their own money?" he asked very seriously.

"It looks like it Charles. I know you and I have talked, and you have prepared for this kind of thing at least a little, it is happening. How bad it gets I am not sure, but I am not taking chances and am pulling everyone in. I would tell you that securing those two places is a must if you want to help keep this community going. Tell Mike to secure them regardless of what the board of counsel says and deal with the backlash later." I said.

"Ok, I will tell him. I get it why you are 10-8 now. Keep safe and keep us informed, we are on the Same team bro." he told me.

"I know and I am sorry I had not reached out, just moving a million miles and hour here and my family is the priority." I told him.

"No need to apologies bro, I know you got our backs. Be safe." He said.

"Watch your six." I said as I hung up.

"Undersheriff pissed off?" Bill asked.

"NO, more like agitated and stressed" I replied to Bill.

"What did you tell him to secure?" Bill asked.

"Walmart and Sam's Club" I said.

"Smart. I hope they listen to you." Bill said.

"Bear 17 this is Bear 6, immediate reaction needed. I say again immediate reaction needed." blared from the radio on the Tahoe. My mind reeling as it registered gun fire in the background of the call.

I looked towards Bill, and he was already grabbing his kit like I was. I threw my gear on and jumped into the driver seat. My heart was already racing as I had just heard my wife calling for help on our secure team frequency.

Chapter 9

"Bear main copies all" Came the reply in my ear before I could key the transmit button. "QRF Execute! Execute! Execute! Gate is opening now. Bear 24 guide to target from ATAK. Acknowledge."

"Bear main this is 24 acknowledge. I have target and will vector. Break, Bear 6 sitrep" Bill radioed.

"Bear 24 we are currently being engaged by three, I say again three tangos. They have small arms and have us pinned at Bear 56's front door. Bear 56 has sustained a GSW to her left leg, not serious. They are to our Northeast behind a brown sedan." came the sitrep from my wife. She sounded calm and I was proud she sounded that way.

"24 copies all. We are coming code 3 in the black Tahoe. ETA less than 5, can you hold?" Bill radioed.

"Roger, they lost interest of advancing on us when one of their own was taken out." Came the reply.

"24 copies all. Will advise as we arrive. Please give updates as needed." Bill called out on the radio.

As he was doing this the truck radio blared on the S O net, "All units be advised we are receiving multiple 911 calls of shots fired at Cross Road apartments."

"435 code to location" came the call from a deputy with multiple others responding the same way.

"Bear 17 to S O, we are code to that location." I radioed.

"435 to Bear unit, is that where she is at?" Came the call from the Undersheriff.

"Affirm 435. Be advised we are coming in hot. S O 10-3 the air. I say again 10-3 the air." I radioed as I drove at nearly 90 miles an hour towards my wife as she was in a life-or-death struggle.

"All units the Air is 10-3. I say again the air is 10-3." came the call from dispatch.

"Bear is 97" I called on the S O net as I pulled into the apartment complex and immediately saw the three tangos to our front. Their weapons started turning in our direction as I hear Bill come up on the Team Net.

"6 this is 24 we are on scene and going to clean this mess up get ready to move." was his call.

While he was saying this I had already braked hard to a stop and thrown the vehicle into park. In practiced motions we exited the vehicle and started to acquire targets with our weapons.

"435 is 97" Echoed in my ear as my eyes steadied the red dot on the tangos face and my first shot broke from my weapon the squeal of tires trying to abruptly stop behind me. My round found the face of a younger looking Hispanic male and he crumpled to the ground already dead. The tangos next to him started to squeeze their pistols triggers but it was already too late for them.

"Bear 24 this is Bear 2 we are set to move and my vic is directly behind the tangos." Came the call from Luke echoing in my ears on the Team net. My radio was set to scan the frequencies but transmit on S O net.

The other two tangos took a round each from Bill to the face split seconds apart. I was just finishing taking up the slack in my trigger when I registered the hit to my targets face. My trigger broke and that tango took a second round to the face. I instantly started searching for other targets but saw none. I yelled clear and Bill did too.

"Bear 2 and 6 moving with 56 in tow" came the call in my ear from Luke on the team net.

"Bear 17 to S O all is 10-4 here. You can 10-2 the air. We have 4 times code nine here. All units can cut back scene is secure" I radioed.

"10-4, the air is 10-2 and scene is secure with 4 times code 9." the dispatch echoed.

"435 to S O rescue is cleared to come into the scene." radioed the deputy.

I turned to see the deputy walking with his long gun at the low ready towards me with a look of serious focus on his face.

"What the fuck was that shit? What the fuck is going on here" He asked as he neared me looking towards the three tangos we just bagged and saw the other one laying closer to the house. As he looked Luke and Rae exited the house helping carry Paula under their arms their weapons hanging on slings around their chests.

"Relax, those are our people coming out of the residence and they were pinned by that group of MAM's there" I thumbed over my shoulder.

"What the Fuck is a MAM? And you did not identify yourselves or yell commands at them." the deputy said. As he finished, I noticed Luke and my wife loading up Paula and getting into the vehicle.

"They can't leave here." the deputy almost yelled.

"Look they have a wounded person and are taking her to get medical treatment." I said, raising my hands talking calmly.

"That vehicle is part of the crime scene! It can't move! We have medical responding, and they can get treatment from them." He yelled.

"401 to S O. 97 with 410." I heard in my ears.

"17, we going to bounce this zoo before we are locked in?" Bill asked on the team frequency.

I reached down and toggled my radio to get on just the team frequency. "All Bear units at the scene extract to compound. 24 nonchalantly get in the vic while I try to defuse this deputy and the undersheriff who is sure to be here any second." I heard two clicks in my ears acknowledging my transmission"

"What in the complete fuck Wayne!!" I heard boom from behind the first deputy and knew the voice to be from the Undersheriff.

"These MAM's" thumbing towards the bodies "Military Aged Males" I corrected for the benefit of the deputy and undersheriff who had not served in the military "engaged my team who was here to extract a person and bring them to my location. My team radioed for help, and we responded. As we arrived on scene, the said individuals turned and pointed their weapons at us, which was a fatal error on their part. My original team sustained a GSW to the leg and is leaving to seek medical treatment. I am about to extract from this location also to assist my team in getting medical treatment. Barring your questions we are leaving Charles." I stated.

"You cannot leave" stated deputy 435.

"Deputy, I have no beef with you as Charles, excuse me, the Undersheriff can assure you. Times are different now and going to get worse and if you can't figure that out with the day you have had today, I honestly cant help you. Now Charles, I am leaving, and you know where you can contact me and find me, I have things that need to get done and this shit right here is just the start and you know it. Do you have anything for me?" I asked as I moved towards the Tahoe.

"No Wayne I don't, was it Rae that got shot?" He asked.

"No, it was Luke's Girlfriend. Thank you for asking. I will have statements for you from all parties and we can go from there. I am sorry it is like this, but I am not going to go through the standard protocols because nothing about these times is standard. Start wrapping your head around it Charles, this shit is for keeps. I am out of here." I turned and got into the Tahoe and left. In the review mirror I could see the first deputy on scene animatedly gesturing with his arms as I am sure he was telling his boss how we exited the vehicle and executed the three guys in manner seconds. To this deputy I am sure it looked like we executed them because of our years of training taking effect and our actions fluid and deliberate.

"Bear 6 this is Bear 17, sitrep" I radioed as we cleared the scene and got moving. I had turned the lights out and was heading back to the compound.

"Bear 17, Bear 56 is stable and going to be alright. Bear 2 is upset as to be expected. Thanks for the help." came the reply.

"Bear 6 no problem. We will AAR once we get refit at the compound. Break, Bear main any traffic for us?" I radioed.

"Bear 17 negative" came the response from Craig in the operations center.

"Bear main this is Bear 2 ETA 3 Minutes to gate. Can you bypass for us as we arrive, please?" Luke called.

"Wilco" came the reply from Craig.

"10 minutes out for us main, you can track us on ATAK and bypass gate for us too please." I called on the radio.

"Wilco" came the response from craig again.

"How bad is this going to blow back on us Wayne?" Bill asked.

"I am not sure Bill, I mean the world is going to shit but the system is still operational, and we just told it to fuck off." I said.

"Was Charles pissed" Bill asked.

"Oh yeah, he was pissed. Though he did ask if it was Rae shot, so he was still concerned for us. So not so pissed as to come after us but we did tell him and everyone to fuck their system. And that poor new deputy just watched us dump three dudes before they could even acquire us and shoot. You should have seen him all animated in the review mirror as we drove away.' I said.

"Luck was on our side they got surprised and had no training. That poor third guy got a round from both of us I saw." Bill said.

"He did for sure because my trigger was breaking as I saw your round hit him. At least our years training didn't kick in and we dumped any extra rounds in them to make sure they were in deed dead." I said.

"That would have just set that first deputy on the scene off even more. I bet that was the first time he had seen anyone killed or even dead for that matter." Bill said.

"I would not take that bet. I will say he is going to see a lot more in the coming days though." I responded.

"I would not take that bet because in the coming days things are going to get worse and it is wild it is this crazy already and we are only on day two." Bill said as we pulled through the compound gates, and I watched as they all started to close behind us.

To the East I could see the sun starting to reach the horizon and the beauty of the day ending was not lost on me. The AAR needed to be for the entire day, and we needed to get everyone from the compound to gather to talk through the day's events and to set forth in what this new world might be. God, I hoped it stabilized.

Chapter 10

As I looked around the large training room, I saw mostly familiar faces who I had known for years with a few fresh faces here and there. After we had gotten refitted from going out to grab Luke's group I had asked everyone to come to this meeting. In all we had 126 members on the compound, this included the young adults and kids too. The age range in our big group was from 55, yeah I was the oldest it looked like, to 6 months old. Twenty-six of the group are under 13 years old which means the next generation was already a part of the compound. Most of the adult members had served in the military in one capacity or another with my core group all serving on tiered operator units. This helped our group with the knowledge of how situations can become kinetic. Military service does not make a person better in my eyes, it does however open the eyes of the person who served to new ideas easier often.

"Ok everyone let's get this shit show started" I said to the group with my voice slightly raised to be heard over the hum of small talk.

"I want to welcome you all to the compound of Bear Tactical and Aeronautics America. Over the years I had been preparing and thinking through plans and ideas should the world take a turn for the worst, like it looks to have done yesterday. Wow, just yesterday." I said looking around to the group who looked as shocked as I was it was just yesterday that the market started to collapse. "To a few of you this might seem like it is not needed or way over the top, and I can honestly pray you are right. In my many years of talking this over, planning it with my wife, then my team and also with Mitch, it has always been a question of when do you circle the wagons. When is the time to act, and for me it has always been that if you act too soon what does it hurt? If it gets better, we can all head home and restart what we had already been doing, but, and it is a big but, what if it continues to get worse, that the world as we know it is no more. That yesterday was better than today and today is better than tomorrow? And that is why we are all here, to make sure we came together, that we got settled and that we are ready for what tomorrow brings should it be worse than today. You all knew of the compound, knew of the Shit Hits The Fan plan. Knew what this" I waved my arms all around us, "is about. It is about the next generation, which we have 26 sitting in this room with us. It is about helping them have children and that they may have a good life despite the turn for the worst that our nation might see, and now, sadly is seeing. It is going to take long hours, sweat, and sadly blood as we have already seen today, to keep this group moving in the right direction. This compound is not run by my choices and decisions but rather a group effort with a core group whom you are all familiar with. I am not going to get into the nuts and bolts of how we come to decide things in this meeting because I just wanted to welcome us all together and talk about the last two days and wait for the President to speak in the next ten minutes of so. This is why we have the Screens on the news around the room and will turn on the volume to watch. After his address if you are a family member and want to stay for the rest of the meeting, I welcome you to stay, if you want or need to get the kids back to your new homes, I can understand that too. I will end by saying thank you. Thank you for seeing that we need to protect the next generations future and coming to the compound and becoming part of my family. I will stop with that and wait for the President to address the Nation and then those who want to leave can go and then we can start back up talking through the last couple of days thank you." I stopped and looked around and no one moved. They all just watched each other, looked to the screens, and stayed standing or seated.

As the screens switched to the Oval Office, we turned the sound on and watched a very tattered and stress looking President begin to address America.

"My fellow Americans, the last two days have been unprecedented in the history of our nation as the stock markets turned sharply downward sending the people of this great nation tail spinning into panic. This fear and panic have spread far and wide, even reaching into other nations. The SEC has informed me that this morning the circuit breaker that aids in stopping a complete crash of the market malfunctioned and failed to stop before another sharp downturn took place. They took immediate action and stopped trading for the day to assess the malfunction and fix the issue. They have assured me the problem has been fixed and that we can open the markets in the morning as normally scheduled and my advisors have urged me to do just that, open the markets. With their advice and guidance, we have devised a plan to help ease the panic and fear, the first step was what we have already implemented, the travel restrictions. These restrictions are to stop the movement of possible agitators and those who might try to travel to the bigger metropolitan areas to take advantage of the situation and cause problems. The restrictions have helped to stop those would be problems and will continue for a few more days as we settle back to a steadier and more normal climate in the nation. The next step to help ease the fear is to limit the transfer and movement of money out of the banking institutions. This step has already commenced with my address to you. Effective immediately, all accounts are limited to a single fifty-dollar withdrawal per day, or a two-hundred-dollar transfer to another account. This measure is to stop those with large sums of money from withdrawing vast amounts while leaving those with smaller accounts nothing to withdrawal. While this measure might seem drastic, it is to help those with less money gain access to these funds. Many have tried to get money from their banking institution of choice only to find that others have already taken and horded this money. My administration will not tolerate the hording of assets in any shape of form. We are a nation built on the foundation of working together to help one and other and we will continue this today and into the future. I ask you, the American people, to come together and start to help those around you. These two steps combined, with the market opening in the morning, will help stop the panic and fear and bring us together. May God bless you and the United States of America. Thank you."

The camera cut to the media announcer who immediately started to recap the President's address as we muted the TV.

"Well, that is kinda what my team had expected him to say to the nation. Anyone wanting to leave and take care of family please feel free to head out." I spoke.

I looked around the room and again everyone stayed where they were and did not move except to look around at one and the other.

"Ok then, I guess you all want to talk about or listen to what the last few days have been for all of us." I said.

I heard many say "Yes" in the group and saw a lot of heads nodding.

"Ok, I will keep it short then and we will have internal After Action Reviews (AAR) to follow this bring group conversation. For my group it started when I got to work yesterday morning with the collapse and then the market closing. For me it was like a warning bell sounded in my head because the stock market had continued to grow for years with no real concern despite all the turmoil around the world and I had talked at length with my wife about it tumbling to the ground." I saw a hand shoot up in the group and I pointed and said, "Go ahead."

"I am Sally, and I came with my husband Neil." a blonde female I had never seen said as she stood and continued, "He works on the aircraft for Mitch. I am a day trader and had worried about this happening and watched as the market has been changing. The first day and how it continued is because of exactly what you said but I will define it better, growth and greed. I will tell you that this is not going to get better and the crash we saw this morning was not because the circuit breaker failed like the President and media are pushing, it is because the market sold out so fast that the system in place took that long to stop it after the sell offs had already started. The money measure is just going to make people more upset as they see that money as theirs to take and have as they wanted it, and I think they are right so this is going to get bad. You did not have us come here early and anyone that thinks that will see when they open the market tomorrow. The last two crashes will be nothing compared to the morning." She said and sat.

"Welcome to the compound and the family Sally" I said looking at her and Neil. "Could I ask you to link up with Luke our head intelligence when you get a chance?" I asked her.

She nodded her head saying "yes" and I continued. "The warning bell increased in intensity as they reopened, and the market continued to crash. I called a meeting and the market crashed and closed yesterday. To me it had started, and I did not want to wait, that and the run on the banks caused me to call a meeting of our group and we all agreed to commence the SHTF plan. As we did this, I got my dad out of Commi Cali and had to deal with a few issues until this moment. One being a guy with a gun this morning across from a bank being destroyed as my family drove by it coming here. I stopped to assist the Sheriff deputies arriving on scene to make sure they did not get popped by this turd. The second issue was far more dynamic and kinetic, the shoot out earlier this evening. Needless to say, these two days have ramped up far faster than I had thought they would, and my mind kept asking if I acted too soon and this will blow over. At least it did until the shootout. Now I am certain we did the right thing by getting us all here and thank you Sally for thinking so too. I am glad we are all here, so has anyone else had issues getting here?" I asked as I looked around.

Mitch stood and started, "First Thanks brother, for talking to me all these years and getting my mind to this point. Second, thank you for having my team, now our family here together to help our children and their children to have a future. It has been years in the making to get to this point, and we are here because of your urging and pushing just in case you always said. I know Melinda had more than a few times she wanted to kick my ass for spending what we have spent to build all this, but she too is more thankful than ever we have this, that we have us. Getting out of Texas was easy but not easy if that makes sense. My girls had never flown a Nap of the earth flight before, well none like this sustained except my wife. And thankfully I had the hawk at our home to load out and my wife is my co-pilot, so getting to it and taking off was easy. We immediately got called to land as we gained altitude near our home in San Antonio and the local radar painted us. From that point on we went low and continued out west to here. Coming in was no issue and the local tower did not even call us as we landed here. Many of my team had to push the envelopes and a few almost got caught taking off. In the end we all got here and have a story to tell. I want to try to keep it short so that the teams that made contact today can have an AAR and then down time. This leads me to a question on many people's minds, Chow." He smiled and sat looking my way with a big grin on his face. He was a food junkie and that was the smile looking at me, a kind of feed me look.

"The chow hall in the bunk house will open in the morning and start serving three meals a day. I think the drink bar is already up and running with soda, juice, milk, and coffee. Am I right Stephanie, Bill, Rae??" I asked looking at the three of them.

"Yes, you are right" Rae said as she stood, and I saw she was looking sexy as hell like always. "Three meals a day, breakfast, lunch, and dinner buffet style. Maria, are you good for starting in the morning? I know you already set up all the drinks." Rae said, looking towards Maria.

"Yes, breakfast will start at 7 in the morning, then lunch at 11:30 and diner at 5 if that is good." she said staying seated.

"Great, thank you Maria." Rae said. "I want to thank all of you for being part of the compound family. You are all amazing and I am glad to have you here and excited to get to know all of you better as we move forward into these new times. If anyone needs anything, please let me know." Rae said turning towards me and catching me staring at her ass. She rolled her eyes at me and sat.

The room had a slight rumble to it as little side conversations started. "Ok, does anyone have anything pressing?" I asked. No one stood or said anything my way and the rumble got a little louder. "Well then, I need to see my team in the Headquarters conference room in ten minutes. Thank you everyone." I ended, turned, and walked for the door before anyone could stop me. I was hoping Rae had followed on my heels and as I turned to look, she was right there smiling at me.

"Looking good sexy man of mine" she said looking at me like a piece of meat.

"Oh my God, stop. Just because you saw me in action earlier and it still has you all hot and bothered now doesn't stop me from remembering you almost got shot today." I said not being able to keep the smile off my face.

"Yes, well you look sexy as hell leading too, ya know" she said getting closer to me.

"I love you wife of mine and I am glad you did not get hit earlier. Lets go to the conference room so we can talk through what happened and plan for the repercussions of leaving the scene." I told her as I gripped her hand and we walked towards the headquarters building.

"Love you too" she said holding my hand in hers too.

"For fucks sake, keep that lovie dovie shit in the bedroom" Came shit talking from Craig behind us.

"Never" came a chant back from both Rae and I as we looked back in Craig's direction. He smiled and rolled his eyes at us. We are known to be very outwardly loving towards one and other and gave zero fucks who cared.

We went into the building and turned to head to the conference room. As we did my phone began to vibrate. I looked down to see it was Zack. Zack was the boyfriend of Chelsea and they both where friends of ours. Zack was a golf pro at the local Military school's golf course. He was an avid outdoorsman and camped and hunted regularly. In the last couple years, he had been taking courses from my company at no charge and planned on being part of the compound family when SHTF. It had started with a conversation at wine night with an invite to come shooting and turned into him becoming a very competent rifleman and part of the group. I had honestly forgotten about Chelsea and him with all that had been going on.

"Hey Zack, how are you?" I asked as I answered.

"FUCK!" Rae said and pulled out her phone. I put my hand on her phone and gave her the wait a minute signal.

"Things have been a little on the chaotic side but not terrible." he responded.

"I see, well I fucked up and didn't let you know we are circling the wagons and started the SHTF plan. So um, yeah sorry." I said to him as Rae looked at me with a WTF look.

"So Zack, get your shit together, turn on your TAK tracker and team radio and get Chelsea and Alec here. If you have any problems call me or call on the radio. Bear main is up and listening." I told him.

"Fuck, I can bring my dad still too right? He asked.

"Damn, yes sorry. I just have a bunch going on man and was not excluding him just forgot about him too. Yes, all of you are welcome and part of the plan still." I said.

"I am glad to hear this because I thought you decided to not have me or us come. Thanks Wayne I will get off here and get going so we can be there before it gets too late." He said.

"Sounds good. Sorry again Zack." I said.

"No problem see ya soon." He disconnected.

I looked to Rae and said, "ok now call Chelsea and tell her that Zack is coming to her place to get her and Alec, that she knows what was on the list and bring it."

"She has no idea Zack has been training with you as much as he has, he kept it a secret from her you know" Rae said as she called Chelsea.

"Really? We have talked about it at wine night, and she has no idea?" I said as we sat down in the conference room, and everyone else was doing the Same.

"No, not really. Zack just talks about range time but not that he has been training in room clearing or CQB or anything. I mean she knew from Bill and Craig and the guys at the wine nights that Zack knew everyone, but I just don't think she got the whole picture." Rae said.

"Zack and Chelsea coming in then?" Bill asked.

"Yeah, he just called, and I had left him out of the loop, so I dropped the ball getting them here too." I said to the group.

"Hey Chelsea, No I took the day off. Yeah, we are at the compound. No, you are still invited. In fact, Zack will be there with his dad shortly, just do as he tells you and see you later this evening. I have to go. Yes he is getting you. Ok see you soon." Rae put her phone down and said, "Sorry."

"Well at least they are coming now," said Craig.

"That is true. Ok let's get this over with so we can all try to get some rest because the morning is going to be shit. First, Luke how is Paula?" I asked, looking at Luke.

"Hhmm, well the gunshot wound was nothing more than a graze kinda threw and threw in the thigh." he started when Frank interrupted him.

"It was a deep grazing wound to the thigh with slight muscle damage but will heal with no lasting impairment. Rebecca and I irrigated the wound and cleared it of any debris from the clothing stuck in the wound, stitched her up and now Rebecca is looking in on her to make sure the pain is not too bad, sorry to interrupt Luke" Frank said.

"No worries that is your area and all. So, the wound is not serious, but she is still pissed off, first that she got shot and second because she blames Rae and I for it. The guy that shot her was aiming at me, he was her old boyfriend who was still obsessed with her. Rae dumped that guy after he got a shot off at us. I had just seen him when he fired his round and I had started to move. I think that is why he hit Paula instead of me. Anyways, Rae was also yelling gun as this was all going on. So, it was chaos and dynamic all at once." Luke said.

"Yeah, I think I saw him at the same time as Luke and just yelled gun and brought up my gun and cleared the sight picture and squeezed off a round. It just all happened, and I can't tell you that I even thought about it. I heard the bang or pop or whatever you want to call it from his weapon and next thing I know he was dropping from a round in his face from me." Rae said matter of fact.

"I think you saved my bacon Rae with your reaction time and then seeing the other guys near that car. You called it out and the training just seemed to take over for you. Very smooth and deliberate actions. Anyways, you dropped him, and I heard Paula screaming she was hit. And then you called out the other guys, so I pushed us back through the door and into the apartment. They started shooting and screaming at us for shooting their guy and I looked at her wound and started to dress it. Rae jumped on the radio and called you guys in, and we tried to not get shot by the three of them outside. I think they thought better of advancing on us after seeing their guy get smacked in the face at the start because they just fired off from the car, I think I returned fire maybe once or twice, but it was more aimed at the car as I had no clear target." Luke said.

"I saw them and yelled out and Luke turned and said back and pushed us all into the apartment. I heard Paula screaming, she was hit but was fixated on the guys around that car. I took one shot at them and hit the car just below the guy I was trying to get. Luke told me to call it in and I called for help, and we kept an eye on the three of them as they kept yelling at us and shooting now and then. Bill came up on the net along with Craig and said you guys are coming. I gave the information as best that I could when asked. It honestly is all a blur." Rae said and I held her hand, it was her first actual contact and firefight, not to mention her first kill.

Craig jumped in, "I heard it and immediately called for QRF to execute on the radio. And started to make sure the gates had no one around them before I used the bypassed to place them in the open position to allow the QRF out faster. I called Bill to tell him to vector you guy in using the ATAK system as I saw it was clear and I opened the gates and waited for the QRF to clear and close the gates right behind them and monitored the situation."

"I heard the call and immediately acknowledged the call and then asked Rae for a sitrep. You did a really good job of telling us all you knew under the stress and it being your first time, case of beer by the way" he said looking at Rae and me and we all had to laugh. In the teams when someone did something for the first time, and mostly if they said it was the first time, they owed the team a case of beer.

"For sure" Rae blurted out with her big smile on her face.

"Anyways, I vectored Wayne in and we screamed to the area in that Tahoe with lights blazing like a the police car it looks like." Bill continued but I interrupted him.

"I had actually called in to dispatch and put us on as a unit waiting in case something bad happened with Luke's mission. So, the Tahoe was a police car Bill, as you started gathering info from Rae I called on dispatch, well more like I heard the call out of shots fired and then called out that we were responding to that call. I went through the entire protocol of arriving on scene and keeping the air clear and everything, trying to go by the book. Then as we pulled in those turds turned and started to aim at us. I just let the training take over and exited the vehicle, acquired the target, stroked the trigger and dropped the first one transitioned to the last one standing and Bill's round punched him in the face at the trigger broke and the guy took two instead of one to the face. It was over before it really started. I called out all the info on the sheriff's frequency and then that deputy was yelling behind us." I said.

"Yeah, I thought that fucker was going to shoot us honestly. He was yelling and all scared shitless. I think it was his first time seeing a person killed and being in a shooting. Either way he was yelling up a storm. Then Charles showed up, he was calm and all but he did not like you telling him it is a new world and you did not have time for the standard protocol of a shooting." Bill said.

"You told him that?" Jeff asked.

"Yeah, I told him it was a new world and I had better things to do then deal with that shit, or something along those lines." I said to Jeff and the group.

"How do you think that is going to fly" Jeff continued.

"Honestly Jeff does any of us give a fuck how it is going to fly right now?" I asked him directly.

"No, we don't, but that will not stop the bureaucratic machine from continuing on and that means you deliberately left a crime scene, and I can see the local city council and their shrill of a police chief making a stink with the district attorney." Jeff said.

"Oh Yeah, for sure." Paul said.

"I know guys and we will cross the bridge when it happens. We just do not have time for that and they need to understand that the normal rule of law is soon to be out the window and the rule of war is coming." I said to the group. "Am I wrong?"

"No" was unanimous around the table.

"While all that was going on Paula, Rae, and I extracted from the apartment and the area and headed back to the compound. Rae called it in, and Frank and Rebecca were waiting when we arrived. They took her into the medical room and fixed her up. She is now back in our room and like I said a little pissed." Luke said.

"Yeah, she kept say to me that I killed her ex over and over." Rae said.

"Yeah, she told me that we showed up and he came to try to get our stuff and wanted her back. I told her that he picked the wrong people to mess with and that his little gang had no clue what a real group of hard hitters looked like. Then they stepped way out of their league and paid the price. I might have been a little too hard but fuck that guy and his group." Luke said.

"Did he run with a big gang? And is this going to cause us any blow back besides the local law enforcement?" I asked.

"I pulled his record, and he ran with the biggest local Chicano gang but was a small timer. My assessment is it could come back to us. Sorry Boos." Luke said.

"So be it." I said.

"Is she going to be a problem?" I asked.

"NO, I think she is in shock." Frank said. "She might have still had some feelings there for that turd but she was pissed he shot her too. So, I think it will be ok." he finished.

"I think she will be good to do Boss, just pissy at me for a bit." Luke said.

"The shit this President and his administration are doing right now is not going to smooth things over at all." Stephanie said.

"I agree and think it is going to just make it worse like Sally said in the compound meeting." Craig said.

"I guess we will see in the morning, but I bet it has already caused trouble. Luke?" Stephanie pressed.

"It has and cities are slowly eating themselves with the riots and unrest. By morning I assess that all the major cities with more than 150 thousand people will have serious issues." Luke said.

"Ok, moving on then. Do we need to set up a watch tonight?" I asked.

"Already done." Craig said. "With the AI and they system you and Troy set up around the compound we will get alerted far before anyone could get into the compound baring an air assault or parachute insertion."

"I think we have those covered too guys," said Troy.

"How Troy?" Jeff asked what we all thought.

"I have four cameras pointed to the sky and they overlap with the other cameras to have complete coverage of the area. The AI knows what helicopters and parachutes look like and will alert should one come into the bubble I built." Troy said smiling.

"Wow" was the reply from most of us.

"I think we should all have our light kit in our rooms. I know we could use the tunnels to get to the building and team room from the bunk house but let's keep a little firepower close to home. I don't think we need to worry about anything yet, but I have been known to be proven wrong. Agreed?" I asked.

"Agreed" came the replies.

"Am I missing anything" I asked the group.

"I do not think so Boss" Luke chimed in with head nods around the table.

"Shit, yeah I am. I need statements from Rae, Luke, Paula, Bill, Craig, and myself done tonight and emailed to me so I can send them to the Sheriff and Undersheriff." I stated.

Grumbles of ok came from the group. "Night all and thank you." I said.

I turned to look at my beautiful bride. "You ok sexy?" I asked as I held her hand and looked into her eyes.

"I think so, you had always talked about how killing a person changed you and I never put much stalk into that, but it does. I get it now if that makes sense." she said.

"It totally does, and I am here love, always and forever to listen, talk and whatever you need. I am sorry you had to be a part of this kinda club baby doll." I told her pulling her close.

"I know love and I am blessed to have you. Let's get this statement done so we can go hang out with the boys and maybe have some us time too." She said.

Chapter 11

We had finished our statements and were heading back to our compound home when Rae took out her phone because it was vibrating. She showed me it was Chelsea and answered.

"Hey lady what are you doing" Rae said. "Yeah, we can let you in the gate, I thought Zack knew the code." She continued as I could not hear Chelsea talking.

I pulled out my phone and called Craig and he answered on the first ring.

"Hey" Craig said.

"Hey, are you in operations? and does it look ok at the gate? Zack knows the code but is having Chelsea call Rae" I said to Craig.

"I was just calling you. Yeah, I am here. Something doesn't look right about the way they are in the vehicle." Craig said to me.

"Buzz them into the secondary and lock it all down. We can go have a little look see. I will be in the control room in a minute." I said and hung up.

"Tell them we are buzzing them into the compound and hang up." I said to Rae.

"OK, Wayne said they are buzzing you guys in see you in a minute." Rae said and hung up.

"Ok, what the fuck is up?" Rae asked sternly.

"Craig said it looked weird and we know Zack has the code." I said as we both started moving swiftly towards the headquarters building and the operations center within.

"Let's go to the team room and grab out gear and then we can see about operations and go from there." I told her.

"Ok, do you think it is that serious?" Rae asked.

"I honestly don't know but have learned better 'to have and not need than need and not have' she echoed my words with me. We went straight to the team room and our cubbies; she had a small one inside of my big one and grabbed our kits. Bill, Frank, and Jeff were already finishing their load outs and we all headed to the operations room. As we went in Rae stopped, took out her phone and flashed me the screen, it was Chelsea.

"Everyone quiet!" I yelled to the operations center. You could have heard a fly fart it got so quiet.

"Answer, act like you are heading out to meet them and put it on speaker" I told Rae.

"Hey Lady, was just coming out to meet you" Rae said into her phone as she punched the speaker button so we could hear.

"Um yeah well the gate is messing up and only opened the outer gate. So, you need to get the other gate open for us so we can get to our room. We are tired and ready to get in and relax." she said sounding very stressed.

"Shit, it locked up again. Hold on" Rae said as she acted like she was looking for me. I gave her the keep going kind of hand gestures. "Wayne, the stupid gate is locked up again and they are stuck behind that damn second gate. Please get it opened for them." She yelled at me.

"Ok baby doll, sorry. I will get it open for them and have them in here shortly. Tell them I am sorry it is doing that" I said as me and the team started to move out.

I came out of the operations center and turned left and out the side door and headed to a vehicle. I looked at the group and saw we had all put on hard plates and helmets and had out night vision gear.

"Shit did we call Paul?" I asked noticing he was not with us.

"SHIT...ok I will call him and have him be a QRF just in case." Bill said.

"Ok, so did she sound stressed out to you guys?" I asked the team.

"I don't know her that well but she sounded like something was going on for sure." Bill said as he had his phone out.

"She sounded frazzled" Jeff said.

"She sure as shit sounded pissed to me" Frank chimed in.

"Yeah, something is going on." Said Craig.

"I never heard Zack at all. So that has be worried, but he is driving I could see that on the cameras." Craig said.

"Bear main, Bear 17 here, anything change at the gate?" I said into the radio.

"Negative 17" Came the reply from my wife in my ear.

"Ok, pull up the four cameras and look hard into the vehicle. Then cut the lights to the entire compound. Let's go dark on them and see what happens as we drive up." I told her on the radio.

"Ok let's drive the golf cart and then get us a view at the show." I said getting in the cart.

"Lights going out in three, two, lights out" Came the call in our ears and the compound went dark. We all lowered our night vision and kept rolling.

"Call coming from Chelsea." came the radio traffic in our ears.

"Hey Chelsea, Yeah Wayne must reset the system and will have it open in a minute. See you soon." I heard Rae say. "Getting restless at the gate, oh and the back of the vehicle has opened and two guys are crawling out. Both have long guns." came the call in our ears.

We all double clicked to acknowledge her report as we started to get close to the front gates. I had arranged the entry point, so it had two pedestrian gates on both sides of the large vehicle gate. "Ok so it is confirmed we have tangos trying to get into the compound. Jeff, you get overwatch on the right berm in the shooting spot we have there, Bill you are with me, and we will assault through the left ped gate. Frank be ready for casualty response." I told the team.

"Ok" I heard everyone. "ROE?" Jeff asked.

"Paul is set and has a 249 ready to respond just in case." Bill said.

"Paul and his damn little machinegun" I said rolling my eyes behind my nods even though no one could see them and continuing "No quarter" I told them. They all nodded, and we started moving slowly.

"Long gun guys have laid down next to the vehicle on each side pointing their weapons at the big gate." came the radio traffic in our ears.

Again, we all double clicked to acknowledge the information.

"I see a guy leaning forward from behind Zack. He looks mad and pointing at the gate." Came more info in our ears.

"Jeff that is your target. We are going to try to get in the gate and around without the guys outside the vehicle knowing. Once you are in position let us know if you have a shot on your target. We can initiate on your shot. Questions? Concerns?" I asked everyone and then pushed transmit on the radio. "Bear main, only give info if situation is dire, we are getting set and need channel free" I radioed.

"17, Tango acquired. MAM with pistol. Will be tricky but doable." Came the call from Jeff.

"Let us get through the gate, if it looks like it is going to slip sideways on us then it is go time on your shot breaking and we will bang and clear at that point. Other wise when you see us set on our targets you initiate with your shot and we will clear" I called.

"Sounds good, 27 out." Came Jeff reply.

Bill was at the PED gate and slowly entered the gate code in the keypad. The gate made a small click sound and I cringed hearing it. It sounded like a bat clanging on the ground to me with my amplified ears, but I squeezed the shoulder of Bill to let him know I was ready and to go. Bill moved steadily and opened and pushed through the gate weapon up with me right behind him my weapon up and ready. The area was awash from the headlights shining on the secondary gate and the Denforster privacy fence screen. The entire compound fencing had this privacy screening on it to help shield what was happening in the compound. Thankfully Zack had pulled right up to the second gate to minimize the light in the area.

I pushed the aiming IR laser pressure switch and the laser that only our night vision could see appeared on my target. Bill moved against the fence towards the first vehicle gate and the far side of the vehicle where the other guy was, leaving me the first guy on this side of the vehicle. I placed my laser on the back of his head and settled in my firing position. We were far off Jeff's line of fire behind the vehicle to ensure not to cause any concern.

I heard the snap of the round fired from Jeff's suppressed rifle almost exactly as I heard the window being broken by the bullet as it went through it into the vehicle cavity. My trigger broke and I heard the sound of the weapon discharging combined with the grewsome sound of the round impacting and destroying the head of the guy laying in front of me. The sound of a bullet hitting flesh is something hunters have heard, and it is a very unique sound, hitting the head has a more distinctive sound that is hard to describe unless you have heard it before. I swiftly moved to the vehicle and swung the side door open and came face to face with Alec looking at me with wild eyes and blood on his face. I had transitioned to my sidearm without even really processing that I had done that. I cleared the vehicle and saw the guy who had the gun with his head wrecked and blood draining from the wound.

"OUT!" I boomed to Alec as I grabbed him and moved him out of the vehicle and then grabbed Zack's dad and pulled him out too. Frank was behind me pulling them out and away from the vehicle towards the rear. I jumped in and looked for targets as I cleared the back of the vehicle, and it was empty.

"Clear" I called and could hear screaming from Chelsea in the front seat.

"Clear" came the calls in my headset as the radio echoed loudly in my ears and brought me back to the brutal realities of this moment.

I swung the door open to Chelsea calming down but still very shaken. "Hey, you hit Chelsea, Zack?" I asked. I could see Zack exiting the vehicle and coming around the front to this side of the vehicle. He opened her door and was looking her over.

"Hey, Hey, are you hit!" he said loudly to her, grabbing her head and pulling it towards his and looking her in the eyes.

"FUCK!" screamed Chelsea more as Zack held her head in his hands looking at her face to face.

"I know but are you injured, are you hit?' Zack repeated to her.

"Get her out of here and go with Frank, Zack" I said to him and looked back at the mess of a man laying with his head spilling out in the back seat of Chelsea's smaller SUV. The pistol still in his hand gripped tightly. I could see what looked like tattoos covering his hand in my night vision.

"Bear 17 to Bear elements. Clear the area and report." I said into the headset.

"17, I have zero movement outside the gates, Bear main can you confirm on camera?" came the call from Jeff.

"27 this is main, I confirm what you have reported and see no threats outside of the gate or the entire compound." came the response from main.

"21 is clear and assessing for injuries" came Frank's response.

"24 G2G." came Bill's response which meant good to go.

"Bear 06 head this way and hit the lights. Open the secondary gate and when you come bring another vehicle this one is not ready for passengers and may never be again." I radioed my wife.

"Wilco" came her response to me.

"Lights are coming back on!" I yelled out as I flicked up my nods on my helmet. As I did the lights on the compound came back on and the darkness of night turned to stunning daylight for a minute in my eyes as they adjusted back to normal lighting conditions. I could see more clearly now that the guy in the vehicle with his head wrecked was a Hispanic male with a lot of tattoos all over his arms and even what was left of his head and face.

"They looked a lot like the guys we encountered earlier today at Paula's place which means they came looking for us most likely. 24 get face photos and thumbs on all these guys so we can have 2 run them in the system and see if they are friends of the group we bounced earlier today." I said into my radio.

"Roger" came the reply.

"Bear 28" I radioed Paul.

"17, what do ya need?" came back instantly.

"Get with Adam and see if he has a place to plant these bodies with the backhoe." I transmitted.

"Gotta ya" came Paul's transmission.

I saw a vehicle heading our way as I looked around and saw Chelsea holding Alec closely with Zack near them and Zack's dad standing by them. Frank was looking them all over and asking questions as I walked closer to them. I knew that they had never been exposed to this kind of violence and carnage as far as I was aware, and we would need to pay close attention to them.

"Hey guys, I hope you are all ok" I said as I got a lot closer to them.

"That...that..was like a video game but right in my face." Alec said.

"Yeah buddy, sorry about that but we needed to make sure you didn't get hurt." I said.

"Don't be sorry Wayne, they got what they deserved" came Zack's reply.

"Yeah they got it for sure. Can I talk to you a second?" I said to Zack as Rae got out of the other vehicle and walked up and hugged Chelsea and Alec.

"Sure" Zack said as he stepped to the side with me.

"What happened?" I asked him.

"As we turned onto the road to come to the gate this vehicle was stopped in the road kinda sideways. I thought it was weird and slowed down and before I knew it a guy had a gun at my window and the guys with the rifles were on Chelsea's side. I did not want to chance us getting shot up so I didn't gun the vehicle and get out of there." as he said this, he pulled out smokes "mind if I light one up?" he asked.

"No, go ahead I am sure you need one." I said.

"Oh yeah, that was way more intense and stressful than I thought it could have been. So, they held us at gun point and took all our stuff out of the back and threw it in the back of their car." he lit his smoke and took a drag. "They moved us around and got us set and then that shit bag with the pistol started asking questions about if we were coming here and on and on. Then they told me to drive and go to the gate. I told them I had to call to get in and they didn't believe me but finally relented and made Chelsea call. I can see that it worked and you knew something was not right. Thank you Wayne for taking them clean and saving us. I am sorry I got caught slacking." Zack said looking me dead in the eyes.

"Man, you did a great job, and this was my fault. I did not think there would be blow back from the shit that happened earlier today. Looks like these guys are from that crew." I told him.

"What? What happened earlier today?" he asked me.

"We went to get one of our the girlfriends of one of our guys and it went sideways. We had to drop four of these guys and it looks like they found out who and where we are at. Sorry you got caught up in it Zack." I told him.

"It is their fault" if pointed towards the carnage "and you don't need to be sorry. Glad you got us out of that jam cleanly. So, thank you and thanks for having us as part of the group here." he said.

"Family. We," I pointed to the entire compound around us "are all a family now. This is going to get far worse, and I honestly can't believe it hasn't been a full two days yet and people are going crazy. I am sure that the police are going to have a load of questions and want to make a stink about us killing the four guys earlier today and we are just going to act like tonight never happened, ok?" I said looking around.

"Well I can do that, we will see what happens with my dad and Chelsea and Alec." Zack said, looking their way.

"We will see for sure. Let's go grab another vehicle and find these guys ride and your shit." I said. "28 bring another vehicle and make sure you are kitted. We are going to take Zack to go get their gear from these guys ride we bagged" I radioed.

"Wilco" came the reply.

Two hours later we had taken the attacker's vehicle and dumped it on the other side of town with the keys in the ignition and brought back all of Chelsea and Zack's stuff. We unloaded it and brought it to their rooms. We had talked to Zack about rooms before and touched on it with Chelsea but never really went in depth with it. Zack had been spending time training with us on his off days and seemed to adapt quickly and was honestly a pretty decent shooter for a guy that was just an outdoorsman and golfer. So, we gave them rooms that adjoined with a door like in hotel and put Chelsea and Alec in one and Zack and his dad in the other. This way they would be able to adjust how they saw fit and we did not put pressure on them to be more than they might want to be.

It was getting late, and we had all talked and decided that tomorrow was a new day, and we did not have to conduct an AAR after this right away. We elected to all head to our compound homes, rooms really, and retire for the night. I was lying in bed with Rae talking to her about the day and what was to come.

"Well, this shit is sure going way faster than I had thought" Rae told me as she was snuggled next to me.

"Right?" I replied. "I mean we talked about how it could happen quick, but this is crazy. I mean we have not even really looked at what was happening around the area and the country since the meeting earlier. I bet it is getting even more crazy now."

"I could see the news reports while the shit at the gate was going down and in the operation center. Cities are in full blown chaos. The headline was 'Fear and Panic grips the Nation' on the news channel." Rae said.

"They are still pushing the fear and panic shit?" I asked.

"I don't know, just saying what I saw, the volume was muted and the captions where not on, so it said that, and they showed a few cities, but I turned my focus back to the cameras on the gate and seeing you guys take them down." she said.

"Yeah, the gate went smoothly as it could and poor Alec and Zack's dad getting that guys blood all over them. No other way to get it done though. How is Chelsea love? She seemed very shook up. Alec? Zack seemed ok but I am sure it will hit him harder later." I asked her.

"She is more pissed off now than upset but I am sure she is shake up and it will get to her. Alec seems ok, kind of put it into a gaming experience it sounded like to me. Like he was in a game, but it was more realistic. I will keep an eye on them for sure. What happened to get them like that?" she asked me.

"Zack said they had an ambush with a car sitting in the road with their flashers on set up on the road around the corner that turns onto the road that leads to the compound. He drove into it and slowed and then had a gun pointing at him with the other guys pointing at Chelsea and he said he didn't want to risk them all getting shot so he stopped. He thought it was a robbery and not to get here." I told her.

"Well, it was quick thinking to not give them the gate code and alerting us that way." Rae said to me as she snuggled a little closer.

"How are you doing love? It is one thing to go to other places and have encounters like this but we are here at home, in our own hometown. I mean I am shocked it is going like this and that things have already gotten to this point." She continued.

"I had not really thought about it being here at home honestly, and I had it in the back of my head that it sure seemed to be moving quick, almost too quickly. Like these guys coming here, I think we need to talk to Luke, and have him look hard at Paula. I am worried she is a loose link and that maybe we had an issue with this group before the crash even happened. Are we going to call this 'The Crash' you think? Like some of the other books we have read about SHTF, it seems they always have a name for the incident." I giggled as I held her closer to me, feeling her warmth and love close.

"The Crash is so plain" she giggled as she felt me holding her close. "I guess we will have to see what sticks and use that as the incident name, but I still hope that things calm down and this isn't really it, I think for me I am still in denial and want it to go back but deep down know it is here. It has finally happened, and the reality is I don't know what this is." she said and continued. "So, I have duty in the kitchen tomorrow morning. We are going to start doing three meals a day and get the plan rolling with that. Everyone seems to understand their roles so far and Mitch's people are going to fit in nicely it seems. Thankfully the plan has duties set in it and we all kind of already know what our immediate roles are going to be."

"I think I was in shock until the gate earlier, then it all just clicked over for me. Now I am in operational mode. So, if I come off that I am short you will understand, I am in that zone now and the balance will lean towards keeping us all safe. Shit like the gate was easy, it is the coming days that are going to be very trying even for me love, family is going to start wanting things. Our new family's family. The roles and responsibilities are going to get people upset, I am sure. The shooting today is going to come back to us from the law side because things are not completely falling apart so no one is seeing the writing on the wall, it is going to get really bad. And that includes Mike, Charles and the likes from the local law. We will see what it looks like day to day, right? The bast part is I have you, my love, right here." As I said the last part, I leaned in and snuggled with my beautiful wife hoping she caught the signals I was giving, I needed all of her. She did and the night ended late with our love joined together in both body and spirit.

Chapter 12

The morning came far earlier for Rae and I than we wanted as the alarm brought us back from the darkness of sleep, and it was not something either of us wanted it seemed. I was moaning and groaning and had to go take the morning

Motrin as the kids woke up grumpy because there was no school, they said. Part of me wanted to let them sleep, to be kids, to enjoy the time they had but we needed everyone, including the kids, to get on schedule and start to do the things that needed to be done. Everyone had a role and a chore if you want to call it that. To the youngest age, no one was exempt. This was part of the SHTF plan to keep us all going long term and not just for a few months.

The compound was supposed to be our entire world and help keep us all alive long into the future, the key was doing all the things that needed to be done. From farming, to ranching, we will need all the food, livestock and such to keep going, sure I had plenty stored, but it would be the end of us all should the world around us completely collapse and we did not start to grow for the long term because no matter what you might have stored, it won't last forever. With that in mind we tried to build the most comprehensive plan to sustain us for the long term. As time moved on and should the world around us really collapse, it reached far beyond the compound.

Our compound family, this group, is all that matters at the moment. As the days moved forward, we would look to establish the group leadership, and what that looked like. Our core group would meet daily before we had breakfast. When it came to the safety of the group no one but I made the final decision. I would take input, and ideas, but in the end if we failed because of security, it would be my failure to bear. The hope, my hope was that good men would rise and help me to build and continue forward no matter what hardships got in the way. I use 'Men' but in reality, it is not about if you are a man or a woman, but rather if you are good.

Good men, which are the corner stone of life, can fall short and make mistakes but it is what they do when these are made. It is the will to do what is right, no matter the cost. The will to do what is right for self or your family is different than what is truly right and good. I hoped I could be a good man, to not let the needs of my family outweigh the right things to do. I was thankful to have such a great group to move forward with and help so that we could all be good men.

"You ok love?" Rae asked me bringing me back to the here and now.

"Yeah, was deep in thought I guess." I responded.

"You had the million-mile stare. What or where did I get you back from?" she continued.

"I was thinking about being a good man. How I hoped, we as a group, could continue to be good men." I told her.

She grabbed me and pulled me close and gave me a gentle kiss on the lips and said, "My love, you have always been a good man. A man that gives completely for others and this is not going to change that. I love you."

"I love you too sexy and thank you. I try to do the right thing and I can only hope that it will continue. I know I just want to continue and make the best of what this world throws at us." I said.

"I must go sexy and get to the kitchen. I should have already been there." She said as she headed to the door.

"You are late to the first shift?" I said as she was leaving.

"On time is what love?" She said as she pulled the door closed.

"It is late" I said to the door as my phone vibrated. "Hey, morning to you" I answered.

"It is morning for sure boss. There is a Sheriff unit across the street from the gate. Troy said it has been there for an hour or so. I thought you should know." Craig said.

"Thanks, I will call Mike." I said.

"Ok. See you in the main conference in a bit?" he asked.

"Yeah, I will be there shortly." I said and hung up then looked up Mike's personal number and called.

"Hey, good morning, Wayne. I was just going to call you." Mike answered.

"I see, and would that be a good call or a bad one? Since a unit is outside my gate Mike." I told him.

"Well, the shooting yesterday with you and your people and you guys just leaving and then the lady with the gunshot wound did not go to a hospital Wayne is a problem. I read all your statements, and they are a great start, but we need to interview everyone and need all your weapons. You know the protocols for all this Wayne, not following them and putting me in this position is not a good thing. The DA is pushing me to put an arrest warrant for you, and everyone involved yesterday if you don't come in and comply. I told him that things are different in your mind, but he doesn't care and the Mayor is wanting your head, you know he hates you after you confronted him in public and made him look ridiculous. So, he has his Chief ready to raid you if I don't get you in to answer all the questions. Though I think the chief would call you and have a talk because almost all his people and for sure all his swat guys know you and have trained with you. Regardless Wayne, what the fuck is going on man?" he nearly shouted the last sentence from his frustration.

"What the fuck is going on is the world is crumbling and has been for years Mike. I have tried to tell the county board along with you and Charles that it was going to come to this. We are here regardless of if you can see it or not Mike. This shit is for keeps, you don't see it yet, but the low Lifes have already seen the writing on the wall and are starting. Yesterday was a start, not sure exactly why they went after one of my guy's girlfriends besides it was his ex-girlfriend. Either way they took a shot at my guy and my fucking wife. They fucked up and their timing was rather fucked for them too because we are all playing for keeps. My gloves are fucking off Mike. I see you as a friend and I hope to keep our community going." I said rather briskly as Mike interrupted me.

"Hey, hey, hey, ok Wayne. I get it. I do. I put a unit at your place to warn you so we could talk. I have put a unit at Wal Mart and Stew's too and they had to call in back up last night because people came looking and it turned a little disorderly. We had to arrest five people and they ended up all being armed. Nothing crazy but you are right they are going to start going after those places and most likely the others you had told us all about in our meetings. I know you saw this coming and are ready." Mike said.

"Let me interrupt you back, I am not ready Mike. I prepared sure, but no one, me included are ready for it to come and the way it is coming like a freight train too." I said.

"Well, it is not here yet, so people must follow the law, you included. I know you are a good guy Wayne and that you just want what is best for your people. I do. So do the right thing and not make this worse than it needs to be please." Mike asked.

"Mike, the law does not require anyone to be interviewed unless they are in custody which requires a crime or probable cause of such. I get it you don't want to go down that road, and I will ask you, if we submit our weapons to you and shit goes sideways, will we get them back from you in a timely manner?" I asked him.

"Well, the weapons are to be in our custody until the investigation is complete and then returned. With the District attorney being a friend of the Mayor, I would say they are going to try to go after you guys' Wayne. So, I think you knew the answer before you even asked and put me in this hard spot. What are you hoping for Wayne? How does this play out in your head, and make it ok to you? I know you are a constitutionally solid guy, and behind the law 100 percent, well I thought anyways." Mike responded.

"Oh fuck off Mike. Don't start with that shit now, the United States in in complete Chaos, Our community right here is fucking starting in the chaos too. I saved two of your deputies shit yesterday possibly. So don't you dare fucking question my allegiance to the constitution and law. The Laws you are looking at are not the laws of man and what will keep us alive in the times to come sir. I made sure you got statements from all of us involved, I did my best to not be a complete ass and disregard your efforts to continue like nothing is wrong, when the world as we know it is falling around us even as we speak. So don't you dare question my choices to switch gears and realize these are new times. Your jail cells are going to over fill quickly Mike, and sadly we are going to lose people in our flock in ways we only imagined in bad dreams. Wake the fuck up already and get with it. Do as you feel should be done Mike, just remember that many of the federal, state, and local laws are not constitutionally sound and have gotten by for years from people neglecting to stand up. I stood up yesterday, and from here on out, no law that doesn't meet constitutional muster will fly in my book. Make sure you tell the DA, Mayor and his crony police chief that. Make sure they understand when you play back this call to them exactly what I mean. The Constitution of the United States trumps all laws imposed upon We the People. My rights are mine, and from this point forward I will rely on the constitution and the voice of my group to guide me. I am getting off my soap box and will get back to you after I go talk to the group." I said.

"I, um, I know you are a Constitutional guy, I will make sure they know what you are talking about. I want this community to continue on Wayne, through whatever it is that is coming, but I don't think it is going to be as bad as you think and that you are making a grave mistake here. That being said, I will let the DA and the rest know what you said. I look forward to working with you, not against you Wayne." Mike said.

"Charles, you listening to this?" I asked into the phone.

"I am here like you thought Wayne and I will talk to Mike. I know you and I have had a lot more conversation about this and I will give Mike the scoop since I know that is why you asked if I was listening in." Charles said.

"Thanks brother, I know you will try to let them know what I am talking about. I have to go talk to my group, just want you guys to know that I understand this is business. I know that business is business and not done lightly. I also want you to know the rules are different now for me and mine. I hope you two get it." I said.

"We do" echoed from both of them as I was hanging up the phone.

I had mindlessly walked from my compound home to the headquarters building and the main conference room, and everyone was looking at me as I ended the call.

"Was that the Sheriff and Undersheriff?" Paul asked.

"Yes" I said as I rubbed my face and put my phone on the conference table.

"So, the Unit out front is for a reason?" Craig asked.

"Have a seat everyone. Is Mitch coming or did we invite him?" I asked as the door opened and he walked in.

"Speak of thy devil and he shall appear." Jeff said.

"Fuck off Jeff", Mitch said as he came in and sat smiling.

"Well, well the devil is pissy this morning" Chimed Bill.

"Ok, glad we are all in an ass grabbing mood, but I did just get off a call with the sheriff that was anything but pleasant." I said.

"Well, you knew he wasn't going to let it fly that we left and did not give up our sidearms or anything else" Craig said.

"Yeah, but the mayor and his new chief along with his henchman the DA are all gunning for us now. Talking about warrants and shit. I explained we are in a new world now and the likes, but he wasn't ready to hear it. You heard me at the end telling Charles in my own way to talk to the Sheriff, who is a very close friend of his, so maybe he will see the light." I told the group.

"And what is the light Wayne?" asked Stephanie.

"That we are willing to talk to the law, but we are not turning our guns into them and following all the made-up laws. Things that have just been let go and everyone complied as a good citizen to the state. Many have truly forgotten about the constitution and how it was to govern the government and not how they ruled us. So, am I wrong group? Should we turn in all the weapons used at the shooting and comply with all the things they are going to demand as the world crumbles around us. What does this group say?" I asked, looking at the faces looking back at me.

"You know my answer boss" Luke said.

"I want the group to hear your thoughts Luke, along with each of you on this issue. We are a group, and I am not the king or dictator." I said.

"For decades the US has stepped on the people and used us to the gain of its needs. Many of the laws in the books are not constitutionally sound and would crumble under a constitutional scholar magnifying glass, but alas many of the courts have become more and more political. With Covid and the restrictions they imposed, many started to realize what was happening and question it. And at the time the government used what authority they had to thwart this but as time has moved forward from, that world pandemic, people have awoken to realization that they are not heard. What happened yesterday was my fault, I did not see the issue with her Ex-boyfriend, and it now is costing us. Regardless of that, they are looking at the laws in place to take the weapons used in the shooting, until the case is closed, which we know the current DA will try to push something if he can, and since we left, they are going to focus on us being the problem instead of the victims. Again, a societal issue that is at our doorstep. So, I am against what the sheriff is pushing because of the DA and Mayor because it is simply unjust." Luke responded.

"Ok, so you feel that we have slowly ended up in this way because as a society we have looked the other way?" asked Adam.

"Not the other way Adam, we have been somewhat complacent in the process to ensure we are represented as we would want and that our voices are heard." Frank chimed in.

"That is part of the problem true Frank, but Adam, the societal decay and making the victims the bad guy is just part of the equation. The bill of rights is not about what rights we have as people, it is about our unalienable rights given from God and restricting the government. The government and the people have slowly turned to thinking that the government is the power and we the people must do as it says. It is the duty of the people to throw off the yoke of a tyrannical government, but many have forgotten. I am preaching to the choir here as we all know this. Or I think we do." Luke said.

"Ok, not your fault Luke but we can get to that. So, Stephanie, your thoughts to this?" I moved the conversation forward.

"The rule of law is an important thing in the overall realm of the community and as such I do not want us all to be seen as law breakers and that is surely what is to come from the mayor and his little alliance. In the light of what is happening in the world, I think we did the right thing, and we should not comply with giving up our weapons or doing anything beyond that which we feel is constitutionally warranted." Stephanie said, looking around the group.

"But is what we are doing constitutionally sound?" Troy asked.

"Yes, but the laws that they most likely are going to use are not built from the constitution but rather a need for process and thus decorum." Steve said.

"What do you mean by process and decorum Steve?" I asked.

"The laws are not clear from state to state or federally on the process used to investigate and process the scene or a crime or a shooting for that matter. It is in fact different from district to district as many may only take the weapon used if they feel a crime was committed in the process of the incident. So legally they have no true law to stand on, unless they push for a crime. So, because the DA and the Mayor, and thus his

Chief of police, are not fans of Wayne and the company we have built, it most likely will be processed as a crime until proven innocent." Steve said.

"So, Wayne, do you think we are doing the right thing by standing up to the mayor and making waves" Miguel asked.

"Miguel, I think we are in new times and had it not been when the world as we know it is collapsing around us, we would have given up all our gear then and gotten it back when it came back to us. We are, however, in completely uncharted waters right now and I am not even certain what is going on in the world and our country as we talk about this. I do know we, the group, killed three more of these shitbag turds last night at our gate. And I know we called no one and took care of it ourselves. Those are the times we are in and facing hard questions. So, I will leave it to the group to decide if we are doing the right thing. Have I done us wrong? I do not think so, but this is a group thing and not me thing." I said looking around at each of the members of the group. "Please answer that and make certain we are all doing this the right way. If I am not, please make it right and known."

"I agree with you Wayne and think we are in uncharted waters, and it is going to be a wild ride." Craig said.

"I concur with Craig" came Bill's reply.

"Same boat," said Paul.

"These uncharted waters may surround us, but we are all Good Men, and we will make the right choices, as a group, if need be, but this has been the right moves, Wayne." Came Jeff's reply.

"I think we are trying to do the right thing and keep our group safe also, I think we continue as we are Wayne." said Stephanie.

"I am here because you accepted me as who I was and have always treated everyone with the utmost respect and these times call upon us all to continue that. The law will soon be who has the biggest guns or the most people as times continue towards a total collapse. We need to be strong. Stay the course." was Troy's input.

"As the 'Cherry' you always call me I am the newest member of this compound and group as a whole and like Troy said you have accepted me and Angelica with open arms and made us feel like a part always. I think we need to move forward thinking about the long term, which it seems we are doing. So, I am down to continue but want to make sure we are focusing on long term effects too." Tod said.

"I understand what you have said and am with you too Wayne. I think we continue forward like Tod said but making sure we look at the effects that our current choices might have too." Miguel said.

"I am in agreeance with the current thoughts and moving forward." Steve said.

"I concur with the current group thinking. I am looking at long term effects of each thing we do and can speak on that when asked." Luke told the group looking around and focused on Tod.

"For the long-haul" Adam said.

"You know I am in this for all the marbles Wayne, have been for a long-time brother." Mitch said.

"Indeed, for the long-haul Adam. I think the country and in turn our community is soon to be rocked by a new reality, and we are ahead of the curve on realizing it. We need to prepare in kind because the shit is sure to come floating our way" Frank said smiling.

"Ok, so I am going to call Mike back then right now while we are all here and tell him the deal. Concerns? Questions before I blast him on speaker?" I asked the group looking around the table. All I saw was shaking heads. "So, we agree I should call him, and we all listen to the conversation and move forward as we have been doing?"

"Yes" echoed from the group.

"Let me get his personal number up here on my phone and dialed on the conference room phone. Here we go" I said as we all heard the phone ringing.

"Hello Wayne, I have you on speaker phone and have the entire group we talked about earlier on with you" Mike said.

"Oh nice, the entire group is on here from the company." I told him.

"Great, so what are we going to do about this?" Mike asked.

"What we are going to do Sheriff is follow the laws of New Mexico and these criminals" the Da started.

"STOP! You sir do not get to call these people criminals when it looks to be that the criminals are those dead gang members from picking a fight with the wrong group. This group here on the phone responded to a shots fired call and neutralized the threat at that scene. You have heard the 911 call, the Sheriff Office dispatch radio traffic. You have read, hopefully, all the statements from this group and the witnesses on the scene. All preliminarily indicate that the subjects approached and started shooting without warning at members of this group and they returned fire, retreated, and called for help as the gang shot at them and came after them. All of Wayne' group are sworn reserve deputies and Wayne and Bill were logged in for duty before anything happened. So don't start calling people criminals in here with me present." came a sharp rebuke from the Undersheriff Charles.

"Are you going to let him talk to me like that Sheriff?" came the response from the DA towards Mike.

"I think we all need to slow down and talk this through with cooler heads. What the investigation is showing is that no crime was committed by this group that responded as law enforcement officers to the scene of a crime in progress. The issue becomes that after actions of these reserve officers and that they did not follow protocol. For that I am suspending them pending an internal investigation. Wayne and Bill, you are both suspended immediately, and I will send it in writing to your email. Do you both understand your powers as officers of the law are suspended and you no longer have these powers?" Mike asked and stopped.

"This is Wayne and I understand I am suspended Sheriff" I said.

"This is Bill and I understand I am suspended too Sheriff" Bill also said.

"This is a farce and laws have been broken, Chief this was in your jurisdiction, you need to take over the case as soon as possible due to conflict of interest" the DA said.

"Sir, the Sheriff has been transparent and had my lead detectives helping with this case and what he said is exactly what my guys have told me. The protocols are not law sir, and as the preliminaries suggest, no law was broken." The Police Chief said to the DA which surprised me and the rest of my group.

"What, they, no, they broke the law, they killed these poor Hispanic guys because they are white extremists. This is a travesty of the law, DA you need to do something." The mayor said loudly.

"Wayne and the rest of you. I am so sorry that you are being labeled by the mayor as white extremists. Let me get these people out of the room and I will talk to you and the group with the chief of police give me a second." Mike said.

"I am not going, hey get your hands off me, hey you can't do this. DA you see this?" We heard the mayor saying.

"Shut up Stewart, you are a fool and have no idea what you just did to yourself and me too for that matter. Just shut the fuck up already." I heard the DA saying.

"They are hurting me, ouch, ouch, you see this DA??" the mayor was yelling now.

"For the love of God mayor, you do realize they all have their cameras on, right?" I heard the Da farther from the phone now and barely.

"WHAT?" I heard the mayor say as a door slammed in the background of the call.

"Oh my god Wayne, you should have seen that in person brother." I heard Charles' voice.

"Did you guys ambush them?" I asked as I looked around the table at shocked faces looking at the speaker in the center of the conference table.

"Wayne this is Chief Campbell, we have met a few times in passing but you have trained about 99 percent of my guys in one way or another. They all have nothing but praise and good things to say about you, even the ones that don't have much good to say about anyone else. That combined with the Sheriff immediately asking me to have two detectives help with this investigation since yourself and Bill are reserve deputies has had me in the loop the entire time. We just gave the case to the DA with no charges warranted and the mayor lost his shit in here before you called. I had been told he did not like you and had a vendetta against you, but it was truly unreal to see it manifest itself firsthand." The Chief said.

I could hear the Sheriff and Undersheriff laughing in the background while the police chief was talking to us. When the chief stopped Mike started, "Hey guys sorry about all the crazy shit and you not knowing what was happening. Wayne, you called me while I was sitting with all of them and turned the phone on speaker at the request of the DA before we had handed him the case. So, I just played along with you and what you thought was going on. Which it was but wasn't you could say" Mike said as I heard Charles giggling in the background along with the chief.

"Joke is on me then hmm?" I asked.

"Not a joke Wayne, you and Bill are suspended while we do an internal investigation and determine what should happen to you both for failure to follow protocols." Charles said.

"But the mayor and the DA just showed their hands and let us know what they think of you guys and how they are going to approach this. Well until they realized that the chief here was part of the investigation from the start. Not that it took much investigating, I mean it was a cut and dry thing they neighbors have cameras, so it is an open and closed case for sure. The DA might try to push an angle, but you guys are good for the shoot. Chief you have anything to add?" The Sheriff said.

"Only that I am sorry you think I am this mayors stooge because I am really a good cop that follows the law and constitution too. I hope we can meet face to face in the coming days and talk about this group of yours and what the community is going to look like in your eyes should this country crumble away as you said." The Chief said and made me feel bad I had assumed.

"Chief I am sorry I assumed and made an ass out of myself. I would love to have you out with the sheriff and the undersheriff to talk about the coming days. Let me know what works for you guys and we will make it happen as we have no schedule." I said.

"Sounds great Wayne, we will be in touch I have to go talk to him about this internal investigation in your lack of following set protocols." Mike said and hung up.

"What in the actual fuck just happened?" Jeff asked.

"We got got," Frank said.

"We truly did get got by them, make a note of that Luke, they are far more cunning than I had given them credit for." I told the group looking at Luke.

"Noted" Luke replied.

"Let's go get to breakfast and see how it is going and watch the market open" I said standing.

Part of the plan was for this group to meet every morning for a quick update before we went to eat. The idea was to let others eat first before we showed up. It also fell back to my days in the Army when leaders ate last. I just hoped the entire compound was full of leaders. True real leaders. I hoped this, tried to build this, so I could learn new things and that the reality was that true leaders had to know how to follow to be good leader. Thus, we would all be able to guide and help one and other through all things. Just like being on a team, everyone had a job but we all cross-trained and knew how to do each others jobs too. Consequently, we could all lend a hand when needed. I wanted this family to be able to guide and lead itself in the right direction always. Time would tell if we could be an effective team and build a lasting community in this volatile world that is crumbling around us.

Chapter 13

We all left the headquarters building and went towards the bunk house and the cafe style cafeteria for breakfast, all a little in shock that the situation was not what it had seemed, and we had gotten caught flat footed. As we went that way, we saw many of the compound families moving around the compound heading off to start their daily tasks you might call them. Right now, the focus is to try to get everyone situated and see if we need other things to complement our current setup. The collapse was in full tilt and the new day was surely to bring new unseen challenges for us all as we started to prepare ourselves and the compound for the unknown future. I was happy we had all made it here but knew deep down that a few people important to me still sat in the wind, my oldest boys.

David was my oldest son from my previous marriage and lived with his wife Emily in Canada while serving in the Canadian Army. His mother and I had met while I was serving in Korea when we married and had him less than a year later. We had my second oldest son, Donnovan, a year after we had David. After the divorce my wife asked to take both boys to Canada and they lived with her there until my second oldest, Donnovan, decided to move with Rae and me to New Mexico after I retired. Both boys decided to serve in the military where they currently reside. I had spoken to both of them about the world going to shit numerous times and what that looked like to me and asked them what it looked like to them. Both had mixed feelings and did not want to abandon their service in the wake of a SHTF scenario.

David was scheduled to accompany the Canadian contingent that was to arrive the following week and his wife was coming along for the ride. He was attached with them as a liaison since it was a new class of protective service candidates coming to get run through their paces. It was a blessing to have the contract to train different contingents of Canadian forces and agencies at the compound and the surrounding ranches. This contingent coming was from the Diplomatic Security Services which was ran out of the Office of Canadian Protocol. They had five trainers, two support personnel and twenty-five candidates along with a liaison. The liaison was usually from the Canadian JTF 2 since they are tasked with counter terrorism and protective services on the military side for Canada. The Canadian military was allowed to operate within their own nation and did not have a Posse Comitatus act stopping them like the United States military did.

Donnovan was currently on a rotation in Poland as far as I knew with his fellow rangers. He was a Squad leader with Bravo Company, 2nd Battalion, 75th Ranger Regiment and loved the fast pace of the 'Bat' as he called it. They had been busy since the Iraq and Afghanistan days, then Syria and other places not named. I was not a fan of him being in the Ranger Battalion and had often tried to get him to go to the 'dark side' as he and others called it and get his green beanie or even go to CAG. His reply was that he liked his guys too much and wanted to continue to do the things he was currently doing. As far as I had known, he was going to be moving to the Regimental Reconnaissance Company since he did go try out for them after he had worked with a team in Syria and had told me he liked what he saw. It was possible he was on a team now, I didn't really talk to him about work, or his brother for that matter, unless we were face to face to try to keep Operational Security (OPSEC) concerns to a minimum while on the phone or social media.

"Hey sexy man of mine" brought me back to the here and now as my wife greeted me in the cafe.

"Hey baby doll, how is it going in here?" I asked going to get a plate of food.

"A few little issues here and there but so far not bad. Maria has this down to a science with Bella. And now Chelsea is here and looking it over too. I am not sure if she is going to focus on schooling the kids or making sure the chow is good at this point" Rae said kind of laughing a little.

"How is she doing this morning after yesterday?" I asked about Chelsea.

"She is good, pissed that they did that to them but glad they are gone and paid for it dearly." Rae said.

"They paid for sure, has the News been talking about the markets opening this morning?" I asked.

"Nonstop, wall to wall talking heads about how it will open and stabilize after the implementations this administration has started." Rae said.

"I guess we will see here in a minute wont we?" I said as I grabbed my food and had a seat near one of the many televisions on in the dining area. I could hear the talking heads chattering on it about the market soon to open and how it was going to be a historic day as the markets around the world had declined but not a drastic sharp decline but a stabilizing decline. Another talking head or analyst was saying that the opening might see a decline but that it should be small with no circuit breakers being triggered.

"Mind if I sit with you Boss?" Luke asked.

"Never brother" I told him.

"I was up early, well never really went down honestly, talking to all my contacts in the field, people around the nation are upset about the cap on withdrawals. It did have the desired effect the administration had in mind and slowed the panic and the chaos in the city streets. That is going to change today boss. All my people that are in the know say that the market is going to close in the first hour and the collapse will be slow but unstoppable now. So, we are going to see a show this morning watching this according to every single person I could get in touch within my contacts list." Luke said as he took a big bite of food off his full plate.

"Unstoppable? What do they mean by that Luke?" Bill said as he sat with us.

"It means that shit is going to hit the fan today and nothing that this administration or anyone else does is going to stop the inevitable, bad times." Luke said around the food in this mouth.

"Your mom teach you to not talk with your mouth full?" Jeff asked Luke as he sat too.

"She tried but your mom liked me to talk when my mouth was full of her." Luke said smiling at Jeff.

"Figures she had always lied to me about that shit, thanks mom" Jeff said smiling back looking skyward.

"So, we are going to truly watch history made as they try not to panic on the air as the market completely goes haywire then." I said more than asked trying to refocus this rag tag group at my table.

"Yes, from what I have been told and could find out, we are in for a wild show today." came the reply from Luke around another mouthful of food and a smile at Jeff.

At that moment the announcers all went silent and that caused us all to look at the nearest TV to see why they stopped talking. The answer was clear, the market was crashing, worse than yesterday morning, it was down over a thousand points in a split second. Crashing was an understatement, it collapsed. The media types all looked shell shocked, even pale as they looked at the information and then one spoke.

"The market seems to have continued on its downward steep trend." the female talking head almost whispered.

"The Level One circuit breaker seems to have stopped trading after three minutes of trading and the Dow Jones down more than 1300 points with the NASDAQ down 892 points and the S&P 500 down also. It seems that traders and the public did not think that the measures the White House put in place last night would help." another announcer said to the camera.

The TV flashed away from the panel of media types and the words 'Breaking News' flashed across all the televisions in the dining area, and most likely the nations as well. Then it came to the female announcer who looked upset but not as pale as a minute ago.

"The stock markets opened just a moment ago to a record sell off that even the circuit breaker could not stop from happening as trading volume was recorded as a record high. Every single stock is down and was sold in numbers that our analysts are looking at right now. We are waiting on word from the White House, let's go live to our correspondent who is at the White House, Steve what have you heard there as the markets have hit the Level one in three minutes and stopped?" she asked him.

"Gretta, we have not been able to get an official statement from anyone here to this downturn, but I will say that Shocked is an understatement here. We are waiting to see if a statement, wait, I have a statement here" he was handed a paper "The SEC states 'the markets are now closed today due to an unforeseen problem thought fixed with the circuit breaker triggers after yesterday. Due to this problem the markets suffered the downturn that should have been caught and the triggers stopping such a deep sell-off from happening.' That is all they gave us as a statement and we will try to get more from the White House, back to you Gretta" The announcer said.

"Thank you, Steve, again if you have just joined us, the US Stock market suffered another downturn as the circuit breakers malfunctioned and did not immediately stop the sell off of all stocks in all markets. According to our analysts here every single stock in all three markets suffered a downturn." the female announcer said.

"It is unstoppable now; thank God we are here" I heard a female voice behind me say. I looked back and recognized Sally that spoke last night at the meeting about the markets.

"Did she link up with you yet Luke" I asked as I turned back from her outburst.

"No but I will grab her after I throw this away." Luke said as he got up and headed to the trash to throw out his very empty plate.

"Now we get to it and go out and grab what we can since we know for sure it is going down" Bill said.

"Yeah, get with Stephanie and see what we have ordered. Anything we can order and have sent next day, do it.

I don't care about the cost and lean on the company credit with everyone.

"Time to spend like we never have before with anyone willing to let us buy." I said then added "group meeting twenty minutes in the conference room with the core group. We need to start moving rapidly."

"Got it. I will send out a text in the core group tab." Craig said.

I got up and found Rae, "Hey love, the ball is rolling now" I told her as I leaned in for a kiss.

"No shit it is rolling, glad you got everyone here and settled" she said.

"We are missing a few still love." I reminded her with a grim smile.

"The boys know how to reach out to you and get here if they want to be here love. I know it pains you, but they want to do their part too you know." was her reply.

"I know love, they do but" I was saying when she cut me off.

"No 'buts' from you mister. They have your heart and desire to serve, and they are. If they are needed here or need us to get them here, they will reach out, or you can call them, but if you do, don't push love. Don't do that to them." she sternly said looking me in the eyes.

"Ok, ok, I won't push them love and I am not sure I could get ahold of either of them, but I am going to try to calling David and see about next week with the protective guys. We have a meeting in twenty minutes with the core group, I will let you know what is going on after." I told her.

"Wild times sexy man, love you" she said with a peck on my lips and walked away.

"Yummy" I said as I watched her sexy ass shake walking away from me.

"For fuck's sake, yuck." Jeff said.

"Stop being a jealous bitch" I told him smiling as we walked out and towards the headquarters building again.

"I got my own hot piece and not jealous of your outwardly public display of affection that NONE, notice my emphasis on none? Need." Jeff poked at me.

"Gotta ya" I said laughing at him.

I pulled the door open and headed towards my office thinking about what this really meant for all of us. Glad I had gotten us all here and ready. I was going to go call David right now so I could keep myself shot with him and not try to pull him and Emily here. Rae was right, I needed to let them do the things they wanted to do, and I struggled with this. I wanted them with me, and knew they made me stronger, us all stronger, but also knew they had their own calling a mission now.

I pulled out my cell and called David. He answered on the third ring.

"Yo daddy O, your markets have crashed." David said.

"Hey kiddo, yeah, they are collapsing slowing only because the SEC put the circuit breakers in years ago, otherwise they would be done, and this slow rolling ball would be barreling down the hill already." I said to him.

"Yeah, well it doesn't look good for anyone that is for sure, and the global economy is going to get hit too. People forget how it is all tied together now." he said.

"Yeah, it is going to get bad quickly now for sure. Are you guys still coming for training?" I switched gears on him.

"As of an hour ago yes, the contingent was still on schedule to come train at your facility, why you don't want us there? Are you needing to cancel?" he asked.

"I was not sure in light of the current economic climate if your esteemed government wanted to send people into America" I replied to him.

"Good one Pops, they had not seemed worried to continue training. Honestly, I think bringing Em down with me in case it does go sideways would be a good thing anyways." He said and it made me smile.

"Yeah, it would be nice to have you both here. Do you want me to send a plane to get your team or you guys have transportation and clearance?" I asked.

"We have everything sent up and have a government plane bring us and our toys. It helped to have Em working on the inside to get us a nice ride. We have reservations at the nice hotel in town, but if that falls through do you have room for us?" He asked.

"We still have room for a few more here on the compound." I replied.

"Just a few? That bunk house is more of a luxury hotel than a bunk house pops, it could hold a hundred or more, I am sure." came his reply.

"We have already circled the wagons kiddo." I said.

"Oh my, well then. So, you are going with the plan then?" he asked me in a serious tone.

"Yes, I already have poppa here too. I pulled the trigger earlier trying to not have any hangups having everyone getting here." I told him a matter of fact.

"And you didn't call me?" He almost sounded hurt.

"I didn't want to sound pushy son, it was hard, but I am calling now and letting you know where my mind is at and that we are well into the plan." I spoke.

"I am coming and will have Em with me and a lot of gear, as the training requires it." he said which I understood as code that he will be packed.

"Sounds good, if plans change or you need a ride for everyone let me know. Love you kiddo got to go, I have a meeting in 5." I told him.

"Love you too daddy O, talk soon" he disconnected.

So, he will be coming and have a pretty big size group to train as of right now, must bring that up in the meeting and get Stephanie to put that plan together. I got up and headed across the hall to the conference room and immediately noticed the TV was going nonstop with talking heads and their feeding frenzy chatter.

"This is the worst crash since the great depression" one announcer said.

"This is not a crash, just a bad downturn" another chastised him.

"You can keep with the talking points, but I am done with that nonsense, this is a crash. The market is collapsing and we here" he pointed to the other talking heads "are part of the problem feeding the public garbage. I am done with that." The screen instantly went to the Breaking New Markets halted after circuit breaker failure. When it returned to the talking heads at the table the announcer that said it was a collapse was missing.

"Sorry for that outburst from our correspondent, he is obviously over stressed from this steep downturn and the pressures of the job we are doing here at CNN." the female talking head said gently to the camera and her audience.

"We are going to go live to Steve at the White House any moment as the press secretary is due to open the daily meeting." said another correspondent.

I sat down rivetted to the TV shocked that CNN had failed and one of their own had said the word collapse on the air to the world. Not just collapse but that he was not going to stick to talking points and the market had crashed. He was done with CNN for sure and would never be seen on that network again, I was sure. I turned from the TV and most of the group was looking at one of the three monitors in the room and most looked shocked like me. I grabbed the remote and muted the screens.

"Fuck me, he said crash and collapse on the air to the nation and the world. It is fucking on for sure." Troy said a little out of character.

"They sure as shit cut the feed quick on his ass, as he was about to speak some truth to that group and the world it looked like no less." Tod said.

"He certainly was going to let it all out and off his chest, wasn't he?" Frank said.

"He was only saying what was truly happening and this administration is trying to stop what is now inevitable, a complete collapse. My contacts are saying that all the agencies are working on measures to stop unrest as they know it is coming. The word is that the continuity of government is being moved to secure locations starting today. I talked to Sally a little bit before heading over here and she is going to help with my analysis of this from now on, boss. She is a solid asset and has a lot of contacts inside the SEC and trading in general. She knows her shit and will be of great value to us. Anyways, she said that exactly what happened was going to take place and the devaluation of the dollar had started and would continue today. Most likely BRICS is going to make a move to try to overtake the dollar with a gold backed currency they have been developing for almost a decade now. That is from her, and I have not looked at this angle, but it makes sense to try to get away from the dollar since the country system is collapsing. More to come on that issue. Either way, my sources are saying today is going to be bad and from here on out have no real ability to see how it can get better, in other words it is here to stay, and the shit has hit the fan." Luke spoke directly to us all.

"Brazil, Russia, India, China, South Africa and others that have joined will push out their currency finally then?" I asked.

"That is what Sally was telling me, I am new to this side of it all, though I have knowledge about the dynamics of BRIC and how they affect national strategic thoughts, I by no means know anything other than the basics and will dig in today." Luke replied to me.

"Great, let us know what you find out at the next meeting. Not that it matters that much. Stephanie, are we liquidating our currency and switching to metals?" I said switching gears.

"We are going to use the money we currently have on hand to purchase locally whatever we think we need beyond the shopping spree we completed the first day." she said.

"Do we have a lot of currency on hand still?" Bill asked.

"Maybe 100K in currency" Stephanie told him.

"Dollars?" Craig asked.

"Part of it is in Euros too for any over sea contingencies." She replied to Bill.

"Wow, that is a lot of cash we can spend. Do we still have lists? Things we need?" Craig asked the group.

"We could purchase building supplies. Pipes, wire, and the likes. It will be useful to come later when we want to build other things. Let me loose with the money at Home Depot." Adam said with a gleam in his eyes.

"Easy cowboy" I mocked pulling back the regains like he was a wild horse running loose.

"We could use a few tractor supplies and such too." He said.

"I have a lot of maintenance supplies and needs coming in today on freight that I had ordered day one. Look over the orders and see what we missed please." Stephanie said to him.

"I can do that, but seriously I think we could go buy most of Home Depot if this is really the end of the world as we know it. This is not an EMP so things work and we have power so long term we could use a lot of things. How much can I spend at Home Depot?" Adam asked the group.

"You can max out or commercial account we have with them." I told Adam.

"Wholly shit, max it out? That is like almost 250K I can spend." Adam blurted out.

"Yes, get it all, but I need you to think about making a huge storage building first. I know we still have a lot of room in the vehicle areas, but I want you to build me a huge storage building. If you can get it from another company then do it, use the company credit card or apply for credit with them, Stephanie can help as can Craig. This goes with all of you, if you think we need it or need to stockpile it, order it and get it sent next day or priority, we can use it all one way or another. I want to build a community and sustain the one we currently have here, the compound and in town. Despite the eminent collapse, we must move forward and continue to build upon that which we already have. Adam, are the green houses already up?" I said.

"They are getting finished today. We had all that started day one and are putting all the water and electric into them. They are state of the art, Rae went all out." Adam said.

"Yeah, she got me to let her get all those when she talked about long term food production. I think she did good with that." I said.

"She did very well with that system for sure and the growth from those greenhouses should be able to continue year-round." Steve said.

"I need to get together with all the people that came with me and build a list" Mitch said.

"I can help with that Mitch, and we can streamline the purchases that they need to get. If they are local, we can try to get it all curbside pickup. If they need to try things on, we can figure out transportation for them which will be Bill's side of the house." Stephonie said.

"I think if we have anyone go outside the wire, compound I mean, we should start thinking about security with them. Things are sure to get more volatile as we move forward and a group playing with a lot of cash might cause attention that is not wanted." Jeff said.

"That is a good point, I can be a part of that team that goes out with them." Paul said.

"Craig, how does it sound to have Bill and myself as a QRF when people go out to get things. We can have Paul and

Frank be the close protection detail. They can go completely grey man covert and no outwardly forward presentation of security at this point. We have all done this before and need to start acting like anything outside the compound is an unknown threat. Luke start working up threat assessments for shopping areas and what the likely known threats would be. We start doing this now, as if we are deployed in a shithole. Every single one of you has at least one deployment, many of us have been to shitholes more than once, time to treat this current situation like it is, hostile." I said seriously as I looked around the group.

"I can start doing this, and I will work on the manning of the operations center 24/7 from this point forward. I think we need to break out the radios and get everyone set up with a personal compound radio. Then we have coverage in case the phones are not working. Troy is the intercom system on the compound working?" Craig asked.

"It was working on the last monthly system test which was a week ago. I can do a test and we can give everyone a heads up that we are going to test the system." Troy answered Criag.

"Great, we need to make that happen today then." Criag said.

"So, purchases, radios, intercom, what else people?" I asked.

"Mitch, are all your people armed?" Bill asked.

"All of the adults, minus a few I would guess, are armed with a pistol for sure." Mitch said.

"I know you have had maybe five of your people training here off and on along with your wife and daughters." Jeff said.

"I have taken all your courses as has my wife and about a handful of my pilots. Though they are going to be primarily for flight, they can defend here too." Mitch said.

"If anyone needs training, they need to get with me, I can start a daily training session." Jeff said.

"Let us all get our feet planted under us and then we can expand on what we have and how we can enhance it, Jeff." I told him. "Don't get me wrong, I want to train us all and get everyone up to, well close to, the same level of knowledge. I want teams established with all adults, an adult is anyone over 13 years old in the compound, to know what to do if we need them to act. This will start once we get everyone settled into the daily tasks. Does the compound family know that they are assigned daily tasks? If not make sure they know where to find the daily task list outside the dining hall area? The clock is ticking people, the real shit started when that news talking head spoke the truth for the first time to the world and the market collapsed this morning. Let's get it done and start working through our taskings." I said looking around at the group.

"Mitch lets go figure out what everyone might need from your team. I suspect they might need more than we might have thought about since the compound is somewhat new to a lot of them." Stephanie said.

"Sounds good" Mitch said and got up with Stephanie.

"Craig, you need to get your operations people settled into the positions while I need you" pointing to Adam "to get the storage unit I talked about started after you finish the green houses."

"On it Wayne" Adam said and left with his team.

"Are you making me a FOB bitch stuck in operations?" Craig asked me with a fake sad face.

"No, we will need you too for tactical and security operations and our six-man team is still a thing with two squads. I just need you with all your knowledge in that operations center to make sure we have the right people doing the things we need doing. Troy, we need to lean on the cameras with the AI. Anyone outside the compound that has a weapon, that system needs to alert us. Is it still tied to the compound radio system?" I asked.

"Yes and no, I need to put alerts on a frequency that will not cover, no, no, I can put it on the main channel and program it to stop anytime another radio transmits, so yes, sorry thinking out loud. I can get it to alert on the compound main frequency. I will get the AI fence up and running today and we can test it this afternoon, maybe early evening if that works." Troy answered.

The camera system I had purchased for the compound had augmented AI that allowed us to build an imaginary fence anywhere we needed one. What this means is we can put a line that the camera watches and if anyone crossed that line the AI would alert. On top of this the AI was built with a database of known weapons and if we programmed it to alert to a weapon it would alert if it noticed said weapon system. It was a great system and one I had used and recommended to agencies when consulting for security concerns.

"Get it running and we can start to test it and refine our fenced areas." I told him.

"I will get on it now, anything else for me?" Troy said, looking at me.

"Nope that is it buddy." I told him and watched him get up and leave.

"That system is amazing, truly a blessing that frees up manpower for sure." Craig said.

"The team is set to standard with 1st squad consisting of Bill, Paul and myself and 2nd squad is Jeff, Craig, and Frank. We will work around issues as we move forward and use everyone for all different details mixing and matching to best fit the needs of the said mission, but this is still the make-up of the team as a whole. Questions on this?" I looked at the guys and saw no questioning looks so I moved on.

"We are the hammer of the group, that can hit hard if need be while Mitch and his pilots are the serious muscle to help us smash anything that needs to be smashed. Our daily tasks are to make certain we are ready to go at a moment's notice with whatever force we might need to use to stop any and all threats to our family. Put your mind in the right mode guys because as we can see things are ramping up and for keeps. We have all done this before and I am preaching to the masses here. Lastly, thank you. Thank you for trusting in me and my vision and being by my side all these years guys, it means a lot to me, and I don't say it enough. So, thank you."

As I said that I looked around the table to each member of the team and made eye contact.

"NO thank you for having me, Wayne" Bill said.

"Ditto" Paul chimed in.

"I would not want to be with any other group of guys." Frank said.

"I think we are all grateful to be with one and other for sure." Jeff said.

"I just needed to say it out loud guys. Without you guys here this would not have worked or been possible, and that goes for everyone, and I will say that to the entire group, but you guy" I got cut off by Bill.

"Oh, my, God, stop with your sappy shit and save it for Rae" Bill said.

"Right" Jeff said starting to smile and making like he was puking.

"Alright then fuckers, let's get this day rolling." I said as I stood and headed for my office.

When I got to my office I sat down and looked around. My walls had different art, mostly military depictions on them, along with military awards. My desk had a few framed pictures of family and one of just my beautiful wife, Rae. Family was my world and I had done all this for them. My wife, boys, buddies, they were all family in my mind along with their families. It was a huge extended family, and it was what kept me going often. The boys and Rae kept me alive more times than I like at admit if I was honest. When the darkness came knocking, I knew I always had to keep going to the light because they needed me. Maybe the real truth was I needed them far more than they needed me and thankfully I had them despite me.

I found the remote for the TV set in my office and turned the volume on, where it already had CNN tuned in. I had caught a lot of shit over the years from so many people about having all the televisions in the compound tuned to CNN if they had news on. It was not that I liked anything they stood for or pushed on that network, it was just easier to listen to their spin than it was to listen to the spin of other networks. And I will be honest, I thought they covered more of the things that the public seemed to immerse themselves in. The headline across the channel was 'Breaking: Fear and Panic about markets and banking grips the nation' and three talking heads continued to talk about what just happened and the future.

I heard a knock at the door and Rae walked in and sat, more like planted her ass, in the seat across from me. "Ugh, I hate this." she said heavily.

"What? The news? My office? Me?" I said slightly smiling trying to make it better.

"Smart ass" she said smiling pointing at the TV "this is real. I hate that it has finally happened and was hoping it would settle down. It is not going to settle down and going to get way worse now." she finished.

"Yes, it is love, but we are prepared and in a far better place to try to stay safe and continue life the best we can, as a family." I told her as I got up and went around and knelt next to her chair and grabbed her hands. "I love you baby doll and we will try to get through this mess, together."

"I know we will love, it just pains me. For years we had talked about what if. You had me read and got me on board to do all this and thank God you did. Now it is here, and I am not ready. I am not prepared. This." I cut her off at this point.

"Sshhhh, my love. Minute by minute, day by day we will move forward, it is all we can do. We have done all that we could to try to prepare and we are still doing love. Together as a big family we will get through this, one way or another." I consoled her.

"I love you man of mine, thank you." she said as she leaned in and held onto me.

"Thank God for that love baby doll. Now that we have that settled are you armed right now?" I changed gears and moved forward on her.

"Yeah, I have the SIG 365 on me and an extra mag in my pocket, why?" she replied.

"We are going to have everyone trained to start carrying from this point forward. I think a sidearm and at least one extra mag should be the standard." I said.

"Sounds good to me." she replied.

"The balloon has gone up and we are going to start focusing on the plan today moving forward. Switch the mind to operational mode if you haven't already." I told her.

"That happened the minute I went with Luke to go get Paula and glad I had because my reaction was good when it was needed." She said.

"How are you doing after that sexy? I know we have trained over and over but that was your first real rodeo and I know it was the first time you killed someone directly." I asked.

"I thought about it a bit, and you are right, it changes you. I can't put words to it how it made me think. During it, the training took over and I just responded to the threat and did what was needed to end it, but after, I just, my mind pulled on me and made me think about how I had ended another life. I know that guy had it coming and started it and that made it easy, almost too easy for me to write it off as a done deal kind of thing. I am not sure I am making sense here, but it is not an issue as much as I know I did it and can do it again when needed. So, it changed me in a way I can't put to words, but not in a bad way. Shit I am rambling." She stopped.

"Not rambling, just telling me in your own words where you are at on it and I appreciate your openness with me like always. Sorry I had not asked about it more." I said as I got up and went back to my chair.

"I want you to be at the core group meetings in the morning, you are my second and we need to establish that from this point forward. We built this from the ground up and I need you with me from here on out, please." I told her.

"You know I will be beside you always love." she said.

"Great, let me bring you up to speed. The team is set as normal with Bill, Paul and me on first squad and the other three on second. If, more like when, people leave the wire security is a must. Paul and Frank are going to be doing close protection with whoever goes out from this point forward and Bill and I will be on QRF. Craig is getting the operations center rolling hard and all the people working in there up to speed. So, after we are done talking, you need to go get with Craig and settle in TOC bitch." I said smiling as a term of endearment.

"TOC bitch, really?" she said smiling at me for giving her hell.

"It really is going to be your bitch to run with Craig and Stephanie helping and Luke giving you the 411." I told her.

"I know that but wow, TOC bitch. You suck husband of mine." She said as she got up and intentionally shook her ass walking out of my office looking at me over her shoulder.

"MMMHMMMM, yep I am watching." I told her as she was looking away and left my office.

The tactical operations center or TOC for short was the heart and soul of a well working military unit, and that is what we used to model our group. Rae was going to be the head of the center and thus I was giving her hell about being a TOC bitch, which is a way of saying you are stuck being a rear echelon mother fucker, or REMF. It was a long running joke between us as I was always outside the wire running ops and she was working in an operations cell getting flights and tracking things. She was excellent at it and thus my number two and running the show in there for the SHTF plan. She had a good group working with her. Stephanie was her logistical person, while Luke was the intelligence side of the house, Troy was her network guy with radios and computer issues, Craig was her operational guy that helped with the hammer side of things. In all we had a solid group set up and the family members augmented positions in the center. Everyone had primary jobs, then secondary jobs and then taskings too. If we planned to survive long term, we would all have to work hard, and eventually we would have to grow to a much larger community. No one could survive long term alone if the world truly turned completely sideways unless they happened to be in the middle of nowhere. Even then they still would have challenges alone that they would not face if they had a group.

I spent the rest of the morning going over security concerns and making a list of things I knew we could use more of that we might be able to get ahold of and have shipped to us rapidly or purchased outright locally. I also went down into the bunker and had a look around. Things like batteries also were on my mind as I had looked at a selection of them in the long-time storage area in the bunker. I had stockpiled tons of batteries for all different things such as flashlights, remote controls and even tools. Should the world go to complete shit, gas would only be around for so long, though we might be able to keep a small refinery running that could make gas but that was a big might if it got really bad. Before I knew it Rae was back in my office.

"Lunch time" she said as she walked in and continued "Going to be like old times heading to the chow hall for a meal with you on the FOB"

"It will be but instead right here on our own compound with the whole family. Speaking of family, how are the boys and are they going to have school here like we had planned?" I said getting up and walk towards the exit and the dining area in the bunk house.

"Chelsea wants to do the school thing, but she likes the idea of being in the kitchen again too. We have two other teachers from Mitch's team so we will be able to do it whether Chelsea wants to teach and over see it or not." Rae said.

"She would do well taking on either of those roles, what does Maria think about her having Chelsea in the kitchen too?" I asked.

"Maria loves the help and has cooked with Chelsea before, so they work well together, I think that makes Chelsea want to be in the kitchen more. So, we will see how it pans out. I know the other two teachers had planned on starting school for all ages next week regardless of if Chelsea is over seeing it or not. It will be in the big classroom in the Training building." Rae told me.

As we walking into the bunk house and turned towards the dining area there was a line and we stepped to the side and found a bigger table and sat down for a minute to let others go get their food. Melinda, Susan, and Amanda all came our way with trays of food.

"Where are all the kids?" I asked them.

Melinda nodded over to her right "they are all over there together like a herd of starved cattle eating everything."

"They seem to love Maria's food for sure." Amanda said.

"I can't blame them, it is pretty damn amazing for sure." Came Susan's two cents.

The ladies all sat down, and their husbands showed up and sat with no food as they too seemed to want to let the line get smaller. It was nice to see everyone settling in and going about their own business getting lunch and making sure that their families got taken care of too. Lunch went smoothly and we all talked about the coming days and what it might look like. The subject got changed on us men a few times when it seemed we got to doom and gloomy for the ladies. It was a nice lunch, and I would say Maria was going to make me fat with this chow. The kids had it right, it was amazing. As the chit chat slowed down my phone buzzed.

"Hey Troy, what is going on?" I asked.

"Nothing crazy, just wanted to let you know I think we are ready to give the camera fenced areas a test and they are set to detection mode for weapons. I gave the command all outside the established perimeter." Troy said.

"Awesome I will be over to the TOC in a minute, and we can go from there." I said hanging up.

"Troy told me he was almost done when I came over to get lunch." Craig said.

"Did he eat?" Rae asked.

"Yeah, he had food he was munching on, I think he slipped out and got a meal to go, that kid is go, go, go when it comes to his tech shit." Craig said.

"He is good at what he does that is for sure." I said as I got up and ready to toss my plate.

The group did the Same and we all went out into the sunlight and the breeze that had picked up a little more into the afternoon. Everyone said they would see us at evening chow and headed in different directions except for Rae, Bill, Craig, and I. We all went back to the Headquarters building and the TOC to find Troy and get this test started. Troy was at the camera station watching the feeds and looking at his monitor while eating some sort of snack bar.

"Hey, ya already to test out my work and see if we can find any holes?" He said to us all.

"I doubt you have any holes. I think we should make a few calls and alert them to the testing we are going to be doing on our perimeter and that way we don't get anyone coming in hot to a guy with a gun call." I said to the group.

"Already called dispatch and let them know so the bases are covered. Do you want to test the runway side of the perimeter?" Troy asked.

"Yes, I think we need to cover the entire perimeter and look to see if we have gaps, which I am pretty certain we do not. Then we need to wait for it to get dark and test it all over again in the dark." I said.

"Sounds good to me" Bill said heading towards to team room to get gear.

"Just grab a shotgun for now. We have tested the gun software pretty in depth already and know a gun is a gun to it and we found no gaps with the many different styles of guns we tested on it." I told Bill as he walked out.

"Wilco" was his reply.

"I think we will do the shotgun and a pistol to test spots and see. We will just try to breech too with no gun and see if it alerts differently." I said.

"It is set to alert armed intruder or just intruder. Do you want it to alert the entire compound?" Troy asked.

"For the first test yes. But we are going to do it over and over again so after the first one lets turn off the compound PA alert and just let it alert on the radios." I said.

"I think we should just do radio alerts for these tests so if people hear the PA they know it is most likely real" Craig said.

"I am open to doing whatever we think is best for the alert, I just need to know it will alert us here and the word will get out." I said to Craig.

"Let me give you the run down on the fenced areas and how I have them set in the system so we can start the field testing and get it completely running. Inside the fence at the vehicle barrier is a digital fence. If a person makes it that far the alert will sound on the computers here in the TOC, radios, PA system, and cell text alert to those on the text alert list that a breech has occurred. It will also alert us to the section of the breech. It will sound like, 'Breech, Breech, Breech sector 2. Breech, Breech, Breech Sector 2.' Just outside the actual fence line is the digital fence that will alert that someone is at our fence should they cross it and approach the actual fence itself. It will sound like this, 'Fence alert sector 2, Fence Alert sector 2' This alert will alert on the computers in the TOC, and radio alert. Again, mind you this is just a person and no weapon detected in these alert series. I have the system set to detect any person or vehicle that is from this digital fence outwards to a mile. This alert will only sound in the TOC and sound like 'person/vehicle alert'. If this person or vehicle stops moving for more than 30 seconds a second alert will announce the location of a stopped vehicle or person. Again, this is if no weapons are detected." Troy said looking at all of us.

"That is awesome, so now give us the scoop on if a weapon is detected and those parameters in the system" Craig told Troy.

"If a weapon is detected from the digital fence just outside the actual fence outwards up to 300 yards it will alert 'Gun, Gun, Gun sector whatever' in the TOC and on the radios. If it is inside the digital fence and almost to our actual fence it will alert 'Gun, Gun, Gun, shelter in place. Gun, Gun, Gun, shelter in place' on the PA system. All radios will get the same alert, but it will say the location and this is so the intruder does not know we know where they are currently at. If the system detects a person between the vehicle barrier and the fence line it will alert 'Lockdown, lockdown, lockdown. Armed intruder inside the wire. Lockdown, lockdown, lockdown armed intruder inside the wire.' This alert will go to everywhere and any computer hooked to our network will get it blasted along with all the tv sets in the compound." Troy finished.

"What in the Fuck!!" I heard come from a female voice loudly behind me. I turned to see Sally near Luke watching the TV.

On the TV I saw the standard Breaking News flashing on the screen under the announcer on the screen. I could not make out what was being said on the TV.

"What is going on? Turn it up or recap for the rest of us" I said.

"They are reporting that the stock market is going to be closed for at least a month according to a source they have inside the SEC. That the problem with the circuit breaker is far worse." Luke said. "A source told me this earlier today but I could not confirm it so it is just on my speculations list. It seems it might be a little more than a speculation now."

"This is going to cause the other markets around the world to crumble." Sally said.

"Tell me what that means to us Sally." I said to her.

"It means the dollar is toast and not going to be worth much come a few hours from now. It is going to start a global panic and not just a national panic." she said to all of us.

I punched in Stephanies desk number on the phone in front of me and it rang and picked up, "Stephanie, how are we coming on all the purchases we have wanted to make? They just announced on"

"I saw it and we are finishing all of it now. The local cash purchases are tomorrow. Adam bought two huge storage metal building sets and picks them up tomorrow also from a local vender. We should be ok no matter what happens." She said cutting me off.

"Ok, Thank you." I said and heard her hang up the phone. Seconds later she came into the TOC too from her office.

The volume on the TV had been turned up and I could hear the announcer talking to another party on camera about what this meant to America.

"I will tell you it is not good for America at all, and the American people need to" and they cut away from that party and the announcer apologized for the technical difficulties and said they would be right back.

"Ok, lets get this test going. We need to have it done and in place no more than two hours after the sun goes down. The shit is starting to hit harder on the fan which will make the people restless. Let's go people." I told the room.

We worked the rest of the afternoon probing and testing the AI camera system in all different places and ways. From vehicles, bikes, kids, you name it, we did it. The system was amazing and alerted to each test and was really giving us ideas to push the system even further with digital fences and parameters. As the evening progressed it was announced that once again the President was going to address the nation at 9 PM Eastern Standard Time, which was 7 PM our time. This was perfect because we could get the testing done as the sun was setting early today and we could have everyone gather in the bunk chow area so we could talk after the address was done.

"Rae could you get the word out for everyone to be at the bunk house chow area for the address so we can have a group discussion after please." I asked.

"Sure thing" she said and started to get that task done.

Evening chow came and went quickly and was an amazing ham steak style meal with burgers and fries as an option too. Everyone seemed to be enjoying the food so far, but we were still eating food out of the huge walk-in freezer and coolers we had stocked heavily this week and hoped to continue to get shipments if they would come, then if they stopped coming it would be time to switch to all the other good we had stored. I doubted quality would go down that much since the dry stock we have was very substantial. Time would tell that I knew.

The testing after dark went as planned and I found myself sitting with my immediate family and the rest of the compound family waiting for the President of the United States to address the nation. After the address we would have a conversation as a new family bounded in the uncertain future we faced together. The announcer on the screen said the address was about to begin and the screen switched and when it did, I was shocked to see it was not in the White House at all, in fact I was not sure where it was at. The President walked to the podium and began.

"Good evening, my fellow Americans, I come to you tonight as our nation, as you, face an economic downturn unprecedented in the history of our great nation caused by fear and panic. This fear and panic caused three days of unrest and uncertainty and this uncertainty fuels other nations to become uncertain too. The decisions we as a nation make from this moment forward will determine the future for decades to come. I have been meeting with my administration and key members of the SEC, FDIC, FRB and other heads of the largest banking institutions throughout the day. I have been told that the market slide caused by the fears and panic of the two days prior combined with the crucial circuit breaks failure has simply broken the system we currently use to regulate and keep a complete collapse from transpiring. To prevent a complete collapse from occurring and on the advice from my head cabinet members, the SEC and other agencies mentioned I have elected to close the US stock markets until such time as I can be assured the events of the last three days cannot happen again. This measure is not taken lightly and will surely affect the global economy in a negative way, but it will surely not be nearly as bad as if we continue down this road and the unthinkable happened, a total collapse of the markets. The road ahead of us as a nation might look grim right now, but rest assured we will work through this together, as a United America. The travel restrictions implemented will continue through this weekend and be lifted Monday morning. The restrictions on money transfers and withdrawals will continue until the stock market system is fixed and open again. These measures are to help all Americans to be able to gain currency for themselves and not just those that have more means than others. We will get through these unprecedented times stronger and more together than ever, for we are the United States of America. God bless you all, good night."

The camera cut away from the president to the new anchor with a panel of analysts as one began to speak, "The President of the United States of America has just closed the US stock markets until a fix can be made. We had been reporting that the market was going to be closed but was unsure for how long, and tonight we are not clearer on how long that might be, Harry, what does this mean for all of us?" he said turning towards another panel member and I muted the system and stood up. As I stood the room was starting to rumble with small talk.

"OK, OK, OK" I said loudly raising my arms trying to get a hold on our group before it devolved into small clusters of conversations. "We already knew this was most likely what he was going to come on the air and tell all of us. Nothing really to bomb shell in this speech." I was saying when a pilot named Percy stood up.

"Sir, He was not at the White House, and he did not say anything about his location. I think you already noticed this because I saw you physically flinch when the camera first cut to the podium at the beginning of the address. So, I think we need to talk about that right from the beginning." Percy said to me.

I sighed and put my hands together in front of me and rubbed them as I began, "you are right I did notice right as the camera switched. It was not the White House, and I am honestly not sure where it was, and we could speculate all night on the possible locations he addressed the nation from. What does it mean to you that he was not at the White House since you brought it up, Percy, right?" I redirected it back at him.

"Yes, sir I am Percy, one of the pilots on Mitch's team. I think it means he knows a problem is coming and has flown the roost." He said to me and the group.

The low rumble started again, and I raised my arms up to signal for it to stop and I started "we are all here because we have prepared for the unthinkable, that we have, I have for decades hoped never happened, our world goes to shit. Here we are, together because we think it is here, and well, it is sadly here. I am sure many of you hoped, even prayed, it would not come to this, that the shit wasn't hitting the fan, that we just got to do this coming together thing, and it would all blow over. Well, here we are, and it is not blowing over. NO, it is blowing right into the fucking fan. Sorry about the language kids." I said looking around sheepishly. "But I might cuss and use foul language because I am passionate about us. About you and your future and the future of your kids and your kids' kids. You are all here to help this family" I waved my hands around towards the group "continue no matter what happens outside this compound. Thank you all for coming. For trusting in one and other enough to make this community possible. Look around you, some of the faces around you might be new to you but make no mistake they are family. They will die for your spouse, for your girlfriend, for you without question because you stood up and came here, to this compound, this community, this family. As the President said just a few minutes ago, the decisions we make will have lasting affects for decades to come. I want us all to prosper, I want us all to live happy full lives, and I want to do it all with you, with us, as a family. I am passionate about family, and make no mistake about it, we are all family now. Sure, we have teams, people we have known for a long time we might lean on more, but in time each and every person in this room and on this compound will contribute to the success or failure of this family, our family. So, from deep in my heart, thank you for being, no, for becoming a member of this family with all of us. These uncertain times are not as uncertain for me and this group. I hope you feel it as much as I feel it, we are strong, we have amazing people in our group like Sally who knew this was a problem with the markets and explained it to us today. Or Maria who is making sure we are all getting fed this amazing chow" the group cheered a little to the great chow and Maria blushed and waved a little wave as I continued "Thank you all for what we are doing now, and for what we will accomplish in the future. Together, as a family, we are the strongest. Tomorrow is a new day, and we will see what it brings to us, rest assured that we all will face whatever that might look as one, shoulder to shoulder. Craig has a few things to say and then we can open it up to the entire group and try to get things covered that need to be covered, Craig" I said and sat. As I sat people started to clap and cheer, which really caught me off guard, but I was glad they felt good about our new family.

"Well said Wayne, family" he said pointing to us all "sadly it is time to put on the game face and the big people pants. Together we need to prepare our minds just as much as ourselves and with that comes the small things. As you leave the chow area and head to whatever you are going to do, please stop and check out a radio from Troy in the back" Craig pointed to Troy in the back, and he waved at the group. "Everyone needs to get a radio. Troy will issue adults, that is anyone over 13 years old, one type of radio. If you are under 13 don't get upset, you get a cool radio too just like we have trained, or you have been told about before. We need you to make sure you have your radio with you everywhere you go, always, even the kids. This is to make sure you can get any information that needs to be put out. Each radio will get a charger with it that you can put the radio on at night and keep it charged. If you are in your room at night, you do not have to keep your radio on since we have the PA system that can put out information and this allows you to put it on the charger. I know you are aware of the radios and how to use them, and that brings me to the next point. It is time to always carry a sidearm with you. If you have been trained then it is time, and it makes me sad to have to say. I think most of you have heard this one before but here goes, it is better to have and not need than it is to need and not have. So, with that, start carrying your personal sidearm everywhere all the time. Parents, I will leave it up to you when you allow your children to start carrying them and not dictate to you about that matter beyond saying that anyone over 13 is part of the security of our family. We face uncertain times but thankfully we face them together as a family like Wayne said earlier. Thank you, Wayne" he finished and looked to me.

"Thank you, Craig, Mitch do you have anything?" I asked him.

"I do thanks, Wayne. Look at you all, my huge extended family. For those on my team, please open your minds and embrace this family, and talk, join together, learn, expand, and teach. Together we are going to beat whatever is thrown our way. I thank you for coming with me and helping this huge family continue far into the future. Thank you." He finished pointing at me as he sat.

"Questions, Concerns, Comments" I said as I stood up again.

We talked formally for more than an hour and then well into the night less formally, as people came and went and got to know one and other better. Concerns where addressed, questions answered, radios issued, and life seemed almost normal as the night wore on and the family grew the bonds needed to get through all that was going to get thrown at the fan. I made my rounds getting to know the newer faces better and watching as the bonds grew between new and old. It was a great sight to see, a community, a family growing stronger. God knew we would need as much strength in the coming chaos that was life. Rae found me and told me she was tired and needed to get to bed, and I followed her up to our new compound home where we found time for one another, and sleep took us both hard.

Chapter 14

I woke startled and in the haze of sleep noticed my alarm did not wake me and it was 4:45 AM, which was not a normal thing for me. I could not remember if I was dreaming, and I did not hear anything loud that would explain my sudden abrupt awakening. I was wide awake and knew sleep was not going to come back to me, so I decided to get up and make the rounds in the compound. I have learned over the years that if you wake before your spouse and try to be the ninja and not wake them you are more likely to be loud than just moving around and doing the things you needed to do.

Don't ask me why it works like this, but trying hard not to wake your spouse always worked the opposite way for me and I inadvertently made a louder noise than I would have by just doing my normal thing. I put on my clothes and EDC stuff and moved to the mini kitchen, if you want to call it that, and started coffee.

As the pot brewed, I took out my phone and looked through the headlines, and it seemed that the global economy was not handling the crash well. China had called for an emergency meeting of BRICS and was looking to push for the immediate release of their new currency to the world due to the pending economic crisis that jeopardized the value of the dollar. All the world markets have steadily lost value, and with the US markets closed they chose to close for the remainder of the week to adjust. The value of the dollar was at an all time low and some of the news articles hinted that it would cause deeper crisis in America due to prices rocketing higher from inflation. I had to put my phone away because nothing was positive to read, and I did not need to start my morning completely negative. I was thankful to see the coffee was done and I made a cup and slipped out of the compound home.

In the hallway I turned on my radio and started for the headquarters building and the TOC. I wanted to have a look at the night time crew and see if anything was stirring this time of the morning. As I got to the TOC I saw Criag was already in and headed over to him to see why.

"You are up early" I said to him.

"And yet you are here too, what woke you? Couldn't sleep" Craig replied.

"I don't know what woke me, no cold sweats, no dream, no loud noises that I could hear, and yet I was wide awake from whatever it was." I told him.

"Sounds about the Same for me, maybe our old operational watches in our heads?" Craig said smiling.

"Maybe so, what is the word in here?" I asked.

"Cameras are running amazingly. I don't want to jinx it, but damn you did good with this system brother. It has not alerted to anything not human, and we have had a lot of dogs, cats, racoons, and even a few foxes on camera. A few cars passing now and then and it alerts to them as they pass and we all are getting the alerts in here. It might be a game changer kind of system, and I am glad you told us all to fuck off and purchased it." Craig said sipping his coffee.

"I remember you as the leader of the 'we don't need that kind of system' here crew" I said smiling the 'got ya' smile as I sipped my coffee too.

"Yeah, yeah, I just admitted I was wrong, give me a break." He told me.

I glanced to the TV set that was muted and the screen flashed Breaking News. I turned and found a remote and unmuted the TV.

"Chase, the leading credit card company by far with more than 149 million cards in circulation, just announced a halt to all credit services. They issued a statement that due to the US stock market closure they are going to pause their services. The statement goes on to state that this pause will be through the weekend and most likely services will be continued starting Monday morning." the news caster said looking at the camera and continued. "We have reached out to them for further clarification but have not been able to get a response yet this morning."

The view on the TV split into two and another face was on the opposite side of the screen. "I am joined this morning by Brenda Singleton who is a financial analyst correspondent for us here at CNN, good morning Brenda." the male caster said.

"Morning Ben, this pause of service is unprecedented in the history of Chase and a true sign that things are not normal. What exactly this means for the economy is not certain, what is certain is that millions of Americans are waking up this morning with less buying power in their pockets as we approach the weekend this Thursday morning." the female caster stated.

I muted the TV and looked at Craig, "Well this morning is starting with a bang. What time are the people who needed to buy things planning to head out?"

"The first group was going to go out at zero six, which is Adam and his guys. Then at zero nine we have the other shoppers, they have two vehicles and the third is the protective team. Does this change things?" Craig responded.

"We need to make sure they all have cash, because if Chase is doing this, I am sure the rest of the card companies are going to follow suit. Do you think we should have a bigger security team?" I asked.

"We do have Adam going out with his team, maybe they can respond along with you and Bill as the QRF if things do go sideways for the other group?" Craig thought through it out loud.

"I think that would work, but the time are they heading out, I mean Home Depot opens way earlier." I said.

"Shit yeah, they are going to be done and back earlier. We could use them as QRF if they get back soon enough and have you and Bill going out with the group?" He said more than asked.

"Maybe we make you and Jeff QRF and have Bill and I close protection with Paul and Frank heavy protection?" I said.

"I think we should leave those two close protection and move you and Bill heavy protection, that would help with kit management as I am sure they both have their close in protection gear set already, as I am sure you most likely have the QRF set, am I right?" Craig asked.

"Yes, that would be correct we are already set up, that makes more sense. So, lets bump you and Jeff up to QRF, Bill and I can cover the QRF for the Home Depot run since Adam and his guys can operate and handle most situations and don't need us to babysit them closer" I replied.

"Sounds good then. Do you think we are going to see more trouble today?" Craig asked as we both sipped our coffee and looked at the TV.

"Plan for the worst, hope for the best right?" I responded.

"Gotta ya" he said.

I headed out of the operation center and over to my office and started to look through my lists and see if I needed to get anything locally. I turned the TV on, and the news was about the Chase credit card pause. I sat heavy in my chair and watched the two talking about how this was going to affect the citizens of America, and the female caster said something that caused me to take pause.

"Right now, many people are going to be caught away from home with no money or funds to possibly make their way home. Business travelers, family members taking trips, all of them potentially using their Chase issued credit cards to do this since the Governmental restrictions on withdrawals have limited how much they can use or spend. It might be a hard weekend for many, Ben." she said.

I muted the TV, leaning back in my chair and closed my eyes thinking to myself. So, this was something I had not thought about much until that new anchor said something, people are going to start to be stranded. No, things are going to slowly start to come to a stop. If companies are using credit cards for fuel to move products, then they can't get fuel starting right now. It is going to start an avalanche and thankfully we have already circled the wagons. Man, this shit is moving very rapidly.

"Hey dad, you ok?" My son Anthony said startling me.

I opened my eyes and looked at him, he looked a little worried. "Yeah, sorry was thinking here and didn't see you come in. What is up buddy?" I asked him.

"Mom woke us up to start the day and told me to come see if everything was okay because you had already gotten up and left. She said thanks for the coffee too." He said to me looking a little less worried.

"Yeah, I woke up pretty early and just got my day rolling, nothing to worry about with me. How are you handling all this?" I asked him.

"I'm good." He said in his normal way.

"I am good meaning? I mean we are here, and things are different, and you are not going to school. SO, it is a change, what is in your head?" I asked him.

"Honestly, it just seems like a weekend, and we are here doing training like we have before. Nothing is really feeling different, though it is nice to see the other people again." He told me.

"Oh yeah, I forgot you have a thing for Casandra, Mitch's daughter" I busted his balls.

"She is a nice girl and looks great too, so what is wrong with me liking her?" he said all serious to me.

"Nothing" I said holding up my hand like I was stopping him mocking that he was aggressive to me.

"Whatever dad, I am going to go get my chores done and see what the others are doing." he said as he turned. I caught his eyes rolling at me when he did. Deep down I was glad he liked Casandra and thought that if they hit it off it could be a cute relationship. I'm not sure my buddy felt the same way about his daughter possibly dating my son, who knew if his daughter even liked Anthony.

I got up from my desk and headed to the conference room in anticipation of the morning meeting with the core group. I ran into my wife in the hall as she was coming to the meeting from now on.

"Hey hubby, I see Anthony found you. You got up early, everything ok?" she asked, walking up for a quick peck morning kiss.

"Everything is ok, no huge issues but that is going to change rapidly today. I just woke up early and was wide awake, so I came to check on things before the day really got going." I responded.

"Change rapidly?" she asked quizzically as she sat with me at the conference table. Luke was already here too.

"Hey Rae, Boss." Luke said as we got situated in our seats.

"Hey" we both responded to him.

"Yeah, Chase stopped their services this morning, so no credit cards from them are working over the weekend." I told Rae.

"Not just Chase anymore Boss, all of them. NO credit services this weekend." Luke said.

"What?" Rae said in a louder tone.

"All of them followed suit then?" I asked Luke.

"They put out their own statements about thirty minutes after Chase did. All about the Same. Services would be reestablished Monday kind of story. I have reached out to my contacts and have not gotten much back from them. One wrote and said she is going to be off the grid for a bit and would talk when possible. That contact works for a senior senator and the message was code for they are in the wind. So, the President being at an undisclosed location for his speech last night makes sense and the continuity of government plan has already moved them all." He said to us as others filtered into the room and sat.

"No credit cards are working now?" my wife asked.

"That is my understanding of it" I told her.

"What" was echoed in the room from a few of the others as they sat.

"Let everyone get in here and we can start the meeting and talk about this together. It is going to get serious much quicker that we had all thought it might." I told those assembled already.

After a few minutes everyone was in the conference room, and I got up and closed the door, stealing ourselves from the rest of the building and anyone who might walk by and hear the conversation.

"Morning everyone. I started my day early and found Craig already had started his day early too. We saw breaking news flash on the TV and unmuted the set. It was an announcement that Chase was pausing services throughout the weekend. Luke just informed me that all credit card companies have followed suit, and no credit cards are operational at this point. Earlier in my office it struck me at how much this is going to impact the nation over the weekend. I do not think most trucking companies have cash with their drivers and most people do not have cash reserves, so that means using credit cards to purchase, that also with the withdrawal and transfer restrictions people do not have much money to use. This will cause stranded people and trucks, shipments stopping in the middle of transit, and more I am sure I have not even thought about." I said looking around the group.

"So how does that affect the teams going out to purchase things this morning?" Adam asked.

"It will affect the Home Depot Commercial account because it is CitiBank, and you will need to take more cash and not have as much buying power unless they allow you to do an invoice purchase. You need to ask when you first get to the store about the invoicing, I can get you cash, but only about 30K." Stephanie told him.

"Ok, I guess we will see and can adjust what we purchase from how they allow us to go forward." Adam said.

"Luke, what do you have for the group?" I asked him.

"Continuity of government plan has been confirmed activated from a contact of mine. This tells me that the government knew that the credit was going to get shut down, or possibly asked to have it turned off. I will try to get more on this and find out what my sources might know. I have threat assessment packets for the purchase teams going out today for the locations they are going to visit. I have gotten intel that foreign governments are moving military assets in the pacific and the eastern European areas. More to follow on this later as I develop the situational awareness better." Luke said to the group.

"Stephanie, how does the credit stoppage affect my group of people? Mitch asked.

"I have enough cash on hand to cover anyone that was going to go out and use credit cards Mitch, so not really at all. It will help us liquidate the cash anyways because the way things are looking it won't be worth shit soon anyways." Stephanie said.

"Thank you" he said.

"We are all family here Mitch, no need to thank us." I said and got a nod from him.

"I will be helping with Melinda and your group today, Mitch." Rae told him. "We should not have any real issues barring outside entities."

"The security plan for the purchase teams has changed" Craig said continuing "Adam your team needs to make sure they have their full kit heading out if they haven't already. Bill and Wayne, you are still QRF for them. Rae you will have Frank and Paul doing close in covert protection with Wayne and Bill covering heavy from a chase vehicle and Jeff and myself being QRF. Adam, when your group returns you can help if a QRF is needed by being a secondary response QRF team. The plan was changed in light of the cards being turned off and people might get a little more upset from this and cause chaos." Craig said.

"The camera system is working super." Troy said with a big smile.

"That it is for sure" Craig said.

"As you can all see, Rae is going to start attending these meetings. We have started this baby from the ground up and it is only right that she has a seat beside me in this morning meeting because if it wasn't for her, none of us would have this place to circle the wagons in. As we move forward, we need to think about how the leadership is going to work, the plan lays out that I was to oversee security measures but nothing really about who was in charge." I spoke.

"Stop." Mitch had his hands up. "I nominate you as the leader of this rag tag group."

"I second" Craig said rapidly as Bill said right on top of him.

"All those in favor" Stephanie said.

"Ye" resonated in the room loudly as all said it with conviction behind it.

"Opposed" Stephanie said looking around with a smile because of the dead silence.

"Motion carries and you are elected the official leader of this 'rag tag group' as Mitch called us." Stephanie said.

I looked around the group humbled that they would allow me to lead them, all of them gifted leaders themselves. "Thank you all" is all I could muster.

"Speechless Boss" Luke said.

"Cat has his fucking tongue" Bill said.

"Well, now this 'who is our leader' bullshit is dead. Can we get some chow now?" Paul asked.

"Anyone have anything else?" I asked the group standing. It was like a signal because everyone jumped up and started moving with 'nope' heard all around. Rae stood and gripped my hand tightly.

"You got this man of mine" she said as we watched the group heading out towards the exit and the bunk house.

"I was hoping someone else, maybe Craig could be the official group leader." I told her as I looked in her eyes.

"They would never have that love, you have brought this group together, built the company and then the compound from all these people. They have followed you and want to continue to follow you. Like I said, you got this. Let's go find the kids and have Breakfast as a family, Ok?" she asked.

"That sounds wonderful." I said as I held her hand tighter and walked in the cool morning breeze. The New Mexico air was getting brisk as winter was heading our way.

"Glad I put on the jacket this morning" Rae said snuggling closer as we walked across the area to the bunk house entrance.

"New Mexico winter is closing in for sure, I mean it is December already." I said.

"Yes, it is, and I hate it." she said passionately. She was a summer girly and hated cold weather and winter. I was the opposite of this, and often said you can only get so naked in the oppressive summer heat.

As we entered the bunk house we went and found a table again and this time picked a small corner table with only four chairs. Rae went and found the boys with the group of kids, many young adults among them that I could not come to grips with not being kids and brought them to our table.

"We will eat breakfast together then you guys can go hang with the other kids." I said to the boys.

"Sounds good dad" Anthony said.

"Ok" Owen said. He looked a little upset.

"What is wrong kiddo" I asked him.

"Crystal was going to sit with me" Owen said.

"OOOOHHHH, Crystal." I said with my giving him shit voice.

He put his hand on my lips saying "Dad, stop" as he looked her way.

Crystal was Bill and Amanda's youngest daughter. They had grown up around each other most of their entire lives and Bill and I often joked about them getting married one day. The joke was on us recently as they had started to like one and other and Owen had asked her to be his Valentine's this year. She accepted and they have been kind of a thing since. Now that we all lived on the compound together, I guess it might grow stronger or break, time will tell. Either way I was here to give him shit for sure. After all, isn't that what good dads do to their children?

"Both of you stop" Rae said to us.

It was nice to have this time, this moment with them all. My mind focused on them, the love I felt inside for them. I could only hope we got to have these moments long into the future, knowing deep down time stood still for no one.

"Let's all go stand in line as a family and talk about what our day is going to look like." Rae said standing and we all followed her to the line.

"I am getting with Neil, he is an aircraft mechanic, and he is going to show me around the Super Tucano today." Anthony said.

"No shit" I said.

"Yeah, I went to the hangars yesterday after my chores and he asked if he could help me, I introduced myself and told him I was looking at the A-29 and had always wondered about working on aircraft. So, he showed me a little yesterday but was busy and asked if I could come back today and I could help him." Anthony said.

"That is super cool son" Rae said flashing her amazing smile.

"I am excited for sure." Anthony said.

"What are you doing Owen?" Rae asked him.

"I am celebrating no school and getting online with my buddies" he said sounding excited.

"Don't get used to it kiddo" I told him.

"Why are we going to go back to school then? It sounds like school will close soon anyways from the other kids talking dad." He asked.

"School is going to start here in the compound next week." Rae answered.

"OH MAN, school here ugh" was Owen's response.

"Yeah, but you are going to start learning new things and everyone one is going to be in a big class learning together." I said to him.

"So, no more math?" he asked excitedly.

"Sorry buddy, still math but different types that will be used more commonly." I said as we went to the plates, and I grabbed them and started to hand them to my family.

"Thank you. Ok boys get what you want to eat and head back to the table." Rae said.

We had a nice family breakfast talking about the compound house, games, friends and the likes. It was good to have this time and be together. I was thinking about making it a normal thing but knew life was going to get more complicated in the coming days and did not want to make promises or set up things that we couldn't make happen. So, I just enjoyed what time I got, and we would make the best of it as it came to us. We broke up so I could go be ready in stand by for the QRF and we said our loves and headed in our own directions with full bellies.

"Love you" Rae told me as I went into the team room and she continued to the TOC.

"Love you too." I said over my shoulder.

I went into my cubby and grabbed the gear I had set out and started for the door and the vehicles. If we had not been suspended, I would go 10-8 with the Sheriff dispatch but instead would just be standing by and ready to respond should Adam and his team run into an obstacle. I put my plate carrier and helmet and made sure the headset was turned on. I did a radio check with the TOC and that was good then checked to make sure my ATAK was linked. All the systems where green and I looked over to see Bill was ready to go too. I had heard him give a radio check and saw him on the ATAK.

"Bear 70 this is Bear 17, over." I called Adam.

"Go for 70" Adam replied.

"QRF set, make sure you have your ATAK turned on, I did not see you up on the network." I transmitted.

"70 copies and is making sure it is up now, I see you in the network should be on and g2g now." Adam radioed.

I looked down at my screen and saw all his team on my ATAK screen and transmitted, "17 has you all on ATAK and standing by, out."

I reached in and turned the vehicle radio up, took my helmet off, unplugging the ears from the system, and setting it on the seat. No need to sit with it weighing down on my head until it was needed, and I could use the vehicle radio to listen for traffic on it.

"Let's hope nothing happens" Bill said.

"Don't you fucking jinx us." I said to him.

"Bear main this is 70, we are on the move and should be at destination in 20 mikes" Adam called they had left and rolling.

"Main copies" I heard the reply.

Right on schedule about twenty minutes later the radio came alive again, "Bear main, 70 going to be on handheld comms, will advise if we have any issues." I heard Adam's radio call.

"Main copies." was the reply again.

"So far so good" Came from Bill.

"You just have to keep pushing our luck with your shit don't you fucker?" I said rhetorically.

"Nothing is going to happen" He kept pushing.

"Bear 17 this is 70, over" came over the radio about an hour and a half later.

"Go for 17" I said into the vehicle hand mike as I grabbed my helmet and plugged it in and placed it onto my head.

"We attracted a crowd. We had to pay cash and a guy was watching us and made a call as we left and loaded up. He is currently following us. No hostilities, I say again no hostilities at this point. You can track us on ATAK. We are currently suiting up should the party get spicy, how copy." Adam's transmission sounded in my ears through my headset.

"Good copy, have you 5 by 5 on the ATAK and tracking. We are going to move to intercept and extricate the tail, how copy Main?" I radioed.

"Main copies and opening gats at this time to save you some time." Came the reply from the TOC.

I double clicked my transmit button and looked over at Bill while I closed the driver's door and we started to move. "See fucker, you jinxed it" I said to him.

"No, it was going to happen, people see that kinda cash, so I already thought it was going to be a shit day, this is just the start of a long day. I know it, you know it." Bill said matter of fact.

I accelerated the Tahoe out to the gate slowed and headed right out onto the surface streets. As we tracked Adam's team on the ATAK the radio came to life again.

"Bear 17 the party is getting bigger, a second vic, looks like four people in this vehicle. Unknown if they are, strike that. Armed, we see weapons." I heard Adam on the radio.

"17 copy, we are 6 mikes out, Maintain southernly travel on the road you are currently on. We will intercept the lead vehicle. How copy?" I replied.

"70 good copy, 6 mikes out to intercept. How do you want to work it?" Adam asked.

"I think we do it while you are at a stop sign and we pull up noise at them and pull them all out at gun point. Have a talk and then get you off the x and we will follow back slowly. 3 minutes out. Next 4-way stop be ready" Came my reply.

"We are set" Came a quick response.

I could see them moving towards us in the distance. Adam's team was in the lead with one of our trucks and a trailer behind it looking loaded down. Behind them you could see a truck and then a white SUV, maybe a suburban, as they got closer you could see it was full of men and they all appeared to have long guns.

"Looks like long guns, no chances here people, if they make any movements that look hostile dump them and we will deal with it as it happens." I signaled as I neared the stop sign "Execute. Execute, Execute."

I pulled through the intersection and nosed my SUV push bar at the truck behind Adam's truck. I saw Steve and Tod exit their vehicle and move towards the back on both sides, weapons pointed at the driver. He was completely shocked, and his hands instantly went shooting in the air. I was out of the vehicle and going around the back towards Bill's side as I heard him giving commands to the people in the other vehicle.

"DON'T FUCKING MOVE!! Release your weapons and let them drop." Came from bill as he was moving forward towards the other SUV. I could see the driver and his hands had already went in the air, his passenger in the front seat did not know what to do. His OODA Loop broken, he just sat dazed big eyes staring at us focused on the weapons pointing at him. I could make out the other two in the back and they seemed as shocked. I started to boom commands.

"HANDS! LET US SEE YOUR FUCKING HANDS EMPTY! DROP THE WEAPONS!" I commanded as Bill and I pressed forward with Steve already pulling the driver of the first vehicle out and was flex cuffing him face down. Time seemed to freeze, as the two guys in the back seemed to move in slow motion. Hands going up and the guy on the right side who I was more focused on had nothing in his hands.

"Don't shot, please don't kill us" the driver on the ground was saying over and over.

"24 hold. 73 you got eyes on them?" I called out to Bill and Tod.

"17 I got them" came the reply from Tod.

"Everyone in the vehicle keep your hands up and don't do anything dumb." I commanded. "Listen to what we tell you and this will be over, and everyone can go home safe, got it?" They all nodded and a few yelled "Yeah don't fucking kill us."

"No one is killing anyone as long as we all stay cool. Driver, put the vehicle in park with your left hand then reach down with the Same hand and undo your seatbelt. Got it?" I commanded.

He nodded and did as he was told.

"Now reach down with your right hand and open the door and step out. When you step out put your hands in the air and get on your knees." I told him.

"24 you secure all them as they get out. 73 keep those still in the vehicle covered from that side." I told Bill and Tod.

Everything went smoothly getting them to exit the vehicle. We gathered them all up and put them on the side of the road next to their front truck. It looked like a construction crew, three older looking white guys and two middle aged Hispanics.

"70 get your guys out of here and RTB." I told Adam as they all started moving.

"Bear base this is 17, all 10-4 here with 70 going to RTB. My element is going to have a chat and then RTB also, how copy?" I radioed.

"Main, good copy" came the reply in my ears.

"OK guys now that we are here, what the fuck did you guys want with our work crew?" I asked this motley group.

"What are you talking about man, we were just driving, and you came out of nowhere guns pointed at us" Came the guy that was driving the lead vehicle.

"Oh yeah? And it just happens that you started at the Same spot as our guys and going this Same direction out to the middle of nowhere on the outside of town? I don't like dishonest people, so think it through a minute." I said.

"We are going to call the cops on you guys, you are going to be in big trouble assholes." Came from an older white guy we pulled from the tail truck.

"Good Idea, let me call the sheriff" I said pulling my phone out and hitting the dial button to the Sheriff's personal number. It rang three times, and I thought Mike was not going to answer when his voice filled the speaker.

"Hey, how are you doing in these crazy times?" he said when he answered.

I hit the speaker button "Sheriff this is Bear 17, I currently have five individuals flex cuffed on the side of the road because they decided it would be a good idea to follow my guys after they purchased building supplied at Home Depot with a large sum of cash. They have two vehicles and the four in the rear vehicle all had long guns as we interdicted them. They are getting pissy and said they were going to call the cops on us, so I took it upon myself to let you know." I said this looking at the older guy in the eyes.

"Mike these fuckers just jumped out and pointed guns at us acting like they are cops and now have us hostage. I demand you come arrest them and get us right now!" the older white guy said.

"Mister Galagher, is that you sir?" Mike said.

"You know damn well it is me Mike, these mother fuckers need to understand who the fuck I am, and you need to get guys here right now." Galagher said.

"Bear take me off speaker please." Mike told me.

I took my headset off my ears and deployed them on the back of my helmet and then took the phone to my ear. "You are in my ear, and I am walking away from the group." I told Mike.

"What the fuck Wayne? This day is shitty enough already without you calling me, and to have that fucking uppity shithead in flex cuffs, dammit." Mike said sounding pretty upset.

"A guy from this group was at Home Depot called when he saw my guys pay out with cash. Then he followed and the second vehicle with all these other guys was tailing our guys too. We took them down and pulled them out. I wasn't going to call you at all but this Galagher guy, I assume he is the mister Galagher of the construction company here in town, started with this call the cops and get me arrested shit.

They did not have good intentions Mike" I said as this Galagher guy lipped off.

"You are full of shit, you pointed guns at us for no reason!!" he yelled.

"Look Mike, I am going to leave these turds right here on the side of the road with cuffs still on and you can send a unit to cut them loose. Do me a favor, explain to them things are different now, because these fucks have no idea the hornets' nest they are fucking with right now. I will call you later because we need to talk and you might want to get the chief on the call too, or we can meet and have coffee? Either way guys like this fucking wanna be big shot are going to get people killed" I said.

"I will come cut him loose myself, where are you at?" Mike asked.

I told him the location out on the south end of town, and he said he would be there in less than ten minutes, and I hung up.

"You have no fucking clue who I am telling Mike I kicked a fucking hornets' nest, you are the one that kicked it mother fucker." Galagher said.

"24 lets load up. Sir, I am going now. I hope that you can see the light when Mike comes and talks to you. From the sounds of it, you are not going to see the light and we will be seeing one and other again. I promise you, if we do meet again and you are armed, it won't end well for you. Have a great day" I said and walked away. As I did, a very upset man let loose with a bunch of nice things to say about me and my family, the one that stuck was he was going to kill us all.

Words he would regret to have ever spoken in time, he just didn't know it yet.

"Bear main, 17 is clear and RTB at this time." I called over the radio as we left.

Bear main copies." Came the reply.

We made our way back to the compound and reset after going out. I went and found Adam and his guys unloading the supplies.

"How did you make out in getting the things you wanted?" I asked.

"It is not as much as I would have liked to get but I have a good stock now in case we need to fix things or even build a bunch of things. Electrical, plumbing and the likes are in what we bought. Thanks for coming out and getting those guys off us. Do you think it was going to get bad?" Adam asked.

"Well depends on what you mean by bad, the guy following you was Mister Galagher and a few of his guys." I spoke.

"The Mister Galagher? From the construction company?" Adam asked.

"I think so, I don't know the guy, just heard things about him and might have met him in passing at some of the events here in town. Looked like him to me." I said.

"He is going to make a big deal out of this then." Adam told me.

"He already is trying, told me I was going to get arrested once he talked to the cops. I called Mike on the spot. Sounds like it is going to be interesting with him and that he thinks he is king shit." I said.

"Oh yeah, he thinks he is a God here in the area and most people give him what he wants, so it could be very interesting for sure." Adam said.

"As we left him sitting there cuffed, he said he was going to kill my family, so he has already stepped over the line and has no idea what he has gotten himself into." I told Adam.

"Oh, he done fucked up" Miguel said walking by with a load in his arms.

"Yeah, he did and doesn't even know it yet, oh well. Can you make sure the green houses are done today and then get the storage unit going, or is it not here yet?" I asked.

"It will deliver today sometime, it was from a local company that had a larger unit in there inventory they are happy to have sold." Adam said.

"Great, thank you for doing the things you are doing. All of you, great job and thanks." I said looking at Adam's team.

"Thanks for having our six boss" Tod said.

"I am sure you could have handled it, just better safe than sorry" I said walking back towards the staging area I had the Tahoe in for QRF.

I went over and took off my chest rig and stowed it in the driver seat and then headed for the TOC. I left my gun belt on as I headed into the TOC. It was humming with activity. I found Luke in his area and asked if he could do a workup on this Galagher guy. He asked me if I wanted a targeting package or just an information work up, I told him to do a targeting package. With the attitude this guy gave off along with the threat to kill my family in the face of a guy that had him detained was over the top and I knew it was going to end up going kinetic. I then went over to the cameras and found troy with a few other people talking through the system and the way to operate certain cameras at one time.

"You need something Wayne?" He asked seeing me watching.

"No, I was just listening and learning things too Troy, thanks." I told him.

I then moved over to Craig and asked, "ow are things?"

"They are good, and the other shopping group is getting ready to head out in about thirty minutes" he said to me.

"Good, I hope it goes smooth, but something tells me it is going to cause issues with a big group paying cash." I told him continuing "This incident with the Galagher guy is going to be a problem."

"Bill came in and said the Same thing, that this guy doesn't understand how far out of his depth he is and threatened to kill your family, our family" Craig said.

"Yeah, I think it will become an issue we might have to fix, I hope not but the reality is he will push until we have to react." Craig said.

"Let's go listen to the conop in the conference room and ready to roll" Craig said.

We walked into the conference room and the mission brief to go out shopping was being briefed. We had four vehicles going out, two with two passengers and the other two with four passengers each. Paul and Frank would be in the lead vehicle, Rae in the next with her group then Melinda in the next with her group. Bill and I would be in a trail vehicle loosely following them. The idea was to lead them into the shopping area and then Paul and Frank would follow them around observing the group in the store from a distance. This would allow them to observe any perceived threats and relay information to Bill and I in the parking lot should a heavy response be needed. Everyone understood the plan and we all went to load up in our vehicles and head out on the next mission.

Bill and I would do this movement with our helmets off so as not to draw attention to ourselves while sitting in the parking lot and driving around. We went out and put our kits on and tested the radios and the ATAK system to make sure we had all the trackers running. The system was such a blessing and for those that have never used one or been exposed I would recommend they look at the system. Everyone got mounted up and our first stop was going to be Target.

As we all got on the move my phone rang and I picked it up on the vehicle system. It was the sheriff, this should be good I thought. "Hey Sheriff, how are you?" I said.

"How the fuck do you think I am doing Wayne?" was his response. "Galagher is a royal pain in the ass to begin with, now he is fuming and wants you arrested. I asked what he was doing following your guys and he said he wasn't following your guy and you just all pulled out weapons and held them against their will. I saw all the weapons in the vehicle he was riding in like you said they had and pointed to the weapons, and he got quiet." Mike said.

"He is going to be a problem" I said to Mike.

"He is going to most likely be a pain in the ass yes, I tried to explain to him that you are not the people to mess with and he asked who he thought I was talking to. Bottom line is he will not listen to reason Wayne." Mike told me flat out.

"He told me he was going to kill me and my family Mike" I said as I drove two blocks behind our group going shopping.

"Damn, he has no idea then what he is getting himself into." Mike said quietly.

"No, sadly I got the feeling the only way he will understand is at a very dear cost" I responded.

"Please use restraint Wayne. I know you are already in war mode, and I don't need more bodies stacked up from you and your people." Mike said.

"We are not going to let people push us around Mike, and we sure as shit are not going to get robbed or let someone think they can have that which is ours. We are out on another shopping trip right now to Target." I let him know.

"The PD has a unit there with an officer, so you shouldn't have a problem there or any other place to shop as we are trying to secure those and keep it peaceful. We had an incident when they first opened this morning because people did not have cash and got upset. So now the Chief and I have placed units around the area in shopping areas to help stop this kind of problem." Mike told me.

"I would love to meet with you both after this mission is done if you guys can spare the time." I said to Mike.

"I will get ahold of him, and we can try to come meet you wherever you might like." Mike said.

"Sounds good. Maybe an hour and a half two hours then?" I asked.

"Great, talk to you in a bit Wayne" Mike said as he hung up.

The entire time I was on the phone with Mike the convoy was proceeding towards town and Target. I maintained a healthy distance behind the group and tried to blend into the traffic. I was glad to see that the roads still had people out moving around and it was not a ghost town like the days of the Covid pandemic and the stay-at-home orders. Traffic seemed lighter than normal, but we still had traffic out and that was a nice thing to see so we did not stick out like a huge 'here we are' kind of thing.

"You want more than you and I at the meeting with the Sheriff and police Chief?" Bill asked.

"Yeah, I think I will have Craig and Jeff come along with Paul and Frank after we get this group back and tucked in at the compound. The more the merrier right" I said.

"Are you thinking they will be a problem, or it be a trap?" he asked.

"NO. Not at all. What makes you think that?" I said watching the group pull into the Target lot and the radio traffic signifying we are at the first target coming across the vehicle radio.

"You are taking the whole team, so I thought that was a lot, why all of us then?" Bill asked as he scanned the area and we parked with a good view of the entire lot and the front of the store.

"I want the entire team to hear what they have to say and to be able to ask questions. I feel like we are going to get asked to help them do things, and I want the team to hear what they ask, I am thinking about bringing Mitch, but they have no clue we have air assets with us, no need to show our hand." I said.

"Do they know Mitch and that him around would mean air assets?" Bill asked as he continued to scan. Our group had entered the store with Paul walking in first, then the group a little bit after and Frank trailing behind.

"Mike has been on a few trips with me on one of Mitch's birds. I honestly can't remember if they met, but I still think it is better to keep our abilities as low key as possible. Am I wrong about that?" I asked Bill.

"No, you are not wrong about that. Better to hold our hand close to chest I would say" Bill pointed to a guy I had already been watching "He has been watching people going in and after our group went in, he got out to head in." Bill said.

"Yeah, he was in that white truck over there." I said pointing.

"Yep, and once our group got all the way in he got out and headed in." Bill confirmed.

"Bear 28 this is Bear 17, be advised you have a possible hostile just now coming in that has been watching people come and go. White male, middle aged, black hat, jeans, green shirt, over." I said into the radio.

I heard two clicks and then another two clicks acknowledging that both Frank and Paul heard my transmission. I looked at Bill and we both took our helmets and put them on. Better to be ready and possibly noticed than not ready and slowed down when needed. We sat observing people come and go from the store for another thirty minutes before the radio came alive with a transmission.

"Bear 17 and 24, subject is very interested in our group and trying to not look suspicious. The subject is certainly armed as his pistol is printed on the right hip side. As of now no hostile intent has been perceived. He is not the only one watching us, the store security has approached the group a few times asking how we planned to pay since it was cash only and the group had so much. Will advise as we approach the registers, maybe 5 mikes" Frank said.

"Understood" I radioed back.

"This might be a shit show hmm?" bill said more than asked.

I sighed deeply, "I really hope not. I just want to get this over and head back without too much drama."

"I sadly think those days are over man, it is shit show central from here on out." Bill said watching the door and getting his kit how he wanted it.

"Stop jinxing shit you fucker. If it goes down, I am going hard to the door. Wait, is that officer Hernadez in his unit pulling up to the front right now?" I asked as a Police unit pulled in and drove up to the front of the store.

"It looks like him. Yea it is him" Bill said as we watched him get out of his unit and look around.

I unrolled my window and waved my arm at him hoping he would see me, and he did and waved. I waved him over towards us as I pulled close to the front of the store. He walked up to Bill's side of our Tahoe.

"Damn, what the fuck you guys all kitted up for?" Officer Hernandez asked, looking around after looking in at us.

"We have a bunch of spouses inside shopping about to pay cash for a larger amount of stuff, which might cause unwanted problems." Bill said.

"No shit, I have Target here and the store across the way I am supposed to watch, I came back over here because Target security had called in to dispatch about a big group with a few larger full baskets that they were sure could not be paid cash for. This you guys?" the officer asked.

"Guilty, but we have the cash." Bill said smiling at the officer.

"Yeah, you guys certainly will have the cash." He echoed back.

"You have trained with us enough to recognize Paul and Frank, right?" I asked Hernandez.

"Yes" he said looking my way "why?"

"They are inside doing close protection with the group and pretty well armed and I don't want you to mistake them for a threat. They are currently watching the store security freak out and another armed guy has been watching the group." Bill told the officer.

"Ok, I will go in and let security know you guys are legitimate. Please let me handle things before you jump out boys come rushing in, ok?" he asked.

"No jump out boy shit from us, we are here only if it gets really bad, Paul and Frank can handle almost anything besides heavy contact." I said smiling at him as he rolled his eyes and headed into the store.

"Bear 28 and 21 this is Bear 24, you have officer Hernandez coming inside. Security was overly concerned with the amount of inventory we had in our carts and the ability to pay." Bill radioed.

"Fucking figures. He knows we are in here?" came Paul's reply.

"Yeah, we intercepted him and explained the situation." Bill said.

"Roger that" Came the reply and I heard yelling in the background.

"You hear the yelling?" I asked Bill.

"Yeah" Bill said as we watched the door and waited.

"Bear elements be advised, people are upset we have so much cash. It is turning into a shit show. Good thing officer Hernandez is here." came a report from Frank.

"Copy" was echoed by the TOC and us as we sat and waited.

A bit after the situation report from Frank, the middle-aged guy in jeans came out and got in his vehicle. He started it up and moved it closer to the two vehicles that the ladies in the shopping group rode in.

"28 and 21 be advised jeans guy has moved his vehicle next to both of the lady's rides. Please close escort, I say again, close escort them to their rides. We will advise." Bill radioed.

"Wilco" came from them both. Ten minutes later the group exited the building with Paul in the lead and Frank in the rear where Hernandez was talking to Frank. I could see the annoyance on Frank's face from here as it was a distraction he did not want during the exfil of the group.

It all seemed to happen at once as Bill keyed the radio and announced "GUN" into it. Paul had already seen it and was yelling "GUN" to the group. I gunned our vehicle and came barreling in between the group and the jeans guy who had pulled his gun and was exiting his vehicle. Officer Hernandez was quick and had moved directly towards the threat as had Paul, both had their side arms out and pointed at the jeans guy. I had come to a stop with the front end of the vehicle pointing directly at the subject who was already bringing his weapon to bare on me. Bill and I immediately swung our doors open and fluidly exited into a kneeling position on the outer edge of our open doors on either side of the Tahoe.

"Drop the fucking gun now!" I heard officer Hernandez commanding from behind me.

I heard doors slamming and ladies yelling "what about our stuff" then wheels squill.

"Bear 06 clearing with all on board. Expect rapid exfil to your location bear main, how copy." I heard my wife say in my ears over the radio.

"Bear main copies. QRF will intercept you in your exfil and escort." was the reply.

"Bear 06 copies" was all I heard from my wife.

"Drop it right fucking now or I am going to kill you motherfucker!" I heard Hernandez yelling.

Reflexively I had exited the vehicle and taken a kneeling shooting stance at the far edge of the vehicle with my rifle. Once again, I found the red dot of my Aimpoint Micro T on the bridge of another guy's nose. He looked completely shocked that so many guns were pointed at him. I could see the determination briskly drain from his body as the pistol fell from his hands and they both shot into the air.

"Good Now turn away from us and get on your knees." Hernandez commanded him.

"We got cover Hernandez you can hook him." Bill called.

Hernandez moved forward and holstered his weapon and then cuffed him. He then got him to his feet and frisked him. We could hear the cavalry coming from the sirens and understood it was best for us to all put our weapons away. Hernandez called out that he had non law enforcement help and that the subject was in custody. Units from the PD and sheriff started arriving. I asked if we could secure our purchases and Hernandez told us to go ahead and do that. He then had arriving officers get quick interviews from all of us on their body cameras so we could leave. It took an extra hour and, in that time, the chief and the sheriff had shown up, so we got to kill two birds with one stone you could say.

"You guys are like shit magnets aren't you" The police chief said.

"More like trouble seems to find us Chief" I said.

"Or you are looking for trouble" the Sheriff said sourly.

"I think by now you know I try to steer as far away from trouble as I can Sheriff" I responded. "But I am ready should it find us."

"Well officer Hernandez was very surprised you did not kill this guy he told us." the Sheriff said.

"Why is that?" Bill asked.

"Because a few wives, and especially his wife" chief pointed at me "was in the group that guy was going after."

"His weapon was trained on us, and luckily for him not on the group or Hernandez is right, we, I, would have dropping him." Paul said.

Holding up his hands, "ok I am not trying to cause or say you are trying to get into a shootout, was just making a point. Sorry." the police chief said.

"Ok, so this is cut and dry and we need to get these items back to our place, but I want to know what you guys had hoped to talk to me about today." I said to the chief and the sheriff.

"Can we just follow you guys out to your place right now and sit down and talk?" The Sheriff asked.

"I don't see why not, let us load up all this stuff and we can head out." I said.

We all loaded up the two vehicles and started heading towards the compound. As we did, we radioed that ww would be having company and to get all the hangars closed and most of the people hanging out away from the view of the chief and sheriff. I did not want to have to answer questions right now about who this or that was or explain why we had new people around.

Since this shopping mission had gone sideways it had taken well past lunch to get ourselves out of the parking area and returning to the compound. I was thankful I had eaten a good breakfast and that I had a couple cliff bars in my vehicle to snack on. I let Paul and Frank lead as we went back to the compound. As we pulled through the gates, the TOC had opened them both as we pulled up, we drove up to the roundabout in front of the Headquarters building with the

Chief and sheriff following us. Paul and Frank drove over to the motor pool staging area between the Headquarters building and the bunk house. We all exited our vehicles, and I told the Chief and Sheriff to follow me, we were heading to my office to have this conversation and see what they had up their sleeves.

Chapter 15

The chief and the sheriff followed me into the Headquarters building of my business, all the office doors and the TOC doors closed as I guided them into my office with Craig and Bill on their heels.

"Gentleman welcome to my office and the headquarters of my business. Sheriff, I know you have been here a bit, but Chief I think this is the first time, can I get either of you something to drink? Sweet tea? Coffee? Water? Soda?" I asked.

"I am good Wayne" the Sheriff said.

"I am too" The Police chief said.

"Well then, what can I do for you guys then?" I asked.

"I have been explaining some of the conversations you have had with myself, Charles, the city council and the county board about things like we are currently involved in happening to the chief here. How you tried to get everyone to work on plans and be ready and for the most part everyone has essentially blown you off." the sheriff said.

"I don't take it as a blow off honestly, I know that preparing for the eventualities of things like an economic collapse are not easy or fiscally sound practices of cities or counties. I also know that some of the people that I have talked to or have been a part of the conversations have prepared for themselves, and that is a start. So now we are here, and it is just now starting to sink in for many, that this shit is going to be bad, is bad, and then the credit card companies turned off the credit of every American. Now everyone, even the rich, are in the Same boat if they have not prepared. People are going to be stranded, truckers are not going to be able to continue to deliver their loads, it is just going to snowball from here." I spoke.

"Truckers, wow, you are right, they are, they are going to not have any way to refill their tanks when they run empty. At least not until Monday when they allow the credit cards holders to start to utilize their credit again." The chief said looking a little stunned.

"How do you fuel your unit's chief?" I asked already knowing the answer.

"We have fleet cards that we gas at the local pumps. Right now we are using the county fuel station since our cards are not working." He said.

"I got emergency authorization to fuel his unit's for the weekend from the county board." the Sheriff said.

"And when your stores run dry Sheriff, then what?" I asked him.

"We won't run dry because we get weekly deliveries that come out of Artesia just down south." the Sheriff said.

"How does the county pay for these shipments?" I asked him.

"I do not know, that is a good question. I am sure we could work something out to make sure it is paid and we can get the fuel we need." the Sheriff said.

"I am sure it can be worked out too, but it should already be in the works to make sure that you can get the fuel you need before you need it. This is all part of the planning process and working through the problems that your city council and the county board did not feel need to be worked through. Food, water, sewage, electricity, and so much more need to be worked on and planned out. The public is already starting to look for ways to get by. This Galagher guy, he was already going to start taking things from people or get the money they had to use himself. He is going to be a problem." I said.

"Now wait a minute Wayne, he said he was just going to check on a site he had out southwest of here and they had the weapons as protection." the sheriff said.

"You really believe that bullshit?" I asked him.

"No, I don't, you are right. He is a hot head and known to cut corners and use his influence to get the things he wants. He is good friends to more than one city council member and county board member. So, he is well connected and not happy about you." the Sheriff said.

"He told me he was going to kill me and my family Mike, so he is a serious threat and fucked with the wrong guy at the wrong time." I told him pointedly.

"He said that to you?" the chief asked.

"Yeah, all red in the face and pissed off I had him sitting on the ground flex cuffed. Did I get it right Bill?" I asked.

"He said you had no idea who he was telling Mike that he had kicked a hornets nest and that he was going to kill your entire family and make you watch. We left then but I am sure you herd him say it all because you tensed up like you wanted to stop and end that threat then and now. I was honestly proud of you for just walking away." Bil said.

"He said that?" Craig asked.

"Yeah, he did, hence Luke is working up a, anyways. He is a problem, and should you not get him and others under control they are going to take advantage of this situation." I said to both of them.

"How do you see getting this under control then?" The chief asked.

"Truthfully, I don't think you can get this under control because it is just starting, and people are soon to run out of food and money to get more. Then it will start to get ugly, and after a while the food we have here on our shelves is going to run out. So it is something that is going to take the community to work on and help with. We have to start growing our own food, and it is just getting to be winter, so that will not be easy. The big marijuana operation on the east side that, damn I can't remember his name" I said, and Mike interrupted.

"Harris farms" he said.

"Yes, the Harris farm could grow year-round, I did a security audit on them and remembered their growing areas and a lot of it was indoors. That could be a start, but it will have to get a lot worse, or people will have to get on board to get things like this rolling." I said.

"You think it is going to get that bad" the chief asked.

"Yes, way worse than we can think of. I honestly did not even think it would be like it is right now, just three days into this shit and it is already snowballing." Craig said.

"And we have been planning and getting ready for many different contingencies for years guys, and Craig is right, I just can't believe we are here at this point this fast. Worse part is everyone here at the compound knows it is going to get worse and still can't believe we are here, at this point." Bill said.

"So, I will ask again, what do you two want to do about this?" I said.

"That is a loaded question now isn't it, Wayne?" the chief said.

"Not as much loaded as it is to the point and not a very easy thing to answer. And then the real question is, when are you going to start doing it? Each hour you wait could be the cause of many to die. So, I am here to help you, but we don't have the answers here, we are going to struggle through it all just like the rest of the area. We are more prepared, and more trained, but that still does not make us ready for everything coming our way. We sure as hell didn't see it happening this fast, that is for sure." I told them.

"Will you help us then?" the chief asked.

"What does the help you think you need look like? I mean I could say yes and then not have the ability or capability to help." I said.

"That we are not sure about, but you have shown that you will help when you can a few times in the last couple days, and well before that training our agencies for a fraction of the price you have charged others. Don't think it went unnoticed, it was known and appreciated by many." Mike said.

As the sheriff finished saying this both his and the chief's cell phones started to vibrate. They both looked at them then reached and turned their personal radios volume up and they both instantly were rewarded with traffic from officers and deputies alike on both channels. It was an officer down and needs assistance call at the Wal Mart on the other end of town. Shots fired and the officer that was calling for help sounded panicked and then you could hear gunfire in the background.

"Craig, get the entire team spun up and open the gates. Sheriff are we all activated?" I said turning to the sheriff.

He looked at me then the police chief nodded at him and then back at me. "Your entire team is activated as deputies. Please help us." Mike said.

"See you there then" and I jumped up and ran to the Tahoe sitting out front that still had my gear in it. The Sheriff and Police chief got in their own units and went CODE, lights and sirens out of the compound. I got on the radio and told the TOC the team would be monitoring the main but working on the SO net. They acknowledged. Bill was already beside me, and we took off after the other vehicles, this Tahoe was the one we had used to get to Luke and Rae in the shootout yesterday. I switched my personal radio and the vehicle radio to the S O Dispatch channel and keyed up.

"Bear 17 SO." I called out.

S O the air is 10-3 phone in traffic." Came the call.

I punched in the S o Dispatch number and got an instant answer.

"S O dispatch go ahead. This is 17 I am 10-8 heading code to code 3 with 24 10-12 in my unit. All bear units are going to be 10-8 per 401 for this rodeo. We are all on S O and in route." I told the dispatcher.

"Got yeah, good luck." and the dispatcher hung up.

I switched to the team channel and keyed up, "Bear units the S O net is 10-3, I say again the S O net is 10-3. I have called dispatch, and we are all 10-8 in route to the call, get kitted and moving. Frank, bring the 249. All acknowledge in order." I ended my radio transmission.

"21 Ack" came the response from Frank.

"24 Ack" Bill responded next even though he was sitting next to me.

"26 Ack" Craig responded.

"27 Ack" came the reply from Jeff.

"28 Ack all" came the reply from Paul.

As I cornered out of the compound, I was already going 60 miles an hour and gaining speed. I initiated the lights and left the siren off.

"Help me, I am hit help me, they are coming. Help someone please come help me" the radio echoed. I found myself pushing the accelerator harder wanting the vehicle to go even faster. The voice sounded scared and millions of miles away and you could hear gunfire in the background.

"Wayne, if we don't get there safely, we are not helping brother. I hear it too, but we must get there safely." Bill said sternly.

I let up a little and hit the sirens. I elected to get on the trucker bypass and the traffic was light. I looked down and we had gotten up to 130 miles an hour and I leveled it there. I slowed slightly and cleared the only four ways stop on the bypass and heard bill yell "Clear" as I pushed back down on the accelerator. I rapidly approached the right turn that would take us down to the Wal Mart and I swung out to maximize the apex turn bringing it back to the inner corner and letting it drift out as I hammered down on the accelerator again. We could see the Wal Mart in the distance and heard many officers calling out 10-97 which meant they were showing up to the scene.

"Help me, I am inside help I hear you guys help" the radio went off again. You could hear the sirens on the transmission and still gunfire too.

"435, where are ya we are coming to help." The radio continued.

"I am" and the deputy started to cough terribly on the radio then very quietly in almost a silent whisper "near register 15."

"24 and 17 are 10-97" Bill radioed as I pulled in and slammed on the breaks and killed the siren. Both Bill and I exited the vehicle as a fluid pair. Years of training took over and we came out in our crouched running stance moving towards the nearest entrance/exit. Weapons at the high ready scanning for targets as we moved. We got to the door and another Deputy was there with his long gun scanning with the sliding doors pushed off their henges and open.

"Blue, Blue, Blue" we said as we came up on him rapidly and continued "what do you have?"

"I saw movement towards the produce on the right but not sure." The deputy said. I knew the produce and bakery were to the right as you went in and all the registers to the left.

"24 cover right as we move and get to the officer down" I said as I started to move.

As I cleared the entry and started scanning to my front, I saw a guy with a gun turn towards me.

"Put the fucking gun down., drop the gun!" My weapon snapped into place with my red dot on the center of his chest as I continued to yell, and the individual brought his weapon up. My rounds broke and two quick rounds impacted center mass and the weapon was no longer pointing at me. I caught movement to the hard right of the target I had just dropped when I saw that movement more clearly it was another man with a weapon and his chest exploded from impacts. The officer behind me put two rounds into that target and we continued moving towards number 15 we could see directly in front of us.

"Two suspects down currently, three officers are inside moving from the north entrance to the south in the front area of the store. One suspect is down in the front area and the other is down in front of the register area between the inventory and registers. How many suspects' dispatch?" I radioed on S O.

"Initial call was two gunmen." Came the reply.

"Bear units assemble register 15. Frank leave the 249 and bring the trauma pack. Ack" I radioed.

I heard a round of double clicks as I saw my team members rushing into the front part of the store from the north entrance Bill and I had come through. I got to the downed officer and was not happy to see how badly he was hit. I went to work as Bill pulled security with the other Deputy and my team was advancing to us. The deputy had a Torniquet (TQ) on his right leg and blood was still seeping out of the wound steadily. I pulled a TQ off my kit and slid it up his leg as he moaned out in pain.

"I got you. We are here. Stay with me, brother. We got you and are going to get you good to go." I told him as I slipped the TQ above the one he had tried to put on. I got it on and started to tighten it. "This shit is going to Fucking hurt like hell. Here we go." I said as I started to torque it down good. He screamed out and I knew I was getting it tight enough then. As he was screaming Frank rolled up on us.

"What we got 17?" Frank asked me.

"Two times GSW. One right leg thigh high that he had a TQ on but it was seeping, elected to go after it first and got it stopped with a second TQ, Other GSW looks like under the vest in the lower right abdominal area. I have not assessed that wound. Patient is yours." I moved back and stood and brought my rifle up.

"Bear team, On me." I said out loud then keyed the S O radio Net, "S O, Bear units are going to do systematic clear and sweep. Hold perimeter. Get life flight staged in parking lot across the way. Deputy is alive with Two GSW's currently being stabilized by medics."

"Deputy" I said looking at the one that came in with us, "Stay with your brother here and help keep him safe, nice shooting by the way. We are going to clear this place. 21 you good?" I asked.

"I got this." He told me as he never looked up and had already started fluids.

"Let's go secure these fucks first then we will clear area by area" I told my team.

It took us more than an hour to clear the store step by step. We secured the two shooters we put down and found one more that was down and taking a dirt nap the first deputy must have gotten. We secured all three and left them in the area where we found them. After securing the front area Frank had stabilized the deputy enough to get him moved out to the Emergency Medical Service guys waiting outside. They got him to the life flight and flew him to the nearest level one trauma center.

The sheriff and police chief both came in and walked around with me as I explained what had happened when we arrived. They saw the gunman where all military aged males armed with AK-47 style rifles that looked Romania to me, but I didn't examine them closely. They thanked us and did not push to get our weapons or anything else from us as we started to head back to the compound. It was clear they knew we had turned a page and things whereas I had been telling them earlier before this call came.

We made our way back to the compound and our families. I was happy we could help but it showed us all that things are slipping more and more away from the calm peaceful place we came to love to live in and into a shittier and more abominable place. We got back, unloaded and brought our kits to the team room and our cubbies. Each of us in our own place thinking through our actions and that it was here, at our doorstep, after years of trying to keep it away. After our gear was stored, we found that chow was almost done for the evening chow, and we all walked over to get a bite to eat. I had to clean up and do a little extra as I still had dried blood from the deputy on my arms and my clothes. I was not worried about the clothes and got my arms cleaned and got in line for chow. Rae found me and walked up and gave me a big hug and looked up in my eyes as I smiled down at her.

"Love you man of mine. Are you ok?" She said.

"Love you too. I am ok, just wild how rapidly things are going to shit." I said as we moved up in the line and before I knew it, I had a tray and food. She had already eaten and was just there to talk with me. We had not seen each other much today as the shopping trip had gone to shit and then the meeting with Mike and the Chief went to shit because of the shots fired call and here we are. I told the guys I was going to talk with her, and they all razed me and gave me shit, but it was all in good fun as we enjoyed spending as much time with our wives as we could. Before long the others significant others were there, and we all just enjoyed the time we could. We all came together, the core group of shooters and their spouses and just talked well into the evening/night. We got word later that night the deputy would live and most likely have a full recovery. That was music, sweet music, to all our ears.

As it got late the group got smaller and smaller until it was just Bill and Amanda, Craig and Susan, and Rae and me. We talked about times we had together and what we thought the future would bring. We had been friends for years because Bill and Craig had been part of the first team, I was assigned to the 1st Special Forces Group when Joint Base Lewis McChord was just Fort Lewis in Washington state. From that point forward we worked together on teams and missions for the rest of our military careers. And now we would face the collapse of the economy together, as we had planned.

"Ladies, guys, I am taking my sexy man to our room." Rae told the group.

"Thank God, I don't need Amanda to get ideas and think I am supposed to cuddle her so much in public" Bill said with a shitty grin on his face as Amanda nudged his shoulder.

"That ship sailed a long time ago buddy" Amanda said smiling.

"Yeah, we all have huge expectations now, thanks guys" Craig said rolling his eyes making fun too.

"You are all welcome." I said standing and bowing.

The group all laughed, and we said our goodnights. I smacked Rae's ass as we left and headed to our compound home. As we moved down the halls and to the room, I found myself feeling blessed that we had all this. That we had taken the time and money to help stack the odds in our favor in just such an event as we find ourselves now. We got to the room, and I unlocked the door and swung it open. It was quiet and I grabbed Rae and pulled her close and kissed her.

"I love you so much sexy lady" I said to her after another amazing kiss to add to the pile of amazing.

"I love you too" she said as she guided me to the room.

We went in and she closed the door behind her, and we stripped down naked, and I shivered from the cooler air after being dressed and now bare. I jumped into the bed and under the covers.

"You look so yummy baby doll." I said as I admired her curves. She cuddled up next to be under the covers and I held her close and felt her warm smooth skin against me.

"How are you doing with everything so far baby?" I asked her.

"It is honestly shocking me how fast everything seems to be going crazy. I mean it is day three and people are going crazy." She said.

"The shopping trip was crazy babe. From the second we went in, they told us cash only and we all said 'ok' to that. Then as we got carts, they told us again it was cash only and we didn't need carts because it was cash only. I assured them we had cash, and we went about getting the things on people's lists. Then an employee, a lady about my age, came up to our group and was very snobby and shitty and told us we didn't have enough cash and needed to leave because they would not let us steal the stuff. Something about it is not the west coast liberal state and we needed to go back to whatever place we came from. I told her we had more than enough cash and would check out what we had and go give another store our money then and she could escort us to the front." she snuggled in and continued.

"We all walked up front, and I saw the police officer come in and he nodded at Frank who was off behind us. So, then I knew he knew who we were and that this might go alright. But nope, the bitchy ass lady that had escorted us up front told us we could leave now that the officer was here. I thought it was funny as fuck when he walked up and told the lady to check us out, he knew us and knew we had the cash. Babe, it was so funny seeing the look on her face. So, she starts helping another employee check us out and as the total climbed, they got more and more shitty. Telling us and the officer no way we had the cash to pay and was he part of this group that was going to steal from them. On and on it went until I pulled out a few envelopes and counted out the cash to pay the bill. Then they got upset we did have the money. Saying it was people like us that pulled our money out that got us into this mess to begin with and stuff." She leaned up and looked at me.

"I thought by the tone it might get physical. That was when Paul and Frank moved in close and told us time to go and be ready to get in the rides and leave if anything happens."

"Yeah, a guy with a gun had been watching you guys in the store and then came out and got into his ride and moved it close to your vehicles." I told her.

"The guy in the jeans then I would bet" she said.

"You noticed him in the store then, I guess the training worked hmm?" I spoke.

"Yeah, I did and was looking around as we got out the doors and moving to the vehicles. Then Paul yelled 'gun' and we all just went into motion like we had talked about before coming out. Once I had everyone and Melinda did, we got off the X and headed for here. The ladies didn't really see much besides getting pushed into the vehicles and rolling out. They wanted their things and whined about that all the way back. I assured them we would get the stuff, but our safety was more important than stuff." she said.

"The guy had pulled his gun and was getting out of the vehicle as you guys loaded up and rolled. Officer Hernandez gave commands and thankfully we did not have to drop the guy. I think he might have even pissed his pants a little with so many weapons pointing at him. I am sure he saw an easy target to get all your stuff since it was just a bunch of ladies, and his focus was so laser beamish he didn't even see the officer." I told her.

"I am sure it was a huge shock to have two hot sexy men all kitted up jump out to defend the helpless ladies" she said into my ear as her touch sent my pulse racing.

"Two sexy men?" I said as I rolled on top of her and looked in her eyes.

"Yes, but your mine my love and I need all of what is mine" she said as she pulled me to her lips and the night blurred into sweet darkness.

Chapter 16

The alarms woke me today, and I was thankful that it was not visions of battle or anything else the woke me. Sure, I hated the alarm like most, but it was better than a lot of other ways to be woken. Notice I said alarms, that would be because my wife liked, no, loved the snooze button. So instead of an alarm at say 5:45 AM and then a backup at 6 AM, she had the first one and it worked and went off, but so too did the snooze about nine minutes later, and should we not arise then, another would trigger at 6 AM as set followed by the sprinklings of snoozed alarms after snoozed. Sure, it was our problem for not getting right up, but curse be to the snoozes of my wife.

I rolled out of bed and went to turn the water on for a shower as my naked wife walked out to start the coffee.

"Yummy" I said watching her walk by.

"Thank you love" she said.

I looked at myself in the mirror and noticed I needed to shave my face because the facial hair was getting long on my face. I could never really grow a great beard, so I had kept a goatee off and on since retiring from the Army. This meant I shaved my cheek area and the rest of the patchy hair that would grow out every day. I had not done it in the last four days, and it was looking a little on the scraggily side, and it was hard for me to allow it to get like this. I had almost gotten it cleaned up when Rae walked by and towards the shower.

"Water is warm" she said.

"It should be almost instantly hot, each room has an on-demand water heater exclusive to the room." I said.

"Then why are you turning it on and waiting?" she asked as she got into the shower.

"Habits I guess love" I said and got in with her.

We often took showers together. It was just a part of who we were. I had no idea how this was not a common thing, as my parents had showered together when I was growing up too. Regardless of whether it was normal or not, it was a part of us and our time together. Just another important part of our day together and the bond we truly felt to one and other. We talked about the day ahead and the kids and then got out and ready for the day.

I put on my EDC gear and went to wake the boys. I was happily surprised to see them both awake and getting dressed for the day themselves.

"Morning boys" I told them.

"Morning dad. Hugs?" Owen asked, reaching out with his arms. I would never pass this up because one day, like all the other boys, it would sadly end. The love wouldn't end, just the need to feel the hugs and love as much as letting the words convey it. I held him close and kissed the top of his head, which would be a thing of the past as he was growing like a weed.

"Love you son" I told him.

"Love you too dad." He said.

I turned and saw Anthony getting ready in his room and walked over to him.

"Hug?" I said.

"Um, I am good dad. Love you though." He told me.

I smiled and said "Love you too kiddo."

"Let's all go grab breakfast together," I yelled to the household from the small living room we had.

"Oh, that would be wonderful" Rae said walking in smiling her radiant smile at me.

"It would be a great way to start the day" I said.

"Boys, go grab us a table and we will be over after the morning meeting." Rae said.

"Hold on" I said as I grabbed my radio and turned it on and keyed it up on the compound channel.

"Morning core group meeting will be at 9 AM this morning, Main please make sure everyone knows." I said into the radio.

"9 AM, got it" came the reply.

We all left our Compound home and went down to chow. It was empty and just getting set up, so it looked like we were the early birds that got the worm. We filed through and grabbed the things we wanted, and all sat down at a table over in the corner of the dining area. We talked about our day yesterday, about the things we wanted to get done today and about what the weekend was looking like. The kids in the compound family had all started to hang out with one and other and the bonds between them seemed to be growing. It warmed my heart to see that they had all started to build these bonds, as they are the future and why this was all built.

I hoped we could have time like this to talk as a family each day and I was feeling very excited and glad we had gotten the time again this morning. It was like my energy tanks had been filled from just enjoying my family and talking. I looked around and saw other families, and couples sitting eating breakfast and enjoying one and other, some looked tired and ready to go sleep the day away, but for the most part the dining area was alive with smiles and conversation. Seeing this made my energy level go even higher, the compound family was happy.

"You are smiling pretty big hubby of mine." Rae said to me.

"Yeah, I am smiling looking at what we have and thankful" I said.

"It is pretty amazing, isn't it?" she said as we walked to clear our plates and trays.

"Now the key is to keep it." I said as I turned and headed out towards the doors and over to the headquarters building.

We had about an hour until the meeting I rescheduled was to take place and I wanted to get my gear settled back in the team room and make sure it was all cleaned after working on the wounded officer. I am pretty sure my rifle had blood on it from my efforts. I am very glad we were able to save him and clean up the threats. That reminded me that I needed to call the police chief or the sheriff and see exactly what happened at the Wal Mart. Maybe Luke already knew, I guess we will start at the meeting then go from there. I spent the remaining time in the cubby cleaning and refitting the gear with Rae talking to me and making sure her kit was refit too. In that time, I had heard most of the team coming and going doing their thing too. Before I knew it, it was almost time for the meeting. I got Rae and we headed to the conference room.

We entered and took our seats. I looked around at the group and they all looked pretty happy, that is until I came to Luke. He was looking at his laptop in front of him very seriously.

"That bad Luke?" I asked him.

He looked up at me, then back at his computer and spun it so I could read it. The headline read 'Dollar collapsing!' and it caught my attention.

"That does look serious." I said as he turned it back towards himself.

"Not good, I will brief it as we get going." He said looking back at the article and forgetting I was even there.

"Alright everyone, we should get this going since I already pushed it this late." I said as I turned from Luke and back to the group.

"Morning, I hope this morning finds us all in good spirits after a longer day yesterday filled with a little excitement. Stephanie, where do we stand with the shipments and inventory, we have ordered over the last couple days?" I began.

"Morning, yesterday a few of the local purchases arrived, notably the storage unit arrived on two loads. The local dairies have assured me that they can still get us manure when we ask despite these times but do ask if we can pay upon delivery. That should not be an issue as we still have cash on hand. All the other orders have delivery dates and a lot of them are due today. We have topped off all the fuel storage units, including the propane storage unit. As of right now we are still scheduled to receive weekly shipments for the kitchen, and I have not seen a notice saying this is stopping as of yet. This we have planned for continued use until it runs dry. I have had a few requests for od orders and they have been placed and we will see if they get delivered." she rambled off in quick order.

"The ammo order still on schedule then?" Craig asked.

"As far as I know yes, but we are just going by the data sent to us from the shipping companies. As the day unfolds, we will see what it looks like." Stephanie replied.

"Craig, what do you have?" I said, looking in his direction.

"Adam got the green houses completely done yesterday so this will allow the gardens to get started. I will leave that for Rae to talk about, but it is a big accomplishment and I wanted to say thanks to Adam and his team. They have been hammering it out from one project to the next." he said looking at Adam.

"Thanks, we are getting it done for sure and have had a lot of help from the new additions Mitch brought too." Adam said.

"The Canadian Protective Service guys are still coming as far as I know on Sunday. Have you heard different Wayne?" Craig asked me, knowing David was coming with them.

"I talked to David and as far as he knew they had government transportation set up and it was a go." I answered.

"We have plenty of rooms for them should they elect to stay here on compound. The training schedule might be a little harder to pull off with us going fully operational but that can get worked out as we move forward. The operation center is manned 24/7 now and we need to make sure we are looking at the tasking schedules because they have all of us scheduled to pull time in the operation center. I am sure we are dropping the ball on things and as we move forward, we will figure out what we don't know." Craig said.

"Speaking of what we don't know, Luke, what is the new information?" I asked looking back his way.

"The headlines from two news outlets are that the dollar is collapsing. I was alerted to this earlier today and Sally and I have been working on getting information on it since 5 AM when a contact reached out to me. Our preliminary analysis is that it is a slow collapse, but it will eventually be almost useless. With the stock market closed and now the credit card companies suspending operations and despite the dollar being the global reserve currency, the economic value of the United States is crashing. This means the trust of the world in our currency having weight is severely impacted as this crisis continues. Overnight we have seen the start of Hyperinflation with the value of the dollar shrinking. All of this coupled with the high debt ceiling is a recipient for the dollar to collapse." Luke briefed.

"Are we seeing the dollar already loosing value?" I asked.

"The value globally was already declining from the onset of the markets crashing, now with the instability of the credit card companies stopping, suspending, whatever they want to call it, it has caused a problem that no one can simply look away from. Hyperinflation is the most noticeable indicator that we are, that is, the United States, and the dollar, are in trouble. Prices have been increasing slowly over the last year but when the market started to crash the price increased sharply. Now overnight the price increases are more than 40 percent higher than when the day ended yesterday. A perfect example of this is the price we paid for the storage building kit went from 26K to almost twice that at 49K now. That is just one example of the increase in prices across the entire spectrum of products. Now it is hard for the media to not report on this news. I see other major news is downplaying the collapsing and saying that inflation and panic is causing the increases in price. I suspect we are going to see a shift to blaming price gouging and not the fact that the increase is because the dollar is not stable. We will be closely monitoring this. I have built a target package work up on this Galagher guy, he is a real threat, boss." Luke said looking at me and then the others and continuing "His construction company has vast holdings throughout the entire state, and he is well connected to the mayor, which we all know means he is in the pocket of the governor too. He contributed to both campaigns substantially to help secure their victories along with many of the local board and city council members. He pays to get his way, and when he doesn't he goes after those that stand in his way."

"Does your analysis indicate he possesses the ability to conduct direct action against us and the compound?" Jeff asked.

"Yes, he has the means and most likely the money to direct actions against us." Luke answered.

"Likely courses of action?" Bill asked.

"Most likely course of action from him is surveillance, he is calculating so I think he would watch us and look for a way to inflict what he wants. With this crisis ongoing it is possible that he would resort to more direct actions as his past activities warrant this concern also. I am still leaning towards him watching before he does anything else." Luke said to the group but looking at Bill.

"Ok, anything else then at this time Luke?" I asked.

"Not at this time, if anyone needs something from me, I am going to excuse myself if that is ok and go link back up with Sally to assess this latest new blast." Luke said.

"Yeah, I am good with that, I will stop by after this to see the latest." I told him as he got up and moved towards the door.

"Jeff, when the Canadians arrive, we good to train in the normal cycle? I know housing is a little fuller and more people are on the compound, but we are not using much of the ranges or shoot houses, so what is the impact of them arriving in the training aspect?" I asked him.

"The impact should be nothing at all besides getting role players, since we would normally get the part time people to come in. Do you want outsiders on the compound for the training now?" he asked looking at his notes. "It would be five to seven depending on the cycle the Canucks wanted to use."

"Do you think we could just use family members like the young adults we have here to augment the role-playing necessities?" I asked.

"I think we could use them and let's be honest some of our young adults would love the chance to run and gun with these guys." Jeff said smiling.

"Any other training issues?" I asked.

"Yeah, there is. I want to get with you on the training cycle we would like to start putting all our non-shooters through. With the incidents of just the last couple days I think it will be an easy sell to start getting people refreshed and trained in the things we see important. Can I get with." I interrupted him.

"Jeff, no need to get with me, build a training schedule and then get with Rae and Craig and coordinate it to be part of the extra tasks. That way we start getting us all through refresher and other training. Does anyone see a problem with this idea?" I asked the group.

A round of 'No's' came from the group. "Anything else?" I asked.

"Not from me" Jeff said.

"Troy, the system you have developed for the compound with the cameras and the alerts is amazing and thank you for the effort there. Talk to us all about the Network and the star link system and will we see problems anytime soon?" I said more than asked.

"I cannot answer if the internet is going to close, shutdown, die anytime soon, but I do not see anything that would show a problem brewing. I have started to harden our network and build it to be self-sustaining and run on our own servers and Lan regardless of if the outside abruptly shuts down or not." he said smiling.

"So, we are good no matter what happens in the world then?" I said.

"Well yes unless the sun spits at us or a damn EMP is popped off." He answered.

"I have backup systems for everything you are using securely stored, so don't worry about that contingency." I told him.

"For everything" he asked me with a serious face.

"Yes, unless you have purchased something on your own and not through Stephanie." I told him.

"NO, No I have never needed to use my own money to get things for here. So, I take it you had her buy two if I asked for one and so on?" he said a little shocked.

"Yep" I smiled.

"We are good to go then." He said still seeming a little shocked.

"Bill" I said looking his way "How are we looking for weapon systems to fit everyone on the compound out with a long gun? And Ammo?" I asked him.

"I do not have the numbers in front of me, but I know we have more than enough weapon systems to maintain a few companies of infantry.: He said with a grin.

"Alright, need you to break into the more standard stuff and be ready to issue out a weapon and magazines to anyone who is not currently, does not have a long gun. After we determine who is the better aims in the group, we can look at designated marksman Jeff, but right now I need everyone here to always have a sidearm on them with a long gun and kit close by. Between the three of you" I looked at Stephanie, Bill, and Craig "I need to make this happen today along with all the other shit we got going." I told them.

I saw the heads nod at me with understanding. "Adam, thank you for getting so much done and being the go-to crew here right now. I know we all appreciate you." I said.

"Yes, thank you, thank you, thank you for getting the three greenhouses up and going." Rae said smiling widely. She was a green thumb that loved to garden and had been a thorn in my side to buy these expensive Gable 7500 greenhouses a few years ago 'just in case' we might need them. Now we have three 24' x 48' commercial grade greenhouses for her to get production going for the future.

Adam smiled at her, "no problem, Rae."

"I need you to shift gears now and get the storage unit going. Can you build it without a cement floor, or do we need to have that poured then build?" I asked him.

"I would like to pour the cement foundation and let it cure a bit and while we wait, we can build some walls and then also focus on the improvements to the animal areas since we had not been using them but just maintaining them. I want to turn the water on and make sure there are no leaks and such so we can use the time to get everything in the plan moving forward. Can we contract out to have the cement trucks bring the yards we need of concrete?" He asked.

"Stephanie, issue getting this moving and see if we can get it as soon as possible?" I asked her.

"No issue, how fast can you have it framed and need to cement trucks rolling in here?" she asked Adam.

"Tod, we have it almost done for pour?" he asked Tod.

"Yeah, we could pour today." He told Adam.

"How many yards was it?" Adam asked him.

"I would get 65 yards delivered. I think it was like 62 and a half but better safe than sorry." Tod said.

"65 yards as soon as possible then?" Staphanie asked.

"After lunch would be best" Adam said to big smile from his guys since they knew he was looking after them.

"I will call them when we are done here and then let you know the time they are going to deliver. What do you want to do about security when they arrive Wayne?" Staphanie asked.

"Craig, have them pull into gate holding area and we can look in cab and at the truck then let them in. I don't think we will have to worry about infiltrators yet, but stranger things have happened." I said.

"Can do." Craig said.

"Again, thank you Adam and crew." I said nodding their way.

"Mitch, how is the air wing looking?" I asked.

"Air wing hmm" he said laughing. "Is that what we are now?"

"Yes" I was smiling big at him.

"The A-29's are set, and the pilots have gone over them. They want to take them up and run them around so we have not put the armaments on them yet, though they are all staged and can be accommodated quickly. My hawk is ready to go and currently has seats out and fast ropes attached. I have the mini guns installed and the crew have used them and are very familiar with them. I have had all, but one jet prepared for storage. This gives us the ability to still travel a small contingent more than 3000 nautical miles away, even crossing the Atlantic should it become necessary. Your 'Air Wing' is ready and more than capable. I hope we don't need any of it, yet here we are, and I thought this plan was bullshit too, yeah so, I am the fool now." he said shrugging.

"No one is a fool, it has me off balance how fast and crazy it is happening and that it is happening at all Mitch." I said looking at him. "I am sure you and I are not the only ones, but it is from this point forward that we all need to focus and make sure we are trying, no, that we are doing all we can do. That we are putting this family, the compound family before all else. That our futures are truly what we start to make of them. So, I know I have thanked Adam a lot in this meeting, but I thank you all for going with the plan, even if it might have seemed like bullshit" I said smiling at Mitch "and being here doing the things we are."

"Green thumb, what do you have?" I asked looking at my wife.

"Green thumb hmm" she said smiling and giggling at me with the rest of the group. "I am going to focus on just that, my greenhouses. As you all know I am excited to have them up and that I can plant in the winter is a game changer as they are connected to propane and will be heated and have temperature regulation systems. The plan has a growing schedule, and I will stick with that for now and then adjust as we move forward. Don't worry about 'naked' gardening yet, but I am sure Chelsea will bring it up soon enough." she joked. Naked gardening had come up at a wine night at the local winery when the group was all out on a Friday night. It had been a running joke among the group ever since.

"The tasking list has been very successful, and it is a great part of the plan and no real issues have come from people not getting the things done that have been needed done, right Craig?" Rae said.

"I have not noticed any" Craig responded.

"We are continuing to post it near the chow area and people are looking and reporting to the areas to do their tasked duties, even the young adults. School is starting on Monday and the curriculum will be that out of the plan also. So far, we are just using the plan as the guide and if it works not doing much in the area or changing it. I am sure over time we will refine things and change as needed but in the starting phase we are in, nothing seems to need to be moved or changed." Rae finished.

"I know my son, Owen, was not happy to hear school was going to be a thing here but he was happy to hear what we planned to have taught. Time will tell how the school thing goes over, either way please let us know if it is not a good fit and tweaks need to be done." I said to the group.

"Craig and Jeff, I will call David after this and let you know what their plan looks like. Mitch, if we need to go grab them, is that viable?" I said.

"Yeah, the only issue will be air clearance, but you know we can get around that too if we go into one of their bases. No matter, it is doable." Mitch said.

"Anything else?" I asked. Everyone looked around but no one said anything and the meeting adjourned and we all got on with our day. I headed over to my office with Rae following me.

"I am going to go get my 'Green Thumb' on" she said to me and slapped my ass and left me standing there looking at her smile and walk out.

"Love you too" I shouted out to her back as she disappeared.

I sat down at my desk and pulled out my cell phone and found David's contact info but then decided to make it an official call and dialed his office number on the business phone on my desk. He answered on the fourth ring.

"Hello how may I help you?" I heard him say.

"Mister Cook, I am calling to confirm you are planning a trip to the United States despite the crisis they currently find themselves in, is this true?" I asked.

A pause on the phone then "you fucker pops. I was like who the fucking bloody hell is leaking shit to the news." he said to me.

"So, you can confirm then that the protective services are in fact sending people to a location in the US to train?" I continued the questioning trying to not giggle.

"I can neither confirm nor deny. I will say that as of this very minute things are packed to go train, and that everything is a green light at this end. Barring anything to crazy we will all be there Sunday afternoon, and ready to train Monday morning. I think we should all stay on the compound though, if that is ok." He said.

"Yeah, we will add your numbers to the chow count too, so you do not have to go outside the wire and just add a room and board fee to the invoice." I said.

"If things change, I will call but otherwise we will see you Sunday afternoon. Stay frosty old man." he said and hung up.

He is still coming with the detailed trainees, and I will not lie, I was glad and excited to have him and the trainees going to be staying here. If things took a turn to the south, we would have more numbers here and all the trainees have a background in either law enforcement, military, or emergency services. This would be a plus for sure, but the biggest plus was going to be having my oldest son here when things are getting a little wild. It had been a long running joke among my boys, especially the older two, about shit hitting the fan. We would always give each other questions about zombie apocalypse or such and what would we do. Now we found ourselves on the doorstep of the United States collapsing.

The phone on the desk rang and I picked it up and answered, "Hello?" I could never bring myself to get a secretary no matter how big the company had gotten.

"Wayne it is Mike, the county board is going to have an emergency meeting tomorrow morning at 10 AM and wanted me to invite you. They are concerned about the current state of the country and county and how we are going to address different situations." the Sheriff said.

"Why ask me to come Mike?" I said to him.

"They remember you talking to them about preparing and pleading with them to open their minds to the fact that in the blink of an eye things could get bad. They are ready to listen to you now." The Sheriff said.

"I can be there then. You guys doing, ok? Family, Ok? I asked him.

"Yeah, so far we are all ok, family included. Thanks for asking, it means a lot, Wayne." He said.

"Charles good too?" I asked assuming he was listening.

"I am good too asshole" he said knowing I caught him listening in again.

"Alright that is good then. I have to get things going but I will be there in the morning to listen and answer questions" I said.

"Sounds good Wayne" they both said, and I hung up.

The rest of the morning and afternoon seemed to fly by. I found myself helping in the greenhouses with Rae and my dad, then the hangars and saw Anthony in there with Neil, then walking the perimeter thinking. The compound family continued to work through the day as I moved from one area to the next, helping, watching, admiring what we had brought together and accomplished to this point. Lunch came and went and then I found myself at the front gate looking over the cement trucks as they brought in the yards of concrete to get poured today for the storage building. Hours seemed like minutes and before I knew it dinner time was upon us all in the compound. The day was turning to night and many of the tasks of the day had been accomplished. I met up with Rae in line and we talked about all we had done for the day and watched the kids all come together and hang out for chow. Into day four of the collapse and our family was bonding, growing as one. It was an amazing transformation to see us all bond.

"Gun, Gun, Gun, sector 3" squawked on every radio turned on in the chow hall. I jumped up and ran for the headquarters building. I knew sector three was to the south side of the front gate and mostly open field area.

"Bear team full kit response." I said into the radio, and I heard many double clicks and saw most of them moving with me towards the team room in the headquarters building. I moved into my cubby where my kit was already stowed on a ready stand and threw it over my head and grabbed the rest and continued moving towards the TOC.

I was right behind Craig as we entered and he yelled, "What do we have?"

"Looks like a team of two out in the field slowly crawling towards us there." the camera operator said. It was one of the Air wing wives, Lisa might be her name, my mind said. She had the pair up on one of the big screens and they could clearly be seen in the field slowly moving both with what looked like long guns.

"27 get your long gun up, possible sniper threat" I said into my team radio.

"Wilco, sector 3 correct" was his reply.

"Correct" Bill radioed.

"I will go with him and spot like normal" Craig said and left.

"Can you switch to day camera view please" I asked the camera operator. The screen switched from the white phosphor night vision view to a color view, and it was much darker, and the sky was a dark purplish black. Night was soon to be upon us.

"Ok go back to the night vision, then zoom in on these guys and let me take a look at their weapon systems" I told her. The view switched back to the whitish grey view and they guys filled the screen. I could see one of the weapons was a bolt gun and the other looked like an AR-10 possibly. I was more concerned with the sights they might have on the top of these weapons. Night vision scopes and even thermal scopes had gotten cheap enough for many people to [purchase them, and I knew a lot of hunters in the area that liked to go out at night and kill and thin the coyote population.

"Looks like some kinda thermal job on the bolt gun, maybe on both of them." Paul said watching. The entire rest of the team was in the TOC looking at the screen with the two guys on it.

"It looks like the ATN Thor on the bolt gun for sure." Bill said. "I am not sure what that is on the AR-10 there."

"I think they are both thermal jobs" Frank said.

"I concur with those assessments." I said as I keyed my radio "26 and 27 be advised they the threat most likely is using thermal, how copy?"

"Good copy. We are almost in the next on the barrack." came the reply from Craig.

"Are you both running thermal?" I asked

"We are" Came the reply from Jeff.

I knew we had the nice Trijicon REAP-IR system for some of our weapon systems along with the SNIPE-IR. Those and a few other systems were possibly ones to use but I knew Jeff had SNIPE-IR on an older M110 he loved. If I guessed this was what he was running.

"Looks like they had found a spot they like" Frank said.

I looked up and saw they had stopped crawling and were both putting down bipods and looked like they were getting set up. I also noticed they both had suppressors on their weapons. These guys had nice systems that was for sure. From the location they had stopped they most likely could see the top third of the bunk house. It would be a 600 plus yard shot from the location they had stopped in my estimation.

"Over 500 yards from that point to the bunk house" Bill said echoing my thoughts almost exactly.

"27 set, I have them in sights. Bolt guy has what looks like an AGM Rattler on his rifle with a can. AR guy looks like maybe an ATN Thor. They are getting settled into the place they are at right now. From their position they can see into the south facing rooms, possibly even the second level but certainly the third level rooms. I can nail both of them in less than three seconds from my position" Came the report from Jeff.

"17 Copy, do you think they are preparing to fire?" I asked.

"Hard to say for certain. They are settling in and getting dialed in. They will be very hard pressed to notice us watching them because of our hide." Craig replied.

"Could we exit the front gate undetected?" I asked.

"They are not focused on the gate, but it is close enough to their current line of sight." Came the reply.

"Let me talk to the rest of the guys here. If you see imminent hostile threat, you are weapons free." I radioed.

"Copy" came the reply from Jeff.

"Ok, I would really like to take these guys and have a chat, but what do you guys think?" I asked the rest of the team that was with me.

"My vote is to dump them" Frank said.

"I would like the info, but they are setting up and came with the gear to do harm, so fuck em." Bill said.

"If they had night vision and not possible thermal my vote would be to take them down and question them, but you can't hide from thermal." Paul said.

"What if we tip our hand and bull horn them. Tell them they are currently in our sights and if they do not immediately stand without their riffle we are going to kill them. I mean Jeff can dump both of them even if they stand up and run at this range. The only downside would be that they take a shot. Speaking of, radio the compound and into the bunk house that everyone with windows facing south needs to stay away from them and, no tell everyone with a south facing window to get out of their rooms and move to the first floor in the chow area or game area until further notice." I said towards the TOC operations area.

"Got it." they replied.

"What do you guys think then?" I asked my team.

"Ask Jeff and Craig because either we do that or we just have jeff dump them." Bill said with the rest agreeing.

"27 What if we use a bullhorn and call out to them. Tell them to surrender or they die kind of thing" I said into my radio.

The radio came alive in our ears, and you could hear both Jeff and Craig chuckling. "Let's do it" you could hear the smirk on his face in the transmission.

"Let's go do this then." I said moving towards the team room. "I will grab the bullhorn from my cubby and meet you guys at a vehicle. Make it a truck" I then radioed "we are grabbing the bullhorn then going to drive blacked out hard to the berm. Guide us to a stop between you and the targets."

"You are a sick bastard. You know they are going to hear you come rolling up and be looking for a target on the fence when you blast them with the bullhorn" Craig radioed back.

"I know. 27 you target the one that looks in charge. I will give them 5 seconds. I will hit the alert on the bullhorn then start talking. You watch and see who looks like they are in charge and target that one's weapon. I doubt they will give up and will need a little persuasion. If it starts to go sideways just dump them both." I radioed.

"Got it. TOC main make sure the camera is fixed on them and recording." Craig radioed.

"Main copies" I heard my wife's voice and smiled. She knew it was going to be wild and was helping lead since Craig is on the op.

I got out in the truck and had an idea strike me. "Bear main is bear 69 in the TOC?" I radioed.

"Bear 17 this is 69, I am what do you need?" came the reply on the radio. Troy was in the TOC.

"Can I get you to pipe the camera feed to our ATAK's please" I asked on the radio.

"Wilco" he replied back.

As we raced out to the fence in our vehicle, I flipped down my ATAK screen and clicked into the video monitor section and then clicked the camera feed. No shit there lay our two shit birds talking and looking through their sights at our compound. You have to love and hate technology all at the Same time. As we neared the fence, we got told to drive thirty more yards than to stop by Jeff and Craig. AS we rolled hard to a stop, I watched the screen to see if the shit birds noticed our engine noise, sure as shit they did and seemed to get excited and start looking around.

"Here we go" I radioed as I got out and so did the team. We stayed low even though the berm had us out of sight.

As I watched my screen, I hit the alert button on the bull horn then called out, "You two fuckers in the field to my front" echoed out of the bullhorn and I saw both men pull themselves closer to the dirt from my words and start searching in their scopes on my ATAK screen. "You have 5 seconds to stand away from your rifles or you will be killed" As I finished, I could see that they both stayed on their rifles looking. The guy with the bolt gun looked in charge but I was not sure. I reached 5 in my head, and I barely heard the round passing us from Jeff's shot as the bolt guy's gun exploded in his face. I could hear the screams of the bolt guy, and in my screen I could see the other guy roll off his gun and stand with his hands in the air.

The Bolt guy was withering around on the ground holding his face and the other guy was standing with his hands in the air looking over at his buddy. "Guy with his hands in the air, do not move or you will be killed. Tell your buddy to shut the fuck up. A team is going to come give first aid to him and collect you up. If you move at all we will kill you. Nod your head if you understand" I said into the obnoxiously loud bullhorn. The guy standing nodded his head and we got in the vehicle and headed for the gate.

"All cameras show negative activity around the compound, and we have been looking hard. These two are the only ones around 17" came the radio call.

"Copy. Open the gates for us and we will go collect this garbage and be back in. Shut it behind us and when you see we have them collected open it back up so we can get back inside moderately quickly." I radioed and continued "Break, 27 nice shooting. Continue to provide overwatch and dump the shit bags if they try anything"

"Wilco" was the reply.

We raced through the gate area and turned right and flicked on our lights and flooded the area with bright light. The guy was visible to our front left out in the field standing motionless with his hands over his head. His buddy was on the ground and not withering around as much as before and on the screen, he had his hands locked to his face. We rolled right out into the field and came to a stop about twenty yards away from them and offset to ensure that our overwatch still had a shot. We all exited the vehicle and moved like a well-oiled machine into firing positions.

"Keep your hands in the air and move slowly towards us keeping to your left or the front of our vehicle." Paul commanded. Hands up guy started moving towards us and got to about 5 yards. "Stop and turn away from us and get on your knees" Paul commanded again. The guy listened and turned around and dropped to his knees. As he did Bill and I moved forward, and I provided cover while Bill pushed him on his belly and pulled his arms behind him and flex cuffed him. A search of him provided a pistol, a few magazines and a knife. I knew that Frank and Paul had cover on the other guy.

"Who the fuck are you guys? Please don't kill me." the first guy started whining.

"21 move forward and be prepared to provide medical to the wounded guy after we secure him. 28 move and secure this guy and gag him so we can push to the other guy." I radioed the team.

I saw Paul secure the flex cuffed guy and tape his mouth shut. Bill and I pushed up towards the wounded guy and proceeded to secure him. His face was a bloody mess and it looked like one eye was toast. We searched him and found a pistol and a few knives on him. Then Frank started to render treatment.

"Don't kill me. Please help me. Please. I can't see. I can't see. Oh my God I can't see." The wounded guy was blabbering.

"If he is stable let's get them into the compound and we can treat and go from there." I told Frank. "Fucker shut up, you got a warning and are lucky to be alive right now. If we wanted to kill you then you would be dead already. Now if you don't shut the fuck up I am going to kill you right here. Shut up." I told the wounded guy and it worked.

"Let me put a dressing on the fucked-up eye and then we can move." Frank said and worked quick and then pulled the guy to his feet and mostly dragged him to the back of the truck. As we moved Paul had dragged his guy to the back of the truck and threw him in. It looked like the guy had pissed his pants and from the smell it was confirmed. I jumped in the back with Bill and then Paul and Frank got in the cab and started driving us back to the compound.

"Bear on the move. We will take them both to medical." I called in the radio.

"Gates are opening" came the reply from Main.

"When you clear the gate and it closes, we will exit the hide and meet you." came the call from the sniper nest.

"Copy" I said as I looked around at the mess in the bed of the truck. It was going to be a really long night after all it turned out.

Chapter 17

We drove back through the gate and this time waited for it to close behind us before heading to the Headquarters building and stopping next to the team room doors where Craig and Jeff waited. Jeff grabbed the unwounded would-be sniper and drug him into the team room and a chair that was awaiting him. Frank had help from Bill and I took the wounded guy to the medical room. Since we told him we would kill him he had not said a word, just moaned and what sounded like a cry. We placed him on the treatment table and Frank started walking out towards the team room.

"I am going to dump my kit be right back to work on this guy." He said as he was out of the room over his shoulder.

"Ok. Hey guy" I said looking at the wounded guy.

"Wwhhat?" came his quiet dry response.

"We are going to roll you on your side and cut the cuffs and then we are going to cuff your arms down. Nothing funny or we are going to gut you right here and let you bleed out. You got it?" I asked looking at his good eye and bloody face.

"I, I, won't try anything man. Please. Please, don't kill me. I don't want trouble, I just want to leave. Please don't kill me and let me go." He started whining.

I ignored him and rolled him on his side and Bill cut his flex cuffs. We each took control of a wrist and pulled it to the edge of the bed and Posey cuffed his wrist to the side rail. The Amsco 3085 SP surgical tables had metal rails at the sides of the table below the edge at each panel. Bill took his shears and then cut the shirt off the wounded guy as I grabbed an ankle and posey cuffed it to the table and then the other ankle too. The guy then tensed up and pulled on the restraints a little and realized he was immobilized.

"Oh shit, what the fuck, what, what are you doing to me?" He started whining in an almost shrill voice.

"Shut the fuck up or we are going to gag you. You are lucky you are even alive you fuck." Bill said in a very calm voice that almost scared me.

The guy started to cry as Frank came back in and started pulling out medical supplies and gear. He came up to the guy and looked him over and turned and got a few other things on a tray and turned back to the wounded guy while he was putting gloves on.

"I see my team members got you ready for me to fix up. So here is the deal, you are going to answer our questions. If we think you are being honest, we fix you up good, if not, well if not you are going to be worse for wear certainly. Shall we get started?" He asked the wounded guy.

"What? What do you want to know? I will tell you anything." the wounded guy said.

"Here is an easy one, what is your name?" Frank asked.

"Well, looky, looky here." I heard from the door and turned to see Luke walking in. "Starting without me I see"

"Just warming him up for you" Frank said.

"You going to answer the question asked of you" Luke said as he sat and opened his laptop and typed.

"Yeah, I am, um, Stew, Stew is my name" the wounded guy said.

"Stew what? Last name Stew?" Luke took over. His voice was calm and soothing with a hint of evil undertone.

"Stew Winston" Stew the wounded guy said.

Luke typed into his computer as he asked the next question, "What do you do for a living Stewart Winston?"

"I, ah, I work, um, construction" Stew answered.

Frank started to clean his face and look at the wounds as Luke was asking him questions. His right eye lid was torn open, and his eye looked to have a bloody gash in it. He was blinking a lot and bloody tears ran down his face from that eye as Frank tried to clean it. He moved the torn Eyelid over the eye and placed a gauze pad over it then an eye cup. He taped it in place and looked at the other gashes on his face. The eye wound was obviously the worst.

"Oh yes, I see you work for Galagher construction, is that correct Stewart?" Luke asked.

I turned from watching Frank work and looked at Luke and walked up to his computer screen. He had a few tabs open but one was from Mister Winston's Facebook page. He looked much better without his wrecked face and eye in the profile picture of him holding up a dead coyote it seemed he killed.

"What? Yeah, I work with that company and others." Wayne the wounded guy said.

"Married, two kids, an older boy and a younger little girl?" Luke said more than asked.

"What the fuck, yes, that is me, oh my god, please don't hurt my family." Stew whined

"Mister Winston, we don't hurt people unless they deserve it. Do they deserve us to hurt them? Does your family deserve us to harm them?" Luke continued.

"No, no, they don't deserve to be hurt. Oh my god, no, no, no, they don't." Stew the wounded guy continued as the situation unfolded in his mind.

"Do you deserve us to hurt you more Stewart?" Luke asked as he pointed to another tab, and it was an arrest record for Stewart L. Winston. He had been involved with criminal activity off and on his entire adult life. It looked like he was involved in the methamphetamines trade with arrests for possession and the likes.

"What?" Stew said confused.

"The question was not difficult Stewart, do you deserve to be hurt more?" Luke asked as he leaned in close to him with a tone that made me almost get a chill it was so cold and dry.

"What? Hurt more, no, no, I don't deserve to be hurt at all." Stew said shaking.

"I see Stewart, so why be in a field, at night, with another guy, and two deadly looking rifles? Let me guess, you are hunting coyotes?" Luke continued in his dry tone.

"We, well, we, um, we were, um. We got dropped off and told to watch this place." Stew said.

"Why have those nice big rifles you had if you are just here to watch?" Luke asked.

"Protection, we um, we needed them for protection." Stew answered.

"Oh, protection hmm. Protection from what? What is out at night that you need big scary weapon like yours to keep safe?" Luke asked switching tones to sound softer. I had to give it to him, he was very professional, and I had seen him in far harsher environments doing it for more than a decade now.

"We, um, well, we, um, got told you guys are crazy preppers and hording stuff here and taken all the money from the local banks." Stew said in a disgusted tone.

"Oh ok, so the weapons were to protect you from us, because we are the bad people that deserve to be hurt then?" Luke asked softly.

"No, NO, not hurt." Stew said quickly and continued "they wanted us to watch you. To tell them what you are doing in here. They knew we hunted and knew how to stalk things, so they told us what to do."

"Watch us and report to them, with your buddy? What is his name?" Luke switched gears.

"The other guy is Hen." Stew answered so quietly I had a hard time hearing him.

"Hen? What kinda name is Hen?" Luke almost matched his whispered tone.

"Oh, Um, Henery is his name, but we all call him Hen." Stew answered.

"Oh ok, so you all call him Hen then?" Luke said.

"Yeah, he likes Hen more than Henry. The crew gave him shit years ago, how it sounded like an old person's name. He has been Hen since." Stew said more relaxed.

"The crew?" Luke asked.

"Oh, yeah, um, the crew is the guys I work with, um they are friends too, well most of them." Stew continued to answer like it was more of a conversation now than an interrogation.

"Hen is part of the crew then? And the crew wanted you to come watch us?" Luke asked.

"No, no, no, the crew didn't want us to watch you, the boss did. We just work for the boss and hang out most the time after work too." Stew said.

"So, you hang with the crew and Hen is part of that, but it was not the crew that wanted you here?" Luke asked trying to keep the conversation seeming like it was just that, a normal get to know you conversation.

"Ugh, damn my face hurt you guys have any pain killers or anything to help it. Fuck my eye is throbbing too. Can you get me to the hospital please." Stew said sounding in pain all of a sudden.

"Oh, damn Stew, I am sorry sure let us get you something for the pain." Luke said sounding all apologetic. He pointed to Frank and made a motion with his hand like he was holding a syringe and giving his arm a shot. Frank nodded and got a vial and syringe and gave Stew a shot in his exposed upper deltoid.

"Ouch, damn that pinched. Oohh man that feels, it burns but oh man, that is good though. Damn, what did you give me, oh man, mmm." Stew said after the drug was pushed into him.

"You asked for help with the pain, we gave you the good stuff because you are talking to us about the crew and your boss and Hen." Luke said.

"Mmmm, the boss was right, you guys have some shit here for sure damn. That took the edge off right away, so good man." Stew said.

"So, the boss was right hmm? What did he tell you and Hen was here then? To look for?" Luke asked in a normal nonchalant way.

"Man, he told us you guys had a bunch of things here, that you all have things stored here and keep it for yourselves. And he was right, this is some good shit you hit me with" Stew said with a smile on his broken face.

"The boss tell the rest of the crew things to do while you are here watching? Did the boss tell you to report in about what you see?" Luke continued the conversation rolling.

"I had my cell phone in my backpack, shit did you guys grab that and my rifle and stuff when you took us, I want to get it all back when we are done here, please." Stew said, seeming like this was just a regular normal conversation. I was surprised how much he had changed from the opening of the questioning to here.

"Yeah, you should get it all back as long as you answer honestly with me. With us Stewart, you are doing that right?" Luke said.

"Yeah man, yeah, honest and up front for sure. Great I need to call my wife to let her know I am good too. Can I get the phone son to do that?" Stew asked.

"That might work Stewart, just have to keep answering honest and I think we can make it all work." Luke said, then asked "So who is the boss, the people that told you to come here an watch anyways?"

"The boss is Mister Galagher. He oversees this area man, you don't know that? Big G, they call him. Shit he owns most the judges and the mayor and even the DA, that new police Chief they hired is fucking that up, but yeah Big G is the man around here." Stew said proudly.

"Oh, you work for Big G?" Luke said sounding scared.

"Hen and me both do, you done fucked up. Big G is going to fuck you guys up for this unless I put in a good word for you. You need to get us out of here and take me to the hospital and I can make sure Big G goes easy on you guys." Stew said all serious like he was in charge.

Luke started to laugh, a real deep dark sounding laugh as he leaned into Stew and said through laughter "Stewart L. Winston, you really have zero clue who we are do you?"

I watched the look of fear quickly return to the broken hurt face of Stew as the words Luke just spoke resonated in his drugged mind. The bravado of being in charge, that the name of 'Big G' would save him gone. Stew grew pale and he looked at Luke with his good eye.

"What? Wa, what do you mean?" Stew stammered.

"What I mean is you had no idea what this place 'Big G' sent you too is? It is no secret what this place is, what we do, and who shows up here to get trained. I thought the whole town knew this place." Luke said smiling down at Stew.

"I, un, I have heard things before, but we just came to watch, to do what Big G asked." Stew said.

"Stewart, we have had such a good open conversation and now you want to start to be dishonest with me?" Luke said sounding pained.

"No, no man, I am being honest, please, ok, ok, I knew you guys trained in weapons and shit like that. I knew what ya all did ok. Big G knew too and wanted us to tell him what was going on. Look I will be honest man, sorry, look Big G told me and Hen to watch and call if anyone left. I was being honest man, I was, I just want to get out of here man, I am sorry man please." Stew started sounding hysterical.

"Stewart, slow down and stop with the whining. I ask, you answer got it?" Luke said while smiling.

"I got it man, Honest, got it." Stew said.

"I am going to ask you again, Stewart, and I need you to be open and honest like we are buddies, lost old friends reunited, did you bring the rifles to shot any of us?" Luke said leaning close into Stew

"Man, um, well, um, man, um Big G, um, he told us if we could, to shoot him." Stew said nodding at me.

Luke turned to look at me, he winked, then turned back to Stew saying, "Big G wanted you to shoot that fucker behind me?"

"Yeah, yeah, Big G wanted us to kill him, sorry man" Stew said shifting his good eye to me "it was not personal, I just work for Big G" coming out of his mouth like it was no hard feelings.

I tried to keep the fury I felt in my body from showing and said, "business is business, right?"

"You get it man, good I thought you would kill me right here. Yeah man business is business, no hard feelings?" Stew said looking at me then back at Luke.

"How do you know this is the guy Big G wanted you to shoot Stewart?" Luke asked.

"He texted me a photo, well me and Hen a photo of him. It is on my phone, and he made us look at it and told us to remember it, that he wanted him dead as soon as we saw him. Big G has a real hard on for you man." Stew said looking back at me.

"So, shoot and kill this guy" Luke said thumbing towards me "and watch if anyone came or left, report it back to Big G? That is Stewart?" Luke asked.

"Yeah man, honest, that was what he told me and Hen to do man. Can you let me call my wife man, please." Stew said, almost pleaded.

"No, I can't do that Stewart. Gag him now." Luke said looking at Frank.

Frank shrugged and grabbed gauze and started stuffing it in Stewart's mouth. He instantly started to fight it and Frank leaned down and put his thumb to his wrecked eye and pressed down. Stewart's entire body stiffened.

"Open your fucking mouth nice and big asshole, or I will make sure this eye is really gone. NOW" Frank ordered.

I watched as the poor guy's mouth shot open wide and Frank stuffed it with gauze and then taped his mouth shut. That done we all looked to Luke.

"Shall we all go have a chat with this Henery guy next door, see just how honest Stewart has been with us?" Luke said more for Stew to hear than for us to hear, I think. We moved out and Frank said he would stay there with Stewart to make sure he didn't go anywhere. I gave him the thumbs up, and we went in to see that poor Henery was already having a bad night. Soft jazz music was playing in the small room he was seated in. Henery was naked taped to a chair in the middle of the room.

"Oh my, Henery you are naked" Luke started.

Henery looked up at him with his mouth still taped shut eyes big.

"Take the tape off Mister Henery D. Clawson's mouth so we can have a chat please." Luke said to no one in particular but Craig ripped it off.

"What the fuck, how did, damn never mind you have my wallet." Henery said.

"Yeah, Hen we got your wallet." Luke said and pulled a chair out at the table near the guy.

The look on poor Henery's face was priceless to say the least. Shock, fear, and then he paled whiter than a ghost.

"Yeah, Stewart WAS very helpful, poor guy." Luke said looking at his laptop.

"Was, what the fuck, was, what does was mean, fuck you killed him, he dead? He die from you shooting him? You mother fuckers are going to pay." Henery said, seeming to find his spirit again.

"Hen, come on man, that is pathetic coming from a guy taped to a chair naked. I mean seriously, look at yourself." Luke Said very sarcastically as he continued "Small ass shriveled dick and all, man, what a fucking joke. Jumped up, hands flying in the air giving up pretty much before poor Stewart took the round to the face. And now you want to act all big and bad, get the fuck out of here with this bullshit, Hen."

"You, you mother fucker, just wait." Henery said with a little less gusto behind it.

"I am sitting here waiting. I was waiting when poor Stewart was in there crying like a little bitch asking to live, telling us everything so we would help him." Luke said, still staring at his laptop screen.

"You will see, you all will" Henery said.

Luke turned abruptly and looked at Henery, "When Hen, when will we see hmm? What will we see?" Luke almost shouted.

"You, you will see the end." He said a little softer now.

"Yeah, the end hmm. Sounds scary to me" Luke said shaking on purpose "Look it has me shaking."

"You think you are all big and bad with me taped to this chair, just wait" Henery was saying when Luke launched at him from his chair.

"WHAT THE FUCK AM I WAITING FOR?" Luke screamed in his face.

Henery sat eyes wide looking at Luke just inches from his face smiling at him.

"No one is coming for you Henry. We are going to ask you questions and get answers from you one way or another. If I have to, I will cut little pieces out of you slowly. Look there is a drain right under you in case you piss or shit yourself or if I decide to start cutting you up." Luke said in a whisper near Henery's ear.

"Ya, you, ca, can't do that. I, I work for." Henery was saying when Luke interrupted him.

"Big G? You think any of us give a fuck about him or that you work for him?" Luke asked.

"Um, you, you should." Henery was saying before Luke continued on.

"Big G has no fucking clue and neither do you about who we are or what any of us do or have done. I honestly feel sorry for you, a little pawn in "Big G's' crew sent out here to watch us and see who came and went, and to shoot my friend"

Luke looked back at me and winked and turned back to him and continued "I honestly have zero reason to talk to you Henery. Stewart gave us everything trying to protect his family and save himself. Really, he stopped caring about himself in the end and just wanted his little girl and son to live."

Henery turned starkly white and pissed himself and started to shake and cry. The realization of just what and where he was starting to sink in.

"Let me ask you Henery, did you know who and what we are here? What we do when you dumbly followed your buddy Stewart out into the night with your wannabe sniper rifles?" Luke questioned him.

"Wa, what?" Henery managed to stammer.

"Here I will dumb it down for ya, did you know what the fuck we do here, at this place you find yourself taped to a fucking chair naked?" Luke said pulling his chair over in front of the poor guy and sitting.

"Some training. Like with weapons, teaching people to shoot. That is what you guys do here. That is what Stew said you guys did and so did Big G" Henery said softly.

"Interesting. Big G didn't know much about us hmm?" Luke asked.

"I don't know man, he talked mostly to Stew. Man don't kill me please. Don't cut me up." he started whining.

"Henery, that all depends on you. On if you help us. I already told these guys to kill you, so yeah man, I don't need you at all." Luke said.

"NO, no man, I can help, you don't need to kill me. Please don't kill me, anything man, anything." Henery pleaded.

"Gag this fucker" Luke said.

Craig grabbed him and pulled his head back looking down at him, "open wide please." Craig then stuffed what looked like a sock into his mouth and taped it closed. The jazz music was put back on and we walked out of the room, closed the door, and went to the center of the team room area.

"You still want to call the Sheriff and police Chief boss?" Luke said.

"I do, we taped both the interrogations, correct?" I asked.

"We did" Craig said. "I am not sure that the chief or sheriff will condone our actions. And we both know the DA is in this Mister Galagher's pocket. I think we should put them in a hole here and be done with it." he finished.

"And if the DA knows they are here and hoping they don't come back so he can get a warrant and come search here?" I said.

"Damn, you are really raining on my parade, then it is a big desert?" Craig shrugged his shoulders.

"Can we put these guys on ice, bag their phones?" I started when Bill interrupted.

"We bagged their phones when we exploited their hide sight and grabbed all their shit." Bill said.

We had all been on missions and did sight exploitation whenever possible to gather as much intelligence as possible off targets. Bagging a phone means we put it in a bag that blocked signal in and out, that way their phone was essentially dead to anyone that looked for it, called it, messaged it and so on. It gave us time to get away from a target or stop potential follow-on targets from knowing something had happened. The technology used today allows people, agencies, to track and watch devices, sometimes unbeknownst to the owner of the device. This had helped to target many evil people in the world, and we made sure to not allow the device to give away sensitive information by bagging them.

"Great, so they look like they went dead in the field if they are being watched. Nice work, I do not mean put them on ice, as in dead" I said looking directly at Craig "but we need to find a nice secure area to put them. We have the holding cell, but it is just one big drunk tank cell really."

"I could knock them out with a shot of Inapsine. Should give us 6-10 hours depending on how they are affected. I could get Rebecca involved and we could watch them together once we knock them out." Frank said.

"Do it" I told him.

"Ok so that solves the problem of them two for a bit" Bill said as Frank walked away.

"Boss, I say tread lightly talking to both the law men, but it might be time to figure out if they are going to be on our team or not. I need to go get some rest. It is late and Paula is still a little skittish from the shootout. Can I get to bed?" Luke asked.

I looked at my watch and was surprised to see it was after midnight already, "Damn sorry guys, Yeah, we can pick this up at the morning meeting. I will get with Frank and then think about the call to the law, sorry she is still upset about that. Get out of here." I finished.

"I am going to stop by the TOC and then catch some rack then." Craig said shuffling off.

"Get out of here you two, I will talk to Frank and then get a move on too." I said, looking at Bill, Jeff, and Paul.

"Night then." Bill said.

"See ya in the morning, or more like in a bit" Paul said.

"Bye" Jeff said walking out.

They headed out of the team room and towards the exit and the bunk house. I went back in and found Frank giving the wounded guy, Stewart, a shot, and watching closely as he did it. I knew that we gave him some pain killer and I also knew that a sedative might cause an issue, or at least my layman knowledge thought it was possible. Frank looked up at me watching.

"Rebecca will be here in a minute, and she said we are good to go to give this, which I was pretty sure about but double checked with her, but need to watch him for a bit after it was administered. Can you watch him while I go give a little to the other one?" Frank said.

"Sure" I said and looked at the broken face that was stitched up and the eye cup covering the wrecked eye. As I stared at him Rebecca walked in.

"Hey" I said.

"Hey, so we are now wounding people instead of killing them?" she asked with a smile.

"It just happened" I shrugged at her smiling back.

"What is the story? How much inventory we going to spend on this guy?" she asked flatly.

"No more inventory except to keep him out if need be. They came to watch and kill me if possible." I said, watching her face.

"And he is still alive, wow. Real restraint then, Rae doesn't know this I bet." Rebecca said knowing Rae would kill the guy herself to keep me safe.

"Not yet no. I'm surprised I told you, but Frank will tell you everything in a minute anyways once you both know these guys are out. I know how it goes so beating him too it. Thank you for helping." I told her and walked out before she could give me too much more shit.

Frank was dragging the guy taped to the chair towards me and I went and helped. We dragged him into the medical area and placed him against the wall and Frank taped his head to it.

"Thanks" Frak said.

"No thank you, see you in a few hours" I replied turning and leaving.

I went to the TOC and heard Craig talking to Troy who was still up, and they both seemed to be happy and going on about the video of the incident and then the interrogation. I turned and went to my office and found Rae sitting there, waiting for me.

"Hello sexy man of mine" she said slightly excited with that amazing smile plastered on her face. She knew she had caught me off guard and that was rare.

"Hey beautiful, waited up for me hmm?" I said walking towards her with my arms outstretched. She stood and snuggled into me.

"Yeah, I needed to see you after all this to see what is going on. I heard they came to snipe you love." She said pulling back and looking up at me in my arms.

"You heard that hmm?" I said to her.

"Confirmed now. What are we doing about this love? Who sent them?" she asked rapid fire.

"That Galagher guy sent them, they call him 'Big G' and he supposedly has the Mayor, DA, Judges and others bought off." I told her and kissed her head.

"I am thinking about calling Mike and seeing if he is going to be on our team, his own team, or what. I am torn as I did not want to be dealing with this kinda shit after five fucking days of shit hitting the fan. Hell, love shit is just barely starting to hit the fan and assholes abound." I said disgustedly.

"Why haven't you called yet?" She asked me.

"I think it is a group decision and am going to bring it up at the morning meeting before chow. We sedated the turds

and Frank and Rebecca are watching them in the med room."
I told her.

"Then let's go grab a little sleep and relieve Rebecca and Frank in a few hours so they can rest too." she said, pulling away from me and dragging me out of my office towards the bunk house.

We stripped down and hopped into bed and before I knew it was awoken by an alarm in my ears. Saturday started way too early for me.

Chapter 18

After grumbling a bunch, we both got up and took a quick shower, dressed, and headed over to the medical room. A quick pit stop in the TOC to check if anything was going on and say good morning to the crew on duty. We were briefed that nothing was going on and no motion alerts or visuals of anything that looked out of place. We went to the medical room and saw Rebecca awake reading a book with Frank sound asleep, his head on her lap.

"Morning Becca" Rae said to her as we came into the bay.

"Oh, hey lady, what the fuck are you two doing up?" Rebecca said looking at her watch. Frank steered in her lap and looked up at us.

"Hey guys" he mumbled as he rubbed the sleep out of his face.

"We came to let you guys get a little sleep in your own bed, I want you guys to be able to function a little if we need you today." I told them.

"We are good, honest, you guys can go back to bed." Rebecca said to us both.

"Becca, we know you are good, but it is about being fair to you guys. Wayne and I will take over and then you can come back and watch after these turds for the meeting." Rae told her.

"Alright, we can come back then. Frank and I just checked them, and they got a little more sedative an hour ago because they both started stirring." Rebecca told us.

"No problem. Get out of here." I said.

"Rae, be nice." Becca said.

"Yeah, nice Rae" Frank wagged his finger at me.

"What? Little me can't be anything but nice" Rae told them smiling and batting her eyes.

"Please" Rebecca said walking out with Frank in tow.

Both of our guests were in the same place I had seen them a few hours ago when I left in here for one exception, they had medical blankets pull over them. Stewart, broken face man, was still strapped to the medical table with the blanket all the way up to his neck. Henery, naked guy, had the blanket tucked around his shoulders with his head still taped to the wall. Rae walked around both and gave them a hard stare and I could see the wheels turning in her head.

"What is in that head of yours beautiful?" I asked her.

"I was just thinking how I wanted to kill these two, that they don't deserve to live wanting to kill you." she said without skipping a beat.

"Well, a little blood thirsty?" I said smiling.

"Just want to protect what is mine love, and they wanted to harm that. You know what lurks in my head when it comes to protecting us. Ours." She said looking at me.

"Yes, just remember we need these guys alive right now. No funny business, promise?" I said to her.

"Promise, no funny business." She replied to me.

I settled into a chair and thought about all that had happened in the last few days. It was crazy to think we are here and only five days had transpired since the crash started. I had gotten my dad on the first day from that shithole, California and he seemed to really be glad to be here. The greenhouses going up had him planting his 'tomato' plants, he called them, when in fact it was his marijuana plants. He had been smoking weed since before I was born, and I honestly didn't mind. He still tried to hide it from his grandkids, which I found funny, because it was becoming legal in many places. Canada had legalized it years ago, and they had very little problems since.

"Earth to Wayne." Rae said to me smiling.

"Sorry was thinking about how quick this thing has made a mess of our lives already and it is only like five days since it started." I said smiling back at her.

"Only five days? Really?" She said finding a chair and sitting too.

"Yeah, it is Saturday morning, crazy right?" I said.

"It really is crazy, we thought things could get bad quick, but the market really hasn't completely collapsed. Well, maybe it has since they stopped trading and have not traded more." She was thinking out loud now.

"It is not that bad, but I did not think we would have people wanting to kill us like this" I pointed to the two guys out cold.

"We both knew this town had bad people in it, and we had talked about the big fish in a little pond thing. Galagher is one of those and I remember my dad having issues with him long ago. We should call my parents, I am surprised my mom hasn't called yet." She said.

"Your dad and I had gotten them a lot of supplies love, once your mom accepted, they needed weapons, your dad started preparing on the side with me." I told her.

"Mom told me she had found a lot of supplies that she didn't know they had, asked if I had bought them for them. I told her I didn't know anything about it." She looked at me very seriously and asked, "You bought it all?"

"They have enough food and ammo to last for a year. They even have a smaller Atlas shelter in the back yard." I said gritting my teeth.

"What? How the fuck did you pull that off and not tell me?" she said looking a little hurt.

I put my hands up in a surrender gesture "I am sorry, it was supposed to be a surprise to you and your mom in a few weeks. The bunker was put in and completed when your parents went to the lake a few weeks ago. I bought your sister off and told her that if she said anything I would take it all back. Surprise!" I tried to make light of it.

"No wonder she has not called then. I will call my dad in a bit because he should be getting up to go to work, well maybe. Either way they get up early, so I am going to call them. He might know a little about this Galagher guy too." Rae said.

"Sorry love, I should have told you, but it was not on the top of the list until you said something about your parents, then I was like 'oh shit' and here we are." I said hanging my head a little.

"No reason to be sorry love, I am glad you helped and that they have a place to hide should it get that bad until we

can get them. What they fuck did you use to bribe my sister?"
Rae asked.

"I shamelessly bought a lithograph of that youtuber guy she worships and had him put a personalized message on it to her." I smiled.

"Oh my God, you are shameless. That would surely buy her off. So, they have a bunker and are good. Wow. I love you. Thank you." she said and came and sat in my lap and kissed me.

"I love you too" I said holding her close.

"What to do with this mess here then hmm?" She said as you got back up and pulled her chair close to mine.

"The timing is a little off for me too." I said.

"What do you mean?" she asked.

"Mike asked me, well said the County board would like me to come to the meeting they are having this morning. And then these guys are out setting up to watch us and possibly take a shot at me. Seems like maybe they are connected. Maybe they are all part of a plan, or maybe I am just a little to over-the-top thinking things? I don't know." I speculated.

"No, you might be onto something with that thought. Was it Mike or another person that asked to have you come?" Rae asked.

"It had sounded like a member of the board asked, not sure though. Maybe one of Galagher's bought people is a board member?" I said.

"Could be, could be Galagher knew you had been asked to come and was taking a shot at you? You said he was pretty upset about being left cuffed on the side of the road." Rae said to me.

"He was turning bright red when we left him there and yelling about killing me and you guys." I said.

"So, it could be coincidence, or it could be a plot to get you out and take you down. I guess things to talk to the group about and see what they think then?" Rae asked.

"Yeah, and the reason I have these guys knocked out is to give us the time and get the group together to brainstorm ideas and possibilities." I said.

"Are you still wanting to go to the meeting?" Rae asked me.

"Yes, I want to head to the meeting and part of me wants to take a few of the heavy trucks loaded to bear, but that would be giving away too much, I think. All this is going to be a repeat for you at the meeting now." I said giggling a little.

"I know and love that we get this time to talk alone about things, it has always been an important part of our relationship and love." She said smiling at me.

"As I love it too and respect your insight and thoughts on all the things we talk about, and that we can work out issues and plan for the future, and so much more." I said looking at her.

"The problem is, well really, comes down to what are we going to do to fix this problem or issue. I do not think that the shit has hit the fan hard enough to let you guys loose and raid his place and seed the earth with his blood, but I might be wrong about that." She said to me.

"You are not wrong that the collapse and the way society is not paying attention to it and moving along in day-to-day life. This credit card stoppage, and the withdrawal limit have caused pain, but most are just moving forward. All that said, can we afford letting this problem fester?" I told her.

"You know we can't, but how to deal with it is the real issue." Rae said.

I got up and checked on both our would-be snipers and they seemed to be out cold and breathing, good enough for me. Part of me just wanted to dig a hole and move forward, but that was a simple answer to a far more complex problem. It was getting closer to meeting time, and I was surprised that the time had went by so fast talking and thinking this through with Rae. I walked out and over to the team room and started a pot of coffee, which we had slipped out of our compound home forgetting to make. I am sure that it will get drunk by the guys, and I would let others know it was in here when we went to the meeting. AS I was getting a cup of the coffee Rebecca walked by but stopped and stuck her head in smelling.

"Is that coffee?" She asked me.

"Yeah, I figured we might all need a little pick me up after the long night we had." I responded to her as Frank pushed past her and went towards his cubby in the team room.

"Thanks fucker." He said to me as he walked back out and handed a coffee mug to his wife.

"You are more than welcome shitbag." I said back smiling. "Morning to you too, again."

"Stop ass grabbing in your Manship and give me a cup." My wife said.

"Sorry love, here you go. Special cream and all" I said with a childish grin thrusting the cup I was holding out to her.

"Special cream?" Rebecca said rolling her eyes at me then continuing. "How are the two we knocked out?"

"Good as far as we can tell, does it matter honestly?" I responded.

"That depends on what you want to do with them, but I would hope we did not waste the sedative on them if they are just going to get a bullet in the end." Rebecca said.

"It will be a group problem and decision." I told her.

"Yeah, and that is just the tip of the iceberg really." Rae said walking back to exchange duty and head over to the TOC. I knew she wanted to check in with her morning crew and see what the evening crew was briefing out to them. It was always a blessing to know she could run things and had seen it firsthand in a war zone.

"What is the word, you got a plan, Wayne?" Frank asked me.

"Fuck no. I have a bunch of jumbled thoughts and we are all going to work through them in a bit." I told Frank.

"We will certainly try, right?" Frank said sipping his coffee and moved towards the conference room leaving me standing near the big bullet of a coffee pot.

I walked out and stuck my head in the TOC to listen to the brief for a minute. It sounded like the rest of the night had been dead, which is great. I went into my office and turned on the TV and was met with another 'Breaking News' on the bottom ticker tape, which seemed like everything was breaking news to them now. The headline was, Dollar continues to crumble. No surprise guys, I thought in my head not really understanding how the average American could not see just how bad it was. I grabbed my notebook off my desk and walked back to the conference room.

A round of "Morning" was bombarded upon me as I walked into the room from all of the core group already seated. I looked around and it looked like every single person was already seated and looking at me.

"Damn am I late" I responded as I looked at my watch. Nope the meeting time was in 5 minutes.

"No, I think we all know that today is going to be, possibly be, trying." Bill said.

"We have the county board meeting, the two turds on ice in medical, this Galagher fuck, possible shipments arriving, and the list goes on" Craig said smiling.

"Why the fuck are you smiling saying all that?" Mitch asked.

"He is a sadistic fuck, that is why." Paul said.

"Come on, we get to use all the cool toys we have, and that is exciting to me, does that really make me sadistic?" Craig said now grinning instead of smiling so big.

"I do not want to use any cool toys, yet, because I am not wanting to show my hand to anyone unless we really need to do that. Am I wrong to think that things are not bad enough to get out, All, the cool toys?" I said to the group.

"I think that we are at a crucial point, that we could flex and show a little of our hand, but is the flex needed. I see the point you are making Wayne." Jeff said.

"Boss, the target package is built for Galagher, he is well connected and has a lot of friends, or acquaintances, here in the Raeley, and the entire state. He has vacationed with the governor even. I am a little biased and want to execute the target package and rid ourselves of this problem going against my professional analysis of developing the target intentions more. In the end the analytics would suggest that Galagher needs to be dead." Luke said.

"Exactly Luke, he needs deaded." Tod said.

I could not help but giggle at Tod, "Deaded?? What the fuck is Deaded?" I asked him.

"Made dead as shit" Tod said now smiling and laughing to which pretty much the entire group was either smiling or giggling now.

"Thank you for lightening the mood, Tod." Craig said.

"Is this how you all feel? We need to kill Galagher now?" I asked.

"I think that we need to reach out to the Sheriff Wayne. You have had an almost friendship with Mike off and on over the years and tell him all this." Stephanie said.

"I had thought about calling him and talked to Rae about that last night a little. It could be a way to see what team he wants to play with. I was also curious about whether he invited me to the meeting this morning or someone else had. The conversation I had with him seemed another had invited, and he was the relay but not sure. So, the real question is should I call him and see about the meeting? Tell him more or even all of it?" I asked the group.

"I think that he is on our team, but this could be a way to secure him on the team." Adam said.

"Secure him or let him know we know that Galagher is after us and he tells 'Big G' that we are onto him." Craig said.

"Who the, I mean 'Big G' I get it but what the fuck Craig?" Miguel said.

"Let me back up because I am forgetting not all you took part last night. The two guys outside last night had long range weapon systems with thermals on both weapons. Mind you not top end gear but they had pretty nice setups. Anyways, they crawled into a position, and we got the notice as the entire compound family got it on the radio system. Jeff and Craig set up in our counter sniper hide on the bunk house and had a clear shot on them. I elected to use a bullhorn and try to get them to surrender. In the end Jeff had to blast a guy's gun and that fucked that shooters eye and face up and his buddy surrender. We grabbed them and Luke interrogated them. They informed us that mister Galagher was 'Big G' and in charge around these parts and had the mayor, DA, judges, and others all in his pocket. Am I leaving anything out people?" I said looking around.

"Yeah, that they got sent here by their boss, 'Big G' to watch us and kill you, if possible, honey, big fucking deal." Rae said.

"Did you leave that part out on purposed Wayne?" Troy asked.

"Not totally on purpose but know it will change how a lot of you want to handle this, and I want to try to be rational and not lash out at the problem." I told the group.

"Fuck the 'being rational' shit, they came to kill my man, I want to draw blood, I want to have the target wiped the fuck from this earth and anyone associated with him." My wife said, letting out her very vengeful side.

"I am more than aware of your vote to seed the earth with his blood, but is that really the way forward? Are we going to be a group who squashes little problems with the biggest swatter we can find?" I asked the group looking around.

"This problem needs to be dealt with sooner rather than later boss." Luke said.

"I am not saying it doesn't need to be dealt with Luke. I know it should not be left to fester and possibly get more people hurt because the guy does something else. Troy, do we have UAV capabilities? Shit and do we have counter UAV capabilities? Shit I am just adding to it at this point." I said.

"We have both yes." Troy answered me.

"Wayne, we have the Draco in my 'Air Wing" you are calling it, have you forgotten?" Mitch said.

"I guess I have Mitch" I said.

"We have a fully capable crew, and it is loaded with all the bells and whistles since it is the newest U-28a. You spent an arm and a leg getting us qualified on all of it to possibly establish the training modules here. I think Craig and Stephanie are likely more read in on it, but we can watch this guy and track him, and anyone associated with him, and he would almost certainly never know it real time." mitch said to me and the rest of the group.

"How long would it take you to get in the air and start looking at the target then?" I asked.

"Maybe thirty minutes to an hour at most." He said.

"Get it going then. We need to start being better at this, I know we do not have unlimited personnel to run operations. Let's get the bird up and watching. How long can it stay up?" I asked.

"Longer than we would like it to be up." Mitch said smiling.

"This could help with the meeting today too, which is in, two hours and thirty minutes." I said.

"I am going to go and trust you guys can figure the rest out. I want to brief the crew about this mission." Mitch said as he got up.

"Thank you." I said.

"Luke, do we think that the meeting and these guys being sent to watch and possibly take me out are related?" I asked.

"That is hard to say. Boss." Luke said.

"Best analysis guess? Looking for your gut, not your analytical step by step analysis." I told him.

"It sure as fuck is too coincidental." Paul said.

"The likelihood that the two events a very possibly linked is high for me, I think you need to call the sheriff like you said earlier and see who had asked to have you join the meeting." Luke said.

"I can call with you all here and that way if you guys have questions you can ask him too. Remember to not give away our hand please." I said as I dialed on the phone in front of me and used the conference speaker.

The phone rang five times and then was answered, "Sheriff here, can I help you?"

"Morning Mike, it is Wayne and I have you on speaker with the gang. Say hi gang." I said.

"Hi" everyone said.

"Hey all, you are calling early what is up?" the sheriff said.

"We are just getting ready for the meeting today and a question came up if you invited me or someone else did." I said and continued "because we had tried to talk to the county board many times about getting prepared and not that it is here, they are wanting to talk." I ended.

"I had talked at the meeting yesterday how your team had helped at Wal Mart and honestly saved my deputy, thank you all by the way, he is doing better and going to be back to our hospital Monday morning. Anyways, The Land Commissioner said I should invite you, Ronald Felps, to the meeting because you knew a lot about getting prepared." the sheriff said.

"So that was who invited me then?" I asked.

"Yeah, he was very pushy, and the others said alright but that they thought they had it under control. He said the least they could do is have you around to answer questions. So, I invited you. Why?" the sheriff asked.

"And is he good friends with the Galagher guy I left pissed and cuffed the other day after they followed my guys?" I asked.

"Galagher helped get him elected to the position, ok what the fuck is going on Wayne?" the Sheriff asked.

"Is Charles in there with you?" I said.

"No but he will be in a second, CHARLES!" the sheriff yelled.

"What?" You could hear Charles say as he came in.

"I have Wayne on the phone, and it seems we have a problem and our dearest friend, Galagher is part of it." the sheriff said to Charles.

"Oh, hey Wayne, oh that Galagher has a hard on for you buddy. A few people have asked me about you and why

Galagher is upset and talking badly about you all over." Charles said.

"Yeah, well he let his hard on get too close to me last night guys." I told them looking at the group to nods.

"Fuck me, did you kill more people, Wayne?" the Sheriff asked me.

"Nope." I told them as Bill started giggling.

"Is that Bill laughing Wayne? Is that you Bill?" Charles asked and then more started to giggle and laugh.

"Yeah, it is me, Charles." Bill said smiling.

"What in the fuck is so funny about one of the richest and most powerful guys in the Raeley having a hard on for Wayne? Or us asking if you fucking dip shits killed someone else? I think you guys are up to six or seven in the last couple of days, all clean shoots but still" Charles said

"First it was the sheriff's tone for me Charles, like we are looking to go bag people. Second, Galagher has no fucking clue what kinda shit pile he stepped in with Wayne, and really all of us. The Third part I will let Wayne talk to you about." Bill said smirking at me.

"Spit it the fuck out Wayne, what the fuck is going on?" the sheriff said now more serious.

"We had two visitors last night. They had rifles with thermals on them. The planned to watch the compound and possibly shot and kill me. Plans have been averted." I told them.

"You are talking about them in the past tense and yet told me you did not kill anyone, so?" the Sheriff asked.

"One is wounded, and the other is fine. We captured them and interrogated them. We found out their boss is 'Big G' as they call him, Mister Galagher for the rest of us. He sent them with instructions to watch and report if anyone comes or goes and if possible, to shoot me. They, the two goons we have, were asked how they knew it was me and said the boss had sent them a photo and made them study it. Poor guys had no clue and I do not think their boss does either Mike, Charles." I said to them both.

"You still have them there? At the compound?" Mike asked.

"Sheriff they are being held" I said.

"Fuck, so you are not certain you can trust me and Charles but are taking a shot at it hmm?" Mike continued.

"I am sincerely hoping we, you both and I, are on the same team guys." I said.

"Are you serious, you mother fucker?" Charles said and continued "after all the conversations we had and the times we hung out you seriously would even question if we are on the same team, Wayne?" He sounded hurt I thought.

"I am taking a shot in the dark here Charles, thinking you are on my team and so is Mike, but this shit is getting crazier each day and people are the biggest surprise to me." I said.

"We are on your fucking team asshole. Or you on ours, or whatever the fuck you want to call it." the sheriff said.

"Great, now we still have 'Big G' to deal with." Jeff said matter of fact, causing Charles to start laughing.

"Leave it to you Jeff." Charles said laughing.

"I do not find this funny at all." Mike said. "Galagher hates me almost as much as he seems to hate you, Wayne. So, my assistance doesn't really help much. What are you guys planning cause I know sure as shit Rae isn't sitting tight with a guy wanting to kill her husband or family." Mike finished.

"Oh, how sweet, you know me so well Mike." Rae said.

"There is the little firecracker. No more killing, unless, dammit I can't even say needed because you think it is needed right now damn." Mike said and I could hear Charles full-on laughing now in the background. "You're laughing isn't helping a fucking thing, Charles."

"Here is the plan then guys. I will come to the meeting, but we are going to come in with a little team and be very ready and kitted up. I will bring the two pieces of shit we have with us and release them at the meeting. If anything goes sideways, those two pieces of shit get dropped first. I do not want or need a problem, Mike. Maybe either you or Charles need to go talk to Mister Felps and let him know we are coming, and he should have his boss "Big G' come too." I said as all my people smiled knowing I wanted to stir the pot now.

"He might make a move here but I doubt he would be that forward, then again the world is going to shit and it seems he knows this and is starting to take what he wants instead of by it." Mike said.

"Wayne, if you want me to stir the pot I can, but Galagher is a wild card and been a problem for a long time. It sure as shit could go bad quickly." Charles told me.

"My group, stir the pot or no?" I asked.

"Stir" was all I heard.

"You hear them Charles?" I asked.

"Yeah brother, I heard them. I will go let Felps know in a bit." Charles said.

"Anything else?" Mike asked.

"Yeah, could you wait until I text you before you go tell Felps so I can get an asset in position first?" I asked Charles.

"Text me when you are ready." Charles said.

"See you guys in 2 hours or so." I said and hung up.

"Rae, you are in charge of the TOC, unless you can't handle it because I will be in harm's way." I said to her.

"Whatever, I got it." She told me and got up and left.

"Luke, I need you working with the ISR team in the Draco. Dump these pieces of shits phones and get as much info out of those phones as possible, then get ready to give them to Craig so we give them back to them when we release, if it goes ok, them." I said to Luke and he stood and moved from the room.

"Adam, I need your team to kit up and take a vehicle and go try to scope out the area to see if you see a problem already." I said looking at Adam.

"Got it, let's go guys." Adam said as his team got up and shuffled out.

I pulled out my phone and dialed Zack. The phone rang three times and he picked up.

"Morning" he said.

"Hey, I was wondering if you could come over to the Conference room in the headquarters building." I said to him.

"Sure, be right over there" he said and hung up.

"You guys good with him riding along for this op?" I asked my team.

"He is green but knows what to do." Craig said.

"I was hoping to have you and jeff on long sticks to help drop things and was going to have him with one of you for security. Who wants him?" I said looking between them.

"I will take him with me." Jeff said.

As Jeff had said that Zack walked into the room and Jeff turned to see him.

"Speak of the devil" Jeff said and put his hand out to shake. Zack took it.

"Been a bit Jeff, how are you?" Zack said.

"Could be better, come on you are with me we have a mission." Jeff said, dragging him towards the door and then the team room.

"Craig, take Paul with you." I said and they nodded and got up and went towards the team room too.

"That leave you and Frank with me" I said to Bill. "We need to get the two shit heads up and going get our kit on and thing about what we want to bring." I said.

"249 for this then?" Frank asked.

"Yeah, we should bring it and hope not to need it." I said.

"Yes sir, better to have and not need than need and not have." Frank said smiling and turning to head to the team room.

"He loves to have that fucking belt fed shit" Bill said getting up too.

"I am going to head into the TOC for a bit then come grab kit to go." I told Bill.

Troy and Stephanie sat looking at me. You two can be used in the TOC too. Troy, I think we are going to need your help to possibly pipe the shit from the Draco to us on the ATAK. Is it already in the system?" I asked.

"The Draco is in the network already and can give the network a bigger footprint depending on the flight level." He said.

"Let's go see what we got going on then." I said as I slid back and got to my feet.

"Shit do you need to help Luke dump the cell phones?" I asked Troy.

"NO, he is more than capable of doing it and has done that way more than I have even though that is in my job scope" Troy said laughing.

"Makes sense since he has done the intelligence side of this shit more than he ever did his infantry shit." I said.

"He was infantry before?" Staphanie asked as we entered the TOC.

"Yes, it is a small secret though." I said.

"Ok" she said.

I walked up to Rae and asked her for an update on the Draco. And she told me it was airborne and already watching the Galagher home and that his cell signature was at that location. She said Luke was just finishing the phone dumps and would have the phones for me in a minute. I thanked her and went to find Luke in his area. He handed me one phone and it was already back in the bag, this was to make sure the signature from it would not be seen once we left the TOC. The TOC was protected from the outside and cell signals could not get in or out of the TOC. As I waited for the phone, I looked around the TOC and realized that it was operating like a well-oiled machine despite the fact only a few of the people working the shift had been together like this. I was glad we had what we had in our group and amazed it was working so well. Luke handed me the other phone and I left him to do his work coordinating with the Draco and us.

When I entered the team room Frank walked past me and said he was going to wake the turds and would be in medical. I went into my cubby and got my kit together. I was going hard plate and helmet just in case. I dropped the Thorax carrier over my head and tightened down the cumber bun. I checked the ATAK system, and it was green and showed all the moving pieces. I messaged Luke on the system chat to see if Draco was able to intercept the phone calls to Galagher and hit send. I then grabbed my weapon system and had already been wearing my gun belt since early this morning. I hoped this did not get wild.

Chapter 19

I exited my cubby into the team room and went to medical to help get our two want to be sniper turds going. They were half out of it and mumbling through their taped mouths. I grabbed the one we had stripped naked for the interrogation. I saw they he was wearing pants now and moved him towards the exit and the waiting Tahoe we had to put them in. It would be the blacked-out Tahoe with the police cage we had. It had been close to the building from the last time we used it and was not a far walk. I opened the door and placed him in back and belted him in. My ATAK alerted in my ears that it had a message for me, I opened it seeing it was from Luke and we could intercept incoming and outgoing calls to Galagher. I messaged him back thank you and took out my phone.

I messaged the Undersheriff to tell Felps I would be at the meeting in a little bit and wanted to talk to the group and show them something I had found. He replied back that he would tell him right now and I thanked him. I then keyed my radio.

"Bear main this is 17, call should be made to Target phone." I radioed.

"Bear main copies." I heard my wife's voice on the net.

I turned the vehicle on to let it warm up and to make sure the radio was up and running in the vehicle too. I would have it scanning but priority to our group net so if we keyed up in the vehicle it would be on our team net. I looked back and our want to be sniper looked like he was already back out. I got out and walked back to help Frank bring the wrecked face guy. Frank waved me off and said he has him and to grab his 249 for him. I grabbed it and told him I was going to stick my head in the TOC and then head out to him and get going.

As I walked in the TOC Luke waved me over. "Boss, we intercepted this conversation. Felps called and Galagher answered on second ring. Here is the transcript, I printed it so you could take it and have it with you too. It is my professional opinion that Galagher is looking to take over the area." Luke said, handing me a page. I started to read it as I left the TOC and headed to the Tahoe.

Galagher: So do you have anything for me?

Felps: Undersheriff just told me that this guy was coming and had something to show us. What the fuck does that mean?

Galagher: I am not sure, he might not even make it to you guys anyways.

Felps: What do you mean he might not make it to us? He is not that far away from the Board room.

Galagher: I have a surprise waiting for him, well watching him and his people. If they get a chance he won't make it to the meeting. If not, we will know he is coming. Either way I will be coming to the meeting too. It is time I explained a few things to you all about who is in charge.

Felps: Who is in charge, what the fuck does that mean?

Galagher: You will see in a bit, I have to go so I can make it to this meeting too.

"Bear 17 to all Bear elements. Weapons free, I say again weapons free. Any and all hostile threats are to be given no quarter. Any, I say again, any hostile intent is to be met with maximum force." I radioed everyone. I heard many double clicks in my ear in response. I reached the Tahoe and handed the 249 to Frank. He had a serious look on his face and took the weapon and started to confirm it was loaded.

"What is up" Frank asked me.

"This" I said handing him the paper Luke gave me with the intercept on it.

"Well, he doesn't know that his little watching party was busted up that is good." Frank said smiling and handing it back.

"I am more worried about his little party coming to town and what his intent is." I said.

"Do you really think that his party is going to be capable of doing much to us? Seriously?" Frank asked.

"You and I both know it only takes one bullet to ruin your day. None of us are invincible, or bullet proof. And I hate the unknowns that we can't control." I said as we started moving in the vehicle towards the gate.

I pulled up and punched in the code and waited for the bastions to deploy downward then pulled into the secondary holding section waiting for the first gate to close behind me and the bastions to lower and gate open in front of me. My mind was racing with possibilities of what we might be getting into ant then my radio came alive in my ears and the vehicle.

"Bear 17 this is Draco Four vehicles have left the Galagher home and are heading towards the County Building. All four have armed individuals. Shotguns, hunting rifles and some AR's and AK's." I heard on the net.

"Roger, Break. Bear 27 and 26 be in position to interdict them as they are at County building. If this goes sideways, be ready." I radioed.

I heard multiple double clicks in my ear to acknowledge they understood.

"Frank, does it look like the team has a good set up on the County building from the ATAK? I don't want to look and not drive well." I told him.

"They are set up from two angles as we would expect them to do on a target building. Looks solid to me but now I am thinking that you might have wanted me in a support position with this" He said looking at the 249 he was carrying. The 249 is a squad automatic weapon, belt fed 5.56mm machinegun. This one was more specialized and shortened barrel, with a suppressor on it and a collapsable stock. Kind of like the airborne addition, but a little more tricked out with things Frank liked.

"I think in close will work just fine with this group. I am sure they might have a few guys that know what they are doing, but from the sounds of the weapons they have, they are not a highly trained group, which might be to our fortune." I told him as we turned onto the main road leading to the County building.

"Bear 17, I am currently about 2 miles out, sit rep Draco?" I said on the radio net.

"Draco has the four target vehicles about 10 miles out Stopped at a stop light. You are going to get there before them for sure." Came the reply from the Draco.

"17. Copy Break, team on site, I am going to pull right to the front and take these two straight into the building. Weapons free if you see anything that constitutes a threat." I said pulling into the parking area.

"Bear 17 is on the X." I radioed into the net and pulled up to the front of the building. Frank was out and scanning with the 249. I walked around to his side and opened the door. "Get out and walk into the building and into the Board meeting room, it is straight to the back. Do not stop for anyone and walk in and sit in the front row, got it. They both nodded their heads. If you need help then your buddy will help you. We will be escorting you and telling people to get out of the way. Now get out." I told the two in the vehicle.

"Moving" I radioed.

"27, Clear." Jeff radioed.

26, Clear" Craig radioed.

"Draco, on station and have wide view until target vehicles are on X" Came the reply from the eyes in the sky.

We walked rapidly towards the doors and eyes turned to look at us and they were all looking shocked. First at the two guys with cuffs and then seeing two guys in what to them looked like military gear escorting these guys inside. The Sheriff and Undersheriff walked towards us when we got into the lobby.

"These the guys you talked to us about?" The Sheriff asked.

"Yeah, they are, I am going to take them in and have them seated at the front. Galagher is coming with four vehicles full of guys armed, they are minutes out. Felps told him we were coming to the meeting, here." I told them as I handed them the sheet of the transcript of the phone conversation we intercepted.

"What the fuck?" the Sheriff said as he handed it to the Undersheriff.

"Damn, let me get some guys moving back this way. What does he fucking think he is going to explain?" the Undersheriff said as he keyed up his radio and asked for all available units to report to the County Board meeting.

"Fuck, the radio doesn't work for shit in here, let me step outside." the undersheriff said as he moved to the doors.

"Draco to team, target vehicles 30 seconds plus minus to the X" came the call in my ear.

"17 Copy, look alive and record all events Draco." I responded.

"Draco, copies. Already recording. Good luck." They responded.

"21 go over there to that corner and watch with the 249, that will give you a bit of cover and allow you to suppress should we need that." I told Frank.

"Who the fuck is Draco?" the sheriff asked.

"Got it." Frank replied as he moved and set himself into a comfortable position to rapidly bring the little machine gun to bare. Just as he was getting settled, we heard then saw the four vehicles barreling into the parking lot then stop out front with our vehicle.

"What a rag tag looking bunch." Came Craig's radio chatter on the net.

"No weapon discipline pointing their weapons all over the place." Jeff said.

"Draco, black out this entire place, no cell traffic out of here, now." I radioed.

"Done." Came the call from Draco.

The Undersheriff was already outside, and I could see him looking at the group, then back at the Sheriff and me and shrugged with a worried look on his face.

"Shall we go see what Galagher and his group might want? And you ignored me about Draco" the sheriff said as he was walking that way.

"Sure, just know I have snipers set up in overwatch and they are going to kill anyone that looks like a threat Mike. Not taking chances anymore. I can explain Draco later" I said moving with him. I looked to Frank and nodded, he had a clear view out of the glass windows and doors that covered the entry into the county building and the lobby area.

As the Sheriff opened the door, I heard the undersheriff asking, "what's going on gentlemen?"

"Hey Charles, oh and sheriff. Can never be too safe, after all, the country is going crazy, and I already got pulled." Galagher stopped talking as he saw me step out and stand there with the sheriff and undersheriff.

"Yes, he" pointing at me "pulled me and my guys at gun point from our vehicle after we had done nothing. And you" pointing at the sheriff "did nothing. So now I am moving around with a bigger group to make sure I am safe. And I am going to make sure everyone is safe since you can't be trusted to do your job sheriff." Galagher said with a thick sour voice filled with contempt.

"Is that so? You are saying the sheriff can't be trusted. Is that how you feel Kris?" the undersheriff said pointing at a guy with a shotgun. "You here to protect

Galagher and help him make sure the sheriff does the right thing?"

"You don't have to say anything to these men. Soon they will have no authority here anyways." Galagher said towards this Kris guy.

I heard steps coming from behind me and saw two more deputies come walking past Frank looking at him all serious then yelled out to the sheriff. "Sheriff, were you need us?"

That is when Galagher saw Frank for the first time through the doors, and his attitude shifted slightly. "What is that guy doing with a machine gun?" he pointed towards Frank.

"He is keeping the peace Galagher, just like all your guys here are trying to help you keep the peace." the Sheriff said.

"You two" Charles pointed at the deputies "go inside the chamber meeting area and secure the two detainees in the front row and make sure they are comfortable, I want to hear what they have to say."

"Ok" they both said and turned and walked towards the meeting room where the would-be snipers had been left to sit.

"So here is the deal, you arrogant prick, you and another guy can come inside armed. The rest of your guys can stay out here." The Sheriff said forcibly.

"Who the fuck do you think you are talking to mother fucker." one of the guys next to Galagher yelled and pointed at the sheriff. I was truly glad he did not point his weapon or he would be dead and the shit would have gotten a little wild. A total of 18 armed guys, including Galagher himself, all stood tensely looking at the sheriff and the rest of us.

"Calm down junior." the undersheriff said to this younger looking guy. It made sense as I looked at him, he looked a lot like his father. "We are not asking you how this is going to go, we are telling you. It is not personal, we would not let him," He pointed at me "have more than himself and another in the building either, so the rest of his team." the undersheriff smiled as he left it at that and stopped talking.

Galagher quickly understood the tone and looked around and did not see anything or anyone that looked like I did. Galagher senior put his hand on his son's shoulder and said, "Easy son, the sheriff will soon get what is coming to him just like that guy there" he pointed at me "will get what he deserves. You can stay out here with the crew and make sure nothing happens. Don't let anyone else in after we go in." He finished looking at the sheriff.

"You cannot block people from attending the meeting Galagher, and you know this. If others arrive your guys need to let them inside. Do you all understand?" The Sheriff asked the group.

"And how exactly are we to be sure there are no more members of this dangerous group that you have already allowed in the build, with a machine gun no less. Is that even legal Sheriff? To carry a machine gun in public, in New Mexico? I am searching my memory of the law and can't seem to think it is, MIKE." the other gentleman, in a suit no less, next to Galagher senior asked.

"Quit the lawyer bullshit, Jeremy." the Undersheriff said. "You know as well as I do that it is legal to own and possess machine guns in New Mexico. As for that person in there with the weapon, he is a sworn reserve deputy and a federal contractor who is more than authorized and capable with it. Enough of the bullshit, we going to have a problem, or can we get to the meeting and get it started?" Charles finished.

"We are not going to have a problem as long as his people and yours don't cause an issue and understand, after the meeting, who is in charge." Galagher said smiling as he walked past us, and the suit followed him.

"Always such a prick Galagher" the sheriff said under his breath well behind him as we turned and followed him and his suit to the meeting room. Galagher was in the lead as he got near the door, he saw the backs of the heads of his would-be sniper team. He stopped in his tracks with his hand on the glass door handle.

"What is wrong? You ok Mister Galagher?" I said to him with a huge smile on my face standing back behind the sheriff with the undersheriff next to me. Frank was still covering the guys out front, and I had not heard anything on the radio in my ears, which was nice because if I did it most likely meant trouble.

"I seem to have forgotten something, I need to step out and make a call." Galagher senior said as he turned from the room quickly and started to walk back towards the exit.

"I am sorry Galagher, but you are going to turn and head back in that room and sit the fuck down." The sheriff said, his hand now on his service weapon still holstered. Charles had pied off to my right and I had pied out to the left as the sheriff said this. "You can make your call from right here, or even in the chamber, I will not stop you and neither will the council." the Sheriff continued. "I know the rules say no phones, but they say no weapons too and we are not going to disarm people when these times seems to be so volatile."

"I um, I am good then, I can make the call seated in the room if it is allowed now." Galagher senior said looking very pale.

"He can't keep you here sir if you do not want to be here." the suit stammered.

"Shut the fuck up and come sit with me." Galagher senior said as he nodded towards the meeting room, and particularly the two seated. The suit visibly stiffened when you recognized the two heads up front that his boss had nodded at. They both went through the door and walked to the right side of the room near the back and sat. Galagher senior pulled out his phone and immediately realized he had no service and leaned over and whispered to the suit who pulled out his phone and they both looked at it.

I knew they would not get service as the Draco was blocking all cell phone frequencies, radio frequencies minus ours and the EMS services, and Wi-Fi frequencies in the area from high above as they orbited and watched. It created a bubble that we were currently sitting in. I took up a position opposite them in the back of the room near the door with my back to the wall. I smiled as I watched them both whispering, and they started to get more frustrated. As they did one of the guys up in the front turned and saw them and started mumbling through the tape. A deputy went and told him to turn around and shut up. The suit guy looked physically ill now. They both frantically tried to use their phones. Then the council started filling in and Galagher saw Felps come in.

"Ronald, is your phone working?" Galagher senior said standing looking at him. Felps saw him and smiled then quickly realized he was just with the suit guy and that the two up front looked familiar.

"Let me look and see" Felps said as he pulled out his phone. "No, it says no service. Maybe the world is going to shit more than we thought it was?" He said kind of not sure what to do as he took his seat looking confused.

They called the meeting to order and then we all stood and said the Pledge of Allegiance. The continued to go through the motions and then a request for emergency Quorum was voted and passed that tabled all the rest of the agenda and opened the floor for the conversation about the current collapse and the counties response.

"Henery Clawson why are you in this chamber with no shirt and tape on your mouth. Does your mother know where you are?" Council lady Bale asked.

"Council, please continue and I will let you all know why these two men are up front in the condition they are in." The sheriff stood and said with his hands spread.

"Council woman Harper, let us please get this moving so we can figure out why these two are here. How is the county currently sitting when it comes to emergency supplies?" Chairman Winters asked.

"Chairman winters, our current emergency supplies are at the standard required levels. The Sheriff has informed me that he and the Police Chief have placed law enforcement at the major shopping establishments in our area to help any unrest that is related to the cash withdrawal restrictions. This crisis is just in the infant stages, and we should look at long term issues and start to think through those ramifications." She addressed stopping and looking at the two would be snipers.

"We have the required crisis inventory approved by the county and in storage then?" the Chair asked.

"Yes" she answered.

"Sheriff, what issues have we had since this crisis began? And why do we have a shirtless man and a man with his eye bandaged and bloody sitting here in the front row?" the Chairman asked very seriously looking at him.

"Chairman, we have had a few issues and two very serious incidents since the crisis started. As most are well aware a deputy was shot and wounded very seriously and had to be rescued by our local team of reserve deputies. Thankfully they got to the downed deputy in time to save him and stop the threat from progressing and harming anyone else. The second incident happened last night, as these two individuals stalked towards a local business with rifles that had suppressors attached. These rifles had thermal sights to allow them to see and shoot in the night. I have video of them both crouching as they walk, then crawl, then slowly shimmy their way into a position and set their individual rifles up facing this business." the sheriff was saying as he got interrupted.

"So, they stalked into position to watch a place, is that a crime Sheriff?" Council member Felps asked and continued. "And why do they have tape over their mouths?"

"The crime was not the stalking, and they have tape over their mouths to stop them from causing problems during the meeting and to not be a nuisance." the sheriff said. "Should I continue Mr. Felps?" the sheriff asked.

As the sheriff said this, I saw Galagher senior get up and start to move towards the doors. "Oh, trying to leave before we start to talk about you and Mister Felps are you?"

"I am not sure what you are illuding to sheriff, but I have things that need to be taken care of and seeing as this meeting has not keep to the scheduled agenda, I have no reason to be here." Galagher said glaring at the Sheriff.

"Trying to run out before the world finds out how you are moving in this crisis then? How 'Big G' is making his moves?" The sheriff said his hand was already resting on his service pistol as he moved forward and ripped the tape off the shirtless unwounded Henery.

"Team, stand by for possible contact starting from inside the meeting." I whispered into my headset to the sound of double click responses. I slowly moved my body to get into a better stance should I have to bring my rifle up and place accurate rounds on targets.

"Big G help us, get us the fuck out of here and away from these people. They are fucking crazy and took us hostage. Get the boys in here and show these mother fuckers who is in charge." Henery was almost hysterical.

"Order! Order!" The Chairman shouted. "I will not have this in this chamber. We need order now. Please stop with this nonsense Sheriff." the chairman looked shaken.

"Fuck your order!" Henery said starting to stand.

The sheriff grabbed him. "Deputies grab this piece of trash and the other one and take them to booking and put them in a cell."

Then Henery twisted in the grip and ripped away. He was met with the two prongs of a taser slamming into his shirtless body and delivering 50 thousand volts to his body, but the volts are not as important as the 1.9 milliamps that courses through the body and locks up the muscles. Henery went down with a thump and smashed his head on the chair and was not only locked up for the 5 second ride the taser gives but knocked out cold. The deputy grabbed him and carried him from the room over his shoulder and the other one walked off looking scared and unsure with his one eye and wrecked face.

"Chairman, my apologies for the outburst, and Mister Galagher you are more than welcome to leave, just know we will be talking about you, and I thought a man of your stature would stay to defend his honor." the sheriff said. I was smiling, Mike was laying it on thick to this fucker.

"You have nothing that will take from my honor and the great things I have done for this town and community sheriff. You are going to be sorry you went down this road, mark my words." Galagher senior said as he headed out the doors.

"Are you threatening me? Council, do you hear Mister Galagher threaten me?" Mike asked the members.

"He did not threaten you sheriff, get over yourself already." Felps said.

"Glad you opened your mouth Ronald, undersheriff arrest him for conspiracy to commit murder." the sheriff told Charles.

"What, wha, what is this?" Felps asked.

"You have the right to remain silent. Anything you say can and will be used against you in a court of law. You have the right to an attorney. If you cannot afford an attorney, one will be provided for you. Do you understand these rights as I have just read to you? And with these rights in mind, do you wish to continue to talk to us?" The undersheriff gave the Miranda.

"You are under arrest mister Felps, for conspiracy to commit the murder of Mister Cook" the sheriff said pointing at me. "Do you wish to talk to us here, in chamber to clear this up?"

"I, I, I want to call my lawyer." Felps said and the undersheriff smiled.

"I will take him to booking boss." the undersheriff told the sheriff.

It was deafly silent in the county board chambers as the other member stared at the sheriff and the chairman.

"17, this is 26, the party is breaking up outside and they are getting in the vehicles. Looks like they are not interested in this party anymore." Craig said on the net.

"17, Draco confirms and will continue to orbit and observe. You want phones and Wi-Fi back up?" came the call from our eyes in the sky.

"Draco, continue mission release all comes. 26 and 27 continue to watch and anything hostile gets taken care of." I radioed and heard double clicks as confirmation once again. I looked around and saw the sheriff was about to address the council.

"Board, Chairman, the two individuals that sat before you looking upset with their mouths taped where caught at the Business of Mister Cook, and they were apprehended and interrogated last night with a small incident. The entire capture and interrogation are available to you all on the share drive and I can show you were. I say interrogation because the team that works at that business are both reserve deputies of my agency and federal contractors that work in counter terrorism operations throughout the entire world. They did not know if this was an attack from a local facilitator or a global facilitator and thus continued as though they had a threat from a global facilitator. When they learned it was local they called me this morning and we coordinated this handover at the meeting. A warrant is going to be produced for the arrest of Mister Galagher senior and it was the intent to arrest him here but with the number of weapons his people brought we thought it could be handled with less possibilities of bloodshed done another way. In the coming days this crisis is going to get worse. The dollar is slowly going to be worthless, and our community is going to get restless. Galagher senior thinks this Raeley is his and has a few of you in his pocket that are still seated in front of me. I will tell you now, he will not be able to take over this county while I am alive, and I can speak for Charles as well. I will not speak for Mister Cook, as he is here and will speak for himself, Wayne." He said pointing at the council and the floor.

As I was already standing, I just stepped out into the aisle and started. "Members of the County Board, we stand on the threshold of a coming storm, a crisis that none of us are ready for because the unknown is just that, not known. The sheriff is right, the dollar is crashing, and we all know the market has already crashed and that is why they are not allowing it to start back up, because it is dead in the water even if they do start it again. So, what does this mean to us, here in Southeast New Mexico? It means what we have is what we have. Soon trucks with supplies are going to stop coming. I see the look of 'that is impossible' in a few of your yes. Already the trucks are stopping because the credit cards they rely upon to fill their fuel tanks are turned off. The card companies say this will not be the case on Monday, and time will tell if in fact this is true. Right now, it is Saturday morning, and the panic and fear is starting to settle in force threw out the world, not just here at home. We have people all over the globe stranded because they have no access to their money and the credit cards they had been using are now turned off." As I said this a few people gasped with the realization of exactly what I was saying. "Yes, exactly, it is sinking in to you now. It is time to start getting this community settled and ready for the real fight that is coming, the fight to stay alive. You are going to see people you had never dreamed could be the way they are becoming, Galagher is just one. He has a few of you, like he had Felps, in his pocket. I will warn you now, my gloves are off and many of you only think you know who I am and what I do. Obviously that knowledge is not what I had thought it might be because Galagher sent two hunters to watch me and possible kill me. Council lady Bale, it seems you know one of the hunters, Henery and his family." I said stopping and looking at her.

"I do know him and his family. He is a wild one at times but nothing to terrible." She said.

"I saw his arrest record and he has not found himself in anything too bad until he was in a field across from my business looking to take a shot at me with his rifle and buddy. These bad times are going to bring out things in people and get them to do things, I would ask you to check on his family, his mom. It might be why he was out in that field. Either way he messed up in a very big way and is lucky he is not dead in a hole right now." I told her.

"Oh, look you are a big Billy bad ass telling us how lucky he is too not dead, what the fuck ever guy." a gentleman with the name Finch, that looked to be about my age but a little pudgier and balder.

"Mister Finch, I am no 'Billy bad ass' as you say. I am however very versed in the skill sets that make me a far more dangerous man that most in this room, to include the sheriff. Am I telling tales Mike?" I said.

"Wayne, this guy like so many others have no idea." Mike said laughing at this point.

"Sheriff, this blow hard is just another bullshit artist like you and your veteran status because you served in the Navy. I have heard of his company that trains people in weapons, your undersheriff does that too, who cares. If you don't have anything else I have better things to do, Chairman?" Council Finch said.

"We are adjourned then" the Chairman said to the council and then continued. "Can I have a moment with the two of you please?" he said to the sheriff and me.

We waited until the chamber was clear and all had left to go to their offices and most likely head home. The chairman waved me forward, "Do you have a few minutes to sit and talk?" he asked us. "Sheriff if you must go help Charles with Felps I understand."

"Wayne you good to talk to him for a bit, I should go get with Charles and when you are done here can you come to my office, I am sure your key will work." Mike told me.

"Sure thing, Mike. Chairman give me a second here to get my team redeployed" I said then talked into my headset, "All Bear Team elements, stand down. Bear 70 take your team and redeploy home. The rest of you come to the Chamber. Draco continue mission" I radioed on the net.

"70, wilco" Adam responded.

"Draco copies, continue mission." replied.

"Ok, what can I do for you Council Chairman?" I asked.

"Galagher is just the tip of the iceberg Mister Cook, and I have to get all this off my chest" He began.

Chapter 20

As I stood and thanked the Chairman, I turned and left the chamber meeting the team out in the lobby to head over and have the conversation with the sheriff. The last thirty minutes were a waste of time and the Chairman's iceberg was nothing more than a melted ice cube puddle with the information we had already gotten out of the two would be snipers in our interrogation. The chairman had no idea truly who we were or capable of, and that was due to my efforts to keep the company in the shadows and not draw attention to myself or those who worked for me. I was truly shocked just how little the more powerful people of the community knew of me or the company I had run for years out of our community. This may be because I did not participate in the politics of the community and only helped the law enforcement in the area mostly, still shocking to me.

"What information did he have? Couldn't have been much since you only talked about thirty minutes" Frank asked me.

"I thought it was going to be big the way he talked about the 'tip of the iceberg', but it was more of a recap to what Stewart, our wanna be sniper, told us earlier. So now the information is confirmed I guess, anyways, let's go see what the sheriff has and wants to do." I said and turned and headed towards the sheriff office, which was attached to the county Building.

I pulled my wallet out of my back jean pocket and used it to open the card key reader door in the sheriff's office side of the building, which was secure, and I helped navigate the security needs for the undersheriff after they took office years ago. I heard the sheriff yelling in his office as we walked down the hall getting closer to him.

"NO! You sir are the district attorney of this area, not the fucking law. I am the law here, and this is my county and community which I have grown up in and helped to protect and build for decades." He was yelling into the phone as I stuck my head in the door frame and looked at him. He didn't skip a beat and gave us all the arm wave to come in and continued his conversation, "So if you and your clan of buddies are not going to do your job, in the current crisis we are in no less, I will figure it out and talk to the chief of police about how to continue moving forward. I cannot believe you are telling me if I pursue charges against Galagher you will drop them without even knowing what the warrant and case would be."

I was shocked to hear the last sentence from the sheriff, but we had information that he was part of the Galagher problem along with judges, so I shouldn't be. The sheriff knew this and looked like he was pressing the DA, though I didn't know if the DA called the sheriff or vice versa. Either way it was unsettling to know that the DA was being this open about dropping charges or a case. Maybe this was because of the current crisis, and they saw an opportunity to make a move to control the area, maybe that was the thought of Galagher and his group, control.

"You sir are not my boss, what? What did you just say to me?" Mike said into the phone and then listened. "So, you are going to charge me, really? I think our conversation is done now, have a good day."

Mike sighed heavily and leaned back in his chair and rubbed his face then said, "hey guys. We have a serious problem now and I am afraid it is going to just get worse and worse now."

"It did not sound good, is the DA feeling his oats and challenging you?" Jeff asked.

"Worse than that." Mike answered.

"How could it be worse?" Craig asked.

"He is going to drop any charges you bring against Galagher and his crew, including the two we brought in to you and Mister Felps" I said leaning forward taking my helmet off for the first time in a while.

"Bingo" Mike said pointing at me and continuing "but wait there is more" he said like a terrible sales spokesman on a tv add "he is going to charge all of you with kidnapping and a host of other things he said."

I pulled my helmet back on my head to use my radio set, "Draco this is 17."

"Go for Draco" came the response.

"I have a new number for you to monitor, prepare to copy." I radioed and then turned to Mike, "what is the personal number of the DA?"

"Send it" I heard Draco respond.

"575-420-2010" Mike read to me from his phone and I replied to Draco.

"Galagher already called that number as he was leaving the county building 17." Draco informed me.

"17 copy, put it on the monitor list from this point forward along with any other numbers Galagher calls or makes a call to him." I radioed.

"Wilco" came the response from Draco.

"Who the fuck is Draco, Wayne. You told me earlier you would let me know" Mike told me.

I gave the look of wait to Mike as I made another radio call, "Bear 2 this is 17."

"Draco is our eyes in the sky." Bill told the sheriff.

"Go for 2" was the response from Luke in my ear.

"Eyes in the sky, what does that mean?" the sheriff said, looking at Bill while I was having my radio conversation with Luke.

"I need you to review target package you worked up and refine the known associates." I told Luke.

"Already on it" Luke radioed back.

"Roger" I said and then looked at Mike.

"I guess it is time for me to let you in on a few secrets you might not know." I turned to Paul and said, "Paul can you go ask the undersheriff to come in here, I think he knows most of this, but I want to say it once and then move forward."

Paul got up and walked out of the sheriff's office and turned left towards the holding cells and where we thought the undersheriff was with Mister Felps.

"Secrets?" Mike asked.

"Not so much secrets, more like information that we do not readily put out there for people to see or know about us or the company I run." I told him.

"You are a weapons and tactics training group, you train some pretty high end guys from all around and even Canada and parts of their army. You guys are not that big a secret, Wayne." Mike said as the undersheriff walked into his office.

"Shit, look at the party in here with all you knuckle dragging fuckers." Charles said as he walked around behind the sheriff and pulled up a chair and continued. "What the fuck guys?"

"I am about to explain a few things about us" I gestured to all the team "that the sheriff and you might not already know."

"Oh damn, this should be good. Felps is down there having a shit fit about calling his lawyer and we are going to pay. Just so you know Mike." Charles said to the sheriff.

"I can only imagine. The DA said he is going to drop all the charges we file and going to file charges against these guys." Mike said, pointing to us. "After we are done with this, I guess we should cut them all loose, I mean we could book them at county but then it will just be a bigger shit show, maybe we can all figure this out together?" Mike told us all.

"The DA is certainly part of the problem then." Charles said.

"Yep, we intercepted Galagher calling him after he left the meeting." I said.

"Intercepted? What exactly does that mean?" the sheriff asked.

"We have a Draco, which is an intelligence aircraft made to gather intel and other things. This is what you asked about and I said I would tell you later, now it is later. It can also designate targets for guided munitions. I have had it up since this morning." I said as the sheriff interrupted me.

"Intelligence aircraft, designate targets, I knew you guys had a lot of specialized training and taught things at your company, but how do you get an aircraft like this? Are you guys' really CIA or something?" the sheriff asked, leaning forward in his chair as he did.

"Careful Mike, they might have to kill you if they answer." Charles said laughing.

"Ha, Ha, Charles, seriously though, what the fuck?" Mike said looking at all of us.

"CIA, get a load of this guy." Paul said laughing now too.

"My company has contracts with the government, along with the Canadian government, to do work for them and train individuals. I also train law enforcement from around the US to supplement and diversify our portfolio. Which makes us look like a more standard training facility to the layman, which is the way we like it. Do you know most of our backgrounds Mike? I ask you because Charles has spent time with most of us watching your guys get trained and going through a few of our courses himself, which gave him the opportunity to talk to us more. Charles, do you know most of our backgrounds?" I said looking at him.

"You guys all worked together on some type of a team at one time or another. I know those teams are special forces because I have read a few of the awards and citations you have on your walls in your office too." Charles said.

"I thought you guys where all retired or ex-law enforcement that decided to get into the training business." Mike said.

"We intentionally stay as vague as possible with our marketing and try not to let it out who we are or what we have done." Craig said.

"Your 'years of operational time' means a lot more than on a beat or patrol then it leads on in your brochure and on your website." Mike said.

"Yeah, we really are not hiding the fact we served but most of us have tried very hard and kept it very low key exactly how we served and with whom." Jeff said.

"So, you guys are all special operations then?" Mike said more than asked looking around at the team, "that makes way more sense now." I could see all the puzzle pieces in his head all come together as his face changed.

"We all had been in that type of unit at one time or another." Craig answered.

"So now that the cat is more out of the bag, we have more assets than normal people might have, well more than a lot of agencies might have. I am not going to go into detail right now Sheriff, but we have the ability to maintain our surveillance and survival. I, no we," I said looking at my team, "have used much of the money and profit generated by the company to stock and equip ourselves and family to hopefully pull through a crisis like we currently find ourselves."

"For years you have tried to get the county to listen to you about preparing for the worst, and it makes sense now because you have been preparing, just in case something like this happened. You got me to listen to you, well Charles made me listen more or less, and I have stocks of food for my family just in case too." the sheriff looked around saying.

"I am glad you have your family in that position, I want to help you, and the community as a whole, to make sure we do not just survive, but that we thrive in this coming collapse. Make no mistake, the dollar is going to collapse, and the economic impact will in turn cause our great nation to collapse along with it. I cannot, no, we, we will not help those who do not first help themselves. That being said, Draco is our aircraft that can listen and do a lot more. We have intercepted all the conversations to and from Galagher on his phone, as I showed you before the meeting one such intercept." the sheriff interrupted again at this point.

"Wayne, what you are doing is highly illegal and you are admitting it to a law enforcement officer. Why are you putting me in this position?" the sheriff asked.

"Because times have changed Mike, soon, the federal government is not going to be able to contain this mess. The dollar is about to be worthless, that is why the credit card companies have stopped service, they know that the debt will not get paid back. With them stopping service people are soon to be stranded all over, many far from home with no money, if they are not already. The only law that matters, that has ever mattered, is the Constitution of the United States. I am not going to sit by with my hands in my pockets while this community crumbles, while criminals plot against me or mine. You will have to make a choice, what team do you want to play for? This is going to soon be a life-or-death crisis and people are going to start killing other people for the can of corn they have if we are unable to bring this community together. I came here this morning knowing it might get a little out of control or wild, and it has not lived up to that, and I am glad. Galagher has ties all the way to the governor, I am sure you already know that, and it is not confirmed he has the DA and others in his pocket working for him or with him. I didn't give a shit about him or what they had planned or were doing, until they targeted me and my family. Now, well now I am still trying to figure out exactly how to approach thing, constitutionally." I said, thinking and trying to control the anger I felt deep inside me.

"Just because you think the world is collapsing does not change the laws around us. I am a huge constitutionalist and have had my run ins with the governor and many others and honestly can't fucking stand Galagher, but that doesn't stop the law, Wayne. It does not take away from the constitution either. Our rights don't change." Mike said to me.

"I am here because you are a good man, both you and Charles are good men, and that is what we need to make it through this crisis, collapse, whatever it is and going to be. If Galagher is really hoping to take over the county, and maybe more, then the rule of law and the constitution do change for me, it becomes the laws of war. I did not start this war, sure I stopped him and pulled them from their vehicle and left them cuffed, but I never threatened him or anyone else." I was saying as Charles interrupted me.

"I am pretty sure you never threaten people, I mean you might tell them the consequences if they continue, but it is a promise and not a threat" Charles told me chuckling.

"I know you are trying to make light of the tough situation we are facing, but this gentleman is truly just the beginning of it. In the coming days, weeks, months things are just going to get harder and harder unless we, the entire community, band together." I told them.

"Come on, you really think this is a war?" Mike asked.

"Yes, I think that Galagher had planned on coming to the meeting and taking over the county and making himself a kind of boss of the area. That is the assessment of my Intelligence analyst after listening to the conversation I gave you earlier on the paper. What that looks like I am not sure, and I have my guy looking hard at it." the sheriff interrupted me at this point.

"Intelligence analyst, are you serious? You are not kidding about any of this are you? What the fuck is really going on here?" He looked at me sternly.

"Exactly what I told you, the collapse is happening and things have changed. As Charles said, we are operators. I am not going to get deep in the weeds on this Mike, bottom line is, you can get on board, or you can get out of the way." I was saying when Charles stopped me this time.

"Hey, hey, hey. Stop with the ultimatums Wayne. We are not going to bend to you or Galagher or anyone else. We are listening and will help you if it is warranted, but don't you dare coming in here and tell us to get on board or out of the way, no matter what you think is happening we are still the law around here, you got it?" He said leaning forward in his seat.

I put my hands up in surrender, "It was certainly not like that, it was more a shit or get off the pot kind of thing. You are and will continue to be the law around here as long as it stays constitutional. I will not tolerate a war lord style leadership or a king on a throne. As I have already said, you both are good men, and that is what it is going to take, and your attitude just now is exactly what makes you good men. I want to work with you, not against you. Together, as a team, not against, not above or below, but together to help this community, our homes, our families and friends make it through what is to come." I spoke.

"So, what does that look like to you then, break the laws that don't work for you? Are the laws going to even matter to you?" the sheriff asked.

"Are many of the laws even constitutional Mike?" I asked him.

"They have been legislated and signed into law, so yes." Mike answered.

"That means that a pistol brace makes a weapon a short barreled rifle? As the ATF has made anything that has a brace on it with no legislation?" I asked.

"I see your point Wayne, and I hope you can see mine. Is listening to people have a conversation on the phone, ok? Recording it? You think that is alright to do now?" he then asked me.

"I think the law is blurred in a circumstance that a threat is planning to take action against someone and by listening you have a chance to stop this threat. It is not like I am just listening to everyone all the time, I only targeted his phone calls after it was proven he was going to take action against me and mine. I believe in the freedom to do as you want, but those actions will have consequences. For a very long time we have allowed people to continue to do things without consequence, those days are gone for me and mine. So, I am here to tell you, we are going to live peacefully and leave people alone, unless they do something to us. I would not be here with my team talking to you if we did not respect you and want you to be a part of our family. That also means we will ask you what you think should be done, if time allows. I am not going to be a war lord, or king, and I am sure as fuck not letting some prick like Galagher be one either." I told him flatly.

"I agree for far too long we have let people get away with things they should not get away with. I just can't sit back and let you do things that I would not let others do too. Do you see that and understand?" He asked me.

"I understand this and will try to always make you aware of the things that are happening, but make no mistake, I am not asking you for permission Mike, I don't need you to show me what is right or wrong, only God gets that option. We, my family, will act and do as we think is best for our survival and follow god's law." I told him.

"I can respect that, Wayne." Mike said.

"Ok, as I was saying, we have assets available to us that make us able to operate on a level few in this community, and possibly this region, can operate at. Charles called us knuckle draggers earlier, because that is what the hard-hitting pipe hitters get called and I take that as respect from him and will tell you, we can strike on a level that both of you would be terrified by. Now, we have held back on doing just that to this Galagher guy and his little group of followers and I want you to help me continue to be nice and not let me do what I truly think needs doing." I said.

"You think he needs to be taken care of? As in killed?" the sheriff asked.

"I do." I said openly.

"Wow. Well ok. That is pretty forward, and I am not sure how to wrap my head around it. A part of me is in total agreement with you because I know Galagher is a prick and wants nothing more than to control things, this county for sure. The lawful side of me is screaming how murder is not ok in any circumstance." he said with deep thought on his brow.

"Is it murder to kill an enemy leader?" Jeff asked.

"This is the United States of America, with laws and the constitution. We are not at war, so stop with this line of thinking because it is just not what we are facing." the sheriff said, looking at Jeff.

"At what point will you be willing to accept that Galagher is at war with us, and most likely the county members against him, Sheriff?" I asked.

"I don't have an answer for that, and I really hope and pray it never gets like that. I appreciate all of your help, but I can't condone the things you are doing right now and am going to be forced to follow the law, so stop telling me illegal things you are doing, and I suggest you take this opportunity to leave." the sheriff said.

"Very respectful sheriff I appreciate it and we will take our leave. We want to be on the same team and hope to be able to help this community and you get through the coming crisis." I said as I stood and put my hand out to shake. He took my hand and shook it quickly and released it. I looked at Charles and nodded as I turned and walked out with my team in tow.

"Bear 17 to Bear Main" I radioed.

"Go for main." was immediate response in my ear.

"Sitrep follows. RTB heading to vic time now." I said into the handmike.

"Roger" came the reply.

"Draco to 17, we just did a quick sweep of your area no threats detected." The call came from my eyes in the sky.

"Roger" I replied.

"Let's get home guys, we have a lot to talk about." I said as I exited the building and headed for the Tahoe. I am not sure what I had expected from the sheriff, but from the way I was feeling it must not have been this. It was still surprising that Galagher had not taken a shot at trying to take over at the meeting. He was smarter than I had thought, and I needed to talk to the whole group about how we should proceed from here. Six days, well the middle of day six, and it was far crazier than anything I could have imagined, and I still had not seen what the news was reporting nationwide.

Acknowledgments

I wanted to take a moment and tell you all thank you so much for joining me on this new and exciting journey. This is my first book in what I hope will become a long series about good people who take the hard right over the easy wrong. With you all along on this ride with me, we can navigate this world and the terrible things that will possibly happen to our characters. I can only hope you are enjoying this as much as I am enjoying sitting down each day and putting my fingers to work on the keyboard, I find myself on.

Made in the USA
Columbia, SC
14 March 2024